Fistful of Colours

Fistful of Colours

Suchen Christine Lim

SNP•EDITIONS

an imprint of

SNP•INTERNATIONAL

Published by SNP International Publishing Pte Ltd
A subsidiary of SNP Corporation Ltd
1 Kim Seng Promenade
Great World City East Tower, #18-01
Singapore 237994
Tel: (65) 6826 9600
Fax: (65) 6820 3341
http://www.snpcorp.com
snpinternational@snpcorp.com

Printed in Singapore 2003
Reprinted 2007, 2008

ISBN 981 248 012 9

National Library Board (Singapore) Cataloguing in Publication Data

Lim, Suchen Christine.
Fistful of colours / Suchen Christine Lim. – Singapore : SNP Editions, c2003.
p. cm.
ISBN-13 : 978-981-248-012-9
ISBN-10 : 981-248-012-9

Singapore – Fiction. I. Title.

PR9570.S53
823 — dc21 SLS2003020238

QUINTESSENTIAL ASIA showcases Asia's most remarkable literary voices. Spanning fiction, poetry, drama, biography and criticism, it explores questions of identity and change in Asia through the singular lives, memories and traditions of its people.

With a host of essential titles ranging from seminal classics to the finest contemporary works, QUINTESSENTIAL ASIA captures the true soul of Asia and promises to inform, provoke and delight.

QUINTESSENTIAL ASIA is dedicated to publishing and reissuing works of literary, cultural and critical interest from new and established writers. If you have a manuscript, book idea or suggestion about a classic you would like to see re-issued, that belongs to the QUINTESSENTIAL ASIA collection, do contact us at:

SNP International Publishing Pte Ltd (a subsidiary of SNP Corporation Ltd)
1 Kim Seng Promenade
Great World City East Tower, #18-01
Singapore 237994
Tel: (65) 6826 9600
Fax: (65) 6820 3341
http://www.snpcorp.com
snpinternational@snpcorp.com

For
My mother,
Sister Damien Murphy (CHIJ)
and
Sister Dolores Healy (CHIJ)

"A Singapore novel, one could say, should capture some significant moments in the country's history. Its characterisation should be authentic, and reflect multi-ethnic concerns. Anyone who looks for historical richness in *Fistful of Colours* will not be disappointed. From the hardships of the rickshaw coolies and *kampung* life to a last display of colonial splendour at a Raffles Hotel ball, the book is packed with the flavours of the past...On that score, the book – launched by National Arts Council chairman, Professor Tommy Koh last week – is a valuable addition to Singapore literature."

Koh Buck Song
Poet and Journalist

"...Lim touches on broader issues – ethnic identity in contemporary Singapore, the relationship between art and history, and the pursuit of personal and artistic freedom. Through the eyes of the younger generation of Suwen's friends and fellow artists, we also get the history of the nation builders – the Chinese coolie, the Malay waiter, the Indian doctor. Beyond the stories of people and places, however, it seems that the unseen major character is History itself."

Professor Ronald D Klein
Hiroshima Jogakuin University

"In the history of Singapore fiction in English, few novels have truly attempted to explore the complex plights faced by women as they struggle to realise their own self-fulfilment. *Fistful Of Colours* is one such novel. If I have to use two words to define the achievement of *Fistful Of Colours* I would use 'gentle honesty', for here is a novel that not only explores the suffering that men and women go through, but tempers the exploration with humanity."

Professor Kirpal Singh
Singapore Management University

"This is a book you find difficult to put down once you start reading. ...the story is built up layer by layer. The present is built on the past and the present is an indicator of what the future might be. On one level we have Suwen's story of her search for the "perfect union of medium and content" in her art. In her search, she delves into the family history of her stepfather, the Ongs. In doing so, narratively, the author is able to bring in the story of the forefathers of Singapore around the turn of the century, the ordinary people responsible for the shaping of Singapore."

Dr Zalina Mohd. Lazim
Tenggara, Journal of Southeast Asian Literature

Contents

PART 1

...and she would paint

Suwen stirred her paint pots vigorously, mixing colours and feelings, angry that her mother was demanding so much from her and furious that she had not the guts to say, "Get off my back! My life is my own business! You have your own life to lead and I have mine! Why should children be tied forever to the mess their parents made? Is this the only way to be filial?"

But she made no attempt to answer her own questions, choosing instead to concentrate on squeezing a long yellow worm out of the tube of paint, carefully mixing in the blue till she got a dull green. The thought of another confrontation with her mother filled her with loathing. All her life, she had wanted to escape the clutches of the womb. Give back to her mother all the gratitude she wanted and then to have nothing more to do with her.

"So you think you're the only one suffering, ah? The only one in this world with problems?" her mother had demanded in her most self-righteous Cantonese voice. "What didn't I do for you as a mother? Did you not have enough to wear? Enough to eat? And a good education? And now you want to run off? After all these years! Now you complain. Just when the mansion is sold, ah! You flog a horse when it is dead! But I tell you, ah! He was drunk. He did not know what he was doing! I am not trying to put him above blame, ah. But you think a bit. That was the only time, was it not? After that, nothing! And you went away, and he paid for your education in England. What more do you want? Did he not treat you like a daughter? You forget so quickly, ah! Before that happened, did he not bring you to the pictures? To the swimming club? And it was I who made him do it. When I married him, I told him about my daughter. And I said to him, you must treat her like your daughter. I, your mother, thought about you! Did you ever worry about me? Go! Leave me if you have to! With two hands and two feet, do you think I will be helpless? In Cantonese opera, we always say, when one's horse is dead, one can learn to walk! You can go away. I will not blame you! So you don't blame me! Who asked you to leave your bedroom door open? You cannot blame me for that! You can blame me for anything else in your life. But not that! I did tell you, not once, but many times. Right from the time you came to live here. This is a big mansion, I said. Lock your bedroom door at night, I said. You never can tell. And it is not because you are not his flesh and blood. Even in the papers got stories about people like that taximan, mah! And those two girls were his own daughters! Some men are like animals. Always after one thing! And only one thing! A man's heart is sharp as a needle in the ocean; it pricks you when you least expect it. You were already a big girl. You got to protect yourself. Your mother cannot be with you all the time. Now if you had listened to me, nothing like that would have happened. Right or not?"

YES! YES! YES! The whole of Suwen's insides screamed. "Do you think I wanted it to happen? That I left the door open for him? On purpose? You are only saying all these things because I am leaving!"

"I know you are leaving. Now that you have wings and feathers, you are ready to fly off. But I have another daughter! I thank the gods for that! Sulin will be with me. I am not as helpless as you think! But remember, ah! I did not abandon you when you were young and helpless! I returned to the farm to reclaim you. I could easily have left you there to grow up like a pigsty girl! Many girls are abandoned by mothers who don't want them! But ah! I have learnt a bitter lesson today. Never, aiyah, never be so responsible. Your own flesh and blood will not appreciate you. I have been slaving all these years. For what? You tell me! For myself alone? I have lived alone and worked alone. Your own father left me alone! Then he came along and wanted to marry me. He even agreed to take you. What more could I ask for? For once think about me! Your own mother, an opera actress growing old. Who wants to marry an old fah-dan? You think it was easy to find a man to give me a home? A woman with another man's daughter? Who knows my pain? The young only know how to complain and grumble. Do they understand old age? You are not so very young yourself! But that is your problem. Water flows downhill, never up. Gratitude! Ha! I dare not hope for it!"

Her mother's words had poured out with such a rhetorical flourish and vehemence that she had had no means of staving off the onslaught. Proverb after proverb, phrase after phrase from classical Chinese literature and operas hit her like cluster bombs, releasing their sticky webs of guilt upon immediate contact with her flesh. How could she fend off her mother's accusations and explain things to her in Cantonese? Even in English Suwen had great difficulty expressing her feelings in words.

More often than not, she would rather paint. Painting as she was feeling and feeling what she was painting, filling huge abstract spaces with colours. Lifted by an inner music, impelled by a feverish restlessness, her hand had painted light and shadows, lines and shapes, colours and textures, her strokes uneven and unplanned, her agitated spirit yearning for the fluidity of dispossession, rootlessness and loneliness. To be free to seek pure form. Free to paint the canvas she was defining and to suffer the loneliness she was choosing.

To the external world, she was an artist of great potential, but to herself, she was the great void. An amorphous being of inchoate dreams and desires. But in some rare moments of intense lucid creation when she was painting alone, her many dreams and desires had fused like colours shading into one another, mixing and merging, so that for an instance, one whole uncomplicated and integrated individual, the artist, had painted in total control, totally absorbed and complete in her artistic powers. Manipulating the brush as an extension of her hand; her hand as an extension of her will; her will, the expression of her being – Suwen. Supreme and solitary she had stood in front of her canvas.

Then she remembered how the front door had opened with a soft click that fateful day. Years ago. And she had looked up from her painting. Must be the servant, she had thought, for everyone else had gone to the temple.

"Siew Chay!"

She froze at the sound of his voice. He had returned. But none of the servants were home. She would have to serve him. No, no, she remembered her panic. She would lock her bedroom door.

"Wen, get me a drink."

He was already standing in the doorway of her room. He came into her room, looking pale and exhausted. Unbuttoning his shirt, he waved her away. "Go downstairs and get me a drink."

She returned with a glass of cold water and found him lying sprawled on her bed, his eyes closed. "Nah, your drink," she coughed, holding out the glass awkwardly. When he sat up, she saw that his fly was opened. She turned her head away just as he took the glass and grabbed her hand, pulling her down towards him. She kicked and shoved him away. The glass was smashed into smithereens. He grabbed her breasts, squeezing them as he tried to plant his foul kisses on her lips. She scratched his face like a wild cat, and pushed him onto the bed. Then she ran into the bathroom and locked the door, her heart pounding with pain. She had tried to scream but no sound came out of her throat. It had been strangled by fear. He was bestial. A beast! The air was full of his immoral snorts and hisses. She shoved a clenched fist into her mouth and bit hard. She would not cry. She refused to cry. She waited behind the locked door. Only when she heard his car driving off did she come out of the bathroom to sit dazed in front of her canvas, returning like one in a dream to the work at hand. And there she sat as the minutes ticked by, her eyes two dark pools of unfathomable depths, her face blank, unthinking and unreflecting, walled in by a will which refused to sob. She took without seeing the tubes of paint and smeared on the canvas a daub of red, deep carmine red. And a daub of blue. Bright royal blue. Then she flung away her brushes like a prisoner, his shackles, and began to spread the paint furiously with her bare hands. Smearing the canvas to cover up the dark cavernous spaces in her mind, obliterating the hated scene before her again and again as her hands moved from tube to palette, from palette to canvas and back again in furious feverish haste. Stopping the gaping wounds. Covering up the putrefaction.

Smearing, spreading and smoothening. Her eyes seeing nothing; her mind thinking nothing.

Nothing. Nothing. Nothing.
This is the way of peace.
Shanti. Shanti. Shanti.
Nothing. Nothing. Nothing.

"The wealth of a nation is in its economy, its people and the arts," the guest-of-honour declared at the opening of the art exhibition.

Over the next few days, members of the public had crowded round her painting to gape and gawk.

"Wah, erotic, man," the less restrained among the crowd whispered to one another. "Now they don't care one, ah. Anyhow also can paint. Last time where got such paintings?"

And there were the letters to the press. She read each of them with a mix of anguish and amusement:

> I am deeply shocked that erotic paintings are allowed to hang in our publicly funded galleries. We expect public officials in charge of our culture to uphold good taste and decorum. TAX PAYER

> Negative and regressive values likely to corrupt the young minds amongst us must be checked. The artist forgets that she is living in an Asian society. She should not adopt Western practices which contradict our Oriental moral concepts. SINGAPOREAN-ASIAN

> I plead for tolerance in this matter. Let a hundred flowers bloom. Let there be artistic freedom. What has happened to our civilised practice of making proper justification for what we vehemently oppose? Must our society repress everything? TOLERATION

> I refer to Toleration's letter. Our beloved Prime Minister has pointed

> out the dangers of Westernisation in Singapore and the pitfalls of being a pseudo-Westerner or geh angmoh. A sense of our Chinese identity and history is of the utmost importance. Our nation is swamped with numerous geh angmohs. They dress outrageously and insist on speaking English or Singlish. They do not want to speak Chinese. They cannot even read the Chinese signs in public places. Some even claim to dream in English! Such people have forgotten their Chinese ancestors and their five-thousand-year-old history and civilisation! I hope the authorities will do something and not let these Westernised geh angmohs paint dirt and call it art! We have a duty to our young. Son of China

And with that, the editor of the paper had closed the exchange of letters in the Forum Page. Suwen, who had maintained a stoic silence throughout that painful period, sighed with relief. It was a good thing that she was going away. Her identity as a Singaporean Chinese was being questioned at a time when she herself was uncertain about her own future. It looked as if she would have to start life anew. In her late thirties. Not a bad age really if one thought about it. Neither too young to be naïve nor too old to be decrepit. Her reflection in the train window showed a woman with dark intense eyes and straight black hair. An ordinary-looking woman.

The station master gave a sharp blast from his whistle. The train jerked forward and began to slide slowly out of the station. As scenes of bushes and shrubs, cars and buses flashed past her window, Suwen settled into her seat. It was going to be a long journey back to Kuala Jelai.

Suwen had never planned to launch herself as an avant-garde artist; she was strongly averse to the stereotypes which such a label was likely to evoke. When she came back from England, she had started out as a simple college teacher with two secret wishes. One was to move out of the Ong Mansion, away from her mother and stepfather to live on her own, and the other was to leave teaching one day to paint full-time. She would never have done this painting had it not been for the betrayal of Mark and Nica. Mark Campbell and Veronica Sivalingam. Their very names pained her. Where once she had felt the bond of a kindred spirit banding together those out to create a brave new world, now, in its place, was an acute sense of distress and an emptiness which her art could never fill.

The critics in the newspapers had been unkind and unjust to her. She was not a person devoid of a sense of her own ancestral roots and history. In fact, her problems had started because she had had too much of it. She had wanted to paint her forefathers. This island's forefathers and its myriad histories. For is not our national history the sum total of ethnic and personal histories woven into a common strand when our great grandparents stepped onto these shores? Mark and Nica had applauded her and cheered her on. Paint the past for what it was. Unadorned by political myths, they had urged. Don't do those pretty murals to adorn the walls of some HDB blocks or MRT stations. How was she to know at the time that history and politics were not enough, never enough, to create real art? Only passion and hate were.

Her own history as an artist had begun one hot afternoon when an old man in Kuala Jelai had ordered her to paint.

"Paint!" the old man had barked as he handed her a brush.

"Paint and wait. Your stomachache will go away."

The afternoon sun was a blaze of heat and light, and she was a lonely, worried twelve-year-old, crouched in the shadow of a row of shophouses. She had grabbed the proffered brush from the old man's hand, vandalising the canvas with a vengeance she did not know was in her. She shoved the brush up and down, left and right, criss-crossing the huge canvas used for advertising movies outside the cinemas. She splattered and painted, blocking out the shapes she hated, the guffaws and giggles she had recoiled from, erasing the very memory of them, willing her brush to form new shapes, new lines and new hues. All that afternoon she had painted and brushed, covering up the ache inside her as she waited for the mother who did not come down the stairs of the Nam Sun Hotel till long after the sun had set.

"Your mother! Where is she now? In the big city of Sing-gah-pore, mah!" her grandfather spat, and puffed at his bamboo pipe.

"Eat big talk big! That is your mother for you. She has never changed."

He was a gruff old man who spoke the unpolished Cantonese dialect of his Toong-koon village in China. Fifty years of toil, first as a rubber tapper and then as a vegetable farmer tilling his own acre of land, had not made him change his habit of speech and the dialect of his youth. Throughout the years, from the time of the British colonial government to the Japanese Occupation in World War II, and right up to the time of Tengku Abdul Rahman and national independence, he had clung stubbornly to his dialect and his bamboo pipe. He smoked his bamboo pipe like the Chinatown trishaw riders, squatting on his haunches, knees apart, with the bamboo pipe, a thick cylinder polished with age, thrust between his knees. He steadied the pipe with his right hand, and in his left, he held the joss stick which he used for lighting the nub of tobacco stuffed tightly into the pipe's opening.

"Eat up, Ah Wen," he said to his granddaughter one day. "Tomorrow you go to school. Study hard. Never be like your mother. Nah! She is stupid."

Then he had lapsed into his usual silence at meal times. He ate quickly, seated with one foot resting on the stool so that his knee, level with the table, was supporting the left hand that was holding the bowl of rice. Now and then he grunted with his mouth full. And she, the granddaughter, seated opposite him, was watching him with the deep concentration of a six-and-a-half-year-old. Grandpa's hands were dirty. Hard, knobby, dirty hands. His fingernails were dirt encrusted. The houseflies hovering above their bowls of rice and fish annoyed him. With a deft practised hand, the old man flicked away a persistent fly with his pair of chopsticks, and then proceeded to convey, quite unperturbed, a lump of white rice into his mouth with the same pair of chopsticks.

He had enrolled her in the village school of Ulu Tampin, and every night, fascinated by the pictures in her English reader, he had made her recite, "A for apple, B for ball. A man and a pan. A pan and a man."

"Good ah! Good ah!" he applauded his granddaughter.

Every day, rain or shine, he cycled the ten kilometres to take her to school and home again. He sat her in the wooden crate, strapped to the back of his bicycle, used for carrying the vegetables from the farm to the market.

"Now hold on tight. Hold my belt, nah!" he reminded her as he pedalled down the country lanes with her clinging to his old leather belt for dear life. The image of the old man pedalling with the noonday sun beating down mercilessly on his back, his cotton shirt flapping in the breeze, would remain forever etched in her memory.

SWAT! SWAT! SWAT!

"Aiyah! These flies are such a nuisance!" her mother grumbled when she visited the farm.

"Nah! Burn some more incense sticks," Grandma said.

"No use, Ma! I cannot stand the smell."

"Spray then."

"No use, I say! Is Pa going to wash out the pigsty or not? The stench is terrible. And today is so hot. I really cannot stand it, Ma."

"Oi! Tiew-nia-mah-ah! This you cannot stand! That you cannot stand! You think you were born with embroidered slippers, ah? You can take your big nose back to Sing-gah-pore! To people like you! Everything in the big town smells good. Even its dog shit and cat shit! But you don't forget, ah! You were born here! Among the pig shit and duck shit!"

SWAT! SWAT! SWAT!

The spirits of the underworld were against her mother. And swat! They were against her too. Chasing her mother away with their smells! She grew up in the belief that her grandparents' three-room shack of wood and zinc was surrounded by spirits lurking among the rubber trees and scrub. Large brown rats lurked in the grass and lallang, waiting for her, and if she were careless and forgot to close the wire mesh gate of the fowl run, the next morning, one of her ducklings would be without its head. Gnawed off by rats with vicious teeth. To her seven-year-old mind at the time, it was a constant battle of wits and evasion between her and the spirits. Sometimes these spirits would send the fruit flies. These sneaky pests laid their eggs in the chiku fruit, and they hatched into wriggling maggots to poison the mouths of the unwary. But the green bottle flies were the worst. They buzzed around the open latrine in the outhouse, dipping their tiny hairy legs into the pit of human waste and waiting for her to fall into it. But no, she had vowed, they would never get her. Rather than confess her fears to her grandpa and face his scorn, she would never ever use the outhouse latrine at night, holding herself tightly, oh ever so tightly, till her bladder felt like bursting, and wait till the orange rays of the morning sun had driven away the awesome shadows of the rubber trees.

When she was twelve, her mother came back to take her away from the farm. It was exactly one year after the death of her grandpa. Villagers and relatives came from far and near to catch a glimpse of her mother, the fah-dan or heroine of Cantonese folk opera. The wives of rubber tappers and farmers, straddling babies to their waists, crowded the entrance of her grandma's house to "ooh" and "aah" over her mother's jade and diamond bracelets, and her dark shoulder-length hair permed into cascading waves. Her mother's face, rouged and powdered, had looked years younger than the farm women and rubber tappers who had grown up with her. While the latter had remained in the village to marry and toil on the pig farms and rubber estates, her mother had escaped to the big city down south where she had joined a travelling opera troupe.

"Ha! Your mother is a flower by the roadside. She will not last! Gone to the city to eat big and drink big! Wait! One day she will come crawling back!" Grandpa had huffed.

At first, the villagers and relatives had agreed with her grandfather and tut-tutted in sympathy with the old man. She was his only daughter and she had brought shame to the family, first, by giving birth to a baby girl without marrying the father (no one knew who he was) and second, by running away afterwards to join a roadside wayang! But all that was before her mother's face started to appear in the Chinese tabloids and racing weeklies like the Mah-piew-poh. The photos showed her dressed in the finery of a Chinese opera actress. So, by the time her mother returned to the farm again, the villagers' views of her had changed.

"Aiyah, our koo-leong, don't go away so soon, mah! Stay the night," they called out to her.

"Such a famous actress to come to our village, we are very honoured," the village headman was smiling and nodding his white head like the village idiot.

"Aiyah, it is so good for my old eyes to see you in person, ah," an old aunt grasped her mother's hand.

"Thank you, thank you, uncles and aunties," her mother giggled coquettishly as though she were on stage. "But too many mosquitoes here, ah! And too hot! My Mr Ong here is a spoilt towkay. He cannot sleep without the air-conditioner, ah!"

The villagers of Ulu Tampin, who had never seen an air-conditioner in those days, could only nod and agree that it was, aye, such a pity. Such a famous daughter of the village and she had to leave so soon. They glanced at Towkay Ong Tay Luck, standing beside his big white Mercedes, but Suwen was very sure that Towkay Ong Tay Luck, whose eyes were hidden by his dark glasses, did not waste a glance in their direction.

"Aye, he is a very big fish, ah," the women whispered among themselves. "From a very rich family in Sing-gah-pore. They own a big bus company there. Who does not know the name of Ong Ah Buck, his father, ah? When his father was alive, ah, the family was even richer."

"She is very lucky. Got fook ah! As they say in the old days, different umbrellas, different handles; different people, different fates," the old aunt murmured.

"They say she is older than him. She is already twenty-eight or twenty-nine."

"Good, she can settle down and marry, man. Already she is nearer to thirty than to twenty. After thirty, ah, no man will want her. And she got a daughter some more! Towkay Ong, some people will think he is stupid. With his money, he can have any chick he wants, right or not?"

Suwen, twelve years old and miserable at having to leave her ailing grandmother, had been listening attentively. She gazed at the thick gold band with the black seal stone on the man's finger and the bright gold watch on the man's wrist. "A Ro-si-lex, thirty thousand at least," an uncle had estimated in an awed whisper. She had never seen so much gold in all her young life. The man who was three to five years younger than her mother did not look at her. He was standing beside the white car, shifting from one foot to the other, looking utterly bored.

Her mother was finding it very difficult to tear herself away from Grandma who was weeping.

"Aiyah, Ma, I will come back. And you don't worry. I will look after Ah Wen, I swear to the gods, ah! Look, nah! Towkay Ong bought this for you."

The old lady closed her fingers over the pair of jade earrings. Tightly.

"Ma, wear them. Pa never gave you jade."

Suwen saw the gleam of greed in the old lady's eyes and was surprised that the look did not match the words coming out of her grandmother's mouth. The words were those of a woman about to die, but the look of greed was from one clinging to life.

"Bury me with them. Aye, I never had a good fate. Always poor in life. You gods, ah, let me be rich in death."

The old lady sighed wearily and closed her eyes, her hand waving them to leave her. Suwen bit her lips as she fought to hold back her tears. Sold for a pair of jade earrings, her young heart raged. If Grandpa were alive, he would never let them take her away.

"Come, Suwen! Get into Uncle's car. We've got to go now," her mother said, and that was how she, Suwen, came to address the man as "Uncle".

When they had driven out of the farm, her mother, who was in the front seat next to the man, turned around and handed her a box. She opened it. Inside was a doll with real yellow hair and eyes of blue glass. As blue as the sky. The eyes could open and shut, and the arms and legs could move! She had never owned such a marvellous doll before.

"Oh, thank you, Mother," she murmured as she clasped the doll to her breast.

"Aiyah, not me! Say 'thank you' to Uncle here. He bought it for you."

Liar! She was screaming inside her head. The man had not bought it. Her mother had bought it and was now pretending that it was from the man!

"Suwen, don't be rude! Say 'thank you'."

"Thank you."

"Thank you who? Say 'thank you, Uncle', mah! So rude!"

"Thank you, Uncle," she choked.

They were now driving down the hot tarmac road, going south to

Singapore. The rubber trees on either side were a blur of grey and green. The doll lay lifelessly on her lap, its glassy blue eyes staring blankly out of its plastic head.

"When we reach Sing-gah-pore, ah, I will buy Suwen some new clothes. Throw away the old clothes. They make her look sua-ku, right or not?"

The man grunted, and her mother carried on her chatter in the Hokkien dialect about this and that, keeping up a continuous drone in the car like the hum of the noonday insects back at the farm. Suwen, who was no stranger to the Hokkien dialect and, like her mother, could switch from Cantonese to Hokkien without much effort, listened listlessly to her mother. The black tarmac road shimmered in the blistering heat, and her eyes hurt when she looked up at the blue cloudless sky. The rubber plantations soon gave way to the flat open grassland of lallang, scrub and bush, and the occasional attap hut.

"Aiyah, so hot and thirsty, my throat is dry," her mother was grumbling to the man. "I am going to peel an orange for you, ah. To suck an orange on a hot day like this is very good for the throat, people say."

She watched her mother take out an orange, peel it and feed portions of the fruit to the man. "Sweet or not? Talk to me, nah," her mother cajoled.

"Sweet, ah, very sweet. Makes me want to suck something else now," the man guffawed.

Her mother glanced quickly into the rear mirror to see if she had understood the man's words.

"Aiyah, speak properly, nah," her mother nudged the man.

"We stop at the next town," the man grunted.

"Aiyah! You can't wait, ah?" her mother stroked the nape of the man's neck.

"Cannot. I bring you to the best hotel."

At this, her mother giggled and fed the man another segment of orange. The man sucked upon it, making loud disgusting noises.

"Mmm, stop that, nah, you," her mother was tittering and giggling like a silly schoolgirl.

In the rear seat, Suwen gazed steadfastly out of the car window, the lallang and scrub flashing past her unseeing eyes. Years later, she would look back at this moment and describe the car as vibrating palpably with crude unnameable desires which she, the adolescent, could sense but could not name. But although she remembered her feeling of disgust at the time, yet the grown woman in her could not help but regret that, unlike her mother, she had not had the good fortune of being caught up in a web of earthy passion like, well, like a cat in heat. And immediately after, she was ashamed of her thoughts.

Suwen was relieved when the car finally stopped outside the hotel of a small town. Nam Sun Hotel Kuala Jelai, the sign said. It was a sleepy sun-drenched place with only one main road. A typical Malaysian town along the western trunk road. The hotel was at the end of a row of two-storey shophouses. Its main entrance was the flight of stairs next to the coffee shop.

"Wait down here and eat something," her mother handed her five dollars. "Uncle and I will come down in a while." Her mother then went up the stairs of the Nam Sun Hotel with the man's arm round her waist.

Suwen turned away from the curious stares of the old men sipping coffee in the shop. She strolled down the covered walkways of the shops, walking in the shade, keeping away from the blazing afternoon sun, past the tailor's, the furniture shop, the motor repair shop, and stopped outside the sundry goods provision shop. Stacks of brooms and brushes, red plastic pails, umbrellas hanging from wire hooks, crates of onions and garlic, and sacks of rice and sugar cluttered the front of the shop. Large green bottle flies like those which buzzed in the open latrines were hovering above the sacks of sugar. Her hand reached furtively into the pocket of her skirt to touch the crisp five-dollar note. Reassured, she pointed to the jars of sweets, olives and red sugar-coated cuttlefish. The shopkeeper took her note and counted out the change.

She started on the cuttlefish. A bus and lorry trundled past as she chewed on the delicacy. Then she dug into the packet of olives, spitting the seeds into the drain as she followed with great interest the steady progress of a bullock cart drawn by two skinny bullocks. The Indian driver was dozing in the heat. Then she spied a Malay hawker selling chendol and ice kachang in the shade of a tree. She bought a sugared iceball and stood beside the stall, sucking her ice as she watched an old man wield his paint brush like a broom, sweeping up and down an enormous billboard, filling up the blank spaces with pinks and yellows, smearing the canvas till there emerged the doll-like face of a woman with blue eyes, red lips and yellow hair.

All that afternoon, she crouched in the shade watching the old man paint as she sucked iceball after iceball till her stomach ached. And still there was no sign of her mother and the man. She held her arms tightly against her belly and tried not to groan. Her face was an ugly grimace, and the old man glanced at her from time to time.

"Want to go to the toilet?" he asked her at last.

She nodded, mute with shame.

"Go to the back there," he pointed to the shophouse.

The "back" was a dark dingy room littered with signs, billboards, tins of paint and brushes, their hues of red, blue and green gleaming in the semi-darkness like the treasures of yesteryear. When she came out, the old man had moved his canvas into the shade of the verandah, and had set up an old billboard in a corner. "Paint!" He handed her a brush. "Paint and wait. Your stomachache will go away."

PART 2

...and she would tell stories

Once a thing is remembered, it is seldom forgotten. It is remembered and recalled in different ways, and in a way which shapes and reshapes the past; the past as retold in stories shaped by the creative memory.

Suwen had swapped stories of her childhood with Mark Campbell and Nica Sivalingam when the three of them were good friends and part of a group of like-minded English-educated malcontents who got together every weekend to grouse about the sanitised politics of Singapore, and dissect the plays they had attended and the paintings they had seen as they drank beer till the wee hours of the morning in one another's pads.

Theirs was a fluid disparate group of artists, writers, people in the media, a couple of lawyers, doctors and college teachers who drifted in and out. The regulars were Nica; her live-in boyfriend, Robert Lim who worked in an American bank; Zul Hussein, writing for the *Straits Herald* and who had just returned from the States; Janice Wong, his fiancée, who was Suwen's colleague; and Mark Campbell who was teaching English Literature in the same college with Jan and Suwen.

Nica, who knew a lot of people and who was a well-known sculptor on the local art scene, was the one who held the group together, while Robert, earning the most among them, supplied the beer, cheese and wine.

"Hey, I don't mind," he laughed when Suwen tried to thank him once.

"It's my job. Besides, I'm known as her constant companion now."

"Eh, why you talk like dat one ah? Wan' to buy beer, buy lah! Don' wan', done! Ne'er mind one what!" Nica quipped in Singlish, imitating the twang of a popular entertainer.

"You complaining or what?" Jan joined in.

"Eh, you got hear me complain, meh? I just explain to Suwen only what!"

"Ya lor! He talk only what and you all jump on him like dat! So unfair one ah!"

Suddenly, all those in the group who had secretly prided themselves in the knowledge that they would never speak like this normally were launching into the street-smart slang of the Ah-Beng-and-Ah-Huay variety. Mark was laughing even as he was feeling a little, just a little, excluded, like the new kid in the playground who had not cottoned on to the jargon of the dominant group.

"Eh, man, you one kind one! Why you don' talk like us? You talk like us, sure win you many friends in Singapore, you know or not?" Zul was also hamming it up.

Mark laughed. He had corresponded with Zul before coming out here. Like pen pals. A former Campbell, a distant cousin of the family, had been the benefactor of Zul's father. Since then, Zul's father had made it a point to write to the Campbells at least once a year. This slim connection, plus his feelings for Suwen, had led him to come out East to teach and to write a story or two, he explained when pressed by Nica.

"Psst! Suwen! You're sure he's not one of those patronising asses from the British Council?" Nica hissed in a loud stage whisper meant for Mark's ears.

"C'mon, Nica! Give the guy a break. He's okay," Zul laughed.

Suwen's pad was their occasional meeting place. It was the refurbished garage of the Ong Mansion. "My home's my garage, my garage is my home," Suwen used to sing to annoy her mother.

"Your home, ah, is this mansion! As long as I am in it!" her mother would inevitably remind her in her self-righteous Cantonese tone. "If I don't die, you will have this roof over your head. But the day I go to my ancestors, your Uncle's vixens will throw you and your sister out, ah!" Her mother's voice quivered each time she talked about Ong Tay Luck's mistresses.

Suwen could never bring herself to think of him as her stepfather. In her mind, he was either "the man" or "Ong Tay Luck", son of the rickshaw towkay, Ong Ah Buck.

With the passing of the years, her mother had become more and more obsessed with the mansion, the symbol of her marriage and authority as the first wife. She took to heart the saying "she who lives in the big house has the big say in all family matters". Her greatest fear was that her husband might change his mind and his will, and that the mansion would pass into the hands of the sons of his other "wives". Her fears were real enough for sons will always be more important than daughters if only because they bear the family name. Ong Tay Luck had had one mistress after another, changing them the way he changed his cars. Once every few years. And in the process, he had sired many offspring who had claims to his properties and businesses. It was in the nature of things Chinese for the men to behave like this, Suwen thought with some grim amusement. Monogamy and fidelity belonged to the poor. The Chinese rich could father as many children as they pleased with as many women as they pleased.

She slipped behind the bushes and took the path leading to the servants' quarters and her garage. She had converted it into an art studio with a bamboo partition to screen off her bed. This will be a good day to bring Mark and Nica over to the mansion, she thought as she was undressing. The man won't be home. Those two can see her mother's rosewood altar for themselves. Mark was interested in taking a look at her mother's ancestral hall.

The rosewood altar with inlaid mother-of-pearl was a testament to her mother's sheer inventiveness and penchant for embroidering facts. She was a born storyteller who had eagerly embraced the current practice of the Chinese Singaporean peddling the myth that they were the inheritors of an illustrious five-thousand-year-old civilisation. Never mind that their forebears had been the dregs of society. Never mind that they had never seen rosewood furniture, much less possessed it. These forebears had left China to carve out a new life for themselves, and their descendants, the inheritors of their wealth, should follow likewise, albeit symbolically, to carve out a new family history to match their wealthy new life.

So her mother had gone about the business of collecting Chinese antiques and rosewood furniture with the seriousness of a historian using artefacts to recreate the ambience of a rich past. "Like the Aws and the Tangs, ah! Their mansions are very nice. So many things handed down, one generation to the next. Our living room must also be like this," her mother said.

Her mother had bought the rosewood altar at a sale in Malacca for a mere six thousand dollars. It had once been part of the furniture belonging to a prominent Baba family that had since come down in the world. Her mother had the table transported back to Singapore and installed in the room which she now referred to as the family's ancestral hall. From then onwards, Suwen had heard her claim, without batting an eyelid, that it was a family heirloom, brought over from China as part of her mother-in-law's dowry.

"Made by Shanghai craftsmen, ah! Very old already! But then, ah, you cannot throw away things just because they are old, right or not? It was passed down from my mother-in-law. Her mother gave it to her, ah. And she gave it to me, mah!" her mother had once explained to a friend in her affected Hong Kong-accented Cantonese which she had acquired as part of her upward mobility. "My mother-in-law was the daughter of a small mandarin in China. Not a very important judge," her mother continued modestly, "but still a kind of scholar, mah. And their family brought out this rosewood altar when she married our patriarch. To put her ancestors' memorial tablets, ah! Aiyah, where can you find such filial children nowadays? Young people are so different now. Over here is our patriarch, the second towkay, Ong Ah Buck. My husband's father. He was very respected by the British in his days, ah! First Chinese to start a bus company here." At this juncture, her mother would pause and point to an ornately framed photograph of a portly man in a long silk gown and jacket, the kind worn by learned gentlemen like Sun Yat-sen and Chiang Kai-shek at the turn of the century. Next, she would point to another photograph which showed the patriarch in a Western suit of white, complete with bow tie, bowler hat and walking stick, posing quite self-consciously next to an Englishman, heads taller than him. "Aye, this is our most treasured photograph, ah," her mother would begin modestly. "It was taken when my father-in-law got his decoration. The OBE, ah! The gwailo king, King Gee-orgee, ah! Number three or number four. Aye, but people like me, don't know English, how to remember such things?"

Mark and Nica enjoyed her mother's tales of the good ole' days with Suwen acting as the translator. For her part, Suwen had shrewdly detected a potentially rich theme for her art. To look at these good ole' days with eyes clearer than her mother's and to paint the personalities and events as she imagined them. Not for her the stiff formality of the poses caught by the salon photographer. She would capture them unawares in daily life. There was more to the stories of Ong Ah Buck than was purveyed in her mother's tales, she told Mark and Nica. The patriarch might be the enterprising pioneer in trade and transport. But he was also the father of many bastard children. Similarly, his wife was not the cultured gentlewoman suggested in her mother's tale. Albums of photographs kept in dusty drawers and forgotten told a different story.

The Story Behind The Photographs: How Ong Ah Buck The Rickshaw Puller Became The Rickshaw Owner

There was a black-and-white photograph of sullen rickshaw pullers and their rickshaws parked in front of a shophouse in Pagoda Lane. It was the only photograph in the Ong family album which showed its patriarch as a lean hungry-looking young man eking out a living as a rickshaw coolie. What the photograph did not show was daily life in Chinatown; what it was like to live in a dunghole in the early nineteen hundreds.

Five o'clock in the morning. A succession of choking coughs and yells, and the persistent tick-tock-tick-tock of the noodle hawker hitting his bamboo sticks. "Hot tea! Hot tea, ho!" The tea boy bellowed from the corner coffee shop which had opened for business since four that morning. Down the narrow lane of a row of four-storey tenement houses, a woman on the third floor pushed out a bamboo of fresh washing. Her neighbour on the second floor swore and yelled out in Hokkien, "Who's the mother pig with no eyes? Can't she see that her wet clothes are dripping on mine? My clothes were dry! I hung them out last night. Now curse the sow! They're wet again!" Whereupon the woman on the third floor screeched in Cantonese, "Samsui-por! You think you are the landlady, ah? You wash your clothes and I wash mine! Who are you to tell me where I can hang my clothes? You fat sow, you!"

"Pooi!" Out came the prompt spat of venom from downstairs. An empty can was hurled out of the window. It landed with a loud clatter on the lane below. "Oi! You stinking cows! Let's have some peace!" a man yelled from across the lane. "Egghead! Don't put your mouth in! If you don't open your mouth, no one will say you are dumb!" the Cantonese woman answered. A baby wailed. An old man coughed. It was the dry rasping cough of an opium smoker. The residents of Pagoda Lane were dragging themselves out of bed just as the grey dingy light of dawn was seeping through the cracks of shutters and matchwood-thin partitions.

Pagoda Lane was a leprous gully of four-storey lodging houses with dark warrens of tiny cubicles into which ten, twenty or thirty men were cramped into every bit of conceivable space. These cubicles, with or without windows, gave out the same dark malodorous stench of urine and phlegm, mixed with the sickly odour of medicated oils on festering sores and rheumatic limbs. Other than the prostitutes in the cheap brothels and the few long-suffering wives who seemed to be forever pregnant, Pagoda Lane belonged to the Chinese male – the rickshaw coolie, the odd-job labourer and the half-starved sinkhehs, newly arrived from China. Lean, brown and sinewy, always at the edge of hunger, these Chinamen were squeezed into dark dingy holes, lured into brothels, gambling dens and opium dens ruled by the brotherhood of the tongs. Every night there was fighting when the men, half-starved and short-tempered, got drunk on cheap beer and fought over the few available women. Often they were maimed; but sometimes they were killed. Life in Pagoda Lane, pre-war Singapore, was harsh, brutal and short. And the colonial police, made up mainly of Indians and Malays, were fearful for their own lives and limbs. They would only patrol the gas-lit lane in twos or threes, marching down the narrow gully in a parade of duty, seeing nothing, hearing nothing and doing nothing.

Like the hundreds of thousands before him, Lim Ah Buck (before he became Ong Ah Buck) was a sinkheh living in Pagoda Lane. You would find him hidden among the numbers and digits in the record books of the Colonial Immigration Office, a dot among thousands of other dots: young Chinese male, aged seventeen or thereabouts.

Since his arrival in the colony, he had eked out a living as a rickshaw coolie in Chinatown. On the morning before he changed his family name from Lim to Ong, Ah Buck woke up with a curse and a yell. He had banged his head on the bunk above his. "Son of a bitch!" he muttered. He couldn't wait to get out of the rat hole the next day. He rubbed the bump on his head gingerly, cleared his throat noisily like the rest of his roommates, and spat out a gob of thick green phlegm into the spittoon. Then, placing his nose between his thumb and forefinger, he snorted and rubbed the snot onto the plank which separated his bunk from that of his neighbour's. Having completed this part of his morning ablutions, he stood up, lowered his trousers, and emptied his swollen bladder into the spittoon.

Seventeen other men in the crowded cubicle did the same, some using a rusty tin can instead of a chamber pot. Ah Buck let out a loud yawn, scratched himself and, pulling up his singlet, began to mop his armpits, damp with the previous night's sweat. The gods, he cursed under his breath, he wouldn't want to spend another night in this dunghole. His ancestors had blessed him with the ruddy health of an ox, and although he had pulled a rickshaw every day with never a day of rest, he had never been sick. Unlike his neighbours, men in their thirties and forties, rasping like winded beasts of burden. At twenty-four, his broad chest was brown and sinewy even though it was glistening with the red angry warts from the bites of the bedbugs.

The wooden partitions and soiled bedding were fertile breeding grounds for bugs and fleas. These mites hid between the layers of faded wallpapers and in the cracks of the bunks to lay their eggs by the millions. Ah Buck had spent many a warm sleepless night watching the blighters creep out of the chinks and cracks to crawl over the sweaty bodies of sleeping men who tossed and scratched in irritation. He recalled with childish pleasure the night of a hundred bugs. It was his single most enjoyable experience in the first year of his arrival. He was seventeen then, and he would have howled with hunger pains and loneliness had he not tasted power that night. The raw naked power to crush the life out of another life! A horseless carriage driven by a crazy angmoh had run into him. He had ended in the ditch with a swollen knee and his rickshaw had had a twisted wheel. That had cost him three days' earnings! He had had nothing to eat for two days as a result. His belly was aching with hunger pangs that night! Then he saw the mites. He pressed his thick forefinger upon one. A mess of dark blood. Then he pressed another. And another. And another. Flattening and squashing each fat blob into a bloody mess. Till his fingers were black with the blood those vermin had sucked out of him and his mates. The gods! Sons of a mother pig! But those bugs had saved his sanity!

"Ah Buck, remember this old bull here when you are a rich towkay," Lau Goo wheezed like a tubercular patient. "It is my chest again. Ah, what to do? Not enough to fill my belly."

"Don't worry. Tonight you can eat all the meat you want," Ah Buck gave his old pal a friendly jab in the ribs. "There will be braised pork, salted pork and roast pork. Eat your fill, old man. When Towkay Ong asked me what I wanted for the feast, I thought of you at once. We dream of roast pork every New Year. But we only had money for salted eggs. But tonight, old friend, eat all the roast pork you want."

"Ugh! Only a gutter rat will give up his family name for a piece of sow's meat!"

"Which son of a bitch said that?" Ah Buck yelled. His scowling face was dark with rage. But not one of the sullen faces answered him. "Pooi! You swine!" he spat. "Want to talk, talk in front of me! Not behind me! Cowards! Repeat it and I will squash you with my fist."

"Aye, let them say what they want," Lau Goo wheezed. "Even the gods in heaven cannot shut the mouths of all men."

After that, Ah Buck left the lodging house, "Swine! Sons of sows and bitches! Die without sons to lead your funerals! Pooi!" He swore and cursed the men – over and over again. He coughed out a gob of phlegm and sent it flying through the air into the murky depths of the drain. "There! Stay in the longkang forever! Rats will never rise in prosperity!" He wiped his mouth with the back of his hand. And that was how Ah Buck left Pagoda Lane.

Another photograph showed the first Towkay Ong, short, bald and stout, the man who had plucked Ah Buck out of the filth of Pagoda Lane and installed him in Telok Ayer Street as his son-in-law. The first Towkay Ong, owner of twenty-five rickshaws, no mean wealth in those days, had no male issue. His wife and concubines had given him nothing but worthless girls. And having no surviving brother of his own, he loathed the thought of having to pass on his worldly possessions to some male cousin, three or four times removed. In his desperation, the old man had hit upon the traditional Hokkien stratagem of chew-kia-sai, inviting an impoverished young man to marry into the family. As the old Hokkien towkay perceived it, such a chew-kia-sai son-in-law, bonded by the solemn oath to give his firstborn son the surname of Ong, would keep the family fortune intact and within the bounds of his immediate family. But the sly old fox knew how to use the power of wealth, going one step further, pressing the matchmaker to find him a young man willing to change his own surname as well to make doubly sure that the Ong name and line would continue.

From the point of view of sociobiology, it was a brilliant stratagem worthy of Sun Tzu, the Chinese military strategist. Towkay Ong's adaptation of the Hokkien tradition of chew-kia-sai was indeed much better than adopting a son, and letting the adopted son marry someone entirely unrelated to his blood. His way ensured that at least half his genes would be passed on to the next generation through his daughter and his family name continued.

At first, his problems were almost insurmountable. His favourite daughter was fat, ugly and born with a harelip. Moreover, the girl was born in the year of the Tiger when there was a terrible drought in China. It seemed like a double curse. No right-minded parents would want their sons chewed up by a tigress, and if their horoscopes clashed, worse things might happen. So, at twenty-four, Ong Geok Neo was considered way past the marriageable age for Chinese girls. And her matchmaker despaired of ever earning the hefty red packet which Towkay Ong had promised her.

Towkay Ong, however, was a persistent man. "Ask around some more," he told the matchmaker. He was not giving up yet. This was the daughter whose birth had changed his fortunes from poverty to prosperity. "She brought me fook and luck. She will do the same for her husband," he said. And indeed it was widely believed that the girl's harelip which had marred her face had something to do with her father's luck. However, in a community of clans like that of the immigrant Chinese, impoverished young men willing to give up their surnames were extremely rare. Their family names were their only links to home in China, and the Hakka and Cantonese young men in Chinatown rejected Towkay Ong's proposal outright. The social stigma and the guilt of having betrayed one's kin and clan to bear the name of another were too great for many a lonely young man to bear.

But Ah Buck was no ordinary lonely young man. He had more dreams and a greater lust for wealth than most young men. Perhaps. It was difficult to tell just by looking at that lean hungry face in the picture with the rickshaw coolies. Perhaps he did not care what others thought about him so long as they did not utter those thoughts in his presence. It was not for nothing that he had escaped death and famine to come to the colony to learn and earn, he had said in his later years. Better to cheat a little like the rat and enter heaven first than be stupid and honest like the pig and enter heaven last. Of all the twelve animals in the Chinese horoscope, he believed that the rat was the smartest. It had jumped onto the nose of the water buffalo and thrust its body forward just before the water buffalo was about to become the first animal to enter heaven. Consequently, the rat became the first and the water buffalo became the second animal in the horoscope. Push forward, if not, you will be pushed backward, he said.

All his young life he had watched in helpless rage as greedy landlords and ruthless bandits robbed his father of everything, and droughts and floods destroyed his crops. In the year of the drought, his father's harvest of rice was seized by the landlord's paid underlings. In that year, two of his sisters had to be sold. "We got to eat," his father snarled. The drought continued. The family lived on grasshoppers, field mice and roots. A baby brother died. The following year, the rains came. The rice plants grew green and tall. But the pending prosperity brought back the warlords and their bandits. They killed his father while he was harvesting in the field. His sisters were raped and kidnapped. His mother died of heartbreak. And at sixteen, he was an orphan with no possessions and no illusions. An old villager brought him to the port of Canton and sold him to the captain of the ship which brought him to Singapore.

The ship's hold was so packed with bodies that there was crouching room only. The men retched and groaned as their ship was tossed about by thunderous waves. One day, Ah Buck found himself squeezed between two corpses. The two men had died in the night. Dead men did not need clothes and shoes. So Ah Buck stripped them and hid his booty before calling the sailors. He even helped them heave the bodies overboard. Throughout that month-long voyage across the South China Sea, he must have helped the sailors throw overboard more than two hundred bodies. There was more room in the dark hold after that for the other two hundred who survived.

The photograph in the dusty album showed a plump Chinese bride dressed in rich brocade and pearls. The bride and groom sat side by side, unsmiling, so that unless one looked at the face of the bride closely, one hardly noticed the harelip.

Before this picture was taken, Miss Ong Geok Neo had knelt before the altar to offer the gods and ancestors libations of tea and wine. Then she kowtowed three times, knocking her head upon the wooden floor, and the ritual combing of the maiden's hair began, a custom brought into the family by her Cantonese mother. Her elder aunt snipped off the ends of her long black locks, combing as she sang in provincial Cantonese:

> Loy-ah-loy! Nae first comb, comb each hair
> Till husband and wife grow white and old.
> Nae second comb, comb it long
> Till sons, grandsons and great grandsons
> Fill and bless your days.
> Nae third comb, comb it thrice!

May health and wealth and honour
Come your lord and master's way.

Then the mother plaited and knotted the daughter's hair into a neat chignon resting at the nape of her neck, a style worn by the married women in those days. She stuck a gold and jade hairpin into the chignon, intoning in a sing-song voice, "Daughter, from tomorrow you will no longer be a maiden. For tomorrow, you will cross the threshold into duty and responsibility."

The women poured out more libations of tea and wine for the God of the Earth and the Goddess of Fertility, chanting:

Bow to heaven and pray to the gods.
Pain, aye, pain is the woman's lot.
Pain goes with her when she leaves her mother's side;
Pain lies with her when she lies in bed each night.
Pain is with her when she carries her child;
Pain is with her when she is without child.
Aye, Geok Neo, may the gods bless you with sons!
Sons aplenty like the seeds of the pomegranate.
May you sow his seeds and reap his sons,
Else you lie with pain and he lies with another one.

Geok Neo rose upon her tiny bound feet, weeping the silent tears of a bride, fearful of the pain she was about to endure in the nuptial chamber. And the older women, freed of their menfolk, plied her with stories about the peccadilloes of young men, carefully refraining from talking about the pain and loneliness of married life on this auspicious day.

That same night, it was the turn of the men to enjoy themselves. Towkay Ong had invited friends and relatives, as well as Ah Buck's coolie friends for a feast. It was a pre-nuptial feast strictly for the men. A bigger wedding dinner would be held the following night for everyone (men, women and children). The wealthy Towkay Ong was following the tradition of his village back home in China in which it was customary for rich families to host at least two feasts as part of their wedding celebrations.

"Wah-lau-ah! Chunks of streaky pork in brown sauce! Ah, how my mouth waters," a young coolie grinned. He loosened the belt of his trousers. "Oi! We better eat and eat, ah! How often do you see one of us become son-in-law of a towkay?"

"Aye, such things are fated," Lau Goo said. "Ah Buck has a very good life line on his palm. I brought him to the fortune teller myself." He took a sip of rice wine. "Aye, we are good friends, very old friends. You have porridge, I eat porridge. You have rice, I eat rice. We are that kind of friends, I tell you."

"Oi, old man, don't dream, ah! Now he is the rich one and you the poor one. Things will be different," the young coolie grinned. "Friends are like that in this world, don't hope for too much, old man."

The painted eyes of the Chinese tongkangs berthed along the boat quay gleamed in the flickering light of the oil lamps hanging from the posts along the waterfront. Ong Prosperity Rickshaw Shop was bright with gas lamps and two large red lanterns heralding good luck and harmony. Impoverished coolies, whose daily fare was a bowl of rice with salted vegetables and egg, crowded round the tables. They crouched on their haunches on the wooden stools and tucked into plates of fried pork fat with innards, stewed pork with garlic, chicken stewed with ginger and mushrooms, delicacies which they had never eaten, not even during the Lunar New Year.

"Will you give up your family name for this?" the inquisitive coolie asked Lau Goo.

"I came to eat. Not to gossip," was his gruff reply.

"My friends! Relatives! Eat up! Eat up!" Towkay Ong called out. "My new son-in-law, Ah Buck here, now also called Ong, ah, is going to help me. Good friends! He will need your help!"

"Yaaaaaam seng!" the men toasted the groom and his father-in-law. "Once again! Yaaaaaam seng!"

When dinner was over, the men smoked their bamboo pipes and swapped lewd stories about the women they had bedded. They guffawed over bawdy jokes, slapped their thighs and jabbed their neighbours. Then tables were set out for card and mahjong games. The men betted noisily and the clacking of the mahjong tiles went on till the early hours of morning.

"Remember your old ox here," Lau Goo whispered as he took his leave.

"Old friend, you are like a relative to me. I will never forget your kindness in those early days," Ah Buck said.

"We wish you well, young Master Ong!" his coolie friends called out.

"Thank you, thank you."

Master Ong. The name had such a sweet ring of authority.

A year later, Ah Buck wondered whether his marriage to a tigress was accursed. His wife had miscarried.

"Aiyah, a son, ah," the old amah who assisted the doctor whispered.

"Aye, choy! Choy! The gods bless us! Nothing like this has ever happened to my other daughters," his mother-in-law wailed.

"Stop this noise!" Towkay Ong barked. "See that your daughter eats the right food. Not rubbish!"

The family engaged a temple medium to cleanse the house. Rid it of evil spirits. Towkay Ong donated a large sum of money to Lung Shan Temple and engaged a monk to chant prayers and intercede with the gods on his behalf.

Six months later, Geok Neo was with child again. But two months later, she had another miscarriage. This time she was inconsolable. She wept every day. Her mother brewed bowls of evil-smelling herbal soups and forced her to drink them. Again, a temple medium was engaged to cleanse the house and pray over her. Towkay Ong doubled his donation to the temple. But he seemed to have lost hope of ever seeing a grandson who would bear his family name. He took to his bed and left the day-to-day running of the rickshaw business to Ah Buck. When Ah Buck protested that this was too great an honour and too heavy a responsibility for him to undertake, Towkay Ong said, "I know I have other sons-in-law. But you are the only son-in-law who bears my surname."

"Oi! Hot water, oi! Make way! Make way!" the young waiters in the teahouse yelled at the top of their voices. "Siew-mai! Char-siew-pow! How about some egg tarts, uncle?" the waiter, bearing a tray of steamed buns and dumplings, asked.

But Ah Buck did not have the heart to eat.

"But you eat, Lau Goo, you eat," he urged his friend. "It is good to see you again."

"Wah-pia ah! It has been more than a year!"

"I know, I know," Ah Buck agreed. "But as I said before and I say it again, old man, you are like a relative to me. I depend on you to do this, and I thank you first,"

"Aye, small matter. What are old friends for?" Lau Goo mumbled, his mouth stuffed with dumplings. It had been years since he had had a meal like this. "When do I see you again?"

"Aye, I don't know, ah. We have been very busy at the shop. A new shipment of rickshaws have arrived from Japan. And the old man is sick. But he wants them assembled before the Lunar New Year. He has been nagging me. Even on his deathbed, ah, he will be telling me: Ah Buck, business is business. You are one step behind only, and the person in front will snatch the profits from under your nose!" he mimicked the querulous voice of his father-in-law. "And the old man does not know that I have to watch my backside. I turn my eye only, ah, my brothers-in-law will bite me."

"Wah-lau ah!" Lau Goo laughed. "What a fighter you are! You must be making pots of money."

"Aye, no! Running a business is not so easy," Ah Buck parried, for he wanted to avoid at all cost the notion that he was making money. It would never do for this would encourage borrowing. Money and friendship just did not mix.

"So how is the wife?" Lau Goo was asking him.

"Aye, no change, ah! She cries every day. The old lady is bringing her to the temple every day."

"Does your wife know that you are making a memorial tablet for your parents?"

"She doesn't have to know."

"Aye, I don't want to offend you, Ah Buck. But between old friends, I can speak plainly. It is time, ah, to place your own parents on your family altar, right or not?" Lau Goo was shaking his head at him. "Who can tell what unhappy spirits can do to the living? Your wife, ah…"

"I know, Lau Goo, I know," he answered his friend impatiently. "But I cannot do it until my in-laws go to their ancestors too. My surname is now Ong!"

"Ha! Ah Buck is what we Cantonese call a good-for-nothing son! If I were his father, ah, I will haunt him. What! Give up my family name? For what, ah? For a rickshaw and a tigress of a wife? One day, ah, she will eat him up! Ha! Let me eat plain rice porridge every day and keep my own name, lor!"

"Oi! Big mouth! You don't open it, no one will say you are dumb!" Lau Goo yelled from his bunk bed. It was warm inside the cubicle and he was fanning himself furiously with some newspapers to ward off the mosquitoes buzzing around him.

"Hey, old man, oi! Open your eyes wider! I know he is your favourite relation. I wait to see if he will come back one day to help you. Money is bigger than a friend to that man, ah! He is what we call a cross-the-bridge-and-pull-away-the-plank type of man!"

"Pooi! Egghead! What good is a family name if you have nothing to eat? No hope of rising in this world? You think it is respectable to die like that old pig, Ah Tu? He had a good family name! But did you see his wretched body in the latrine? Blood and pus everywhere! His legs and balls were swollen. He was bleeding from all the holes in his body. Even his eyes! Now that was a fool! And a filial son! He did not take up Towkay Ong's offer. Every cent he earned, he sent back to China. But last week, ah, Ah Tu drank a bottle of bleach and went to his ancestors! You are so sure you won't end up that way? Laughing at Ah Buck like this?"

"Oi! Watch your mouth, you crazy old man! If not for your age, ah, I will push my fist into your face!"

The young coolie stormed out of the cubicle. Its heat and stale air were making his temper rise. Lau Goo fanned himself and shook his head ruefully.

None of the young coolies liked to be reminded of their bleak future. They harboured fantasies of wealth in their opium-induced dreams. But somewhere inside their heads, they knew that Pagoda Lane, like Sago Lane and all the other lanes in Chinatown, was full of stories about rickshaw coolies who had fallen into the solitary impoverished half-mad grooves of life in this island colony. The city itself was a dog-eat-dog world. Most of them died like beasts of burden. By the roadside or in the deathhouses in Sago Lane. Worn out by hard labour, opium and loneliness. Some became characters like the rag-and-bone man who stacked his prized rubbish under his bed. Bundles of neatly folded newspapers, paper bags, gunny sacks and clocks which had stopped. In Lau Goo's cubicle was another silent solitary figure with a surly sullen face. He was a nightsoil collector who worked among the backlanes of Chinatown in the dead of night, emptying buckets of human waste into two steel drums which he balanced from a pole slung across his shoulders. Like the rag-and-bone man he was a former coolie too. The poor fellow had lost his father and two brothers in a traffic accident and two gang fights. After that he had slaved for ten years to earn enough money to return to China to see his aged mother. But one day, to his horror, he found that his entire hoard of Straits dollars had disappeared. He had stuffed the money into his mattress. The mattress had been slit open and the money was gone. Gone! He had shrieked and banged his head against the wall till it bled. But there was nothing he could do. The money had disappeared. Tenement houses were full of such thieves. One could not be too careful. The poor fellow blamed himself for having talked too much and too often about his plans. Henceforth he forswore speech and became Ah New the Dumb.

In 1920 or thereabouts, Ong Ah Buck moved his family into a two-storey shophouse in Telok Ayer Street. He had done well, he thought. In just over a decade, he had risen from half-starved coolie to rickshaw owner with thirty rickshaws for hire. This cluttered shophouse was palatial compared to,his filthy cubicle in Pagoda Lane. On the ground floor was the rickshaw repair workshop which doubled as the sleeping quarters for his coolies at night. The family occupied the upper floor which had a large sitting room to house the gods of wealth and prosperity and the ancestral tablets. The memorial tablets of Ah Buck's parents were not installed on his family altar until eight years later when the first Towkay Ong and his wife passed away. During those eight years Ah Buck suffered in silence the taunts of those who said he was unfilial, and his wife, Geok Neo, suffered one more miscarriage and the birth of four girls.

On the day when the family ended their mourning for Geok Neo's mother and took off their black clothes, Ong Ah Buck spoke to his wife.

"I have mourned your parents in sackcloth for one full year. Like their son. Their memorial tablets are here. On our altar. Their spirits..." he was overcome by a sudden fit of coughing. He could not go on even though he had rehearsed this speech over and over again in his mind. "Nah," he growled, "take this. I want my parents' spirits to come home."

He thrust the wooden tablet into his wife's hands and left the room.

Geok Neo sent for the Taoist priest. A simple prayer service was held, and the red wooden tablet with the gilded Chinese character Lim was placed next to Geok Neo's parents' memorial tablet with the character Ong carved in camphorwood.

One year later, a son was born.

"Oi! Master! Master! Good fortune, ah! A son! A son!" the old amah yelled from the top of the stairs.

Ah Buck pushed past his coolies and raced up the stairs, two steps at a time. His heart was pounding. Ah! His parents' spirits had blessed him. He had made the right propitious move in bringing them home to rest upon his altar. Years of waiting and four useless females who had to be married off as soon as they came of age! If Towkay Ong had not been his benefactor, he would have taken a concubine or two. Other men poorer than him had done so. It was too bad that the old towkay did not live long enough to see the grandson who would bear his surname.

He pushed aside the curtains and strode into the darkened bedroom, shuttered even in mid-morning to keep out the air which might harm the newborn. When the beaming midwife put his tiny son into his brawny arms, Ah Buck said nothing. His happiness was choking him. He held the wrinkled bundle awkwardly for he had never carried any of the girls before. His heart was rejoicing. A son at last to sweep the ancestral graves on Ching Ming day! A blessing, a blessing! He gazed at his son's tiny pink face and broke into a smile. He handed the boy back to the midwife and, turning to his wife, he said, "You rest", and left the room.

Geok Neo's harelip puckered and creased into a tearful smile. She hugged her baby son. Her taciturn husband, silent when the daughters were born, had acknowledged that she had fulfilled her duty. With just two words: You rest. She would remember those two words to the end of her days. The only kind words he had ever said to her.

When the baby was one month old, Ah Buck gave a large dinner party for the Ong relations, friends and business associates to celebrate the boy's birth.

On the morning of the dinner, he brought home a large red parcel and a nine-year-old girl, bought from a ship captain.

"Nah, take them," he said to his wife.

Geok Neo opened the parcel. Inside was a new memorial tablet for his parents. It was made of rich camphorwood and was just as elaborately carved as the one for Geok Neo's parents.

"Ah Buck, what do you want me to do with it?"

"You should know. Call the priest."

"Our son will be named Ong Tay Ik. You don't forget his surname is Ong," she reminded him.

"And you don't forget that I was born a Lim," he retorted.

"What is your name?" Geok Neo asked the girl.

"Ah Chun," the girl whispered in Cantonese.

"You can't speak Hokkien, ah?"

The girl shook her head.

"Ah, you can learn. The young amah, Lan Chay, can teach you. Come closer, let me look at you." She spoke in Cantonese but when she spoke to her daughters, she switched back to Hokkien.

"Don't tease her, girls."

"But, Mother, she is filthy and smelly," her eldest daughter exclaimed.

"Look, Mother, she is eating her porridge too fast. Like a hungry ghost," her youngest daughter laughed.

"If she lives with us, she will not be hungry. Your father gave her to me. She will be my maid. But ha! He thinks I am stupid. He wants me to change his parents' memorial tablet. Raise it to the same level as my parents'. Ha!"

The trapdoor above her opened. Blinding light. "Come up here!" a man barked. "Up! Up!" She climbed up the ladder. Into a very, very bright and strange place. The noise and people confused her. She shut her eyes. The sun was too bright. She opened them again. "Walk! Faster! Follow your master!" the man barked at her again. She ran and cringed against the wall. The strange dark people scurrying up and down the ship's planks, the honk of the cars and the gharries and buggies frightened her. She shied away like a young animal in fear. As she trotted beside her new master, she clung tightly to his hand, afraid he might let go of her in the midst of such frightening chaos. Her head was spinning. Once again she felt the rolling of the ship. Her stomach started to churn as the thunderous waves crashed over her. The floor beneath her seemed to be moving. She clung to the wooden post and retched. Another wave crashed over her; she threw up again and rolled across the floor. A crash of thunder. Lightning pierced through the cracks. She was thrown onto the floor again. She clung to the wooden plank; the ship was splitting and huge waves threatened to swamp her. Was she going to die? Mother! Mother! Where was her mother? Why did they sell her?

"Oi! Wake up! Wake up, girl! You had a nightmare," the amah shook the skinny body.

"I want my mother," the girl whimpered.

"Aye, umbrellas have different handles, people have different fates. Some of us lose our mothers at a young age," the amah muttered in Cantonese. Hearing the familiar dialect, the girl stopped her whimpering. "If we had been born into a rich family we would not be sold. But we were born poor. My old man sold me too. No food to eat. Aye, day in day out, flowery porridge. Just bowls of hot water and a few grains of rice floating in it."

The amah wiped away the tear at the corner of her eye seeing her own life being replayed by the little girl.

"Aiyah, wipe away your tears. No use crying."

Ah Chun lay down again and turned to face the wall. The tears trickled down her face even as she tried to stifle the sobs racking her thin frame.

"Ah Chun! Where are you? Come here at once!" Geok Neo shouted. The stubborn girl was never around when she was wanted. When the twelve-year-old finally stood in front of her, Geok Neo felt like giving that sullen face a hard slap. "Come here! Why are you so slow? Didn't you hear me calling you? Answer me!" she shrieked, "Char-boh-kan! Answer me, you slave!"

Ah Chun stood with head bowed, waiting for her mistress to stop shrieking.

"Answer me when I talk to you!" The hard hand of her mistress lashed out. Her cheek stung. But three years of frequent slappings had hardened her. She did not cringe. Neither did she cry. Ah Chun held on to the cup of scalding hot tea. If the cup should fall and break, she would be beaten again.

The eldest daughter of the family ran into the room, trailed by the girls and the boy, Tay Ik, now three years old. Another boy, a baby of two months, was sleeping in his cot next to the mistress.

"Mother! Mother! Ah Chun stole my comb!"

"I did not! Towkay-neo, I swear I did not steal it!" She had seen that pretty pink comb with the red flowers but she had held it in her hands only for a while. She did not take it.

"Liar! Liar! Thief!" the girls and the boy shrieked and danced round her.

"Thief! Thief!"

"Give me back my comb, you thief!" the eldest daughter of the family, also aged twelve, pulled and tugged at Ah Chun's plait.

"Ouch! My hair! Ouch! Stop pulling!"

Ah Chun felt her arm shoot out of its own accord. The eldest daughter gave a yelp of pain. Her nose had been hit.

"Aaaah! Mother! She hit my nose! It's bleeding!"

"You she-devil, you!" Geok Neo shrieked. "There has been no peace since you came! You bring me nothing but bad luck!" The baby was bawling again.

The boy was sickly but Ah Buck did not seem to care. He had not come home again last night. She had sat up till three this morning, waiting for him. What more did he want? She had given him a second son. But why should he care now that his vixen outside had given him a son too? She worked herself into a rage thinking about it. The sight of the bondmaid Ah Buck had bought for her when the first son was born made her angrier still.

"Bring me the cane!" she shouted.

Ah Chun cringed against the table as the thin cane sliced her cheeks. The next lash missed her as she ducked under the table.

"How dare you run away?" Geok Neo screeched. She yanked the bondmaid from under the table and whipped the little witch, the bringer of bad luck, again and again.

Each time Ah Chun was caned, she shrieked and wailed till the whole neighbourhood of Telok Ayer Street heard her. How she howled like a wounded mongrel over the unfairness of life, lamenting that the Ong daughters had a mother but she, Ah Chun, had a mother too! Why, then, why, she cried to the gods in heaven, was she beaten so hard and so often? How could the gods in heaven let this happen to her? Didn't they have eyes? When the baby cried, she was beaten! When a cup was broken, she was beaten! When the master did not come home, she was beaten! She was beaten for everything which went wrong in the household. Must she be beaten too if the people in the house could not fart?

But the more she wailed and lamented over the injustice of things, the harder the blows arid lashes fell upon her. Consequently, her face, arms and body were covered with angry red welts. Never scream when caned, the old amah advised her. Never, never answer back when scolded. Never cry when beaten. And never, never inch away. You move away, you will be beaten harder! These and many other such commandments were hammered into her by her mistress. Bong! Bong! Bong! Like a blacksmith's mallet, hard, hot and heavy, the blows from fists and canes fell upon her. Day after day, month after month. And gradually over the years, they shaped and moulded her spirit. As she grew older, she cried less. Her screams and screeches became softer. At first, they were heartrending cries. Then they became loud sobs. A year later, her sobbing turned into whimpering and snivelling. This went on for a long time. Her whimpers used to drive the other servants up the wall. "Shut up! Stop your snivelling!" they shouted at her. "Eat! Work! Sleep! That's our lot!" And when this did not stop her whimpers, the amah slapped her. Eventually these whimpers were slapped out of her, and Ah Chun moved about the house like a mute and "Ah Chun the Mute" became her nickname.

All wise men know that it is easier to create a slave than a truly free man. So it was not by education but by the natural process of attrition that, by the time Ah Chun was sixteen, she was as mute and meek as any other sensible bondmaid in the neighbourhood. She spoke only when she was spoken to, with her eyes humbly lowered, not daring to look the speaker in the face. This was a trait highly prized by the owners of bondmaids, for it was said that only the bold and the wilful slave would dare look her mistress in the eye. By this criterion, Ah Chun was the perfect slave. She crept about the house with her eyes averted, filling her days with constant fetching and carrying for her mistress, the four young misses and the two young masters of the Ong household.

Five o'clock in the morning. A loud yawn. Ah Chun stuffed newspapers and faggots into the wood stove, and lit a match. A burst of flames. She puffed and fanned till the sticks caught fire. Then she wiped the soot off her face and washed herself. By the time the old amah came into the kitchen, she had already set the kettle and pot of porridge on the stoves to boil.

"Ahh! Ah Chun, go quickly! I hear Towkay-neo calling you."

Ah Chun quickly filled the porcelain basin with warm water and carried it into her mistress' room.

"Good morning, Towkay-neo," she greeted Geok Neo.

"Hmm," and Geok Neo placed her pair of dainty feet upon the footstool.

Ah Chun kept her eyes lowered as she unwound the length of cloth to reveal the not-so-dainty but bent and contorted feet of her mistress. Feet which had been tightly bound since the age of five to prevent them from growing any bigger. To the modern eye, they would appear to be horribly misshapen. Ah Chun, however, was looking at them with the eye of tradition as she bathed them lovingly each morning, sighing over those small beauties. Chinese tradition dictated that small feet were beautiful, a sign of one's class and wealth. A woman with small feet need never labour while women with big and unbound feet should work like slaves. And, knowing no better, she accepted the injustice of fate and blamed it all on her large feet.

"Let the rains fall, let the storms blow; in fine embroidered slippers, her dainty tiny feet would go," she hummed softly under her breath.

"Stop making so much noise, Ah Chun. Have you boiled the porridge yet?"

"I have, Towkay-neo."

"Brush my hair quickly. Aunt Ee Poh is coming this morning."

Ah Chun brushed and combed her mistress' hair, rubbing the long strands with fragrant oil. How thick and black the hair had been a few years ago; now they were thinning at the temples.

"Aiyah, Geok Neo," Aunt Ee Poh huffed as she came into the room. "You are my niece, so it is my duty, ah, to see that that ingrate, Ah Buck, does not cheat you out of your father's fortune. That Ah Buck has changed, ah! Anyone who's got eyes can see that! Your uncle, ah, tells me that he goes to Keong Saik Street every night. Aiyah, those roadside flowers will wheedle every cent out of him! He is like a bull chewing a chrysanthemum and treating you like his common roadside flowers!"

Aunt Ee Poh who liked to talk went on and on till the tears welled up in Geok Neo's eyes.

"He did not come home again last night," she sobbed.

"Ha! Now I know why people call him Tua Lui Buck! His big eyes roam everywhere. From woman to woman! They tell me, ah, a she-fox in Keong Saik Street has blinded him. He visits her every night!"

"What can I do, Aunt Ee Poh? You tell me. I have given him sons!"

"Aye, what you need is a concubine. A man's a man. All the same. When you are not well each month, what can he do? Naturally, he goes to look for someone else. When your uncle was young, he was like that. Ah, until I gave him a young concubine, ah."

"But I gave him sons!" Geok Neo said, for Aunt Ee Poh had no sons.

"Aye, when a man is rich, son or no son, his heart will not stay still. A young concubine will take care of that. It is any time better than those she-foxes, I tell you. A she-fox, you cannot control. But a concubine, chosen by you, ah! Her you can control, right or not?"

Aunt Ee Poh's argument was irrefutable. It was female wisdom handed down through the generations.

"My niece, ah, listen to your old aunt. You need a concubine. Young and pliable. Someone you can bend. A char-boh-kan is the best. Like my Ah Kiow. A char-boh-kan is always below you. She can never take your place. And since you have bought her, she is yours. You can do what you like with her. And if you raise her to be your husband's concubine, aiyoh! She will be eternally grateful to you. In your debt, so to say, right or not? From a lowly char-boh-kan to rich man's concubine, wah! Big jump, ah. And you have tradition on your side. Her children will have to call you mother. You will always be the mother of all the children born under your roof. Nowadays, ah, we are lax. But in the old days, back in our village, a char-boh-kan cannot even go through the front entrance. Not even when she is dead. Her coffin will have to go out by the back door, ah! Concubine or no concubine, that was the custom, ah. But if she were lucky enough to have a son, and he is filial and sits astride her coffin, then, and only then, ah, can her coffin go out of the house by the front door. So, that is why you, the wife, must have full control over all the children. Your own as well as hers, right or not?"

On the morning of the Mooncake Festival, Ah Chun rose before dawn as usual to sweep the stoves, light the fires and boil porridge for breakfast. The old amah came into the kitchen.

"Aiyah! Still unwashed? What are you waiting for, girl? A matchmaker to attend to you? Shoo! Go and get dressed. It is your big day today, mah!"

Ah Chun's heart was pounding with childish excitement when she donned her new samfoo. Such a lovely red cotton jacket. Almost like the expensive silk samfoos the misses wore for the Lunar New Year. And oh, such delicate white and blue flowers. She liked the crisp feel of her red cotton pants too. Long enough to cover her ankles but not so long that she had to roll them up like the hand-me-downs which she had been wearing. This was the most beautiful suit of samfoo she had ever worn in her entire life! She looked at herself in the mirror. Aged sixteen and a half. A woman already, Towkay-neo told her. Ready for marriage. Her dark eyes clouded at the thought. The old amah hobbled into the dimly lit storeroom.

"Aye, poor girl, ah," she sighed. "You have no mother to comb your hair for you. So I have to do it."

But the old amah, who had never been married before, did not know the ritual song well enough. So they had to make do with a disjointed fragment in Cantonese.

"Aye, comb your hair. May you grow white and old. Comb your hair again. The gods bless you with sons and gold. And, aye! The gods bless you, Ah Chun. From today, your life will be different. You are going to be a married woman. Wear this rose and jasmine. They will have to do in place of a gold hairpin, ah!"

"Thank you, Lan Chay. Will the master beat me tonight?" Ah Chun sobbed. "I don't want to stay in his room."

"Aiyah, stupid girl! Choy! Choy!" the old amah scolded. "No tears! No crying today! Your auspicious day! You will count yourself lucky, ah, if you are allowed to stay in his room one whole night, ah!"

Ah Chun wiped her tears and took one more look at herself in the mirror. A thin brown face with high cheekbones and dark apprehensive eyes stared back at her.

"Aiyah, hurry! You look good already. No need to look any more. I have to return this mirror to Miss, ah. I only borrowed it for you for today."

At six-thirty, the hour deemed auspicious by the temple medium, Ah Chun left the shophouse by the back door. Neither sedan chair, matchmaker, friends nor roast pig and firecrackers accompanied her on her wedding walk from the back door, round the block of shophouses to the front door of her master's shophouse. Then she re-entered the shophouse by the front door, hoisting a bamboo pole across her slender shoulders. A bucket of water hung on each end of the pole and she crossed the threshold of the house like a labourer, an apt symbol of her life to come. A bondmaid on becoming a concubine must be reminded that she was not a pampered mistress nor an honoured second wife, Aunt Ee Poh said. This time-honoured ritual of carrying water would serve as a reminder that a concubine's status was only higher than that of the servants but lower than that of the children. Painted on the buckets hanging from each end of the bamboo pole were the characters for gold and silver. This was to symbolise the concubine's auspicious entry into the family, bringing gold and silver, ushering in the gods of wealth and prosperity. As Ah Chun stepped across the threshold, she spilt water, and as she went up the stairs and into the living room, stopping in front of the family altar.

"Good luck is coming! Good luck and fortune, ah!" the old amah cried. "Gold and silver spilling all over the house!"

Tall red candles and sticks of fragrant incense invited the gods and ancestors to gather round to receive the kowtows and libations of wine from the new concubine. The master and the mistress sat on two rosewood chairs in front of the altar. The misses, girls in their teens like Ah Chun herself, crowded into the living room, curious and giggling. They were the only witnesses at the ceremony. Geok Neo had refused to spend any money on a feast. The eldest Miss Ong looked on with serious eyes for she was the same age as Ah Chun and the matchmaker had already found someone for her.

Ah Chun stole a glance at her master. The towkay was looking kindly at her, she thought. But Towkay-neo's face was stiff like an opera mask. Ah Chun knelt down before them and kowtowed three times.

"Towkay and Towkay-neo, please accept your lowly maid's cup of tea," she murmured.

"First kowtow, you serve and obey," the old amah chanted in a ceremony conducted in two dialects, Hokkien and Cantonese.

"Second kowtow, you serve without delay. Third kowtow, you will bear fruit and bring them good fortune every day."

Then Geok Neo took out an embroidered slipper and hit her three times on the head. "Hitting you is reminding you who you should obey. Under my hand and under my feet, you are the concubine today. Serve your master and serve me well," Geok Neo chanted in Hokkien. "I name you Sia Liew the pomegranate. Be fruitful and bear us sons."

That night, Sia Liew the pomegranate lay on her mistress' bed and waited in the dark for her master. When he finally came into the bedroom, he said, "Take off your clothes." She could hear his heavy breathing as he groped about the bedclothes and lay down beside her. She closed her eyes when he grabbed her. Towkay-neo had told her that a good woman should never look at the man. "Open wide your legs," her towkay growled. She clenched her fists and thrust them into her mouth when he rammed into her. She bit hard. Inside her head, she was screaming over and over again, "A whipping is worse! Ten times worse! Ten times worse!"

When it was finally over, her towkay turned away and fell fast asleep, snoring beside her. Then the bedroom door opened and Towkay-neo came in. Sia Liew the pomegranate scrambled out of bed. Hastily, she wiped away the sticky mess seeping down the insides of her thighs and pulled up her pants before stealing out of the bedroom like a thief in the night. A bondmaid could sleep anywhere, Aunt Ee Poh said. On the floor or under the table. Anywhere. And so from that night onwards until the birth of her son, Sia Liew the pomegranate slept on the floor of the passageway outside her mistress' bedroom. Whenever the master wanted her, Towkay-neo would come out and awaken her with a kick. And when it was over, Sia Liew went back to sleep on the floor.

Whenever that happened, the old amah would sing softly in the kitchen, "Aye, aye, aye! Umbrellas have different handles, people have different fates. Ah so, that's what we Cantonese say."

"Now if that wasn't marital rape, what is?" Nica Sivalingam asked. "Long ago, yesterday, today and tomorrow, what's the diff? Women will always seek love and security. And the men – sex and sex and sex. Copulation to be precise."

No one in the group which included Mark Campbell, Robert Lim and Janice Wong said anything in response. They were quite used to Nica's forthright speech and equally forthright views on sex and art by now. Sometimes Suwen had even wondered whether Nica's mixed Baba Chinese and Indian heritage had something to do with it. Perhaps the necessity of having to straddle two or three cultures within the home had forged a strong personality.

"Here's your drink," Robert handed her a glass of sweet apple wine.

"Thanks," Suwen nodded absent-mindedly and returned to watching the hamsters. Nica's pet hamsters fascinated her. They were kept in a large black cage in one comer of her studio apartment. The male was sprayed a luminous green and the female a luminous pink. Pink chasing green and green chasing pink, round and round the toy merry-go-round in the cage. Then Mark switched off the lights and the luminous balls of pink and green glowed dramatically in the dark as they chased each other round the cage.

> "And the seasons, they go round and round;
> And the painted ponies go up and down.
> We're travelling on a carousel of time.
> We can't return, we can only look behind
> from where we came;
> And go round and round and round in a circle game..."

A husky voice was crooning from the cassette player which Mark had switched on.

"All our life, we go on looking for someone who will love us. Love chasing sex; sex chasing love," Nica said.

"Hmm-mmm," Mark was humming the song softly.

"Nyet! C'mon, Mark! This is so trite, man," Robert laughed. "Play something more jazzy. Boring lah!"

"I still think the hits of the sixties have something to say to us," Mark countered, ready to launch into one of their usual entertaining debates on pop culture.

"Yes, Mark, but we are not talking about songs now," Nica pointed out impatiently. She was not going to let the men change the subject. "From time immemorial, the guys go after sex, love or no love. No diff to men. Right, Mark?" Nica's voice had a hard teasing edge to it.

Suwen waited to see if Mark would allow himself to be drawn into a sexist argument which he could never hope to win. Not if Nica could help it. And Nica always got her way. Robert had given up long ago trying to win an argument with her. How she wished she had Nica's magnetism, for the men usually did what she wanted in the end.

"The men here go to Hatyai. In droves," Nica was saying. "They have their bit of fun. Then they return to their wives the next day. As if nothing had happened. And it's true. Nothing had happened. A f--- or two don't count. For the men. Right?"

Mark and Robert were silent. Janice was glad that Zul was not there with her that night. Nica was fun to be with when she was light and gay. But not when she was in one of her dark moods. "Zul is not very comfortable with her," she had confided to Suwen once. "But I like the crowd round Nica. I don't want to hang out with teachers all the time. It can be so boring." And Suwen had agreed, thinking of all those women who could go on and on about jewellery, clothes, bargains and mothers-in-law, the staffroom talk seldom rising above exam results and grumbles about the Ministry. The arty crowd she had met in Nica's apartment was different and therefore more stimulating. Nica was the consummate artist, full of sudden changes in her moods. To Suwen, she was the sculptor or dramatist in performance art who could change the shape and mood of a roomful of people simply by saying something provocative.

The air was heavy with the approach of rain, and the night breeze wafting in through the window was warm. From the light of the street lamps filtering through the foliage outside, Mark could see the profiles of the three women. Their delicate Asian features belie their strength, he thought; there's flint beneath their silken exteriors. "Well," he said, "I don't mean to defend my sex, but as with all generalisations..."

"Mark, I know what you want to say," Nica's voice rose above the music when someone, probably Robert, lowered the volume. "Present company excepted, okay? But in general, men are shallow. You guys can't help yourselves. It's your biology. Your sex organs are outside your bodies. So you can't feel as deeply as we do. I mean, to put it crudely, between the thrust and the spasm, it's all over for you guys. We are the fortunate ones. Ah no, Su and Jan! I can see your smiles. Even in the dark. I know what you two are thinking. But I'm not thinking of our grandmothers and their bondmaids and suffering. I'm looking at us biologically. And biologically, we are the lucky ones. Our sex organs are inside us. So we can feel more deeply. Sex affects our entire being. It strikes us in the heart. In our very core. For us, sex and love come together. Like a two-edged sword. The day a woman enjoys her first sex-love encounter, she's cut in two. But the guy remains the same. He spends a night, a hundred nights, with a woman. Then he goes away. His life and body don't change. But a woman's body does. She can conceive. And carry the fruit of those hundred nights in her body. Nine months long. Inside her body. Look upon it as a curse or a joy. It depends on whether one is loved or not, doesn't it? But curse or joy, the fruit grows in her. And never quite departs from her. Not even after an abortion."

PART 3

...to sculpt and shape

Nica was the kind of artist Suwen wanted to be if she could ever resign from the college. Bold, frank, honest and utterly at ease with people, she had a wide circle of artistic friends, art collectors and dealers. Everyone who had anything to do with the arts in Singapore seemed to know Nica. She was one of those fortunate persons, born into the limelight, attracting people the way a candle attracted moths. She gathered to herself circles of friends and acquaintances wherever she went; people cheered and applauded her outrageous sayings and risqué jokes. When she got up to speak in front of an audience, she became like an animated piece of art. Everyone's eyes were drawn to her. Her large dramatic gestures swept through the air like bold brush strokes creating asymmetrical designs. Her heavy bangles of Indian silver, carved ivory and tortoise shell with coloured stones caught the light as she moved. Her scarves and necklaces draped about her neck created a tension of colours, fabrics and stones.

When she walked, her small breasts thrust forward as if to assert that she was a woman but, beware, a highly volatile one.

How Suwen had often wished for that supreme self-confidence. As if the world existed for one to sculpt and mould. She watched without rancour and envy the way Nica could hold the attention of others by swishing her skirts and her scarves with the subtle disciplined grace of the artist and dancer, and sighed with the resignation of an onlooker who knew her place on the sidelines. It was not as if she had not longed secretly to enter that charmed inner circle of the art world in which she could paint and earn a decent living as an artist. But she knew that she was not as fortunate as Nica. Robert Lim, Nica's live-in companion, was devoted to her. He was from a wealthy Chinese family with many business connections. Robert brought the wealthy but hip art dealers and collectors to Nica's parties, and they, in turn, became the added incentive which drew together other sculptors, painters, designers, media people and so on. These parties, held four or five times a year, were unlike their quieter Saturday gatherings. They often left her dazzled and delighted. They were like the Bohemian evenings of the rich arty crowds in London which she had read about. And Nica, in the midst of these events, seemed to her to be living an artist's life of heightened sensibility and sensuousness. "Sculpture, more so than painting, is a sensuous art," Nica said.

But then Nica could say anything. Nica had the confidence which she, Suwen, lacked. She had often seen Nica walk down Orchard Road, ever so confident that her lithe dancer's body was a natural construct built for admiration. She, Suwen, on the other hand, had never felt that way about her body before. Not ever. She was more like a raindrop, falling like millions of other raindrops to join the common pool of humanity flowing into the wide open sea.

When the storm had passed, Suwen went for a walk on the beach with Nica the next day. The sun was rising above the waters. Bars of yellow and orange nudged away the dark grey clouds of the night before and fell upon the beach, gilding the poor fisherman's weathered sampan. The leaves of the crab apple trees gleamed red and gold as the thin swift waves, pierced by the morning light, raced, curled, and spread out their latticed fans of foam. Down by the rocky embankments, the waves hurled themselves upon the shore and, drawing back, teased the beach of sand, leaving behind a long black undulating cordon of driftwood, bits of cardboard, newspapers and the ubiquitous pink plastic bags of Singapore's picnickers.

An old Malay fisherman stood with sun-browned arms outstretched, holding the bamboo poles of his net. He held it up against the light, shaking out the minute shrimps, squids and other sea jewels of jade, ruby and sapphire onto the waves of dancing lights which, quivering, ran towards the shore, racing ahead of the morning breeze. Not to be outdone, the sea breezes rose and flew round and round the angsana trees in bloom, shaking down showers of golden blossoms upon the feeding crows and quarrelsome mynahs. The birds fluttered and pecked among the rubbish bins. Two schoolboys sauntered by and threw a stick at them. With a flutter of black wings, the birds scattered to the tree tops and waited, in wary silence, till the boys, laughing, callous, male and supreme, had strutted off. Then the birds returned to the bins to scratch and scold, and to pick at the insides of the swollen things washed ashore, the rotten fruit peels, mouldy rice and crumbs of half-eaten sandwiches.

Nica led the way to the far end of the beach, clambered atop the rocky embankment and crossed the monsoon drain to the finger of wasteland as yet unclaimed by man and industry. Here the sea breezes whispered among the bushes and tall grasses while the birds, hidden from view, chirped erratically from this bush, up that tree, high among the casuarinas or down below the thorn bushes with the bright yellow flowers. A lonesome oriole trilled and whistled an instant, and held its breath. The pain of apprehension hung in the momentary silence which followed. Suwen looked up and spied, high up swaying on the tip of a casuarina, a bright yellow bird warbling her response. A flutter of yellow joy, sharp and shrill, now loud, then soft, now alone, then together, the pair trilled amorously from the casuarina to the angsana, and back again. Then, tiring of such sweet rivalry, the golden orioles fell silent and flew away.

Suwen followed Nica on the planks, zigzagging across the muddy puddles, the remains of the previous night's storm. Nica's body moved with the deliberate grace of the trained dancer, her father having insisted that she take up Indian classical dancing when she was young. Her eyes followed the flight of the seabirds which swooped and dipped the tips of their wings into the dancing waves. Then, flicking off the water drops, they flew over the land into the distance, black dots in the sky. But just as they were about to turn away, the birds veered round like a dark boomerang over the trees, and came gliding down smoothly for yet another dip into the water where the Singapore River entered the sea. Then, looking up again, the two of them spotted the hawk. A singular brown dot against the blue of the sky, cruising in ever decreasing circles as it descended towards the trees on the beach. It seemed to be heading towards the bird sanctuary. It was gliding above the casuarinas, sweeping past the angsanas and then as if rejecting the safety of their shadows, headed towards the open sea again. A lone majestic hawk. Brown, singular and solitary.

"That's what it takes to be an artist," Nica pointed at the hawk. "I can still remember how lonely that moment was when I decided to be a sculptor."

"I can sympathise with that kind of loneliness," Suwen murmured, recalling in a flash that hot lonely afternoon in Kuala Jelai.

"My first wish was: I shall sculpt myself away from this house and this town. Away from the narrow-mindedness and pettiness of Alor Star. That provincial town was like a prison to me. Living there was like being under house arrest. The Indian community there was so bloody small. Everybody knew everybody else. No place was safe from prying eyes. Everyone knew I was the daughter of Doctor Sivalingam, chief surgeon in GH. Important man. Got his reputation to maintain. Indian men are as petty as their women. I used to wonder how my poor mother could put up with my father's nonsense. She's from a Baba family. And Catholic while my father remained Hindu. In name, at least."

Nica told Suwen that she grew up in a household where the air of oppressive authority had made it difficult for her to breathe so that, as a child, she was asthmatic and sickly all the time. A weak constitution and the fact that she was the youngest of five girls had made her redoubtable Sri Lankan Tamil grandmother keep her at home to be dosed with herbs, tonics and fuss. By the time she was seven, all her older sisters had been sent away to exclusive convents in New Delhi, and she was brought up as an only child, with all the drawbacks of such a position.

She was her mother's last attempt to beget a son and heir for the Sivalingams. But that failure had led to her mother's fall from grace, and Mrs Sivalingam senior had found her only son's mixed marriage unforgivable and unacceptable. But the deed was already done, and old Mrs Sivalingam had had to accept the unacceptable. If only her boy had listened to her, she moaned over and over again to friends and relatives. She had spoilt him. He was too headstrong and rebellious, and she had given in. His marriage had naturally shocked the Indian community in Alor Star at the time, for the Sivalingams were well-respected, and everyone knew that old Mrs Sivalingam could have gotten a girl from some of the best families in Sri Lanka or India for her son. Instead he had married a Chinese girl from an unknown family.

Then, consequently, the years of friction and attrition between her mother and grandmother had weakened her father's constitution. The poor sod, Nica said. By the time she had reached the age of consciousness, her father was no longer the idealistic young doctor who had set out to defy the prejudices of his community. He had reverted to being his mother's son. Arrogant, selfish and domineering like every self-righteous Indian man who had been brought up by a doting mother in the belief that the universe revolved around him. The father she knew was a man so proud of his Indian heritage that he was determined that his five daughters should be brought up as Proper Indian Girls and nothing else! PIGs! "Papa wants us to grow up as PIGs!" she used to giggle behind his back. For she and her elder sisters were to be as Indian as money could make them. That was why they had had to endure long tedious hours of Tamil lessons and Indian classical music and dancing lessons.

Once her father had smacked her for picking up her amah's Cantonese. Her mother was reprimanded and the Cantonese amah was dismissed. Her grandmother sent for a Sri Lankan ayah. And from then on, she was allowed to speak only English and what her grandmother had proudly called "our pure Tamil". Her father had also whacked her for sneaking into St Anne's Church with her mother. Those early whackings had so lacerated her young sensitive heart that on Sundays, she used to lock herself in her bedroom lest her childish curiosity would get the better of her and she was tempted to follow her mother to church again. Not that she understood her mother's Catholic god any better than her grandmother's Hindu god. As a child she had admired the splendid robes of the Catholic priest. One Sunday, the robes were emerald green, another Sunday, they were blood red and purple. Oh, the passion of the figure dying on the cross! How she had cried when the priest told them the story of how He was whipped by the Jews! And how splendid those priestly garments had looked, shimmering in the stained glass gloom of the old church in Alor Star.

During the years of her growing up, she saw with precocious insight how her mother was being eroded into a pale shadow of her former self, stubbornly clinging to her only possession, her Catholic faith, but always distorting the central message of the Gospel by persistently offering her other cheek to her mother-in-law in the erroneous belief that such a display of meekness would shame her enemy into submission.

"From then on, when I realised what my mother was doing, I vowed never to be meek. Meekness was used as a weapon. I vowed never to be subjected to any earthly or spiritual authority. It was all bull," she told Suwen.

She was following her own will and impulses when she painted those splendid priestly robes and vestments, she said. And then she moulded and shaped those forms with such a vibrant sensuousness that even her art teacher, a man, was embarrassed. What would people say? Her art teacher was afraid that the parents of the other girls might think he was depraved and withdraw their daughters from his classes. So he had asked her to leave. "I've got nothing else to teach your daughter," he told her father, knowing full well that that was not the reason.

"The dog! He had no balls! My father scolded and stormed, of course. He said I should be learning how to cook and sew like my elder sisters. Even threatened to pack me off to Sri Lanka. What would the relatives think? Which nice young man would want me? How could I gad about and make obscene things? That's when I blew my top. What's wrong with the human figure? I asked him. You're a doctor. You've seen and touched such bodies! Aren't the walls of Indian temples covered with half nudes too? So are your Indian artists and craftsmen obscene too? He really hit the roof! But I didn't care. That was when he slapped me. Right in front of many people. But I had already decided to leave home. I wanted to be free. Free like a spirit floating above the Indians and the Chinese. I am neither. Neither my mother's nor my father's daughter. Just me. Nica."

"You are strong," Suwen murmured as her eyes followed Nica's, watching the lone hawk encircling the trees against an expanse of blue and white.

"Can a hawk forget its hawkness and a man his race?" Suwen asked.

"Of course not!"

"But if I had been given away as a baby to an Indian family, then wouldn't I grow up Indian even though I might look Chinese?"

"Like that, of course, lah! But other than that, cannot!"

Nica was adamant. She spoke from personal experience, she said. And she didn't think a person, however highly educated, could forget his colour and his language.

"My first boyfriend was a Chinese. Ti Lung. One evening we went for a walk along Boat Quay. Years back before they developed the place. We were holding hands..."

She could see him still with his straight longish hair. He was her first love. And although the wound had healed, the scar was still there. They were walking past a row of shophouses, young and in love. Boat Quay was splashed with gold from the setting sun. High above them, in one of the cubicles of the shophouses, a lone flute was playing, yearning like a lover in pain. Suddenly this idyllic peace was shattered by a loud crude voice yelling Hokkien obscenities from one of the windows. "Oi! You filthy Kling! You Kling-ah-char-boh! Kee-ho-lan-kan-ah!" Ti Lung let go of her hand at once. Pale-faced and grim, he walked quickly ahead of her, expecting her to follow. "Quick," he hissed, "let's get out of here." A stream of Hokkien filth followed them as they hurried out of the Boat Quay vicinity. That was in nineteen sixty-six.

"Did you two talk about it after that?" Suwen asked, her voice hesitant, knowing that this was privileged information, a side of Nica which the others, including Jan, were not allowed to know.

"Ti Lung and I didn't discuss it. He wasn't the sort. And I was too embarrassed to bring it up. It was awful. And I think deep down I was hurt. He just let go of my hand. Just like that! And damn it! We had made love the night before."

"What happened after that?"

"Nothing happened. We drifted apart. I heard he got married in Perth last month. I sent him a card. It's more than fifteen years ago. We are both going to be forty soon. So what the heck, I thought! I won't bear him a grudge.

Life's too short for that sort of thing."

What she did not tell Suwen was that two months later, she had aborted the fruit of that night because the child's father was such a coward. She could neither forget nor forgive his cowardice.

"We are still very racial and very prejudiced," Suwen was fuming, her dark eyes smouldering with the anger she felt on behalf of Nica.

"It's all right, dear. We know. This is nothing new. Class and race. Old as the hills. My own grandmother forbade me to play with our Indian gardener's children. Why? Because they got lice and they were Klings! But we! Ah, we are Ceylon Tamils, she said. They don't speak good Tamil, she said. But we were supposed to speak a purer form of Tamil. I never forgot that day when she caught me playing with Muthu and Mala. She soaked my hair with some evil-smelling herbs and oil. To get rid of kutus. Head lice, you know."

And that night, her father had taken her aside for a long talk, impressing upon her that she was a Ceylon Tamil and not a common Kling. You will find the term "Klings" used in the history books and letters of colonial gentlemen, he had told her. It was a term originally used for Indian convicts, railway workers, rubber tappers and generally the lower classes of Indians. But her father had been a trifle embarrassed during his talk. He had tried so hard to be egalitarian in his youth only to find that he could not. Yet he would never admit it. He was such a hypocrite. The phrase "lower classes or castes" embarrassed him. Yet he had insisted on telling her that one need not be ashamed of having a convict or two in the family. The white Australians had hundreds of thousands in their ancestry. And Charles Dickens had even written a novel on one of them.

"All bull, of course," Nica laughed. "But even if you challenge him till you're blue in the face, he'd still say no, he has nothing against the lower castes. It's just that he doesn't want his daughter to get head lice."

Suwen laughed too. Nica could be so entertaining, and her humour had bite; she was not afraid to poke fun at herself and her family. Yet beneath that daughter, Suwen could see that Nica was, in her own way, rather proud of her intransigent father and the high respect her family commanded in the community. All her elder sisters had married men successful in law and business.

"But surely caste is not important in Singapore now?"

"No, except in the eyes of some die-hards. People like my father and grandmother are very sensitive to perceived insults, you know. So they always let others know how very important our family is."

"Oh, to prevent insults, is it?"

"Must be, lah! Especially from the angmohs. Not that people like my father will admit it. He's so darn proud that he's better qualified than his English boss in GH. It's something to do with his granduncle. And the Indian Sepoys' Mutiny in Singapore. After that, my father told us, his granduncle and his grandfather made sure everybody in the family went to English schools and studied up to university."

The Story Of Dr Sivalingam's Granduncle

"I believe in equality. All men are equal." My father always begins the story like this. "But the English, oh, they are hypocrites. They befriended us, natives, only if it served their purpose. They've got ulterior motives. They wanted to use us. That's what my granduncle taught us."

My great granduncle worked as a translator in the Singapore Colonial Service. In the Police Department. He got on very well with the Superintendent, an Englishman. On the day of the mutiny, he had been offered a lift to the police station by the Superintendent's wife. He was seated in the front seat, next to Rahman, the Malay chauffeur. Mrs Robinson was in the back seat with her two little daughters. Suddenly, their car was overtaken by a large convoy of trucks, full of Indian sepoys in khaki, some with rifles, some without. One of the soldiers fired into the air. Mrs Robinson and the two girls screamed. Another shot rang out. Mrs Robinson pushed her daughters onto the floorboard of the car and covered them with her body.

"Pulang! Lekas! Lekas!" my great granduncle yelled to the Malay chauffeur. Rahman stepped on it and screeched round the corner as more shots rang out and people were screaming and running helter-skelter.

"Thank God, you're safe, Martha!" the Superintendent hugged his wife and daughters when they reached home. "Thank you, Mr Sivalingam. Thank God, you and Rahman kept your heads and brought them back safely."

"Sahib, the Indian sepoys are killing the orang puteh," Rahman spoke in Malay.

"That's right, sir. It is safer to move your family away from here, sir."

"Thank you, old chap. I will never forget this. Get into the van, Martha. And you too, girls. Hurry. Not a moment to lose. Go to Johnston Pier. All the women and children will be taken by launch to the ships. You'll be safe out there. Thank God Almighty, those blackguards didn't get you! The Fifth Infantry had just mutinied. Mr Sivalingam, I advise you to go home quickly. When your services are required I will send for you."

Throughout the mutiny, Indians like my great granduncle stayed at home. The streets were not safe for Indians. The British soldiers were after them and they could not be bothered to find out, before shooting, who were the sepoys and who were not. All those with black skins were shot on sight. All sorts of ugly rumours about the Indian sepoys made the rounds. One tragic story about a certain Mrs Woolcombe sent the sailors of a navy ship on a rampage. She had thrown herself across her husband's body when the mutineers shot him. A second shot had killed her. The sailors who found her body went on a rampage, shooting at all dark-skinned people.

Many mutineers died or were wounded, and many more were captured. Among those captured was a sepoy who had shot the Woolcombes. My great granduncle was summoned by the Superintendent to act as his translator. The sepoy spoke freely to him because he knew the British would show him no mercy. Those British army types could be very harsh. But he was not afraid; the God of the Prophet Mohammed would protect him, he told my great granduncle. Ever since he was a boy back in the state of Madras, he had heard the call for "jihad" or holy war. His father, grandfather and great grandfather had had to defend their mosques against the Hindu vandals. His family had lived through tumultuous times in a land which was predominantly Hindu, and the young sepoy was filled with the angry righteousness of men long oppressed and suppressed by social forces which they did not fully comprehend, but nonetheless strongly felt.

"Bloody pork eaters! Those English pigs!" the Indian-Muslim sepoy yelled. "Ask the big sahib over there! Did he think we were fools? They gave us bullets coated with pork fat! And they expect us to bite off bits of these before loading our muskets! They have no respect for our faith!"

"You dirty bastard!" an English voice rang out. The young sepoy panicked and ran. A bullet hit him. He slumped forward. Another hit his leg as he fell. The wooden butt of a rifle slammed his back. He was kicked and stomped upon. He lost some teeth when the hobnailed heel of a British boot crushed his face. The heel had just missed his eye by a hair's breadth.

"Shot in an attempt to escape", the English report read; a terse one-liner on the subject.

My father used to say that he didn't care two hoots what the English historians had written about the Indian Mutiny. He was adamant that had the British been a bit more knowledgeable about and sensitive to the people they governed, none of that bloodshed and violence would have happened. But the English of the Empire days had always assumed that everybody should live like them.

After the mutiny, all Indians in Singapore and Malaysia were tarred with the same brush and regarded with suspicion by the Brits. My father told us that my great granduncle was never invited back to the Superintendent's bungalow again, and his wife even sacked their Tamil gardener and washerwoman. My great granduncle could not tolerate the insidious discrimination against the Indians in the colonial service. So he resigned and went into business. And that's why my father has always maintained that we are not the descendants of Klings. Those sepoys were the Klings, not us.

"It's a pity we don't discuss such things in school. Not even in college history class," Suwen said.

"Don't you know," Nica's eyes lit up mischievously, "our history academics are competing to see who can write the most boring inoffensive history of Singapore?"

"You, ah!" Suwen shook her head. "You let your tongue run away from you sometimes."

"Sorry lah! It's the Indian part of me. My Chinese side is more prudent and kiasu."

Suwen soon slipped into the routine of meeting Nica without the others, on the Friday evenings or Saturday mornings when Robert was away or Jan was with Zul. At first, she was shy and feared that she might prove to be a disappointment and a bore. Nica, after all, was an accomplished artist and sculptor. She was talented, interesting and forceful. People admired her for her strong character and her fearlessness to do what she wanted. "I don't give a toss for what the academics say. Those who can, paint. Those who can't, criticise," she laughed. Next to her, Suwen felt weak and pale, like the duller shades of earth colours. The greens and browns of the lichens one finds along the drains, she thought ruefully, whereas Nica's personality had the vibrant reds and yellows of tropical blooms, commanding the attention of others by her mere presence. On meeting her, one knew at once that here was a woman used to taking centre stage. She seemed ignorant of the sad compromises and quiet consolations which others had had to accept as part of their lot on the sidelines or backstage.

Suwen admired her as a model of what the liberated artistically-talented woman could be, the harbinger of dreams come true. For if Nica was seen as a woman marching to her own drumbeat, might not she, Suwen, hope that some day someone would describe her as an artist painting to the melody of her own flute?

At first, she was amazed that Nica was quite taken with her and took an interest in her work. Suwen was a little shy of confessing her own eagerness to learn the fine points of craftsmanship or her secret longing to enter that inner charmed circle of the arty world. Since her return from England, her life had revolved around college and the garage she called home. The routine of teaching and marking from Mondays to Fridays, and conducting extra painting lessons on Saturday mornings, leaving Sundays free for her own artistic endeavours, gave her the illusion of living a full and busy life. The potential boredom of this routine was broken now and then with visits to the theatre and art exhibitions with friends like Jan. It was not a rich life, but it was satisfactory enough to stave off the occasional nagging sense of emptiness, particularly the kind which attacked her during the long school vacations.

"Now that Mark's here, your life will change, what," Nica said, one day.

"No, why should it change?" she protested.

"Don't bluff lah! Of course it will change. Your loved one is here."

"No, listen..."

"I am listening. Tell me about Mark. How did you meet him?"

"Well, actually, we became good friends after a fist fight."

"Oh! A fist fight! How kinky!" Nica cocked her head and gave her a mischievous wink.

"It's not what you think, Nica. I was attending the summer school in Aberdeen. Mark was one of our tutors. The school attracted many people from different parts of the world. From France, Spain, Eastern Europe. Oh yes, and a large group from Czechoslovakia in the charge of an ice maiden. She was their leader and she never smiled..."

"Hey, why so long-winded? Tell me about you and Mark."

"There's nothing much to tell really."

"One month together and nothing to tell? Okay, skip the intimacies and just tell me how you two met."

Suwen soon found out that Nica had a penchant for being disconcertingly insistent on knowing one's life and feelings.

"Stop holding out on me, Su," she said. "You're being silly and secretive over nothing."

"There's really nothing much to tell. Mark was nice and approachable. But one night, I was so furious, I boxed his arm."

"Now that's what I call an interesting story," Nica said. "Carry on."

"You see, we were supposed to take part in a concert. International Night or something. All of us, the participants, had to contribute an item. Most people sang or recited something in their national language. But the three of us from Singapore didn't know what to do. I mean our national language is Malay but we didn't know Malay. And the two girls from Malaysia had already recited a Malay pantun. And two guys from China recited some poems in Mandarin. The girl from Hong Kong even sang an aria from a Cantonese opera. And she was very good. So one of the Singapore girls wanted to sing 'Burong Kakak Tua'. She was from a Baba family. But that's not a Singaporean song, the Malaysian lady told us. Anyway, the two of us didn't know the words. So, in the end, we sang 'Sing Your Way Home'. The applause, well, was lukewarm. Some of the Caucasians wondered why we sang in English. I was so embarrassed. Then later that night, Mark said something stupid. I can't remember his exact words. But it was something like I had no tongue of my own, and that I had to use a borrowed tongue."

Suwen paused; it was an episode she would have liked to erase and forget had Nica not pressed her. She had often wondered whether she had been overly sensitive; after all, lots of people had studied abroad, and they had probably encountered the same kind of problem, too – people wondering about their use of English in those situations where they were representing their countries.

"I remember feeling very low. I didn't know why at the time. I think I even cried a little. It was silly, I know. But the tears just came. I excused myself and left the room. I remember standing in the dimly lit corridor for a long time. But it was dark outside, and I had nowhere to go. So I went back into the room, I looked for Mark. I was very angry by then. When I found him, I just boxed his arm. Very hard. I was mad with him and myself."

"Slow! What took you so long to get mad? I would've boxed his ears right at the start."

"Normally I don't get angry in public. I think I gave Mark a rude shock that night. And I was very blunt. You are a Scot, I said. And your English is not a borrowed tongue? Do you mean to say that English is the native language of the Scots, Irish and Welsh? Some of the Caucasians applauded, I remember. But I didn't care who were listening. I only wanted to remind them that Asians weren't the only ones colonised by the English. Then I left. I didn't want people to see me crying."

"Good for you! So what happened then?"

"Nothing happened. Mark looked for me the next day. He was upset that I had been upset. So we went for a long walk. It was a four-hour walk, I think."

"Crazy girl," Nica shook her head. "Why do you let such things upset you?"

"I don't know. But I've been thinking, well, not all the time. D'you think language defines a man the way an artist's forms and lines define him? I was born ethnically Chinese. I grew up speaking English. Am I not Chinese still? Or am I just half-Chinese? Not because of a physical change but because of a language change."

"Good grief! I've never thought about this. It doesn't even bother me."

"That's it lah! Most people are not bothered by this. That's why I've not talked with anybody about it. Not even Jan. But I get real mad each time I read in the Forum Page all those complaints about people like us who can't read Chinese. Those people don't think sometimes. Some of us are Babas and we speak Malay at home."

"Ya, like my mum. Her father's a Baba and they speak Malay."

"And I went to primary school in Perak. I had to do Malay. Then when I came to Singapore, we were allowed to choose. That was in the sixties. Late sixties. So I chose not to do another language. Now I'm one of those who even dream in English. Isn't this what one of the Forum Page writers complain about?"

"I don't know why you take such people seriously. Damn it! English is the language we think with."

"I know; it's just that people expect all Chinese to be the hua-ren-chiang-hua-yu sort. Chinese should speak Chinese. I can't speak Mandarin, you see. I can still speak Cantonese but that's not counted nowadays, right?"

"Right. But you're being too sensitive, Su. Once you see what these people are trying to do, you can ignore them. We're living in an age of cultural lobotomy. Forget about your Cantonese, Teochew and Hokkien. Think Mandarin. Drop the dialects. That's what the authorities want. It's a kind of sculpting. Social sculpting. They want to sculpt a new kind of Singapore Chink. The Mandarin-speaking sort. Dialects belong to the peasants. Mandarin is the language of the educated Chinese. You betray your peasant roots if you speak dialects."

"No lah!" Suwen protested. "That's your quirky interpretation. I'm just sorry that I can't speak Cantonese as well as those in Hong Kong,"

"You're sorry! What about me? Nica Sivalingam. Listed as Indian but my second language in school was Mandarin because my dear mother had insisted on it. But she doesn't even speak Mandarin herself! She just wanted me to learn it so she could get even with my father. All my older sisters had to do Tamil. So, by the time it came to my turn, my mum wanted her way. To balance things, she said. My father said that my Tamil is half-past six. But do you think I care? So what if I speak and dream in English? I'm the new breed. At least I have full command over one language. C'mon, Su! We are better off than those who speak a smattering of Mandarin and a smattering of English but are fluent in neither. At least you and I can live, love and lust fully in one language! Yeah! Let's celebrate!"

And that was what Suwen admired in Nica. She was so strong and positive about things.

"My grandpa, on my mother's side, used to work in there," Nica pointed to the former Jinricksha Station, a squat two-storey building, opposite what used to be the Metropole Cinema. "He could speak English, Malay and Hokkien very well. Chief clerk in the rickshaw department."

"So he must've been a sort of go-between. Between the angmoh bosses and the Asians," Suwen said.

"Ya, he was one of those who stuck with the Brits and lost his life during the Japanese Occupation. So, that's why I want to paint this before they change it. Renovate it beyond recognition."

The two women set up their stools and easels in the shadow of the Housing Board flats. Nica put on a cap, wearing it at a rakish angle which made her look quite dashing in her jeans and embroidered smock. Looking at her, Suwen wished she had thought of wearing something like that instead of her straw hat and long-sleeved shirt. Next to Nica's cap, scarf and beads, she was beginning to feel like the meter maid.

"Where did you get that scarf, Nic?"

"Tekkah market. Very cheap."

"But nice. I wish I know how to put together things like this."

"That's what you always say, Su. Just be yourself. You dress okay."

But just as she was beginning to feel confident about her shirt, Nica continued, "Well, some of the time."

"D'you mean that other times I dress awful?"

"Gosh, Su! You mustn't take what I say too seriously," Nica laughed. "Now where were we?"

"About to start sketching," Suwen muttered.

"Right. Before you begin," Nica said in her I-am-in-charge voice, "study the building. Recall its history. Ask yourself: what am I trying to say about this building? Fine architectural details? Play of light and shadows? What? Many paintings of old buildings are just lovely descriptive pictures. They evoke romance and nostalgia. So what? Do they have significant form? Do they suggest the significant past? If there's nothing more, then I say they are touristy stuff. Mere nostalgic scenes."

"Oh, Nic! You're going to offend a lot of people. Talking like this!"

"I don't care. It's the truth, what!"

"I know you don't care. You don't have to because you work alone."

"No, sometimes I teach in the Art College."

"But the people there leave you alone."

"We don't see eye to eye about painting and sculpting. But I can accept that. Why? Are people bothering you?"

Suwen was reluctant to confess her anxiety over her relations with Mark and the other teachers in her college.

"Tell me," Nica pressed her. "There's no sense in bottling your feelings up. Especially if it's over work."

"No, the work's okay. It's the people."

"Is it Mark?" Nica eyed her shrewdly.

"No. I mean yes. Partly him." Suwen felt the warmth on her cheeks spreading.

"Did he ask you to go to bed or what?"

"No, no! Not that, Nica!"

"Oh, then what?"

"You see, we've got quite a few expat teachers in our college now."

"You're talking about Mark, right?"

"Yes. I mean no! You're making me confused. It's not just Mark. There's Dave and Bob."

"So?"

"We, I mean those of us women in the Art and English departments, get on well with them. They're fun. And they can talk. Very well."

"So?"

"So, some of the other teachers, especially the guys are muttering things lah! Nothing serious. But irritating! Actually, the culprit is Peter Kong. I've heard him say things like some people are licking the angmohs' boots and things like that."

"Ugh! He's sick!"

"It's sickening. He doesn't say it outright, you know. He mutters and hums and snorts. But you know that he's making innuendos about you. I try to ignore him. Sometimes I think it's my own hang-up and I'm upset over nothing."

"Just ignore him."

"But it's not him alone, you see. Nobody dared to say anything when these expats were brought in. But I know that some people feel threatened. But they don't speak about it openly. At meetings, they always keep quiet. Then they mutter-mutter among themselves. Peter's group is like this. The other teachers don't say anything too. They just smile and nod but they never sit down with me and Mark in the canteen. Except Jan and the girls from his English department. The men all keep away."

"Ah! Just ignore them! Concentrate on your painting."

They did not talk about it any more. It was obviously a subject which did not interest Nica. For her, it was always art before people.

Suwen studied the profiles of the two buildings, bathed in the white heat of an afternoon sun. Her earliest memory of Tanjong Pagar was that of a dull street. The only building of interest to her then was the old Metropole Cinema which used to screen Cantonese films from Hong Kong. She used to go for film-shows with her mother. She remembered the old amahs who had set up the sweets and peanuts stalls along the sidewalks, mobile stalls made of cardboard and wooden planks placed on dilapidated prams. These stalls hugged the walls of the Metropole, and huddled in their shadows were the old bent amahs stitching cloth buttons to earn a few extra cents. These impoverished amahs had gone off the streets, and with them went the grey drabness of city life at the edge of poverty. The old Metropole was now a splendid white church and the Jinricksha Station was the office of an international company. Tanjong Pagar Road, the scene of numerous rickshaw riots and gang fights, had become a tourist attraction with refurbished Chinese shophouses painted blue, pink and green.

The only way to paint the history of such a place was to do it layer by layer like a piece of kueh lapis, Suwen thought. Bit by bit, the scene peeling away to show the other scene beneath. The whole effect should be like that of an archaeologist dusting away the top soil to show the layers of historical artefacts below. The Jinricksha Station had been a forlorn building awaiting demolition ten years ago. Before that, twenty years beneath the present, it had been a public health clinic for the poor and needy in Chinatown. And if one were to dig deeper still, one would come to the layer, thirty or forty years ago, when it was a thriving busy rickshaw station, where rickshaw coolies used to congregate daily. In the early nineteen hundreds, the Jinricksha Station was often in the news. It was vandalised and almost burnt down when the rickshaw coolies went on strike in the twenties and thirties. It was the hub of the transport business when the Indian gharry drivers stopped work to protest against the horrifying speed of the drivers of motor cars. Those infernal machines had scared the shit out of the horses, they protested. They had endangered the lives of the bullocks too, they said. But the motor car drivers, all of them Caucasians, wrote to the press blaming the Chinese rickshaw coolies for the mess. "The rickshaw coolies are the culprits. They are utterly without any sense of danger. They dash hither and thither across the path of oncoming cars, a danger to life and limb. These Chinamen must be taught our traffic regulations and learn to obey our laws. We urge the relevant authorities to see to this without delay."

Suwen, who was an avid reader, dug up a lot of press cuttings and information about the coolies in Chinatown. Unlike Nica, she would read around her subject before painting it. When they were back in Nica's studio, sipping iced lemon tea, she read this passage to Nica.

"It's by Roland Braddell: 'The rickshaw coolie still speaks no known tongue. If you want to tell the coolie where to go, you grunt hard, then point; if you don't know where the place is, God help you, because the coolie won't. He'll run off somewhere where he thinks you may want to go and grin happily when he's guessed wrong, after which he'll run off somewhere else and grin happily again, and so on until you and your temper are entirely lost. But please don't hit him or kick him as I too often see people doing; he can't help it and he really is the cheeriest, best humoured, most hardworking schoolboy of a fellow.'"

"Nah! What for you read this?" Nica scoffed. "The English empire builders were so darn patronising."

"I'm just wondering. D'you think that this sort of patronising tone has shaped the way we look at ourselves?"

"What d'you mean? You're always talking about serious stuff," Nica grumbled.

Suwen played with the pet hamsters while Nica took a shower. They were going out for dinner with Mark and Robert. The hamsters were still chasing each other on the merry-go-round in a perpetual circle game. Illusion and futility, Suwen thought, humming the song she had heard last Saturday. No escape. One's fate is the cage. One's life and thoughts are predetermined by one's birth in the time and place. A man born during the days of the British Empire would have views vastly different from a man born today.

"D'you know why I keep those two?" Nica came over to crouch beside her, smelling fresh with the scent of aloe vera. "It's to remind myself what living is all about. Ha! You look puzzled." She flung a few pellets of hamster food into the cage. "It's about breaking free, isn't it?"

"But it's not always possible to break free of the forces which shape and mould our lives. You might not even be aware of what they are."

"So? No harm in trying, right?"

"And end up like these two? Round and round to nowhere ?"

"D'you know? Deep down you're a cynic, Su. My grandpa did it. My mother's side. He was a Baba. With all the privileges of an English education. But he didn't think like those patronising asses. Here, read this. You collector of press cuttings." Nica handed her an album of old press cuttings and photographs. "My mother gave it to me when I told her I might paint the old Jinricksha Station."

"May I borrow this?" Suwen's eyes lit up. "It'll be perfect for my History-Art project."

"What project? You didn't tell me! How come I didn't know about it?"

Nica did not seem pleased. Suwen should have told her about it earlier; why was she keeping secrets from her? Was there something to hide? Suwen only managed to placate her by confessing her anxiety: she had not meant to keep anything from Nica. She only wanted to be quite sure of what she was doing; it was an ambitious project for someone inexperienced like herself. She had never really exhibited before. It was just the germ of an idea to marry history and art; in fact, it was Mark who had suggested it. He knew she was interested in digging up the past.

"Okay, you take this. Let's see what you can come up with."

The Story Of The Baba, The Sinkheh And The Rickshaw Strikes

As the traffic in the city burgeoned and the number of rickshaws became hundreds of thousands in the nineteen-twenties and thirties, the cacophony of complaints rose to a high pitch. The English-speaking clerks, mainly Indians and Babas, were flooded with requests for permits, licences, appeals against traffic fines, and letters of complaint, consent or confirmation. Their "In" and "Out" trays in the Jinricksha Station were filled to overflowing with files marked "Urgent", "Immediate" and "Confidential", attesting to the importance of their jobs.

Every morning, the chief clerk himself, Mr Tan Boon Wee, waded through this dusty mess and felt that he had arrived in the world. The mess of files on his desk and those of his subordinates proved it. He had twenty young clerks working under him. He unlatched the wooden shutters and let in the morning light. Seven-thirty, he checked his silver watch against that of the department's clock on the wall. Punctual again, jolly good, he sighed, for he took great pride in his punctuality. He had never been late for work, not even when the rickshaw coolies were on strike and there were no rickshaws for hire for a week.

Mr Tan opened the last shuttered window and paused to gaze fondly at the Yellow Flame blooming in the yard. Then he turned and walked briskly down the rows of desks, stopping now and then to straighten a stack of files or sheath of papers. He liked the outer office of his department to look as neat and tidy as he could make it. He was, after all, the chief clerk there, and somehow he had always felt that the appearance of the office was a reflection of himself. A tidy desk bespoke a tidy mind, his English schoolmaster had said. That remark, overheard along the corridors of the old Raffles Institution, had stayed in his mind for this same Englishman had gone on to add that the Orientals must be taught to live tidily and think logically. So, if tidiness and logic were the accoutrements of an English education, then the young Tan Boon Wee was determined to have them too.

When Mr "Ten" (for that was how his English superiors pronounced his name) reached his desk, he laid out his files for the day with "Immediate" on top of "Urgent". Then he took out his fountain pen from the top right-hand corner of his large desk, which was one foot longer than that of the junior staff, he noted with satisfaction. As was his practice each morning, he proceeded to clean his prized writing instrument with a piece of felt, checked it for ink and filled it up for the day before sharpening his government-issued pencils. This was his morning ritual which he savoured in the half hour before the garrulous Tamil-speaking peons came in to sweep the floor, stir the dust and herald the arrival of the junior staff.

One could tell by the way Mr Tan dusted his desk and straightened his files that he held his post of chief clerk to be of the highest importance. He saw himself as a real and significant factor in the government entity known as the Rickshaw Department of the Registry of Hackney Coaches, Jinrickshaws and Motorised Vehicles. He was the department's only English, Malay and Hokkien-speaking clerk, the go-between of Mr Thompson and the Asian clerks and peons, and the hundreds of Chinese who came each day to beg for a permit. He, the chief clerk, was their conduit to the great white man, seated behind the swing doors of frosted glass with the sign which read "Registrar".

Small and neat in his appearance, he was very meticulous in his work, very precise and correct in his clipped English speech with a facility for those turns of phrases like "in respect of which", "as aforesaid" or "as was mentioned in the minutes of", all of which had marked him as a remarkably good civil servant in the colonial office. He was fortyish and had spent more than twenty years making neat little columns of figures before entering them into the record books, filing away thousands of forms and tallying the figures in his ledger. He could file away an astonishing number of facts and figures pertaining to the ownership, rental rates and licences for rickshaws and their pullers. He handled these bits of facts with such an astounding dexterity that Mr Thompson could never locate a file without first consulting him. And this suited Mr Tan Boon Wee very well for he loved the power and dignity of his position.

In those days when a clerkship in the government service was not something to be sniffed at, Mr Tan belonged to an elite – the coterie of English-speaking Asians reporting directly to the Englishman in charge. And a chief clerkship was a position few Chinese could boast of, even though in the eyes of the China-born who came to bow and scrape before him, he was only a Baba, and, therefore, not a pure Chinese. "He got huan-na blood," they said of him in Hokkien, by which they meant that he had a few drops of Southeast Asian blood. He was unperturbed, however. There was little advantage really in being a China-geh or China-born. His command of English and his Baba heritage which could be traced back to the fifteenth century when the imperial eunuch, Admiral Cheng Ho, visited the Malacca Sultanate, had already placed him several notches above the rest of the Asian populace. Except for some of the white-skinned Eurasians who ranked directly below the Europeans. So Mr Tan had every reason to be contented with his ranking in the colonial chain of being. Although it was not quite the Elizabethan chain, it was still very much an English chain, and his own place was high above the bottom rung.

His pleasant reverie was rudely interrupted by the entry of a China-born and two Indian peons shouting at the man. "Oi! Oi! Tak boleh masok!"

All to no avail. The large Chinaman was grinning and nodding happily, ignoring the shouts and "No Entry" signs as he strode towards Mr Tan. Under one arm, he was clutching a pair of squawking chickens by the legs and, in the other, he held a rattan basket full of boxes and packages.

"Good morning, Mister, good morning!" the Chinaman called out in Hokkien. "Please tell the two Klings I am looking for an important person, ah!"

Mr Tan Boon Wee waved the peons away. The Chinaman coughed and cleared his throat. Like an official messenger about to deliver an important message. "Can you please tell me, Mister, where I can find the honourable chief clerk of this office? His relative asked me to see him."

Mr Tan pursed his lips to stifle a smile. The man's Hokkien, formal and polite as in a Hokkien opera, was incongruous with his attire. He was dressed like a sinkheh fresh off the tongkang from China, in a singlet visible through his thin cotton shirt, opened at the neck, and loose black cotton pants held by a drawstring. He was wearing cloth shoes, made in China, and was obviously ignorant of the rules and regulations in a government office. A stickler for rules and routine, it annoyed him no end that such peasant types could never get it into their thick heads that the government offices only opened at nine. It was barely eight by his silver watch, and only two of the junior clerks had come in.

"I am the chief clerk," he said curtly.

But the Chinaman was either too nervous or too dense for he did not seem to have noticed the curtness in his tone.

"Aiyah! Good ah! Good ah! You must be Mr Tan Boon Wee! I am Ong Ah Buck. Friend of Tan Eng Hock, your relative ah!"

The Chinaman was ecstatic. His voice boomed through the near-empty office. Two more clerks who had just come in turned to look. Mr Tan sensed that his junior staff were curious for he rarely had visitors.

"Tan Eng Hock, your clansman, ah! From Prosperity Rentals, just down my road! He told me to come and see you. He said you are an important man here. You will be able to help me with my licence, ah! I got new rickshaws."

"Right, right, I remember," Mr Tan said, hoping that the excited Chinaman would calm down and speak softly. The junior clerks were taking out their files, but he knew that they were listening.

"Tan Eng Hock did speak to me. And I said I would talk with you," he muttered in Hokkien, his eyes resting on the two chickens still clutched under the Chinaman's arm. The legs of the chickens were secured by a red string as was the custom when presenting fowls as gifts for festive occasions.

The Chinaman, following his gaze, beamed broadly and, suddenly, shoved the two chickens and the rattan basket into Mr Tan's hands. And before a horrified and greatly insulted Mr Tan could stop him, the Chinaman dropped his booming voice to the level of a confidential whisper, clearly audible from one end of the office to the other. "Ah, our honourable chief clerk, please, please accept these small gifts. Very small, my apologies! A small gift to thank you for your help."

Mr Tan Boon Wee felt the rush of blood into his face. He was hot under the collar. His ears burned. A quick glance told him that his junior clerks were looking in his direction in great amusement. He was furious. What a mess! What did the blundering buffalo think he was doing? There was no end to the stupidity of these China-gehs! Bringing him gifts! And him, the chief clerk who had never been tainted by bribes! He who did not belong to those Oriental types who succumbed to a few pieces of silver! And now after what this buffalo had done, word would surely get out that the chief clerk himself was accepting kopi money!

"Cannot! Cannot! Mr Ong Ah Buck, cannot! I cannot accept these things! Get out! Tolong ah! Out!" he heard his own high-pitched voice rising to a squeak.

"But Mr Tan, ah! My licence, ah!"

"Nah! Go! Take these forms. Fill them. Write your name, business and address and so on!"

"Aiyah! Poo-bor-ah! If I can read and write like you scholars, ah, I don't have to come and beg you! Right or not?"

The Chinaman was yelling like the typical illiterate coolie when the two Indian peons came to take him out.

"Son of a sow, ah! These wriggles know me but I don't know them! How can I read these foreign words?"

"Joseph!" Mr Tan squeaked. "Quiet this man for God's sake! Help him fill up those blasted forms!" Mr Tan had recovered his English voice.

Ong Ah Buck refused to budge from the Jinricksha Station. He had been promised a licence and a licence he would get. He sat on the bench in the waiting room with his two chickens and rattan basket. The fowls lay on the floor between his feet. The rattan basket, full of packages of barbecued pork, roast pork, waxed duck, dried mushrooms and bird's nests, was placed carefully on the bench next to him. They had cost him a princely sum. He simply could not understand these Babas. Very temperamental, he raged. They could not be trusted to keep their word. One moment so friendly like a relation; the next moment, they act like they don't know him! Must be the many tongues they speak! Speak one tongue, say one thing! Speak another tongue, they act in another way. Not like us, Hokkiens, straight like our intestines. Say one thing, mean one thing! No change! What we say we do! After a while, however, Ong Ah Buck reminded himself to be patient. A man praying for a favour must wait for the gods to look down from the heavens. So he sat and waited for five hours.

He simply could not see what he had done wrong. In his eyes, he had done the right and proper thing which any wise Chinese seeking an official's favour would do. He retraced his steps once more.

That morning he had alighted from his rickshaw and instructed the coolie to wait for him. Then, clutching the two chickens by the legs, he had carried the rattan basket in his other hand and entered the Jinricksha Station. The front office was a large waiting room with rows of wooden benches in front of a counter with frosted glass panes. Tan Eng Hock had told him to go upstairs.

Ong Ah Buck had gone up the broad stairs with the sign which said "No Entry Except For Staff". It did not mean a thing to him. He could not read English. There were signs everywhere; large black signs like the brows of the Thunder God. The offices were enclosed by walls of dark wood and partitions of frosted glass. It made a man feel trapped and hemmed in. Was this where the great officials worked? He was amazed. Here were books, hundreds of them. And stacks of brown files. And the writing instruments on every desk. He was awed by these trappings of officialdom. His heart was pounding. There was a sudden constriction in his throat. His cough sounded more like a hiccup. The swing doors opened suddenly. The two Klings shouted at him. "Tapek, sahib!" He bowed and nodded. They knew no Hokkien and he knew no Tamil; he could not explain his presence to them. He was looking for Chief Clerk Tan Boon Wee, he repeated the name over and over again lest he forgot.

"I am the chief clerk."

What a short man, Ong Ah Buck had thought, and so much hair oil on his head. The plastered-down hair shone with brilliantine. So this was the man who could speak the angmoh's tongue and do things the angmoh's way. Ong Ah Buck gave a low bow to this representative of the authorities.

"Good ah! Good ah! Mr Tan! I am your humble servant."

Ong Ah Buck had not intended to be so forward. But he was very relieved to find Mr Tan. He had had so much trouble getting his licences.

"Good ah! Mr Tan, good ah! I am Ong Ah Buck, friend of Tan Eng Hock. Your clansman from Prosperity Rentals! Down my road! He sent me!"

Ong Ah Buck knew he was talking too much but he was far too nervous in the room of books and files. He felt he was in alien territory. He mopped his brows and waited for the official to speak. In the old days, back in China, he had heard that peasants hauled before the magistrate must kneel, heads down, and must not look up on pain of death. He made himself look at Mr Tan, the chief clerk. A secret thrill made his heart contract suddenly. He was short of air. He had difficulty drawing in his breath. He clutched his two chickens and bowed again and again. Like a smiling village idiot. So pleased was he with his exalted position. He, the son of poor illiterate peasants, the coolie who had stepped off the China boat with the shirt and pants he had stripped off a corpse, was standing up now like the equal of his high-ranking government official and talking to him like a relation. Aiyah, almost like a relation, he sighed.

"Right, right," the honourable Mr Tan had even spoken to him in Hokkien like a ga-kee-nang, one's clansman. How broadly he had beamed at the kind Baba. Then when he saw the latter's eyes resting on the chickens, he suddenly remembered his manners.

"Ah, please, please, accept these small gifts, Mr Tan," he had dropped his voice to a confidential whisper, bending forward to effect the most respectful bow he could muster. But before he could even incline his head, Mr Tan was already shoving him away.

"Cannot! Cannot! Mr Ong, cannot!" The great man had pushed aside his gifts. The chickens squawked and the Klings had rushed in and clamped his arms like the imperial guards. And he was marched out of the office. He let out a sigh and resigned himself to a long wait.

To a China-born like Ong Ah Buck, the Baba chief clerk was a traitor who worked for the angmoh powers-that-be, making things difficult for his Chinese clansmen. One can well imagine Ong Ah Buck cursing Mr Tan "Poo-bor!" all the way home.

However, getting his licences and treading his way along the corridors of officialdom operating in a foreign language was not the only problem Ong Ah Buck had to face. Illiterate rickshaw owners like him were squeezed between two languages – Mandarin and English. One day, a large Chinese poster pasted outside a coffee shop in Chinatown spelt trouble for him:

> We know that since the English Barbarians established themselves in Singapore, their rules and regulations have been beneficial to the people. However, it is now time for the sons of China to open their eyes and see for themselves that the only rule important to the English Barbarians is making a profit. The Japanese imperialist aggressors have seized a vital part of our motherland – the Shantung Peninsula. We have appealed to the English Prince to cut off trade with these Japanese dogs. But, despite our pleas, the English Barbarians are still trading with them. Their insatiable and vicious lust for profit has made them shut their eyes to the injustices under the heavens! They prefer to be blind than to see how the Japanese imperialist dogs are ruining our homeland! Now, after reading this paper, anyone who does not feel his fierce passions rise has not a drop of China's blood in his heart! All the sons of the Chinese earth must reverently feel

aggrieved. Rise up and fight the Japanese imperialist curs and their supporters!

Ong Ah Buck could not read the large Chinese characters of the wall poster. But Mr Gan, a tea merchant who could read and write Chinese, read them to him. "The foreign devils are cutting up our homeland, Mr Ong. Shantung is the birthplace of our beloved sages, Confucius and Mencius. How can we let those dogs take it away from us?"

"We call on all the sons of China to unite against the Japanese devils!" Mr Kok, the chairman of the Hockchew Rickshaw Coolies Association, read out another poster. He was a stout and hard-speaking man who could read the newspapers even better than Mr Gan, some of the coolies said. "Ha! We Hockchew coolies pull rickshaws. All of them made in Japan! Poo-bor-ah!" He thumped the table so hard that all the coffee cups clattered. "The devils take our land and we still buy from them! I say! From today no more! No more buying of Japanese rickshaws! No more pulling of Japanese devil rickshaws! Those who do so are the sons of dogs."

Mr Kok had spoken in Hockchew so passionately that even the Hengwah coolies had applauded. And the talk in the coffee shop was loud and raucous that night. Feelings ran high. The coolies argued, thumped the tables and shouted abuse at one another.

Two days later, the British Governor signed and issued a proclamation in English which was duly translated into Chinese and posted in the government buildings such as the Jinricksha Station:

The Governor of the Straits Settlements calls upon the Chinese to remember that the British Authorities are placed in this country to afford protection to all classes and races whether they be engaged in trade, manufacture or agriculture. All the people living under the protection of the British flag are requested to obey the Laws, and not disturb the Peace of the community with the grievances and quarrels of their homelands. These people must fully understand that this is not their country. They must attend to their own businesses quietly

> and not disturb the Peace of their neighbours. It is hereby notified by the Governor of the Straits Settlements that all persons found committing acts of violence will be apprehended and imprisoned by the Authorities.
>
> Governor of Prince of Wales Island,
> Malacca and Singapore

On the day of the proclamation, however, more than a thousand coolies had gathered in defiance for an anti-Japanese rally. "Burn them! Nah! Burn them all!" Shopkeepers and coolies hurled out their Made-in-Japan pots and pans, textiles and straw hats. The mob cheered them on. Several bonfires were lit. Twenty Made-in-Japan rickshaws were burnt by the mob. "Curse the Japanese devils! Death to the Japanese devils!" the mob chanted. "Our brother coolies in Keppel are on strike!" announced a jubilant Mr Kok. "The sons of China will not lift a finger to load the ships of dogs!"

Ong Ah Buck called upon his gods and ancestors to protect his rickshaws. The next day, he heard that the coolies had marched into the Japanese brothels in Malabar and Malay Streets.

"I was there, Towkay! I tell you! We went after those daughters of pigs!" Ah Chooi, his hired hand, boasted. "Wah-pia-ah! I went after those Japanese she-devils! I smashed their furniture. Not a stick left, ah! There must have been one thousand of us. The devils attack our motherland, we attack their sons and daughters here! Ten lives for an inch of our earth, Mr Kok said."

That night, Ong Ah Buck crossed the strangely quiet streets in great haste. The dimly lit alleys and roads were eerily empty. A curfew had been imposed. All the shops in Telok Ayer and Chinatown were closed and shuttered for the night. The shopkeepers, sensing trouble in those restless times, had heeded the warnings plastered on their doors. Reports of how hundreds of half-starved coolies had gutted a shop for selling Japanese goods had sent cold shafts of fear into their trembling hearts.

Coming out of Butcher Alley, Ong Ah Buck veered round when he heard footsteps behind him. Towkay Goh, the owner of a large rickshaw rental shop in Tanjong Pagar, was hurrying up the narrow lane towards him. The short stout man was puffing; his unbuttoned shirt flying open to reveal the cotton singlet covering his pot belly. To eat is good fortune, he liked to say, and he had no trouble gobbling up five to six pork buns. But he was generous only to his own belly and tight-fisted with his coolies. He had never allowed a rickshaw puller to owe him more than a week's rental.

"Aye, Towkay Ong, ah! Trouble, trouble," he muttered as he caught up with Ong Ah Buck. "Those hot-headed fools! The moment their minds are off their bellies, they look for trouble! I know what's inside their stinking bellies! First they go after the Japanese devils. Then they come after us! Rickshaw owners!"

"How do you know this?"

"I heard them. The lazy scoundrels! At the Jinricksha Station today. And that pig, Ah Low! He came up to me and said to my face. My face, mind you! And he owes me three days' rent. Your rents are too high! He said that, that son of a pig!" Towkay Goh spat.

"Aye, terrible, this angry talk. I was a half-starved coolie once but I did not talk like that."

"Let me tell you something. I was a hungry man once too. But I worked! I slogged! These young fellows are lazy! It's them Hockchia and Hengwah pigs! Jealous of Hokkien men who have prospered! They don't have a cent to their names! So they don't care. Fight! Fight! they shout. It's them newspapers. All this newspaper reading in the shops is getting to their heads."

"Aye, Towkay Goh, we Hokkiens know how to save and buy property."

"Ha! We know business is business," Towkay Goh tapped his bald pate. "A secure money belt and a barn of rice are better than a thousand books and newspapers, right or not? Those Hockchia fools!" He spat again.

"Not so loud," Ong Ah Buck hissed. He wished he did not have to attend that night's meeting in the clan association to discuss the Governor's proclamation. "What is the latest?"

"Aye, the heads of all the clans have to meet the English lord," Towkay Goh said. "But us and him are like the chicken and the duck. How to talk? Those Babas will talk for us again."

Lau Goo, the coolie friend of Ong Ah Buck, was now grey-haired and shrunken. On the night of the riots, he was crouching beside his rented rickshaw, chewing meditatively on a cud of tobacco to fight off his hunger pangs. He had not eaten since morning, and unless he could get another fare, there was no money for a meal. He rubbed the bruises on his knees ruefully. "Each day, a different fate," he sighed. It was plain bad luck that today of all days he was hailed by a crazy English barbarian who had grunted and gesticulated wildly in the hot noonday sun. How could he be expected to understand the mad dog's bark? He had brought the man, heavy as a ton of bricks, to all the hotels and places which angmohs usually went. But still the barbarian had screamed abuse at him and kicked him. And if he had not pretended to faint, the mad dog would have broken all his bones. As the old folks said, "Bad luck seldom comes singly." So here he was. No money, no meal and no fare in sight. The day had been one of unrest and unease. People had kept indoors and the shops had closed early. Lau Goo looked up and down the road. Few would need a rickshaw tonight. His tua-tow, the leader of his lodging house gang, had said so. And it was so. Since morning he had met only one other rickshaw puller, as desperate as himself, ready to risk the wrath of the tua-tow and the gangs for a bowl of rice. "Don't ply your rickshaw till things are settled," the tua-tow had ordered. "We must be united. Those eggheads who still go out to hire will be beaten to a pulp! And their rickshaws pulled apart. And we don't care who their passengers are! All must wait till we settle things with the English dogs!"

What things had to be settled first before he could ply his rickshaw again, Lau Goo had only the vaguest of notions. He did not fully understand all the arguments, reasons and stratagems he had heard at the lodging house. Men who could read the wall posters and newspapers told his tua-tow, and his tua-tow, a man as illiterate as the rest of the coolies, told them what to do. Just like his parents in China were at the mercy of the petty landlords, coolies like him were at the mercy of the tua-tows and the invisible powers that controlled the city.

And all he had ever wanted, Lau Goo sighed, when he first set foot on this city of golden dreams was to pull a rickshaw for three warm meals a day and save some money to send home to his parents, wife and children, and to return home some day. But now his hopes were fading. The daily rental of a rickshaw was thirty-five cents for each shift of eight hours. During those eight hours, he would have to earn enough money to pay for the rental of the rickshaw, lodging, food, clothes and some money to send home. A rickshaw ride from the harbour to Tanglin, a journey of two and a half miles which took him one hour to complete, cost a passenger only thirty cents. It took him a whole day's work to earn one dollar. And for that he must be on his feet, ferrying passengers for eight hours at a stretch. Lau Goo sighed. He did not mind the hard work if only he could get a fare. He longed for a smoke of opium to ease his weary bones and keep his hunger pangs at bay. After one or two whiffs of that heavenly smoke, he would feel better. But he quickly pushed the thought away. He was beginning to feel the terrible tremor of desire coursing through his veins.

"Don't smoke that damn evil weed!" Ong Ah Buck had yelled at him more than once. More than a thousand times. "Smoke a cigarette if you have to smoke!"

"Cigarettes not the same. Without opium I cannot sleep. The pig next to me snorts all night. His coughing keeps me awake."

"Poo-bor-ah! Stop whining!" Ong Ah Buck had scoffed. "Cover your ears with a pillow. No head, ah? That's what I used to do!"

"That's what I used to do! That's what I used to do! The devils take what you used to do! I am sick of what you used to do! What you did is no better than what I do! You got ears? Can hear or not? No better! So don't act the big lord over me! Go to your wife and towkay! Boast to them of your hardships! But not to me, you son of a pig! I have drunk this bitter brew far longer than you! So don't think you can advise me! Ha!"

"Stop ranting, you old ox! I say what I think!" Ong Ah Buck had yelled back at him. "And I say it again! You should have stayed away from that evil smoke! If not for that, you would have been my foreman now!"

"Pooi!" Lau Goo had spat. "Do you think I have just come out of my mother's womb? At that time, could you really offer anyone anything? Stop acting the big lord! You were hiding under your wife's skirt! Who gave up his family name? Who obeyed his father-in-law like a pup? Say I am wrong, you son of a bitch! Don't come to me with your empty talk! I, Lau Goo, am poor! But I don't kowtow to rich men!"

He had been drunk and miserable that night, years ago, and he had lost his head and said things he should never have said. But words once said could not be unsaid. And he had neither seen nor heard from Ong Ah Buck ever since that night.

"Friends come and go in the city. Each man a different fate, each hand a different palm," Lau Goo muttered a common folk saying to console himself. He was resigned to failure like the helpless millions of this world. At least he was better than the poor old bull who had wheezed and coughed out blood. The man had rented the bed next to his. The old bull's legs and testicles were so swollen with pus that the man had been unable to move for days. His bed stank with the smell of disease. Then, last week, Lau Goo had found the man's body in the communal bathroom, hanging down from the rafters. Dead and swollen as a drowned pig, Lau Goo uttered a prayer to his ancestors and gods. He did not want to die like an animal, worn out by hard labour, with no kin to mourn and bury him. He vowed to work harder, give up opium and save enough to return home.

He got between the shafts of his rickshaw and trotted down South Bridge Road in search of a fare. Ong Ah Buck and Towkay Goh came out of Butcher Alley and saw an Indian man in a white dhoti come out of the Indian Chettiars' temple in South Bridge Road. The Indian hailed an old rickshaw coolie. The coolie glanced furtively up and down the road, undecided whether he should risk danger and break the ban of the tua-tows. The Indian pressed a coin into his hand and clambered into the rickshaw.

Lau Goo put the coin in his pocket, heaved and lifted the shafts of his vehicle. He pulled and broke into a trot, praying that the other coolies would not see him. A body had to eat. Who, in this city, would give him a free meal? He heaved and snorted like a great beast of burden at the thought of a warm bowl of rice porridge at the end of the journey.

"Hey! You fool! You son of a stinking sow! Stop!" a gang of coolies patrolling the dimly lit streets yelled.

Lau Goo broke into a cold sweat and started to run. But the coolies gave chase. "Stop! Stop! You want to die ah!" Their shouts and the clang of steel bars sent cold shafts of fear into the hearts of Ong Ah Buck and Towkay Goh. More coolies had rushed out of the lodging houses to join in the chase. Ong Ah Buck recognised his old friend but there was nothing he could do to stop those gangs.

In the rickshaw, the Indian man was pale with fright. He yelled to Lau Goo to stop as he clutched at his dhoti and tried to jump down from the rickshaw. The poor Indian, as ignorant as Lau Goo himself, was calling out to his gods for protection against those uncouth and wild men who were chasing him. They were as violent as the vagabonds in Madras. He had come to this island to trade, not to be chased by wild men screaming in strange tongues!

"Henti! Berhenti!" he yelled out the only Malay words he knew, and gave Lau Goo a violent kick.

Lau Goo fell and the Indian scrambled out of the rickshaw and ran for dear life. The mob pounced on Lau Goo. A large stick hit him on the back of his head. He reeled and dropped to his knees again. Another blow from a wooden staff fell upon his shoulders. A stone hit his face. Then came another and another. The mob was pelting him with rocks and stones. Traitor! Traitor! F--- his mother! F--- that son of a pig! Their cries and curses filled the air. An iron bar smashed the wheels of his rickshaw. A sudden pain crushed his head. Everything went dark.

Ong Ah Buck and Towkay Ong flattened themselves against the shadows and shuddered for their lives. Ong Ah Buck watched in helpless anger as the animals tore his friend, his one and only relation in this world, from limb to limb. "Lau Goo, Lau Goo ah!" he moaned.

The spirit of hate and violence, in the name of fighting for the honour of one's motherland, had burst open like gangrene that night. Pus was flowing everywhere. Malevolence, malediction and malice filled the air from Sago Lane to Duxton Plain in Chinatown. Balls of pent-up anger and hate exploded like grenades in the hands of desperate men, searing their bodies and souls born out of hunger and despair and bred in the dark warrens of tenement houses and gambling dens.

"Pigs and dogs! Sons of sows! Oh, how they suck us dry!" the great bullhorn voice of a tua-tow bellowed out in the provincial Hockchia dialect, "We give them our sweat and blood! What did they give us? Ask the towkays! Ask!"

"Nothing! Nothing!" the mob roared its reply in the Hockchia dialect which tied them to one another like an invisible umbilical cord.

In the murky shadows, flattened against the walls of the shophouses, Ong Ah Buck and his Hokkien clansman listened to that bullhorn voice with envy, loathing and contempt. Here was a great Hockchia voice, a guttural voice growling like an enraged tiger, a voice which could send out men in the hundreds to burn and assault other men of other tongues. It spoke no Hokkien, no Mandarin. It had no learning. It had, worst of all, in the eyes of the two men, no earning power. The Hockchias were the poorest of all the poor rickshaw coolies in Chinatown. But this Hockchia voice had the power to move poor men. It could repeat what was said in the shops and marketplaces with the roar of a hungry tiger.

"Patriots! Countrymen! Clansmen! Sons of the Chinese earth! We are f---ing hungry! We are the f---ing poor! The homeless and the homesick! But can we, the f---ing poor, make sacrifices for our motherland? Can or not? Say! Can or not?"

"Can! Can!" the mob chanted.

"Can the towkays, who are richer than us, make sacrifices bigger than ours? Say! Can or not?"

"Can! Can!" the mob roared and cheered the voice,

"Then burn these rickshaws! Burn them! Why? Because they are made by the Japanese devils!"

"Burn them! Burn them! Burn the devils' rickshaws!"

The mob dragged out the rickshaws parked along the lanes and alleys, pulling the vehicles apart in a frenzy of hate. Rickshaws which did not belong to them, Ong Ah Buck raged, rickshaws bought by the sweat and blood of other men. And the sudden thought that some of these vehicles could be his hit him like a hammer's blow.

"Stop, you fools! Oi! Stop!"

A large rock struck him on the temple. He reeled and fell against the wall, blood streaming from the ugly gash on his forehead.

"Burn! Burn the devils' things! Burn them! Burn them!" the mob was chanting.

Overturned rickshaws were piled into a heap. The smell of kerosene wafted down the road. The flames of the bonfire leapt two storeys high. Gigantic shadows danced and flickered on the walls of the shophouses. The mob of coolies, half-starved and malnourished, jeered and cursed the Japanese devils and all other foreign devils and imperialist running dogs who had cheated and corrupted their motherland. They carried high upon their shoulders the Hockchia owner of the great bullhorn voice. He was their leader. They were the patriots! China's invincible and loyal sons in the Nanyang!

Ong Ah Buck slipped away. His friend, Lau Goo, had been lynched. There was nothing he could have done to stop it. It was so senseless. He was ready to horsewhip every one of those coolies!

Business in the city came to a standstill. Curfew was imposed.

When law and order eventually returned, many people, in particular the Caucasian part of the population, clamoured for punishment. "The crux of the problem," an English trader wrote to the Singapore Echo, "is that we have allowed these lower classes of the East to gain the upper hand. They have had the audacity to mobilise a force of several thousands to exert a moral pressure upon the colonial government. We urge the government to deal with these coolies and their leaders severely. Violent men who hold the rest of the populace to ransom on account of their numbers should be treated as criminals and punished accordingly. The government ought not to flinch from taking the necessary course of action. And we think the sooner the rotan is used to remind the lower classes of the kind of punishment the police are empowered to mete out, the better it is for all concerned. Far better the rotan in early profusion than a bullet in the last extremity. A hundred rickshaw coolies with well scarified hinterlands are wonderfully effective examples of the kind of action the government is prepared to take in order to secure public peace and good order. We believe that some people in the Asiatic quarters need a little convincing."

That same evening when the letter was published, the English trader was applauded and toasted in the Padang's Cricket Club. 'Hear! Hear!' His Caucasian compatriots murmured appreciatively, for the riots of the Chinese coolies had struck fear in their white hearts.

However, a few days later, a lone voice in the Asiatic quarter cried out against the authorities' treatment of the coolies. Mr Tan Boon Wee, using the pseudonym "Son of a Straitsborn Chinese", wrote in the Singapore Echo:

> Sir, I beg humbly to differ. While I agree that the authorities should uphold the law and maintain the public peace, we ought to consider this problem of rickshaw strikes and riots from another angle. The rickshaw coolies are constantly subjected to the ever mischievous eyes of the peons and policemen whose one duty seems to be to haul these poor coolies before the Tuan Besar, there and then to be taught the law at a cost ranging from $2 to $20! Besides this official surveillance, the coolies are also subjected to the whims of owners of rickshaws and the samsengs who control the gangs and extort protection money from the coolies. Let us bear in mind that we are dealing with poor and illiterate men. These coolies deserve more pity than blame! Those with money and learning should help them instead of thinking of ways and means to punish and fine them!
>
> SON OF A STRAITSBORN CHINESE

"Actually, if we think about it, the past is how our memory shapes and angles it, isn't it?" Suwen asked.

"There you go again! Can you talk without all this philosophising?" Nica dismissed her question. "Now! Let me ask you a question instead. How are you going to translate all this history into paintings?"

"I don't know. I haven't really thought about it yet. It's just a thought. A wisp of something in my head at the moment."

"What? How can you do something without proper planning? Good grief!"

Suwen had no reply to that. How could she explain it to anybody? The images came and went inside her head. Without her bidding. She had tried to capture them in her sketchbook. But each time she tried, she had failed miserably. They never came out the way she saw or heard them inside her head. How to translate that which was inside into something which she could show to the outside world was her constant struggle.

"I know I'm quite woolly about this project. It's very frustrating. I don't even know what I want to do. Except this one thing which I keep repeating, you know. Marry the two things, the word and the image."

"Oh, I know!" Nica exclaimed. "Like a huge photo essay. Words in large print next to the picture. Except that your picture is a painting instead of a photo, lah! It's great! A very workable format."

Suwen nodded silently. She did not have the heart to dampen Nica's enthusiasm and risk argument and distress. Once she had argued with Nica over some concepts in sculpture and Nica had refused to talk to her for two weeks. She was cold and abrupt when she answered her phone calls. She was very busy, Nica had told her and hung up. It was one month before she relented and invited Suwen again to the parties in her studio. The photo essay was not what Suwen had in mind; in fact, she had nothing in mind. Her project was really a search for the perfect union of medium and content. And she was willing to wait for what would eventually emerge. She did not want to upset and argue with Nica, her teacher and model, again. Nica liked her art crisp, definitive and planned. Within a framework which the onlooker could understand immediately; not some wishy-washy ideas of blib-blobs, she had told Suwen.

And Suwen did not argue with her. She went back to Tanjong Pagar with Nica for several Saturdays until Nica had completed her sketch of the Jinricksha Station. They soon fell into the routine of returning to Nica's apartment for cold drinks and a bite after each sketching session. Sometimes Robert would be there, and sometimes Mark came by. In the evenings, Jan and Zul would appear with a hundred sticks of satay and packets of mee goreng for dinner.

From Saturday to Sunday, Suwen pretended that life was free and fluid, eating only when she was hungry and painting and sketching only when she was in the mood. Every Sunday, she clung to this lovely weekend illusion, letting go of it reluctantly on each Monday morning when she returned to teaching in college, tailoring her thoughts to fit into the fifty-minute intervals between each buzz of the electric bell. "My weekend self is the real me," Suwen told Mark. But that was a half-truth. What was closer to the truth was her secret desire to avoid life; to avoid problems and collision with persons which would disturb her closely-guarded fragile tranquillity. Home and family were on the brink of chaos. Her mother's husband might be declared a bankrupt. His businesses were failing and the creditors were moving in like wolves towards a prey. Her mother was going mad with worry and anxiety. Money was in short supply. "A problem of liquidity," an Ong relation in the finance sector said. The Ong Mansion would have to be sold. "Over my dead body!" Suwen heard her mother shouting one night. "The day I die, you can sell! But not a day before!" Suwen could not hear Ong Tay Luck's reply. But her mother's voice was loud and clear. "I know your women and their black hearts! They want me out of here! But I came in here as the mistress of this mansion and I will go out as its mistress! The gods have eyes and the heavens have ears, Tay Luck! They heard what you promised me! Years ago! When I was a fah-dan and you, ha! You were a nobody!"

Such things, however, Suwen would never reveal. She was not in the habit of talking to others about her family or lack of it. One could put it down to natural reticence. But, perhaps, it was more than that. The incident with her mother's husband, "that man" as she had referred to him inside her head, had clung to her like a body odour which would not go away. She lived in fear of it being known, afraid that someone she cared about would get a whiff of it should he come too close and then move off. So, fearing rejection, she kept others at arm's length. But it was an existence of contradictions. An artist sought self-revelation. She wanted to be an artist yet she wanted to hide herself, seeking self-effacement in a kind of hide-and-seek, never quite sure of how far she could go without revealing too much. Many a time she had thought about talking to Nica and seeking her advice for she longed to live like her: boldly and freely with a devoted companion like Robert and without a thought about what her Indian community would think.

"We can change our lives, you know," Nica had said to her one day when they were walking along the beach. "Our lives are for us to mould into whatever shapes we want."

They were strolling barefoot on the white sand by the water's edge. Farther away towards the land, the black crows were fighting over the food scraps washed ashore. There were few cyclists and joggers in this part of East Coast near the Benjamin Sheares Bridge. Beyond the scrub and casuarinas planted along the shoreline, the sun's rays were spreading a layer of gold upon the gleaming towers of Shenton Way.

"When I first came here," Nica was saying, "I missed the Malaysian hills and the ragged roads. They had spelt freedom for me."

"For me too," Suwen murmured, looking down at the bit of seaweed clinging to her feet. "I was miserable when I first came to Singapore. No hills, I was only twelve or thirteen then. And I missed the distant hills. People born and bred here can't understand it. What's jutting into the sky here? These!"

Suwen's hand swept the air, dismissing the tall gleaming towers of steel and glass.

"Why? I like them now. They spell freedom of the city. Small town life is too narrow and gossipy."

"Ya, but these towers are so straight and definite. They're all utility and efficiency. I miss the romance of the trees and the hills of Perak."

"Does Mark live in the countryside?" Nica asked, looking at her shrewdly.

"Yes, on the Scottish border."

"Hmmm, how are the two of you getting on?"

"Okay, we are good friends."

"I know you are good friends, dumbo. Anything else?"

"I don't know what you want to know. I enjoy his company and he enjoys mine."

"Is he the first guy? I mean have you had a boyfriend before Mark?"

"Yes, Miss Interrogator," Suwen giggled. It was beginning to sound ridiculous. Like the two of them were a couple of teenagers instead of women in their late, and she emphasised, late thirties. Of course, there had been one or two young men in her life. Simon and Kok Beng. But, somehow, nothing serious had developed. "I have had many friends who were boys and are now men."

"Very funny, Su! Stop talking like an idiot. You know what I mean. Like Robbie and me."

"Like Robert and you?" Suwen's heart skipped a beat. Simon and Kok Beng had not even come one finger close to that. "No," she answered.

"Then you've had very little experience with men, you poor thing," Nica rightly concluded. "We'll have to do something about that. Jan will be married soon."

"I know. We used to do a lot of things together."

"But Jan's not your type."

Suwen did not know what Nica meant by that but, at that moment, she was not too keen to find out. This spotlight on her lack of a male companion was making her uneasy.

"There was someone else before Robert?" she asked Nica.

"When I was in London, I lived with Jeff for a year. Nearly two before he returned to LA."

"So it didn't last."

"I never expected it to. We agreed to go our separate ways. We still write to each other. Once a year."

"He was your first?"

"Yes, but not the last. But Jeff was very sweet."

"What about Robert? Any talk of marriage?"

"Gosh, Su! No!" Then dropping her voice to a melodramatic whisper, Nica said, "Robbie bores me to tears sometimes. He's nice, very warm and extremely generous. But, I don't know. There's only so much I can stand after a while. He's not a bad sort, really. I always tell him, he's not too bad for someone who's an investment risks analyst."

"But you're not passionate about him."

"Right," Nica sighed. "But I've lived with him the longest. Partly, I think, it's because he travels a lot. So we don't get under each other's skins too often. I mean if he were here all the time, we would've broken off long ago."

They walked on in silence for a while and Suwen was relieved that she had diverted Nica's attention away from her lack of a love life. The sun was beginning to drop below the horizon and a large white cumulus hid it from view.

"Hey, where did those clouds come from?" Nica exclaimed. "The weather forecast says one thing and the weather does another!"

"Come and look at these mushrooms!" Suwen called from under the crab apple tree, pointing to the orange and grey ears growing from its trunk.

"These are fungi, not mushrooms, dumbo." Nica bent down to take a closer look. "Go on. Touch them. They're smooth and spongy."

"Careful there. Might be poisonous."

"No, they are not. Just feel them. Touch is essential if you want to be an artist. Especially a sculptor." Nica was already stroking the ears of spongy fungi. "It's like velvet. C'mon, Su. Feel them. You can't own them until you feel them. Then you can recreate them."

"But I don't want to own them," Suwen murmured.

"But I don't mean owning them like buying something, you know. More like putting one's stamp on them. Like...like the laying of hands, for want of a better phrase. See here." Nica pointed to another part of the tree trunk. "Some people have carved their initials here. Now this sort, I don't approve. It's a cheap grasp at immortality."

"It's okay. I don't want to be immortal."

"Rubbish! Deep down you do! If not, why be an artist? All artists seek immortality."

"But I just want to paint."

"And that's how you seek immortality. Through painting. It's one of the ways, that's all. Others want to create new forms. You have even created new memories and fragments of history yourself. All artists seek to change nature."

"I think nature should be left alone," Suwen murmured her weak protest, thinking of those artists who had twisted plants out of shape and those who had stretched miles of fabrics across lovely fields of grass and wheat.

"If man does not impose his will upon nature, how can there be civilisation? Isn't civilisation the result of man imposing his will upon the natural forces? We build dams, reclaim the land and bulldoze hills and mountains. Without the human will, where would Singapore be? Hey, girl, I can philosophise too. And you call yourself a Singaporean?"

"What d'you mean?"

"Gosh, Su. Use your head. No dictatorship of human will, no Singapore. Simple as that."

"Good. Just life then."

"Ya, life that's bare, brutal and short. Was it Shakespeare who said that?"

"I don't know," Suwen said, unwilling to con cede defeat, knowing that although Nica's argument seemed to be the right one on the face of it, yet, she suspected there were some flaws somewhere. If only she could put her finger on them.

"People who let nature mould them will be subjugated by nature. They are not free. We must mould the things around us instead of letting them mould and shape us. That's why I told Mark the other day the true Singaporean is a sculptor. He shapes and moulds his environment like nobody else!"

"But, when you put it that way, I mean a sculptor is supposed to be an artist."

"So?"

"So, don't you see? An artist is supposed to live in harmony with nature. Not to contend with it. Or...or to shape it according to his will."

"Oh, Su! Don't be such a fuddy-duddy romantic!" Nica laughed. "Even as an artist, you've got to take charge. Be in control."

PART 4

Yellow, White and Brown Reveries

Looking back, Suwen realised that that period of her life had been inextricably linked to that of Jan and Nica by ties of friendship, art, love and hate; each woman, a strand of coloured thread, weaving her loved ones into the fabric of her life, adding texture and colour. Looking back, Suwen realised too that the year when Mark first joined her in college had been the happiest in her life. Those were wonderful days. She had spent weekends painting and sketching with Nica, and her weekdays in college were filled with lively discussions on everything under the sun with Mark, and sometimes with Jan. The nights when she stayed home were spent closeted in her garage apartment, far enough from the mansion and her mother and the numerous Ong relatives who visited each night to commiserate with her mother over the family's impending bankruptcy. In so keeping these things at bay, she had managed in those happy months to wake up each morning full of anticipation for what the new day would bring.

"There's an element of intellectual life in college now," she whispered to Jan one morning.

"But of course! Mark's here," Jan exclaimed.

"It's not just that!" she protested. "But didn't you enjoy that joint student-teacher debate?"

"Yes, I thought Mark and Dave were very sporting. They took their loss so well. They hadn't expected the kids to win, eh?"

"Ya, I think those kids surprised them. But didn't you notice? Only the expat guys came for the debate. The other men didn't show their faces at all."

"Shh!" Jan hushed her.

Suwen looked around the staffroom. She was getting used to the sidelong glances from the women as well as the men whenever she sat down in the canteen with Mark. Nothing had actually been said in her presence, of course. But once, she had heard Peter Kong mutter under his breath, "Not the same colour, man." But when he saw her, he had stopped talking immediately and the men around him would not meet her eyes. She knew what they (the conservative teachers) must be thinking about her: thirty-nine, single and desperate, fishing for an angmoh husband. She saw how she must appear to others, and she was upset. Of course, she tried not to be and tried to play down her own state of romantic yearning, refusing to see her miserable state as anything more than an acute awareness of the hidden prejudices around her. Used to observing others, she now observed herself sitting at the canteen table, opposite Mark, sipping her coffee from a mug. What was so wrong with that? Even if Mark weren't around, she wouldn't have sat down with Peter and his cronies of gripes! For goodness' sake! And Dave Scott didn't count. The amateur spider hunter and collector was too way out for her. Besides, she did not approve of Dave going out with a girl who was a student in another college.

Mark was waiting for her to finish reading his poem.

"Only an amateur's effort," he apologised. His dark brown eyes, partially hidden behind steel-rimmed glasses, tried not to look as anxious as he was feeling.

"When did you write this?" Suwen asked, her own dark eyes narrowing, a little perplexed.

Perhaps she had not expected him to write poetry, Mark thought. "It's been in my head for some time, I guess. But I scribbled it down last night."

"Wow! I never knew you could write poetry. But I must confess, I don't know how to appreciate modern poetry, you know. T S Eliot used to drive me nuts in the U. Is yours free verse or what?"

"I think it's the or-what," Mark grinned. "I wouldn't put a label on it."

"I like this phrase: 'charming slit-eyed smile'. Our Asian eyes are very small, I know."

A pause. Then she read his poem again, this time aloud:

> Where I come from
> Nobody ever dreams
> Of asking how much.
> It isn't done.
> Cost is a very private thing to us,
> Like sex.
> One feels awkward asking,
> Like offering condolences to an almost stranger
> Whose wife unfortunately had run off
> With the milkman.

Then, turning to him, she said, "Oh dear me! We must've appeared crass to you and the other expats."

"Well, it's one of the first things Dave and I noticed when we started talking with Singaporeans. I hope I've not given offence."

"Oh no, but this is not a Scottish voice, is it?"

"You're right. It's more English than Scot. I was trying, well, to see if I could do it from the English perspective. It's...it's probably a silly attempt," he said, and couldn't help seeing how her dark fringe of hair was falling in splendid curls that were almost covering her eyes. He liked the way she would toss back those curls whenever she was agitated. She was still very much like the girl he had met years ago. Just a few more wrinkles.

"D'you know? I've never noticed this cost thing about us. I mean we're such a practical people so used to looking for bargains. So we always ask one another, how much? I've never realised that foreigners find this strange and impolite. I'm thrilled if I find that I've gotten exactly the same thing at a much lower price than someone else. Wouldn't you? C'mon, Mark! Just a teeny-weeny bit pleased?" she cajoled him.

"I must admit I do. You do push a man so."

"Phew! Then you're Scot. Not English at all!"

"Of course, I'm Scot. An Irish-Italian-Scot!" he reminded her.

"And I'm Cantonese. A Hokkien-Cantonese! Don't you forget!"

How could he? She had been constantly in his mind. Since he broke off with Vi. He was here mainly because of her. And he was changing – faster now than at any time of his life since childhood. And he had stopped smoking and drinking too. None of his friends and cronies back in Edinburgh would believe this. And it was not even a conscious decision of his will to give up this smoking and drinking bit. As far as he could see, it was probably just a movement in his evolution, perhaps. Unless he was a spineless blob, shaping and reshaping himself to fit into the spaces that life had presented him, which, if one thought about it, was not such a bad thing after all, for life does demand from us change and response. Still, he would have to examine himself more critically. On this island, in its schools and colleges, the campaign against smoking and alcohol consumption had assumed an almost religious fervour much like any abstinence supported by the clerics. Come to think of it, nothing much was said when one lit up. Just a frown and a glance, swift and furtive, then a cough from one's neighbour. Then another cough from somewhere else perhaps, and another. Nothing more. Nonetheless, one felt the current of disapproval.

Many a time, he had caught himself looking at the woman he had come out East to meet, wondering about the woman beneath the girlish surface. The same olive skin, though not as clear as it used to be. The same almond-shaped eyes and dark wavy hair. Her dressing was much the same as it used to be. She had not changed with the fashions of the times. It had been years since they first met in Aberdeen when she had gone with him to buy a pair of sandals one summer's day. She rode pillion on his rickety bike, clinging to him for dear life as they hurtled down the narrow country lanes. That ride was his clearest memory of her. She was light as a pixie and, later, he had had to wrap his leather jacket round her shoulders to keep her teeth from chattering.

It had been a cool damp day, one of many in the wet summer of that year. And he had lost his head and his heart that summer to Sushila. "Mrs Sanjay", the spinsterish Miss Smith had made it a point to remind him of Sushila's marital status. But he had already broken one of the unwritten cardinal rules of British Council Summer School which discouraged tutors and lecturers from consorting with married participants attending the courses; he had spent the weekend with Sushila Sanjay. They had returned on Monday afternoon to find the British Council blokes in hysterics. There were mumbled reminders of the regulations and disapproving glances, not because he had spent the weekend with Sushila, good God, no, but because he had not taken pains to hide his tracks and be discreet about it like the others. So there he was, feeling sorry for himself and ready to condemn the whole establishment. And to make matters worse, he had somehow left his sandals in Stonyside village, the scene of his weekend escapade. He needed a new pair desperately. But since, like the coward he was at the time, he didn't want Sushila to be seen with him again that day, he had impulsively asked Suwen to go into town with him to buy another pair.

"They found out about my weekend with Sushila!" he had blurted out to that slip of a girl.

"I know! They were looking for you!"

"I won't be coming back!"

"What?"

"They don't want me back next summer!"

"But you're ready to move on, aren't you?"

He remembered that Suwen had tactfully, as usual, encouraged him to look on the bright side.

"How long have you been teaching summer school?" she had yelled into his ear.

"Three years! And I am tired!" he shouted into the rushing air as his bike sped down the road. He had talked on and on, compulsively, obsessively, making his confession of his sordid weekend and seeking conciliation through the calm, sensitive Chinese girl who did not judge him. Her impassive face had shown neither approval nor disapproval. She had sat next to him during dinner that Monday night and, later, she had even come dancing with him and Sushila. And it was partly because of Suwen's tactful supportive presence, he believed, that that was why he did not feel as keenly as he might have the coolness of the British Council blokes and the frost in Miss Smith's communication with him.

"Did I ever write to you about Miss Smith?" he asked Suwen one day when he was walking her home through the Botanic Gardens.

"No, I don't think so. How's she? Still stiff and formal with you?"

"Much the same. But the old girl's married the school inspector from Glasgow."

"Oh."

She had never been much of a talker with him. Except that once when she had boxed his arm over that language issue. They stopped to admire the cannonball tree with large pink flowers blooming from the lower part of its trunk. Suwen touched a stem.

"Ouch! Something's pricked my hand."

"Let me see it."

Suwen held out her hand and Mark held it near-sightedly close to his eyes, peering through his glasses at the minute speck stuck within the lacy lines of her palm.

Suwen gazed at the back of Mark's head. Dark brown hair. Almost black. Quite unusual. Must be the Irish-Italian-Scots genes in him, she mused, trying not to be too conscious of the warmth of his breath upon her outstretched palm.

"Ouch!" she cried when Mark pinched and pulled out the tiny black thorn.

"It's more like a stiff bit of plant hair." He let go of her hand and looked up at the overcast sky. "It's going to pour if we don't hurry," he said, just as the large silver drops fell on them. "Let's get under that tree."

He pulled her up the slope and they ran for shelter under the leafy branches of the julutong tree. The large silver drops soon changed into a shower, splattering the leaves above them. Large drops fell upon them fast and furious for the canopy of leaves above them was soon dripping wet. Her thin violet blouse was soaked. She sneezed.

"This is no help. You're going to catch a cold. Let's run for it, I say."

Mark took her hand and they ran across the grassy slope, cutting through the flower beds, laughing as they ran, heedless of the rain soaking them to the skin. Suwen caught her breath, sensing the sudden release; they were like two children who had escaped from their mother and were now playing a game of catch. Every running step filled her with the thrilling spontaneity which was flooding her being as though irradiating from deep within her. She felt its energy streaming through her heart and out onto her hand held in Mark's firm grasp. He was running beside her, close to her, almost touching her. Her momentary joy was transfiguring all that she was seeing through the rain as moonlight magically transforms a landscape at night, casting the dull, the trivial and the mundane into the shadows. Oh, she was fleet of foot and light of heart! Floating like a wisp of lallang caught up by the breeze!

"Oh, Mark! We're soaked!"

"D'you really care! Race you to the gate!"

Large heavy drops, the size of shillings, fell upon the roads and, by the time they reached the gate of the Ong Mansion, sheets of water had blanketed the neighbourhood of Cluny Road. The two of them dashed through the gate and cut through the undergrowth, running up the stony path which led to Suwen's garage apartment.

"Here, Mark, take this to dry yourself. You're soaked."

He stood by the window, drying himself with the towel she had given him, listening to the gushing of the rainwater down the drainpipes and gutters.

"Coffee?" Suwen asked. She had changed into T-shirt and jeans. "Would you like to change into this?" She handed him an oversized T-shirt. "It's extra large."

That afternoon, the rain came down in torrents. A full-blown tropical storm with horrendous bolts of thunder. Lightning flashed across the windowpanes. There was little hope of the rain stopping soon. And with each passing minute, the shared feeling of carefree play of the previous hour was wearing thin, the veneer of polite talk, skating around trivialities, was threatening to envelop them.

"Any more coffee for you?" Suwen had asked him for the third time.

"No, Su, no more for me."

"Tea? What about some tea? Or, or Milo? D'you drink Milo? I have, er, I have Ovaltine too."

He was smiling. She was getting nervous. This was his first visit to her apartment. Alone. And she was caught off-guard. He wondered about her social life. But he pushed the thought away and, hastily, picked up the thick volume on the beanbag next to him. It was Donald Moore's *The First 150 Years of Singapore*. As the rain poured down all that afternoon, he read portions of it to Suwen to give them something to talk about, at least beside beverages.

"Listen to this. In 1800, the *Royal Engineers' Journal* advised colonial officers to wear plain clothes in Singapore. 'The climate is too hot to allow for waistcoats. Get two thin pairs of riding trousers, and if you are fond of racing, bring breeches and boots. Cricket things are required, also a waterproof.'"

"The English were crazy about cricket in those days."

"Only that class which required servants," he corrected her. "And here, the Asians reign supreme, it says here. 'A European servant is useless. The odds are that he will take to drink and he requires as much waiting on as yourself.' For the bachelor's personal needs, it says here: 'You have your choice of engaging a Malay, Chinese or Kling boy – locally called although said boy may be forty years of age.'"

"It reminds me of America's Deep South. That's what the whites called the blacks too, boy," Suwen said.

"Well, wait till you read this: 'Having tried each class, I would unhesitatingly recommend a Malay. Though, perhaps, not so smart, he's not such a thief as a Chinese boy, or such a liar as a Kling. Moreover, being a Muhammadan, he does not drink as they do; though the Koran does not prevent him from occasionally polishing off your champagne and whisky, beverages which, he contends, the Prophet could have known nothing of when he wrote the Koran.' What d'you say to that?"

"I'd say it's racial prejudice," Suwen answered, getting into the spirit of debate, having forgotten her initial awkwardness over having a male in the house. "You British always pride yourselves as playing cricket and being fair.

But deep down, you're all racists to the bone."

He had to agree with her, Enoch Powell and his "river of blood" speech and the Brighton riots coming readily to mind.

"But it's reading this sort of thing exactly which makes history real and less boring, isn't it? The British Raj and all his prejudices are not figments of someone else's imagination."

He went over and sat on the floor next to her, opening the book at the page which showed a portrait of a dignified-looking Raffles.

"See this eager beaver Raffles here. He was a young shipping clerk who rose to managerial rank in the East India Company. One of the world's first military-industrial conglomerates. And see here. The man wrote to his patron, the Duchess, about building his house on Fort Canning. That's behind the museum, isn't it?"

"Right. It's the park with the sculpture pieces."

"It says here it was the hill where Malay kings were buried. And Raffles wrote here, 'I preferred ascending the hill where if my bones must remain in the East, they would have the honour of mixing with Malay kings.' One wonders how the Malay kings would feel."

"Certainly not elated to have the bones of a commoner among them."

"Hmm, of course, such an audacious wish would never have occurred to him in the first place if there had been no empire or the British Raj."

Suwen nodded. "Who was Raffles? Just the son of an impoverished sea captain. That's all. If you are wondering about the feelings of the sultans, I just wonder how the British royal family would feel if the chairman of Sony Corp suddenly wanted to be buried next to them. Say next to King George VI because the Jap has the money to buy up the whole royal graveyard?"

Heads together, almost touching, they bent over the thick volume, giggling like children over the portraits of the British builders of empire: men with fattish, heavy-jowled faces in dark coats and white cravats who had thought that their mere presence in the East would help raise the level of existence for the lower classes of Orientals.

"They had the cheek!" Suwen exclaimed. Then, turning her dark quizzical eyes upon him, she asked, "D'you really think that the presence of you expats will raise the standard of English in our schools?"

"Well! That's a tough one."

"You don't have to answer it, you know," she smiled primly, a flash of mischief in her eyes.

"One tries one's best to teach." But he was a little annoyed with himself for not being able to give a better answer than that! He could never quite make out whether he had hit it with her or not; his ears were still unattuned to the local inflections and nuances of English as spoken on the island. And, sometimes, it was difficult to ascertain whether Suwen was having a bit of fun at his expense. Not that he minded it terribly. But what irked him these days was something else. There was something indecisive in her feelings towards him. Warm, almost affectionate at times, and then quite unaccountably, she turned cool. Take last Saturday. Suwen had refused to accept a lift from him, insisting on going home with Zul and Jan instead, even though it had been quite late and Zul would have had to go out of his way to take her home. And yet, all evening, Suwen had sat next to him. Quite close. Once or twice, he had even managed to rest his arm lightly upon her shoulders, the nape of her neck resting on him, and he had thought that she was comfortable with him at last, until she had abruptly insisted on leaving with Jan and Zul. He couldn't figure it out. Had he done something or said anything which might have put her off? Or was there perhaps someone else? A fellow he had not met? He wondered if he could find out a bit more from Nica who seemed more ready to talk. The Chinese mind (and one might add, the Chinese heart) still remained an unfathomable mystery to foreigners like him.

"When the Scots lost their lands to the English sheep farmers, they lost their Gaelic tongue too. Right Mark?" Suwen asked him one day when they were having dinner in Nica's apartment.

"Hmm, right. This satay is good, Zul."

"I read somewhere, must be the book you lent me, lots of Scots migrated to Canada and the US because of that," Jan added.

"Those blokes gave the Canadians Nova Scotia," Robert joined in. "The gravy, please."

"Anyone read Prebble's *Clearing of the Highlands*? Very moving account," Zul, who liked to read, was trying to interest everyone into reading the book.

"Nah! I don't read such books," Nica said. "All I know is that Gaelic is a lost tongue now. Killed by the English."

"D'you feel its loss?" Suwen whispered, instinctively lowering her voice tactfully for fear that the topic might be a sensitive one for him.

"I can't really say that," Mark shook his head, running his hand unconsciously through his short-cropped hair. How could he explain to these people that he could neither deny nor admit the loss? He was never one of those who bemoaned the loss of Gaelic, never having grown up speaking the language. And yet, since coming to Singapore, he was becoming more and more attuned to feelings which had lain submerged in his soul and, in meeting Suwen again, he was beginning to feel smitten with a sense of loss he could not explain away.

He took out the letter which an aunt had sent him. It was the faded copy of a letter which a distant cousin, John Edward Campbell, had written from Singapore to his wife in London at the turn of the century. And the aunt, on hearing that Mark was in Singapore, had thought the letter might be of some interest to him.

"John Edward Campbell was a young impoverished clerk. A Scot. Forced by misfortune to come out East."

"Like so many thousands before and after him in the heyday of the empire," Nica quipped.

"One should never keep letters," Robert laughed. "Far too incriminating."

"And their ghosts might haunt one's later life," Mark added, thinking of the mawkish letters and poems he had once written as a pimply youth when his repressed senses were ablaze at the sight of female breasts. Not any female breast but that of Sarah McKenzie: Oh how I'd swoon and sigh; Oh for a glimpse of thy fair breast and thigh! On and on, pages from the sex-starved brain of a seventeen-year-old growing up in a strict Catholic household and too ashamed of his fleshy desires to go to Father O'Reilly for confession. "You might find this useful for your project." He handed his cousin's letter to Suwen.

"Ya, make a letter montage," Nica said, suggesting an immediate framework for it.

Suwen read the untidy scrawl on the page, the unruly print had captured a fleeting moment of someone's life, fossilising it like a leaf pressed into the ancient rock's surface to withstand the vagaries of time.

"'Dear heart,'" Suwen read aloud, "'needless to say, I miss your gentle presence daily.'"

"Oh, how sweet," Jan laughed.

"'I miss those gentle smiles and gentle hands which used to greet me upon my return from work each day.'"

"Gosh, your cousin is a right typical MCP, isn't he?" Nica arched her brows. "A male chauvinist through and through!"

"Give the guy a chance, Nic. The letter was written at the turn of this century," Robert said.

"'But dear heart,'" Suwen went on reading, "'I keep myself busy and try not to fall prey to despair. This evening, I drove through Telok Ayer and Boat Quay. The river was alive with vessels of all kinds. There were the shoe boats of the Chinamen, referred to locally as tongkangs. Then there were the Malay fishermen and the dark-skinned Klings in their sampans and dhows. The Klings from the southern Tamil-speaking parts of India hardly wear any clothes. Their chief item of attire is the loincloth worn round the waist.'"

"It's the dhoti, isn't it?" Jan asked Nica.

"'Most of these men work and sleep in the boats,'" Suwen continued. "'These Klings and Chinamen work as coolies. They haul and carry sacks of goods up and down the gangplanks all day long. At night, when the work stops, this part of the river is considerably illuminated by the innumerable oil lamps which glimmer from the attap awnings of the vessels. It is all very picturesque, certainly, if one ignores the wretched conditions of these natives. Perhaps, native is not quite the word; they are sojourners like my poor self here, but a good deal worse off. And, indeed, these little forays of mine into the non-European quarters of the city are doing me a world of good. The squalor and the poverty I witness in these quarters help to put our suffering in perspective, and has saved me many a time from wallowing in self-pity. I have had the good fortune to engage a very knowledgeable Malay syce who addresses me as Tuan. Yes, dear heart, your humble bank clerk is a tuan besar on this island.'"

"See, that's what I was trying to tell you, Mark," Nica cut Suwen short. "Little English clerks came out here, and suddenly their status and class were raised. They became and acted like lords among us."

It was not Mark's fault, Suwen was tempted to say in his defence. But she did not say anything in the end for fear her comments might be read as a defence of the white skin and provoke Nica to say nasty things. One could not be sure of what Nica might say if provoked. "Hey, listen to this bit," she said instead. "'The dark-skinned Klings are immune to the burning sun and the infernal heat.'"

"Hell holds no terror for us then," Nica laughed and forgot about challenging Mark to another of her debates.

"'A group of dhobies or washermen wade knee-deep into the stream to wash clothes in the midday heat. These stout and sturdy Klings, except for the loincloth round their waists, are entirely at the mercy of the blazing sun. They stand in the muddy waters of the stream, catch hold of the pieces of clothing – shirts by the tails and trousers by the legs – dip them in the brown waters, and swing them over their heads before proceeding to slap and beat them upon a flat slab of rock with the whole force of their robust bodies. This strenuous operation is repeated laboriously, again and again, until each piece of clothing is thoroughly cleaned. And, dear beloved, I can see at this moment the little frown upon your brows at the thought of what this operation might do to the buttons of my shirts!'"

"Well, well, well!" Robert humphed. "That's how the forefathers of Orientals like us earned their living."

"The majority had to slog, what! Except for the noble minority," Nica added. "Anyone for a smoke?"

Cigarettes were passed round, but other than Robert and Nica herself, none of the others smoked.

"I think, except for Zul, none of us are descended from noble families so to speak," Jan said.

"What, Zul?" Robert sat up and Mark was keenly interested in Zul's background too. Although they had corresponded as pen pals for years, Zul had never written anything about his family's background. "Are you descended from Malay royalty?"

"No, no," Zul shook his head, amused at the sudden interest in him. "Jan's not very clear. Not royalty but nobility."

"That's what I said! Robert jumped the gun!"

"I heard royalty."

"Anyway, Zul's great-great-grandfather was a chief in Pahang. Before the British conquered Pahang," Jan explained.

"Oh! So your family was robbed by the British, eh, Zul?" Nica teased, sticking her tongue out at Mark as the sole representative of the former British Raj.

"Oh, but that was so long ago," Zul laughed. "And my father was helped by a white man. This John Edward Campbell."

"Wait a sec! Run that by me again," Robert said. "I seem to have missed something."

"Mark and Zul are related," Jan said, laughing at the look on Robert's face. "Not by blood but by ties. This John Edward Campbell, Mark's distant forebear, helped Zul's grandfather to pay for the education of Zul's father in RI in those early days. Zul's grandfather was his syce. How d'you think Zul knew Mark then?"

"How?" Robert, who liked things to be logical and neat, asked.

"My father believed that he should keep in touch with the Campbell family. He used to write to the family at least once a year. And he made me write too. He likes the Campbells and it's a family joke that if Campbell soup were halal, my father would drink it every day," Zul laughed.

It was a strong infectious laugh from someone who was confident of himself, Suwen thought, watching the smile on Jan's face.

How could she explain it to Mark? This multitude and diversity of her island? Nica, Robert, Zul, Jan and herself were the strands of different histories and cultures woven into this modern fabric of many hues and textures by a loom which was moving too quickly for anyone to have more than a glimpse of its emerging shifting patterns, Chinese and yet not Chinese; Indian and yet not Indian...yet, here they were, the new Asians, and Mark was the foreigner among them. Years ago, in her twenties, she would never have thought that she minded it. The thought had never even occurred to her. Would she ever marry an angmoh? She didn't dare commit herself to an answer. Not now. Not ever. She liked Mark, she quickly told herself. But she was afraid of her own irrational feelings. Once. Only once, she had allowed herself to imagine what Mark might look like stripped of his attire. A white nude male, white as death, with a thick fat organ dangling between his white hairy thighs. And at this point, she had turned resolutely away and stopped her mind from fantasising such nonsense. She could never go to bed with a white man, she told herself. She was too much of a Chink. She put it down to her own innate Chinese snobbery, an irrational memory of the race which inhabited Chung-kuo, the Middle Kingdom. So, she would never dream of marrying outside her own race. She simply could not see herself locked in copulation with a white hairy body. But the minute she admitted this thought, she was filled with shame, ashamed that she, Suwen, was capable of such prejudice against one colour and one race. It did not make sense. She was an educated woman. How she admired Jan!

Now that Jan's engagement to Zul was more or less settled as far as their friends were concerned, Suwen found herself looking at her former classmate and colleague with greater interest. Jan was never known for garrulity, rarely, if ever, saying anything about herself and her family. A trait which suited Suwen fine since she herself did not encourage those girlish exchanges of confidences about boyfriends and family. But among close friends, Jan would open up and regale them with stories about her students. When Suwen left for further studies, Jan was her only correspondent for many years; the rest of her classmates had stopped writing after some time. It was quite natural, Suwen consoled herself, the immediacy of the life around us would consume us; few classmates took the trouble to keep up with one another after school anyway. "So much work lah! Bye! Catch up with you later!" The "later" never coming any nearer. That much she had learnt since returning from England. She had come back expecting nothing. Jan, however, dear sweet Jan, was at the airport to meet her. Up till then, she never knew how the mere presence of a familiar face at Changi Airport could bring so much pleasure. And relief. At least there was someone who wanted to "catch up" with her, and she needn't start life back home as if she were a total stranger in a strange country. Five years was a long time to be away.

"Why don't you join my college as an art teacher?" Jan had asked her. "We've got a vacancy and you've got a teaching diploma."

So with Jan's help, coming home was not so bad after all even though home was the Ong Mansion again. If her mother had not threatened to kill herself, she would have preferred to live some place else. Still, since one had no choice over one's parents, one had to take them as they came. She compromised; took over the garage next to the servants' quarters instead of moving back into the old room upstairs in the main house. She made sure that she went away every school vacation and kept herself very busy, away from her mother and stepfather. Looking back, she was surprised at how quickly the years had slipped away. Like water through cupped hands. In terms of accomplishment, she had achieved nothing outstanding. Groups of seventeen and eighteen-year-olds had passed through her classes, returning year after year to thank her before they slipped behind new masks and new roles after their 'A' Levels. If she had to describe her years from the time of her return from England to this moment, the thirty-ninth year of her existence, she would ruthlessly say that she had been nothing but an interested bystander, living vicariously through the youths in her classes, helping those boys and girls to cope with their romances and getting them ready for their exams. Outside of college, she dabbled with painting and sculpting to keep up with her art. Every Saturday, she went shopping with Jan. They attended plays and art exhibitions together, two single teachers keeping loneliness at bay. Then Jan, who was interested in sculpture, met Nica at an art seminar. She was introduced to Nica and, eventually, her social world widened. Then Zul returned from the States, and her shopping trips on Saturdays ended. Jan was spending more and more time with Zul. She did not offer any explanations nor try to make excuses, and Suwen, out of consideration, did not press her.

However, she could not help but feel dejected, like a little girl at the playground whose best friend had gone off to play with someone else.

Then, one night, Jan phoned her. "Su, can I come over? Now. I need a place to sleep tonight."

Jan's voice was choked.

"Yes, of course! What happened?"

"Tell you later."

An hour later, Jan was in her garage apartment, telling her about Zul and her father.

"He doesn't even want to meet Zul. He was raving mad."

"Exactly what did your father say?"

"Rubbish! He talked rubbish! He's a racist. That's all I can say. And he would've hit me if my mother had not pushed him away. And he fought with her instead."

"I don't know what to say. It must be awfully hard for you and Zul."

"Zul's very patient. He and I have talked about such things for a long time. I'd expected it," Jan sniffed. "My father is threatening to throw me out of the house. And disown me. In public."

"You mean in the press?"

"Yes, he's talking about an ad in *The Straits Times*."

"Are you ready for that, Jan?"

"Ready or not, I'd have to face it, right? I can't stop my father. He's always been pig-headed. And violent."

And that was all Jan would say about her father that night. And although there were copious tears, Jan seemed to be in control. She was a strong and determined woman. Sensitive and sensible, Suwen thought as she lay awake, thinking about Jan when they were in the Vic Street Convent together. It hadn't seemed so very long ago when the two of them were punished by Mrs D'Rose for giggling at the back of the class. Satvinder Kaur had just told them that after her 'O' Levels, she would be travelling to New Delhi to marry a young Sikh banker, chosen for her by her parents. Their teenage eyes had grown round with newfound pleasure as they listened to Satvinder's descriptions of her marriage arrangements. It had not occurred to the three of them at the time, in the sixties, that they should protest against such parental meddling in their lives. Woodstock and the ideals of personal freedom and choice had not touched them yet. They were only in Secondary Four. And while the Eurasian girls in class were already talking about their dates with the SJI boys, the three of them were still naïvely oblivious of the opposite sex. At least one of them was, Suwen corrected herself, for at that time, she had had enough troubles at home with her mother's husband to keep her off the male sex forever. Anyway, she quickly reminded herself, who would have thought that Jan, the girl who was as lanky as a string bean in Secondary 4A, and forever hiding behind her and Satvinder during Maths lessons, would turn out to be so independent and sensible after all. Suwen let out a sigh. While she herself had lacked the guts to walk out on her mother and away from the Ong Mansion, Jan had already struck out on her own when she fell in love with Zul, and when she travelled alone, two years ago, across the Asian continent on the Trans-Siberian Railway. While she, Suwen, had dreamt about things, Jan had gone ahead and done things. She had no backbone, she heaved another inward sigh. Compared with the likes of Jan and Nica, she was just a blob of jellyfish, flapping on the beach, dreaming of freedom riding the waves but had no ability to move on her own accord.

The more she thought about it, the more envious she felt about Jan. How incredible! How very daring! For Jan's parents were Christians. Catholic or Methodist, she was not too sure, but Christians they were for sure.

"And you are studying the Koran?" Suwen asked Jan.

"Sooner or later, I'd have to fit into his family, right?"

She had no arguments against such logic of the heart; people in love with each other shaped and reshaped themselves to sculpt new lives of togetherness, on their own terms, in their own good time. So, whatever fears she might have had about Jan's parents and their reactions to their daughter's change of faith, she kept to herself. She remembered how an aunt in the Ong family was extremely upset when her daughter converted to Christianity. Parents were the same all over the world. If they were used to holding joss sticks to their gods and ancestors, they expected their children to follow suit.

"My father has this cock-eyed view that I'm marrying below me," Jan told her and Mark one day when they were drinking coffee in the college canteen. Ever since Mark, who had been Zul's Campbell correspondent, had joined them, Jan was beginning to talk more openly about her relationship with Zul and the problems she faced.

"Did you tell your father about Zul's family?" Mark asked.

"I tried. Many times. But he wouldn't listen. He's got a fixed mind. And I have learnt such a lot from Zul. His family is very interesting. His father was a teacher, and a journalist with Utusan Melayu who worked with our first president. Tun Yusoff Ishak, I think."

The Story Of Zul's Grandfather And Father

Zul's grandfather, Abdullah Rahman, was the son of a penghulu in the state of Pahang. Way back before the British took over the Malay states in Peninsular Malaya. I am not very sure, but I could be marrying into a prominent Muslim family, you know, marrying above me, although my father wouldn't think so. Anyway Abdullah Rahman never had the chance to succeed his father as penghulu. Abdullah Rahman's father, that is Zul's great grandfather, was one of those Malay chiefs who plotted against the British and got thrown out of power. So, in the early nineteen hundreds, Abdullah Rahman came to Singapore. Without a cent in his pocket. He found a job as a waiter in the Cricket Club, as well as a benefactor in John Edward Campbell. This John Campbell, Mark's very distant forebear or cousin, don't know how many times removed, later helped to pay for the schooling of Haji Hussein, Zul's father. He's about seventy or eighty now, I think. But his mind is very clear. He can still remember many things from the past. The distant past. Not things five minutes ago. He's physically very weak. But he likes to tell me stories when I visit him in the hospital. Maybe it's sort of to induct me into the family culture or what, I don't know. He doesn't talk to Zul much. But he talks to me. And from what he tells me, I can imagine what it must've been like when Zul's grandfather, Abdullah Rahman, first met John Edward Campbell.

It had started one day with a tiger hunt which had gone kaput...

"Boy! Ice! Ayer batu!" the burly Thomas H Thompson, Registrar of Hackney Coaches, Jinrickshaws and Motorised Vehicles had called out peremptorily to the waiters in the Cricket Club. He was not in good humour that day. The tiger hunt had been an utter failure.

"Baik, tuan!" Rahman had hurried over to the white man with a jug of ice.

He was thirtyish, the last of innumerable children fathered by his penghulu father. His impoverished circumstances had forced him to answer to the call of "boy" from the English administrators and traders who thronged the bar of the Cricket Club.

"Good evening, sir," John Campbell greeted the Registrar with all the deference due to a man of his position.

"Aye, good evening, John my boy! Of McAlister and Sons, I'm sure!"

"What an excellent memory, sir," the young clerk in the Scottish trading house murmured gratefully. If this had been London, teeming with thousands of clerks like him, he would never have been noticed by a man of Mr Thompson's stature.

"Ah, my boy, I pride myself in not forgetting a name or a new face in this colony. Especially one mentioned by the missus," the Registrar laughed good-naturedly. "Gentlemen," he turned to his drinking companions, "meet John Campbell of the firm of McAlister."

The conversation round the bar soon turned to the morning's hunt for the elusive tiger.

"A most dismal affair! Nothing was accomplished," Mr Thompson moaned into his glass of beer and asked for another refill.

"I don't understand how the brute could've given us the slip," Dr Johnson, the head of General Hospital said. "There we were with our guns ready to shoot at the drop of a hat! Dying of thirst in the bloody heat!"

"Five and twenty Kling convicts, a whole detachment, mind you, swore they heard the tiger's roar. But what ran out of the undergrowth was a wild boar! I cursed the bloody lot of them," Major Hill of Royal Engineers added.

"The Kling grass cutter swore that the beast could be found taking its siesta in the same spot every day," one of the traders told the company.

"The night before the villagers had lost another goat," another man added.

"The Klings shouted themselves hoarse and, I must add, were quite diligent in beating the thick undergrowth. One of them swore he came within an ace of making the acquaintance of the jungle lord," Major Hill recounted.

"Then it slipped away. Quite unaccountable and extraordinary. There were thirty of us at least in the belukar."

"Gentlemen, I've said this before and I say it again. We should've used the Malay chaps. It's not the practice in these parts to use Klings for tiger drives."

"Why, sir?" John Campbell asked.

"Well, the Malay villagers know the jungles here far better than the Klings for one thing. And, for another, they are a more cautious lot. They'll pray to the jins, the forest spirits. They always ask for a safe passage before entering the domain of the tiger lord. The Malays believe that certain animals have the kramat power to change their appearances to deceive hunters. Who knows? Perhaps that's what the tiger did this morning."

"Now, now, Thomas," Dr Johnson laughed. "As a man of science, I can't let that pass without comment. The jungles here and in the Malay Peninsula are dark sombre places. Even at noon. You'll soon find out, John, if you've been on a tiger hunt. The sun seldom pierces the dense foliage. Shadows lie upon shadows. Quite eerie at times. And it's the silence which is unnerving," he paused and looked at the intent faces of his companions who knew exactly what he meant, though none would admit that they had felt the cold hand of fear. "All kinds of mysterious hidden things seem to slide and slither away in the undergrowth. If you doubt my words, spend a night in the jungle of Seletar. It's camouflage, gentlemen. But to the unscientific mind, it's as if hidden beings are watching you."

"I quite agree, Bill, I quite agree. But, surely, even you will have to admit that there's another dimension of life besides the purely physical," Mr Thompson sounded earnest. "I've lived in these parts far too long to discount such things lightly. When I was in Perak visiting remote villages and trekking through dense jungles, one could sympathise with the Malays' preoccupation with pontianaks, jins and harimau hutans. The jungles in these parts envelop their lives and homes."

Rahman listened to the talk of the white men intently. He could not make head nor tail of it, but phrases like "pontianak", "jin" and "harimau hutan" had caught his attention.

"I was in Bentong Ulumat last year," Major Hill's gruff voice boomed above the hum of voices. "A most ghastly thing happened while I was there. Something to do with a were-tiger. Villagers had been losing their buffaloes for months. Rumour said it was a were-tiger or harimau hutan. Much like our werewolves in Europe. Neither bait, trap nor hunter could capture it. Panic spread, of course. These were extremely superstitious and ignorant people. Those fools kept indoors every night. Tiger traps were set up in every village. Then, one morning, they found a man caught in one of the traps."

Major Hill sipped his beer while his listeners waited. Being a good storyteller, he savoured the anticipation of his audience and he was in no hurry to proceed. He took another gulp, emptied his glass and called to Rahman for a refill.

"Well, the poor trapped man was a simple pedlar. He hawked his petty wares from village to village. 'Could he be the harimau hutan?' the village penghulu asked his people. And those simpletons and fools reckoned that since the man was in a tiger trap, then he must be a tiger! And they promptly speared him to death! Twenty spears thrust into the poor blighter's body. He was dead as a carcass when we found him."

A gasp rose from his audience.

"But how did the man end up in the tiger trap in the first place?" John Campbell asked the question which was on everyone's mind.

"Well, my boy, when you've lived in these parts for as long as I have, you'll soon realise that the Malay villagers have little up here," Major Hill tapped his temple.

The Englishmen laughed as the young Scotsman shook his head. When the others had left and the Club was closing for the night, John Campbell stopped by the bar to ask Rahman about the Bentong were-tiger. He had studied Malay and could communicate in the language fairly fluently.

"Tuan, Bentong Ulumat is deep in the jungle. One week's journey by river," Rahman told him quietly. John Campbell liked his upright bearing and quiet demeanour. "In these faraway parts, a harimau hutan comes out of the jungle. It walks like a man, talks like a man. All your kerbau and other livestock are killed. What could the villagers do? The nearest police post is one week down the river."

"There should have been a trial, Inche Rahman," John Campbell said. "How could the penghulu allow a man to be killed like this?"

But Rahman remained unfazed. Ignoring the white tuan's numerous mispronunciations of Malay words, he explained that the villagers had considered the traditional trial by oath. They had wanted the pedlar to swear upon the Koran in the mosque at first, but it soon dawned on them that such an unnatural creature as a were-tiger would not hesitate to lie and defile the Holy Book in order to save its own skin. The penghulu could not allow such defilement, Rahman said.

"Then why not have the poor man tried in a proper court? An English court in Singapore?"

Rahman, who was familiar with the ways of the courts, at least, the Malay royal courts, looked straight into the eyes of the tuan. For a brief moment, their eyes locked. Then he looked away. None but the most observant would have noticed that in that brief moment, two equals had faced each other – the tuan puteh of Scottish origins and the Malay waiter who was the son of a Pahang penghulu. Neither man indicated that each had noticed anything; their manner and tone of voice remained unchanged. But when Rahman spoke again, John Campbell was listening to him more attentively.

"I beg the tuan to forgive me for disagreeing with him," Rahman began. "Even in the great courthouse here, the orang puteh judges have convicted men of murder when the evidence was not half as strong as this."

John Campbell nodded. "Go on," he said.

"I beg the tuan to look at the case with the eyes of the Bentong villagers. The evidence against the pedlar was very strong. Who in his right mind would spend a night in a tiger trap? And, even more, sleeping next to the carcass of a dog! A Muslim in these parts, tuan, will not let a dog touch him. We don't know the pedlar's reasons for going into the tiger trap. It's his word weighed against the fact. And the fact was his questionable presence in the trap. Who do we believe? In law, tuan, the fact is always heavier than the word. And, in this case, we have only the word of someone we suspect of being a weretiger!"

After making Rahman repeat some of his Malay phrases, John Campbell finally understood. At the same time, he was painfully aware of his inadequacy: his inadequate command of the Malay language and his inadequate knowledge of the people. Like the Major and the other white men, he had made the precarious assumption that the evidence was circumstantial and implying, in the process, that the Malay villagers had little in their brain boxes. How wrong he had been!

So, from that night onwards, John Campbell made it a point to seek out Rahman for a chat now and again when he visited the Club. And that was how, eventually, he became a kind of patron to Zul's grandfather.

Rahman lived with his family in a kampong in old Geylang, within a maze of thatched huts, attap houses on stilts, and muddy lanes crisscrossed with rotting planks and coconut tree trunks. Straggly bushes and creepers hugged the shallow ditches of frothy stagnant pools. Scrawny chickens scratched among the rubbish heap of discarded boxes, cartons and rusty tin cans, and ducks with bristly tails poked their beaks into the grey pools for slimy scraps of food. Dirty little urchins, brown with the sun, crouched near the ditches, oblivious of the flies and filth, giggling and pointing to the thin curls of turd oozing out of their little brown bottoms!

Such kampong scenes have passed away with time; we do not have such kampongs any more. But in those early days, it was Abdullah Rahman's dream to move out of the kampong to a better place some day. He had ambitions, secret hopes and dreams for he never forgot that he was the descendant of a proud penghulu family. He wanted his son, Hussein, to rise above the urchins in the kampong.

"Where's Hussein?" he asked his wife when he returned from work one evening.

"Bapa! Di sini! Already bathed, see!" His son was grinning from ear to ear. The young Hussein knew that his stern father liked to see him washed clean whenever he came home from work.

"Baik! The tuan puteh spoke to me today," he told his wife. "The tuan knows the Guru Besar of Sekolah Raffles. And he has agreed to take our son. We don't have to pay. The tuan puteh will pay all the fees and buy the books."

"Allah is very kind to us," his wife murmured for she knew that Rahman had set his heart upon sending their son to Raffles Institution to learn the language of the white men. "But, Bang, what about his studies at the madrasah?"

"What about it? Nothing will change." Rahman assured his wife that their son would continue attending the religious school. "He will still learn the Holy Book. Going to the school of the orang puteh and learning to speak like them does not mean that our son is going to forget his faith. He's going to their sekolah so that he will not be a waiter or syce like me!"

Before I met Zul's father, Haji Hussein (he's the one who went to Raffles) I had always assumed that only Chinese parents had ambitions for their children. You see how myopic we Chinese can be? Imagine my surprise when Haji Hussein told me that his father, even in those early days, had wanted him to go to Raffles Institution. I felt stupid for being surprised. When I told Zul about it later, he laughed, I think he enjoyed my journey of discovery with his father. Anyway, one day, Zul told me about an early diary entry written by his father. Honestly, I was impressed and surprised. The Malay writings of Haji Hussein must've been elegant and poetic. At least it sounded that way when Zul told me about it. I was just thinking the other day that, when we really sit down and think about it, our feelings whatever our colour or faith are essentially the same, aren't they?

> "...In my old age, my thoughts return to my father and his hopes for me. I can imagine them all now, but, oh, how ignorant I was in my youth! May Allah forgive me. That evening after dinner, my father must have smoked his cheroot as usual in the serambi while my mother was putting my sisters and me to bed. I can imagine a warm breeze rustling among the coconut palms and lallang grass. My father

must have looked out at the kampong of attap houses on stilts, crowding along the bank of the stream of malodorous mud, meandering into Geylang River. This was home to him and our family.

As I write this tonight, I can picture the glow of his lone cheroot and its rings of pungent smoke, keeping at bay the swarms of mosquitoes rising from the stagnant pools of foul-smelling water beneath the huts. His neighbours' cooking fires and oil lamps pushed aside the night's flickering shadows, and in their midst, smoking alone, my father must have felt the stirring of feelings he could not name. Perhaps it was a longing for the home he had lost in Pahang or hopes for me, his son. I can only guess at what these feelings were; feelings not of pride but of hope, a fragile hope and a nagging anxiety tugged his heart – the heart of an anxious loving father.

Now that I have children of my own, I have begun to understand my stern father better, by the grace of Allah. There are in our lives moments which our memories cannot recapture in words; only a recollection of fleeting fragile feelings to which we dare not cling, in case, in our eagerness to grasp at permanence and possession, we lose the very thing which keeps alive our hopes and dreams. So we stand absorbed in the contemplation of these luminous hopes, holding our breath, because we know that fulfilment and forever do not belong to this transient world. And so, this evening, as I write I am stabbed by the futility of hope and the impermanence of joy. I do not think I have fulfilled all my father's dreams. At least not his dream of returning to Pahang to reclaim our family lands..."

When Haji Hussein was a reporter writing for Utusan Melayu and campaigning for a better life for his community, he found out that John Campbell's support for his education had created quite a stir in the European community at the time. But what saddened him most was that, eventually, what had started as an altruistic gesture was turned into something self-serving.

"Well, John!" Mr Thomas H Thompson hailed him. "I've heard about your good deed. So how's your little Malay boy doing?"

"Very well, sir. A fine bright-eyed blighter he is! But how did you know about him?"

"Why, old chap, it's all over town. Surely you don't think such an event would escape the colony? My missus heard it from the Bishop's wife herself. His Grace was mightily pleased. But not all of us, you understand?"

"The deuce of it," John Campbell groaned. "My advice was sought by a native, and I rendered what help I could. I reckoned it would be good for our standing among the natives here, sir."

"Well said, old chap, well said. But," Mr Thomas H Thompson, who had lived in the colony far longer than John Campbell, patted his friend's arm, "intention is one thing, public reaction is another. And, as far as I can tell, the twain seldom meet and concur."

The old colonial administrator sighed. Thomas H Thompson could still hear the shrill voice of his wife at breakfast that morning, recounting her version of the story.

"Oh, that puffed-up John! I'd have to write to Mother about him. She knows all about his impoverished relations back home. I can well imagine what Mother would say about his latest scheme. He's taken into his head that we're not doing enough for our natives! And that's not all! He's going to pay for the education of a little Malay boy. Next he'll be saying we're ill-treating them, depriving our ayahs and syces of opportunities to improve themselves! Here's a man, Thomas, it's very obvious to me if not to you, here's a man who has no notion of our hardships. Does he know what skill and ingenuity are required from helpless women like us to get some honest work out of these people? They're ever so slow. And so uncomprehending!"

There were murmurs of protest and a few voices of support, but many respectable people took offence that a mere assistant, albeit the chief assistant of McAlister, was presumptuous enough to finance the entire education of a Malay boy at the island's premier school. And he was not even the son of a tengku or datuk. "Preposterous!" a matron huffed. "What will it lead to if all of us are required to send the sons of our ayahs and gardeners to school?" Some uncharitable souls even hinted darkly of mischief and misdeeds; perhaps a certain connection with native women, they whispered.

John Campbell, however, weathered this wave of criticism. With the passing of the years, he prospered like any English trader and grew stout. His hair, bleached by the harsh tropical sun, turned a paler brown and grew quite sparse. He was a member of the Chamber of Commerce and had made a name for himself as a shrewd trader of great tenacity although his critics preferred terms like "obdurate fool". These unflattering epithets did not disturb John Campbell unduly. On the contrary, he felt a certain pride in being a subject of controversy. "Have always been so!" he laughed. "I've never been one to duck a problem. However much one would like the goodwill and approbation of others, one should never be swayed by the winds of public opinion," he told his audience at the Cricket Club. And, after a few beers, he would inevitably tell newcomers that he was the first in the colony to support the cause of free native education in a tangible material way when it was still all talk and bluster at the time. "But, mind you, look at Abdullah Rahman's boy now. The young Hussein is completing his studies. By year's end he'd have finished. Then I'd get the young man a place in the Suara or the Echo. And before you know it, he'd be our most valuable source of information. On Malay affairs. Never forget, you chaps, that even the great Raffles had his Abdullah," he laughed.

In those days, whenever John Campbell thought about Rahman's son, the smile upon his lips was as much a reflection of the pride he took in young Hussein's progress as the self-congratulation he felt whenever he thought of his own foresight. This singular feeling like a venomous viral infection had been seeping into his being so insidiously that he had not noticed any change or any coarsening in his own mental composition. At times, he even considered himself as a more superior being compared to his peers; and it was precisely because he believed that "these brown and yellow races can be pulled up, if not by their socks, at least by their loincloths! What they need, gentlemen, is a good solid English education. With an English education, their sons will be gentlemen like us! And we have some of these already. Quiet, polite Oriental gentlemen who speak our language." And to this end, from an exalted sense of duty to himself and the British Raj, he declared that the European trading community should set up a scholarship fund for the sons of poor natives.

And this altruistic act had paid off handsomely for him. His promotion of free native education did not go unnoticed in the colony. The following year, it was proposed to His Excellency, the Governor of the Straits Settlements, that John Edward Campbell, now a full partner in McAlister and Sons, should be appointed an Honourable Member of the Legislative Council so that the government could benefit from his knowledge and contacts with the local population.

"In your telling of the story, Jan, you've made John Campbell into some kind of fraud. Rather harsh, don't you think?" Suwen asked, giving Mark a glance to see if he was affected by what Jan had said. After all, the man was his relative, although one who had died long ago.

"He means nothing to me," Mark assured her. "I didn't even know he existed until my aunt sent me this bundle of papers. She'd thought it might be of interest to me since, like him, I've come to this island to work."

"Mark, you know it's not personal, right?" Jan asked.

"Think nothing of it, Jan. But Zul…"

"Ya, what about Zul?" Suwen was eager to know.

"Men are different," Jan said.

"He thinks John Campbell did a good deed. Action is more important than thought, he says. He doesn't care so much about intention. But, for me, intention is important. John Campbell represents a certain type. An angmoh trader who financed all sorts of projects. Because he pitied us. We the poor ignorant Orientals needed help, what!"

"Don't you think John Campbell could have been idealistic?" Suwen asked.

"Hey, I'm beginning to like this stuff," Mark said, distracting the women momentarily.

As was their habit these days, the three of them were in the college canteen, sipping what Mark referred to as dishwater, otherwise known as kopi susu, local coffee with sweetened condensed milk.

"Watch it, Mark. Liking this stuff is the first sign of an angmoh going to pieces," Jan teased.

"That's right, like one of Conrad's characters," Suwen joined in the game too. "Without the civilised graces of Western society to shore you up, you'll go to pieces and turn local."

"And before you know it, you'll be eating durians by the roadside like us. And going over the clouds."

"That wouldn't be such a bad thing, would it?"

"No, Mark, especially if one is right smack in the middle of an attack on Westerners," Suwen wagged a finger at Jan.

"I am not! How can you say I'm attacking angmohs?" Jan protested in earnest. "I've read John Campbell's other letters. Those written to his brother in his old age. The man had changed by then. Right, Mark?"

"Right, Jan."

"See? People change, Su. We're not static. Here, read this bit."

Jan handed Suwen one of the letters from the bundle which Mark's aunt had sent him. The letter was dated 1935. John Campbell was praising the well-kept garden of a friend:

> ...traveller's palms, pink bougainvilleas, scarlet hibiscus and roses lined the driveway leading to the bungalow. You will be impressed by the garden's sense of orderliness and its regular rows of trees, keeping well away from the unruly abundance of tropical vines and creepers native to these parts. George is understandably proud of his acre of civilised greenery. The homes of the Orientals are in a state of perpetual mess. Children crawling on the dirt floors and mats and things thrown about the rooms in haphazard fashion. Their huts and shophouses are inevitably crammed chock-full with bodies and things. Only the wealthiest among them, who has had the mental agility to recognise and practise some of the manners of the civilised world, has risen above this Oriental mess. And this proves my point that, if officers of the Crown were to set the tone and lead by exemplary conduct, certain Orientals could be taught to reach for the higher levels of civilised life. And, in this way, the Colonial Office need never worry about the loyalty of the more intelligent among its

brown and yellow subjects.

"Patronising is not quite the word, is it?" Suwen said.

"Bastard?" Mark hazarded.

"Well, some of them were," Jan answered him.

"Sorry, Mark. It's not about you. Or even about John Campbell. I think it's more to do with my own unresolved feelings these days."

Suwen looked at her friend; Jan was beginning to open up these days. Love and conflict do strange things to people, she mused.

"Sometimes when one has been made to feel small, one tends to see things differently," Mark began.

"No, Mark. I haven't been made to feel small by an angmoh, if that's what you're driving at," Jan added quickly. "I've seen things in church. At least in the church my parents go to every Sunday. When I was a kid I had to tag along. When I was older, a teenager and more critical I think, I thought the English vicar was more pally with the angmohs, going to their houses for tea. He never visited my parents. They always had to visit him. But those locals who were lawyers like the Subramaniams and Josephs, they got visits. I know because I used to visit Neeta Subramaniam, you remember her, don't you, Su?"

How could Suwen forget the girl? Neeta was the one who brought her to the old Robinson Department Store in Fullerton Square. Neeta was her first encounter with an all-knowing city girl from a rich Indian family who spoke English at home, very much like Nica's family. And she, Suwen, was the new girl in school, from the "ulus" of Perak up north who did not even know how to buy a Marks and Spencer dressmaking paper pattern from Robinson. The store was staffed by English-speaking Eurasians mostly and she did not want to confess that her mother, who could not speak a word of English then, had refused to bring her. Her mother, like most of the wealthy Chinese tai-tais, preferred to shop in the Peking and Metro Department Stores in High Street in those days where the fashionable garments were all from Hong Kong, the Mecca of Chinese fashion.

"As I was trying to tell you," Jan was addressing Mark, "I'm beginning to question why when people migrate here, to Southeast Asia, they want to change it to suit themselves. The Chinese want to recreate a China here, the Indians want an India and the English want another Devon or Hampstead Heath."

"It's natural for immigrants to bring part of the old world with them," Mark said.

"I know, but it's not fair to those who are native here, and I mean 'native' in a nice sense, okay?" Jan wagged a finger at Suwen just in case she had thought otherwise. "I think immigrants and their descendants, us, should change. Not the other way round."

Listening to Jan that day, Suwen was beginning to understand that Jan, unlike most Chinese, was prepared to become more of a Southeast Asian rather than a Chinese seeking to safeguard her cultural self from change.

"I'm very different from my dad," Jan went on. "He went back to Shanghai to study in an English college set up by missionaries. When he was younger, he was quite proud that he was English-speaking. But, nowadays, he keeps talking about China and roots. But to me it's just another foreign country. And that's why, Su, I'd better warn you. There'll be fireworks this Saturday when you come."

"Don't worry, I can take care of myself. You're all packed?"

"More or less."

Zul parked his car in the cool shadow of the Geylang Christian Assembly of Christ Church. Jan had asked him to wait there for her. She did not want a confrontation between him and her father, who was likely to fly off the handle at the mere sight of him. Sighing a little and praying that all would go well for his beloved, he pressed a button, and immediately his window pane went sliding down with a faint hiss. High-tech marvel, he thought and patted his brand new Toyota fondly. His first car had been a scarred secondhand rattle can. But it was a good buy for less than ten grand, all he could afford then.

He looked at the cars whizzing past him. This Geylang neighbourhood was a far cry from the one in which he had spent most of his boyhood. Gone were those familiar landmarks which had given his boyhood a sense of stability because he had once thought they were eternal, suspended in time even though the rest of Singapore was changing. But those totems of his youth, like everything else, had been bulldozed and demolished to make room for the new concrete boxes erected in place of the Flame trees, the angsanas, the lallang patch, the muddy ditch (where he'd caught his first guppy) and the roadside barber's stall under the angsana tree. Ah Seng, the Chinese barber, in khaki shorts and cotton singlet, cut the hair of all the neighbourhood boys, right there where the shops were now. Coarse white powder flying in the air, joking, scolding and cajoling the boys, where was the man now? The price was always fifty cents a haircut for children. How old was he when he was brought to Ah Seng for his first haircut? He couldn't remember; but judging by the remembered scene of his bawling and shrieking when Ah Seng lifted him up and sat him on the high cane chair, he must have been five or thereabouts. "Mali! Mali, Machik! Potong kepala! Lima puloh sen sa'ja!" Ah Seng had grinned wickedly, and he'd kicked the man's shin, all the while shrieking for dear life. "Mak! Mak! Ta'mahu!" He didn't want to have his head cut off! "Bukan potong kepala, Zul! Gunting rambut, sahaja!" his mother had laughed till the tears rolled down, her face.

Other scenes of his Geylang boyhood were equally personal, though largely insignificant to the rest of the world. And that's the thing about memories, fragments of social insignificance unless they were set against a background of war, revolution and such things. Peace and stability make for dull history.

Not far from the barber's stall, there used to be a ditch of dark mud, full of filth and slime. He saw himself squatting on its banks, a seven-year-old trying to catch a fighting spider when he slipped and fell into the soft ooze. The mud sucked and clung to him. He shrieked for help, and Ah Seng came running. The man hauled him up, scolding all the while as he wiped the mud off his clothes with newspapers, "Loo main-main jahat! Tengok-la loo jatoh sekali! Pulang chepat-chepat!"

Geylang Market, a cluster of ramshackle stalls covered by flapping canvases and tar paper, used to be round the corner from where the church was standing now. It was a place of endless entertainment especially when the koyok or

Chinese medicine man demonstrated his gongfu skills to sell medicated oils. The family did not own a fridge then so his mother had to go to the market every morning. But on Saturday morning his brood of brothers and sisters, five of them, would troop to the market with Mak. His three sisters walked in front with Mak while he and his brothers lingered behind, kicking paper bags, sticks, stones, tin cans and whatever their feet happened to meet. The empty tins of condensed milk flung out of the coffee shops made the loudest racket. Nothing except firecrackers could beat the glorious din those tins could make as they were kicked down the backlanes at seven o'clock in the morning. "Bising saja!" Mak would hiss at them as he and his brothers raced down the lane.

When he looked up, the view before his parked car was the neat row of two-storey HDB shophouses which had taken the place of the zinc and wood shops of the Chinese grocers and Indian dhobies. With a sharp pang he recognised what he had known all his life. That, as always, it is the outer physical rim of our social hub which changes faster than its core of age-old prejudices, cock-eyed perceptions and irrational fears. For as long as we mix and mingle in the comfortable confines of the marketplace, all is well; move beyond that into the personal and the intimate areas, then the hub quivers and shakes like a machine into which one has accidentally poured water instead of oil.

Was that his father's warning in the letters? Why else would the old man entrust him with the task of reading them to the rest of the family? His father had always been harder on him than on Yusoff and Rahim. Were these letters the old man's way of warning him against prejudice? He peeled away the years and saw his father coming up the stairs. Bapak had brought some friends home for dinner. The men, as always, ate together, drinking mugs of black coffee and talking in low voices long after he and his brothers and sisters were in bed. He was fourteen or fifteen then, curious about the world beyond the family and the mosque. The murmur of male voices had resonated with purpose and kinship feelings like a strain of music suspended in one's memory and which one recalled before falling asleep. As a teenager, he grew up knowing that his Bapak was involved in important affairs which had something to do with the "ra'ayat Melayu".

Contrary to what Jan and Suwen believed, his father's English education in RI had not blinded him to the faults of the British. Bapak was in the forefront with the likes of Tun Yusoff Ishak fighting for his people's independence. For a moment, alone in his car, he felt pride welling up in him but he quickly pushed it aside.

> "...Like Zul, I too had an English education in Raffles Institution; like him, I too lived for a few years in a Western country. But I lived through troubled times. In those days when I was a young man in the forties and fifties, campaigning for our community's leaders, it would have been political suicide for a Malay to speak and write in English. To understand the language was all right; but to use it in the way you are doing now would be looked upon as a betrayal of one's roots and nature. We Malays in those early days felt like the pelandok, an endangered species of mousedeer, surrounded by crocodiles. We had to rally round our community. As the respected Onn bin Ja'afar said, 'It was time for the frog to come out of the coconut shell,' (*Katak keluar dari bawah tempurong.*)"

He could not help but feel again that sense of fierce male pride and kinship with his father. The older generation was not as soft in the head as he had once thought: too accommodating, always giving in to others. Now, perhaps, he was beginning to see that his father had chosen to fight a different battle.

> "...Your Tok used to say we can be like Si Pelandok and learn to live in the jungle full of crocodiles and other wild animals. It is my hope, God willing, to see my children as survivors. But, one day, you will have to ask yourselves: what do you want to survive with you? What do you want your children (nay grandchildren) to inherit?
>
> I am an old man and the Day of Judgement will come upon me soon. But I comfort myself with these words from our Holy Book: 'If anyone does evil or wrongs his soul, but afterwards seeks Allah's forgiveness, he will find Allah is Oft-forgiving, Most Merciful' (al-Nisa' 4:110). I am wholly and entirely at the mercy of His Most Gracious and Compassionate."

Zul's mind went back to that time when he was deciding whether he should work in the English language press or the Malay language press. He had just graduated from the university, fluent in both languages and, therefore, was in the advantageous position of having a real choice. At that time, there were not that many Malay young men as fluent in English as he was. His father had urged him to work in the Malay press, so when he chose the other, the old man had been understandably upset, and became even more so when he felt slighted by his son. Zul had made a passing remark, picked up from elsewhere, suggesting that the Malay paper his father had worked for was "a chauvinistic venture". The old man had exploded like a mountain on fire. "Ingrate! It was more than that! 1938! We felt like poor people in a great country! (*Ra'ayat miskin dalam negeri besar!*) If my newspaper was strongly chauvinistic, it was only because we, in those early days, saw ourselves as a poor and downtrodden people! We travelled up and down the Malay Peninsula and went to every mosque in Singapore to raise money for the paper. Even ten thousand, we could not raise because our people were poor! But they bought shares. Small shares and supported us! You and your brothers and sisters are living in better times! A better world! You who speak and write English far better than me! You who write for a readership very different and far better than mine! But do not forget this. Our roots are as deep and as long as those trees in the jungles! We have our own traditions going back to the shadows of time!" When his father had calmed down, he, the son, had humbly sought his forgiveness and kissed his hands.

In the car, Zul mopped his brows and closed his eyes as if in prayer. There was still no sign of Jan and Suwen. To the last, his father had talked to him about politics and history. Seldom about personal things. It was one of those things in the eternal father-son relationships. Neither tragic enough to be a tragedy nor comic enough to be termed a comedy. When the old man was strong and well, he was reticent and kept his thoughts to himself. Not once did the old man broach the subject of his pending marriage to Jan. Did Bapak really approve? Why didn't the old man talk to him before he was too weak to speak? Ailing in hospital? Did he want to avoid an argument? Or was it because he knew his son's heart was already set on marrying a Chinese woman?

But he and Jan had waited a long time for each other.

His mind returned to the Padang a few nights ago when he was walking to the Satay Club with Jan. "D'you think we have a fighting chance?" he had asked her. And the roar of the city's traffic in the hours after sunset had seemed muted by the dark trees lining the edge of the Padang. Its muted roar floated above the dark figures of couples huddled on mats on the grass and toddlers running after their parents, oblivious of the adults craving for some privacy. Jan walked beside him, head bent, as if she were intent upon scrutinising the dark shadows on the grass. Neither of them spoke for a long while. Each had thoughts thousands of years away, their inner ears humming with the dim echoes of ancestral voices, the faceless oracles and storytellers of each other's race, speaking to the generations to come, stirring their primal blood feelings and causing unease among the younger members like them who were seeking to break from the fold. And if they broke away, what then? He had posed the question and he had answered it himself: then like Earth's first couple, Adam and Eve, they would have to leave the Garden of Eden to toil and eat by the sweat of their brows!

When Jan spoke, her voice was firm and clear. It had pained him just listening to her. Never had he ever dreamt that love for a woman could cause a man such a tightening in his chest. "Da, I don't know how to tell you this. It sounds funny when I try to put it into words. But I've never felt that I was from China. My father does. But I grew up here. Like you. And you know that in the U, I deliberately chose to read Southeast Asian history. Remember Dr Suhardi? He was a fantastic lecturer. And so inspiring. He startled our class one day. He said that our forefathers must've rejected certain things in the home country by migrating elsewhere to seek a new life. He made me think, you know. What did they reject? Whatever it was, my father is looking for it. But I am not." Was she saying that their marriage would have a fighting chance of lasting? He had asked her, and she had answered him with another question, "Doesn't love have a strength of its own? You don't think we're strong enough?" And they had laughed at themselves that night for talking so unlike lovers. "Not lovey-dovey at all," Jan said. Spouse and friend, he had murmured, clasping his woman's hand in his own.

If Suwen had felt that despite their years together in school, she still did not know Jan well, she felt she knew Zul even less. If not for Jan, she would never have met Zul in the first place. Like most Singaporean Chinese, she had Malay acquaintances and colleagues, people with whom one exchanged pleasantries and grumbled about work and the boss. And on festive occasions, they gave one another pineapple tarts and kueh lapis. Helping Zul and Jan to set up home and getting to know his family was opening up a whole new social world for her. Zul's sister who worked as an art director in Benjamin's was an irreverent cartoonist who loved to poke fun at life down Orchard Road and Shenton Way.

"She hopes to be as good as Lat one day," Zul said.

"Even better," his sister replied pertly and did a lightning sketch of herself receiving a trophy from Lat, the great cartoonist, himself.

"Modesty is my sister's second name," Zul laughed.

"Come, Suwen, come and makan. My brother's satay. Better say sedap or Rahim won't invite you again," Rosnah winked.

"Did your family slaughter a whole sheep today?"

"Ya, we gave half to the mosque. The rest Yusoff and Rahim used for satay. My brothers and sisters-in-law are very good cooks."

Once or twice Suwen had accompanied Jan to the hospital to visit the ailing Haji Hussein. Looking at the frail old man in his white baju and checked sarong, she had found it hard to imagine that this was the man whose oratory had fired the crowds, and that this same man had also brought up from among his six children a journalist, two college teachers and an art director. Another sister had worked in the National Library before her marriage, Jan had told her. Among Zul's three sisters, only two of them covered their heads; the art director did not. On one occasion when Suwen saw Rosnah wearing a headscarf, she was wearing it in such a mod way that one would have thought it was a headdress designed by a New York dress designer gone ethnic.

"I love that," Nica had cooed, and the next Sunday, at an art exhibition, Nica and Jan were wearing their scarfs "Bedouin style like Rosnah".

"Shameless copycats, you two!"

"Rosnah taught me and I taught Nica. Not bad, right? Want to learn?" Jan asked.

She could see that Jan was happy; the obstacles were her parents.

"It's difficult. He can't even eat with us," Jan's mother had whispered to her once. "I don't mind if he doesn't eat my food. But he won't even use my plates. And then I worry. He can take up to four wives, can't he?"

Suwen's eyes searched the lorongs for a parking lot. Lorong 21. Lorong 24. Every inch of parking space in this Geylang maze had a car or a lorry. She was expecting trouble up in the flat. Ah, one empty lot. A tight squeeze. She parked her Suzuki, tore out three one-hour coupons and displayed them on her dashboard. Better be extravagant and safe than be stingy and get a fine, she thought as she got out of the car. Jan's father might take hours to rave and rant. It was not going to be easy for Jan. She lingered in front of the tailor's. A thin film of dust had coated the shop's showcase which had a male mannequin dressed in a Western suit. Not quite up to date judging by its lapels. Wah Onn Shanghai Tailor had been in the neighbourhood for as long as she could remember. She glanced at her own reflection in the glass. Slim woman with worried face. She hated ugly scenes. Please, please, no violence, she prayed. She felt suddenly old and lonely. A friend who was still single; that's who she was. An onlooker.

She hurried down the road. Jan's home was a flat which she shared with her parents and a brother, on the first floor of a row of shophouses built in the nineteen twenties. Jan's father, in happier days, had once told her that, before the war, Geylang was a quiet suburb with lots of trees and shrubs. And there was even a large piece of wasteland behind the shophouses where the Indian dhobies used to hang their washing on ropes strung between the trees. The shops were all family-run establishments like the Chinese medical halls where the sinseh dispensed herbs and advice. Then, after the war, things began to change. The roads were widened and tarred. More buses passed through, especially those of the Chinese bus companies like Tay Koh Yat. In the backlanes and byways of Geylang, backyard factories making noodles, joss sticks and cheap footwear were set up in zinc sheds. A few Western-trained doctors and dentists as well as cabinet makers and tailors from Shanghai also came to Geylang, and their presence in those early years after the war gave the predominantly Chinese part of the district an air of prosperity and of being part of a thriving business community. Quite unimaginable nowadays in a Geylang with its rundown shops, sleazy lorongs of cheap bars and massage parlours. Just two doors away from Jan's parents' flat was a signboard which said in bold red Chinese characters, "Association of Cabaret Dance Hostesses".

"These people spoilt Geylang for us," Jan's father, a retired salesman, complained frequently to whoever would listen to him. "When I got married and we came here to live, Geylang was a good place. Quiet. Market was nearby. And the Methodist Church just down the road. That was why I bought this place. Still a good investment, see." He knocked on the wall and flakes of paint came cascading down. "Walls still solid. During the bombing when the Japs came, this house stood firm."

"But it's not the same now," Mrs Wong, Jan's mother, added. "This place is too dusty. Too many buses and too noisy. If I don't close the windows, I can't hear the TV."

"There you go again, Martha! It is dusty here. It is dusty elsewhere too. Anywhere you go in Singapore nowadays, got dust. The new housing estates worse! You think no dust, ah? Construction sites and hammering. Worse still! You talk rubbish sometimes."

"That's how my parents communicate," Jan sighed. "They don't talk. Mum murmurs and Dad shouts."

Joseph Wong Weng Choy was an impatient and disappointed man, hiding his sense of failure behind his anger. Before the war, he had been a sales clerk with good prospects in a British trading company. His wife, Martha, was a nursing assistant in St Andrew's Hospital. Jan's parents had had the good fortune, in those days, of having been educated in schools run by the Christian missionaries. Both spoke English at home. Jan's father had even spent a year in Shanghai where he studied not only English and Mandarin, but, according to him, also the Bible. Life was good to him then. He went to work in a little black Morris of which he was extremely proud. He rose to the rank of chief clerk and could afford to dine once a month in the Raffles Hotel. "Oh, we could dance in those days. Not like people these days. Just jumping in time to the music. You call that dancing? We danced good and proper in those days. Especially Christmas Eve and New Year's Eve." He was never tired of recalling those good ole' days before the war. The family albums showed snapshots of a well-to-do family. A black-and-white amah carried Steve, Jan's brother, who was born just before the war. There were pictures of smiling faces. Jan pointed to one which showed her father with a pirate's hat with his arm resting protectively upon her mother's shoulders.

"This one here is my Aunt Ethel and Uncle John D'Souza. These others are his friends. British planters from KL. They used to buy things through him."

Then the war came and the Brits left; those who stayed behind were imprisoned by the Japs. Jan could remember what her father had told her. She had heard it so many times.

"I tell you the newspapers should talk to people like me. These reporters so damn young. They write about the Japanese Occupation. What do they know? Before the Japs arrived, bombing every day. It was terrible. I became a fire warden for Geylang. One of the few people who knew what to do in an emergency! Lucky for me, I used to deal with fire fighting equipment and chemicals. In the British company. Very well-known in those days. You can ask the old folks around here how many wardens I had personally trained. Every day, it was hell, I tell you. The bombs fell on us. My wardens and I saved the Methodist Church, I tell you. I even drove an ambulance through the fire. Single-handed, I ferried all the wounded to hospital. Those bastards kept bombing. I didn't care. I kept driving. It was like driving through hell fire."

At such times, Jan could see a faraway look creeping into her father's eyes, and as he puffed and pulled at the cigarette dangling from his lips, the pride in his voice when he spoke was unmistakeable.

"Your mother and I worked day and night. A terrible time. Our neighbour downstairs lost two sons. Next door, Ah Soh lost her father and husband. Those bloody Japs came one day and took them away. Just like that. The Kempeitai. All it took in those days was for someone to whisper something in their ears. And the next day, you'd be gone. Everybody was scared. But I didn't care. I carried on."

"But I was scared," Jan recalled her mother adding. "I kept thinking of Steve. Just a few months old then."

"Yes, yes, Martha! We've been through that! Why bring it up again? You always think I didn't know! You think I didn't think of Steve? You always bring up very unnecessary things!"

"You took some unnecessary risks."

"Now listen. In a war and emergency, you want me to just sit back, ah? Someone's got to do something!"

"Yes, and it's got to be you," her mother continued stubbornly, a note of bitterness creeping into her voice. "I was always the one left. Guarding this home. You went to guard other people's homes. How many nights I was alone with Steve. One woman and a baby. All dark outside."

"Will you just shut up, for God's sake! Why are you going on and on? The war's over. It's over! In the past!"

"You talked about it. You brought it up," her mother retorted.

"You're a damn fool, Martha!"

Whenever this happened, Jan left the room. This was her parents' game. Ever since she could remember, their talk inevitably ended in accusation and counter-accusation, too tiresome for a daughter to recall. The war was the one bright spot in her father's past which her mother was determined to snuff out. Whatever for, she had no idea. The two of them were so childish sometimes. It was unbelievable. She had always thought marriage was love and support. Not this constant sniping at each other!

When her father's British firm did not return after the war, her father went to work for a Chinese company. But he could not fit in. They found him too outspoken and impulsive. Then he tried his hand at managing a small hotel in Katong. That lasted only three years and he was out of a job again. He became a salesman for a few years and then tried to set up his own trading company. When that failed, he packed up his things and left for Hong Kong. He was there for close to ten years and was home only during the Christmas season.

Her brother, Steve, had never cared much for their father. "Stubborn old fool. He never planned. Now he's got no savings. Living off our mum."

"Look you!" her father had shouted one day. "You don't mutter-mutter like a woman. You want to talk, talk straight to my face. Be a man. Don't talk behind my back! What were you muttering?"

Steve had then turned upon their father, his face ugly with resentment and disappointment. "Say what? I say you never plan! If you had planned for me, I could've gone to the States! Like my cousins!"

Before anyone could say anything, their father had hurled his ashtray across the living room. With deadly accuracy, it hit Steve's face and cut his chin. Jan had screamed in fright. She must have been about eleven or twelve then. She remembered how Steve had stoically refused their mother's ministrations. Holding a bloodstained handkerchief to his chin, he had rushed out of the flat. Steve was eighteen when this happened. He stayed with Aunt Ethel and Uncle John for a year before returning home, a dark silent young man who kept out of their father's way.

As Jan folded away the last of her skirts and dresses and packed them into her suitcase, she cringed with pain at the memory of that night. She had tossed and turned, unable to sleep because of her mother's muffled cries in the next room. She knew that her father was taking it out on her mother again. With his fists. Why didn't her mother leave him? Many women would have. How could her mother expect her, the daughter, to remain in this broken nest, watching and yet helpless? Knowing and yet pretending not to know? Why should a woman submit to a man like this? And force her children to respect him?

She was past thirty and she had remained at home long enough, she told herself just as the front door banged shut. It must be Suwen, she thought and went on with her packing. One more lot of books and she'd be through with this place.

"We've brought up a right proper Christian, let me tell you!" Joseph Wong glared at his wife from the top of his reading glasses, ignoring Suwen who was standing by the door. "What kind of a mother are you? Tell me which mother will let her daughter give up her faith like this? Tell me! I want to know! Maybe I am a poor old ignorant man now!"

The man's to be pitied, Suwen thought, wishing Jan would hurry and come out quickly. The father was looking impotent and diminished, a bundle of fury shaking in his cotton singlet and striped pyjama pants. He was not expecting any visitors.

"Listen, Suwen," he suddenly turned to her. "You're the friend. You can be the judge. We brought Janice to church every Sunday. Without fail, rain or shine! Sent her to Sunday School. Sent her for Bible class! We did our best for her! My wife and I! The church can't blame us! No one can. For the way she has turned out! Except for Martha here. She was always giving in to the children." He turned upon his wife again. "You are the one! You never say no! Always acting like a doormat! You forget you have the authority! You are the parent! Weak! Let me tell you!"

Mrs Wong did not reply. Her eyes were red from crying. Suwen took her by the hand and led her into the kitchen, away from her bully of a husband.

"I'll wait for Jan here, Mrs Wong."

"What for I work my butt off to send her to a good school? A good Christian school!" the old man's voice followed them, shouting into the hot afternoon air in the empty living room. "What for? The son's a hopeless bum! The daughter's a spineless bitch! No backbone! If she has any backbone, she will insist on her own beliefs. You are happy now, Martha? Proud of your two children? She is leaving. Disowning us! I can do the same, let me tell her! From this moment, pooi!" he spat, "I have no daughter!"

"What can I say? What does he want me to do?" Mrs Wong was sobbing. "Every night I can't sleep. He scolds me. Keeps me awake the whole night long. What can I do?" she whined. "When he was in Hong Kong, I was left alone here. No money. No news even. Just the two children and me. I worked shifts at the hospital to make ends meet. I let the amah go. Not enough money. I had to do everything myself. And now, he blames me."

"Don't think I am deaf! I can hear you, Martha! Yes! I blame you!" Mr Wong screamed at his wife. He came into the kitchen and Suwen tensed in her seat. No violence, please, she was praying.

"I was working in Hong Kong. For the sake of the family! You understand? I was in Hong Kong working. But what were you doing in Taiwan with Seng Kit? Ha! Tell me! Tell Suwen here!" He turned to her. "Suwen, let me tell you

I was jobless after the war. I am not ashamed to admit it. Times were bad then. Everybody jobless. The British left and there were no jobs for people like me. But I was a responsible family man. I saved every cent I earned in Hong Kong. I shared a room with four men. We slept on the floor. We cooked and mended our own clothes! To this day she thinks I was having a gala time over there. What more does she want from a husband? I wanted her to bring up our two children properly. But did she? Did you, Martha? You, bitch, you!"

"Stop your bullying, Dad!" Jan rushed out of her bedroom. "It's not Mum! It's me, your daughter! Scold me!"

"I have no daughter! I have a bitch!"

PART 5

Montage: Monochrome Memories

Suwen's hideaway, her garage apartment, was in the spacious grounds of the Ong Mansion which was built at the turn of the century by the Ong patriarch, Ong Ah Buck, founder of the family's fortune. However, before the family could move in, Fate struck. The war came and the Japanese Occupation Army took over the mansion. The older Ong relatives used to say that it was fated. Ong Ah Buck was born a poor man and he was fated to die poor despite the fortune he made. He had died on the day the war ended, but in the chaos of the immediate aftermath of the war, the family could not give him a grand funeral. No grand paper mansion was burnt for his next life.

The grand mansion he built was taken over by Ong Tay Luck, the son of his concubine. The building was an odd mix of Victorian colonial and Chinese architectural styles, with a high porch, a façade of colonnades and thick columns decorated with flowers of stone. A pair of granite lions guarded the main entrance. The mansion and its twenty rooms had seen many grand feasts during Ong Tay Luck's better days in the early sixties when Ong Prosperity Company was doing well. These days, however, the mansion looked a little neglected and forlorn, screened off from the road by a thick foliage of trees, bushes, tropical ferns and creepers. Its high colonial-style windows, with their original wooden shutters still intact, overlooked a slightly unkempt lawn lined with pots of orchids and chrysanthemums. A Chinese-style rock pool, the garden's centrepiece, was covered with weeds and moss. Tiny waterfalls still cascaded down the moss-covered rocks and rivulets of green water still weaved in and out among the stones to flow beneath tiny red wooden bridges, past the bent miniature pine trees and broken pagodas.

Mrs Ong Tay Luck, Suwen's mother, stood at the window, looking down at the garden below as the white Mercedes swept up the driveway and stopped by the rock pool. Her husband's stout and portly figure emerged, his ruddy face framed by greying hair, thinning at the crown. A touch of old world Chinese pride perhaps, if not a little intransigence, had made him adhere to the fashion of the mercantile community of his youth: long-sleeved white cotton shirt worn open at the neck, dark trousers of good material, white socks and black leather shoes. He disliked ties. "Not your clothes but your money. You got money, people don't care what you wear. Money moves the devil," he liked to say.

Two boys, aged eight and six, came out of the car with him. They were the children of his third mistress, Madam Li.

"Come, Ah Pa, come! See! Only six carps left," the eight-year-old was peering into the pool of greenish water.

"Cannot be! I ordered them to buy twenty carps," Ong Tay Luck's gruff voice rang out in Hokkien.

He had been quite a mimic in his younger days and was a speaker of many Chinese dialects, picking up Teochew, Cantonese, Hakka and a smattering of Mandarin and English, even Japanese during the war years, in fact, anything which would be of help to his business. He was the typical enterprising Chinese businessman, resourceful as a rat, always seeking for lobangs or loopholes in the city's scheme of things in order to survive and prosper. However, in recent years, his luck had changed for the worse, and he had not the wherewithal to turn his transportation business round.

"Here! Over here, Ah Pa," the six-year-old was pulling his hand. Everybody wanted a bit of him, he sighed as he thought of the sons and daughters, many of them still in their early teens, whom he had fathered in the various towns in Malaysia up north.

"The carp is hiding here, Ah Pa."

"That one not a carp," he laughed. "That one is, ah, goldfish."

"A carp! I say carp!" the older boy pointed to the shimmering fish in the water.

"You must give us ten dollars, Ah Pa! We are right, you are wrong! Ten dollars! Ten dollars!"

The two boys were prancing up and down with hands outstretched. They snatched up the ten-dollar bills and ran off whooping with delight.

"We won! We won, Ah Pa!"

Mrs Ong Tay Luck winced. Grasping little beggars! Always after his money whenever they came over. The greed came from their mother. If she herself had had a son, she would never tolerate the presence of these two monkeys in her mansion. But the gods had given her two daughters! That was her fate. Still, if Madam Li and all the other vixens dared to lay hands on this mansion, her mansion, she would fight them off with claws and nails! Sulin was Tay Luck's daughter, not Suwen, so she did not expect anything for Suwen. But if anything should happen to Tay Luck, then Sulin and her children could get something out of the sale of this mansion.

Ong Prosperity Company was not what it used to be. Ong Ah Buck had changed it from a strictly rickshaw company to a motorised transportation company owning buses and lorries. But that was before the Japanese Occupation. After the war and Ong Ah Buck's death on the last day of the Occupation, Ong Tay Luck and his mother (Ong Ah Buck's concubine) had taken over the running of the company. Through the fifties and sixties, with hard work, shrewdness and enterprise, Ong Tay Luck and his mother became the owners of the largest Chinese-owned bus company on the island. His mother, full of pride in her son, urged him to marry. But when he brought home as his wife, Yoke Kam, the fah-dan of Cantonese opera, the mother was bitterly disappointed. She had hoped that her son would marry someone socially higher. But as her son had so rightly pointed it out to her, objectively speaking, a fah-dan was higher on the social ladder than a mui-tsai or bondmaid, even though the bondmaid had risen to concubine and had become the owner of a bus company. So, as the Cantonese said, she swallowed her feelings and kept her mouth shut thereafter. But she hated her daughter-in-law. And, naturally, her daughter-in-law did not tell her that she had a daughter by another man. So that was why Suwen had to stay at her grandparents' farm for several years, and it was only after the old lady's death that Suwen came to live with her mother in the mansion.

Ong Tay Luck gave his mother one of the biggest and grandest funerals the Chinese community there had ever seen. It was an event remembered for years. More so because, and precisely because, his mother, Sia Liew, was a former bondmaid and concubine. Bondmaids were not entitled, at least in the old days, to grandeur of any kind. After his mother's death, Ong Tay Luck expanded the company's activities and branched into trading and manufacturing. His Ong relations encouraged him. Many worked for him or sent their children to work for him. Every Ong relative wanted a hand in the company's activities. And that was the beginning of the company's troubles as Ong Tay Luck, confident and careless, began to leave his business in the hands of relatives and concentrated on his women and the children he fathered all over Southeast Asia, wherever his business activities brought him.

Then, last year, the government issued a decree that all the Chinese-owned bus companies must amalgamate and merge to form an even larger company. Mrs Ong Tay Luck nee Yoke Kam could not follow all the arguments and counter-arguments over the merits of such a move. All she knew was that what the government said, it would do. There was no doubt about it. And if the government people came in, sooner or later, several uncomfortable questions would be asked of Ong Tay Luck and his relations regarding the company's accounts. She might not know much about business, she told a friend, but she knew when a company was in financial trouble. "How can it not be? I have seen with my own eyes, ah, the vixen's brother taking home bags of coins. To count, he told me. Who knows? Only the spirits will know if he takes out a few hundred coins each time. Fifty-cent coins, ah! You count. How much will Tay Luck lose in a month? I tell Tay Luck. Keep an eye, ah, on Madam Li's brother. You think he listens? If he is not eyeing this vixen, he is off up north looking for another!"

When he came a-wooing her at the Great World Amusement Park Theatre, Ong Tay Luck had promised her this mansion. Why? She was a somebody in those days and he was a nobody. Opening night of "The Scholar's Faithful Wife", she recalled, Ong Tay Luck sent her twenty baskets of red roses. They took up the entire front of the stage. Baskets of bright red roses beneath the pink satin banner with the red Chinese characters: To Miss Chan Yoke Kam: fah-dan. From your admirer. When the roses wilted, he sent another twenty baskets together with a diamond necklace. All the opera workers were impressed. But she wasn't. Those were the days, in the fifties, when she was wined and dined by the rich men of her time. She was the fah-dan of Cantonese opera, playing to packed houses every night here and in every town across the Causeway. Not a week passed without a picture of her in the papers. Those were wonderful days, and Ong Tay Luck was just another rich businessman wooing her like all the others. The mansion was her price. He had to agree if he wanted her. This was the story she told herself these days, and if Suwen thought it somewhat different from the version she had grown up with, it was of secondary importance. Mrs Ong Tay Luck felt, not in so many words, nor was she fully conscious of what she was feeling, that the teller and shaper of her own life story should be none other than herself. If she had been English-educated, she might have said that memories were as malleable as plasticine.

Turning away from the window, Mrs Ong looked at herself in the mirror. Her hair was raven black, dyed, of course. Who didn't these days? Except that mad daughter of hers with the ugly strands of grey! She studied the fine lines and made her lips curl in a smile, dismissing momentarily her downturned mouth and look of discontentment. Bright red lips stood out in stark contrast to the dark curls of her permanent wave.

She heaved a sigh. She was just seventeen when Suwen came. Hardly a woman. Sulin came when she was thirty-two, past her prime, after the loss of two, one of them a son! It was her fate and one had to make the best of it. When your horse dies, you walk. That was what her old Pa used to say.

The sun's last rays stole into the room through the slits of the wooden shutters. Strips of orange light on the floor. She patted her hairdo, gave it a whiff of hairspray and sat in a perfumed haze, dressed in an elegant silk qipao, her daily mode of attire these days lest the world forgot she was once a fah-dan of opera. She was returning once again to the Great World Amusement

Park; the lights were switched on and the stage, which was in her head, shone in the dark.

After the dull grey years of the Japanese Occupation, the Park was humming and buzzing with activities and gaiety. Within its large fenced-in enclosure were the open-air cinema, the getai or open-air stage for singing and comic sketches, the ronggeng platform for Malay dances and the Chinese opera theatre. Tucked in between the cinema, stages and theatres were numerous wooden stalls and zinc-roofed huts hawking cheap plastic wares: pails in gaudy reds and blues, utensils, toys, beads and buttons; aluminium pots and pans; poor quality clothes, towels; the minutiae of dressmaking like cards of bright buttons, reels of coloured threads, rolls of cheap satin lining, bales of cheap checks, packets of metal clips and boxes of buckles and beads. "Lelong! Lelong! Lai! Lai! Ten cents! Twenty cents only!" the hawkers called out to the housewives and their daughters milling under the glare of the naked light bulbs and gasoline lamps. The men were drawn mainly to the games stalls, manned by prettily made-up girls. For the price of ten or twenty cents, these girls handed them air rifles, darts or balls with murmurs of encouragement and sweet glances. "Try again lor! Mister, try again. No try no get, mah!" If he were lucky, a young man could even touch a girl's fair hand as she handed over the air rifle.

Her most memorable night at the Great World Amusement Park was the night when her opera company raised fifty thousand dollars for Nantah. The clans were out in full force. The towkays and their tai-tai, concubines, mistresses, sons and daughters and amahs were there. Young lonely bachelors from the small towns in Johore came all the way to watch her perform, the girls to ogle at and dream about her, and the coolies, amah chays, shop assistants, rickshaw pullers to applaud her and also to support the building of a Chinese university for their children and the children of their children.

The theatre, a large hall with a wooden stage at one end and wooden partitions on all sides, was packed to capacity. A hubbub of voices, catcalls, raucous laughter and the cries of young children filled the theatre. Some boys ran up and down the aisles while groups of little girls in lace and ribbons went over to admire her baskets of red roses from Ong Tay Luck. Their mothers, the tai-tai, sat in the front row reserved for the rich towkays, chatting and nibbling on melon seeds, spitting out their shells on the floor. Towkay Khoo, chairman of the Chinese Merchants' Association, was there. So was Towkay Tan of the Hokkien Huay Kuan Clan Association. He had given thousands of dollars to help build schools in his Fukien province. "That's Towkay Tan Lark Sye, ah!" one of the actors had whispered to her. "He's going to give five million dollars for the new Chinese university, ah!" The first ten rows of seats in front of the stage were all a-glitter with gold, jade and diamonds. Behind these, seated on hard benches were the clerks and accountants of trading houses, the agents of the import-export companies, their assistants, clerks and their wives dressed in sombre floral samfoos. These were the ones whose children, after suffering the hardships of war, were clamouring for a Chinese university education. And, behind them, standing twenty to thirty persons deep, were the amahs, coolies, young servants, maids, porters and labourers who had come to lose themselves in the noise and gaiety of a Cantonese opera as well as to support Nantah.

Towkay Tan rose and went onto the stage to make his speech in Hokkien. She slipped into her dressing room to wait. For more than an hour she sat in her dressing room, painting her face. Outside, the speeches in Hokkien and Teochew and Cantonese seemed to go on and on, punctuated by thunderous applause and cries of "For our children! Right! Right! For our descendants! And our children's children! A place for the Chinese of Nanyang!"

Then the drums rolled and the cymbals clanged! The overture had begun, but before her entrance the lonesome whine of the er-hu had quietened the boisterous crowd. The pipa and the yangqin joined in the melodious refrain; note after note, her singing from the wings pulled the melody higher and higher, till she was holding her notes like a bird in mid flight, fluttering in the air momentarily before plunging down into the depths of despair with the perishing sigh of the flute and her own dramatic entrance as the weeping heroine swathed in pale pink silks. She swooned and swayed like a weeping willow in her flowing robes, daintily dabbing away a tear as she broke into a heartrending song of love and betrayal. A shiver of pleasure and murmurs of praise rippled through the crowd as she let fall her flowing-water sleeves, silks trailing behind her, before lifting them to reveal two fair wrists, each encircled by a band of translucent jade, a present from Ong Tay Luck. Aye, she sighed, those were the days when he would give her whatever she wanted and even what she did not ask for. After that, it was like going down the stairs all the time. Husbands are as faithless as audiences; she was resigned to her fate. A woman tries to be secure but always something else will happen. As they say, men propose but the heavens dispose. The spirits in heaven dispose of us like mere numbers and numerals in a game of chap ji ki.

Mrs Ong Tay Luck returned to her vigil by the window and saw Suwen trudging up the slope towards the mansion. Why couldn't the girl walk straight and proper, she asked herself irritably, spewing out Cantonese proverbs and idioms in her mind, all to do with the upright bearing of scholars. Suwen had been educated in an expensive foreign university, so why was she slouching like a servant girl when she walked? And the girl…aiyah! What girl? Suwen was nearer forty than thirty already lor! Why didn't she marry that lawyer? Why? Mrs Ong raised her eyes heavenwards. Only another mother with old unmarried daughters would understand her feelings! The lawyer was such a nice man. He spoke Cantonese fluently. Owned a house and even a motor boat off Pasir Ris. What more did Suwen want? So choosy. There was also that Baba man. A bit fair with a weak chin. But he was also very nice. And, after that, there was that Indian from…aiyah! Serli Lanka or India! A country she knew nothing about, and that was all she had said to Suwen about him. "I know you, Ma! You don't like black people!" her daughter had screamed at her. But all she was trying to say was that the Indian man had borrowed her daughter's money without repaying the loan. Surely there was nothing wrong in saying that friendship was one thing and money another. "It's a donation! I gave him the money! Don't worry, he's a Catholic priest! He can't marry! He's working with poor orphans." Mrs Ong Tay Luck suppressed a sigh. What to do? Suwen, unlike Sulin, would mix with all sorts. Right now, she was ready to accept anyone who would look after her daughter. Brown, white or black, it would not bother her at all. Many years had gone by since that Indian priest. Nothing happened. Suwen was still unmarried while Sulin had three children already. Mrs Ong was beginning to think that her elder daughter had adamantly refused all offers of marriage just to spite and punish her.

By now there was no sign of Suwen in the garden below. She must have used the servants' entrance again, Mrs Ong thought irritably and hurried downstairs. At the foot of the stairs, she met her daughter.

"Eat till so big, you still cannot remember that the servants' entrance is only for bondmaids and servants."

"So?" her daughter challenged.

"So you should use the front door! Else the servants will have a lot to say about your background!"

"You think I care? That's all you think about."

"You come in here and open your mouth, you start quarrelling with me. What wrong have I done in my past lives to deserve this from you? Tell me! Tell me!"

"The gods in heaven know. I don't know, Ma," she replied in her best Cantonese which was polite and formal, and was bound to annoy her mother. "I came here to look for Ah Siew Chay."

"So! It is Ah Siew Chay this and Ah Siew Chay that! Nowadays you have no mother, ah? In your eyes, I am no longer your mother, ah? Right or not?"

"Why are you shouting? You always said you don't want the servants to know too much, and now you are shouting."

"Right! Answer back! My own daughter comes into the house. Don't want to see me! See other people! And I cannot shout! Cannot say a word against a servant in my own house! Right! This is the right way of doing things!"

"Ma, if you don't like it, I won't come in here any more." And Suwen left. By the back door.

Mrs Ong Tay Luck fumed. Her daughter was always threatening to leave. Ever since that incident. But was it her fault? Even if it was not her fault, she, the mother, had had to shut her own mouth and rave only inside her heart. Not a squeak out of her. Only the gods in heaven knew how she felt. Squeeze your heart and suffer the pain inside, as Ah Siew Chay would say. And that old amah! That! That queen of servants had had a lot to say in her younger days. Did she not boast that she was the favourite amah of her tigress of a mother-in-law? Did she not boast, after the grand old lady had passed away, that she, Ah Siew Chay, was the only one left who could recall the great days of the patriarch, Ong Ah Buck? That boast was to make her feel like an outsider. She had no doubt that that was what Ah Siew Chay had wanted to do all along. The amah was a two-headed snake! If not for the snake's position as the Ong family retainer and housekeeper, she would have gotten rid of her long ago instead of waiting till the old amah had reached senility. Did she not speak with two mouths when Suwen was in trouble? To the Ong relatives, the old snake said, "Aiyah, that farm girl! Not properly brought up, mah! Always tickling and giggling with Master Tay Luck. But she is sixteen, big girl already! And he, only twenty-nine! Things will happen, you say right or not. When you touch me, I touch you. Aiyah, choy lor!" But in front of her, Ah Siew Chay spoke with another mouth. "Aiyah, Ong tai-tai, girls are girls. She is young and doesn't know anything. And men are, aiyah, like this! Very hard for you. Both sides of your hand covered with the same flesh. One is your husband and one is your daughter. Better for you to send her away. Send her to school far away. In another country. Master Tay Luck has money. Make him pay." And that was how she was separated from the girl again, barely a few years after she had come to live with her. Suwen stayed in England for five? six years? She could hardly remember. But in all those years, Suwen had refused to come home for the vacations. When her daughter finally did come home, it was as if a stranger had returned. And if she herself had not suffered two heart attacks, she was very sure Suwen would have moved out of the mansion and stayed away. But who would know a mother's pain these days? She sighed and went back to her room upstairs.

"When both my eyes are closed and you have put me into the coffin! Not before then! What about my daughters, ah? If not Suwen, ah, what about your own flesh and blood? Sulin has two sons! They are your grandsons! This is their roof too! Your vixens' sons are not getting this house! Kill me first!"

Suwen hurried down the stairs and out of the mansion as quickly as she could. The man was home. She did not want to meet him. She did not want his house. No part of it. Her mother could utter whatever rubbish she chose but she would have no part in it. Let the house be sold. Demolished. Destroyed forever for all she cared. It was an albatross. For months, there had been talk among the Ong relations that the mansion, built by Ong Ah Buck, had to be sold. His son, Ong Tay Luck, had not the means to keep and maintain it. "Prime land. Worth millions," a brother-in-law muttered. "Use the money to build up the business again," an uncle said. "Are you selling?" her mother asked her husband. But the man kept his own counsel. Her mother cried and pestered him for an answer. The man walked away. He went off to one of his mistresses and stayed away for weeks. Her mother cried, visited the temples, consulted the mediums and prayed for her husband's business concerns. There were also frantic phone calls to Sulin in Perth. "Come back! Your father is selling the mansion!" Fortunately, Sulin had the sense to remain in Perth.

The mansion was full of bits and pieces, it was true; like one's mind filled with the monochrome detritus of memories pushed into dark corners and recesses. Dark shapes and figures haunted her sleep. She tossed and turned. Her mother's anxiety about the mansion was beginning to rub off on her. She was apprehensive. She sought to lose herself in her work and stayed out, away from the mansion and its ugly debris of tasteless acquisitions and gangrenous desires. There was a reclining chair of teak and cane pushed behind a Chinese screen of carved wood. The patriarch, Ong Ah Buck, had bought it for his own exclusive use. This was the chair on which he liked to take his young concubine, the older female members of the family whispered. When the Japanese officers took over the mansion, they had used this very chair for the deflowering of young girls, the old servants used to tell the young ones. At first, Ong Tay Luck had installed his father's reclining chair in his own bedroom. But when things turned sour between him and his wife, he had had it removed downstairs. Suwen resolutely closed the door upon her fertile imagination, refusing to see what it could show her of things that two people could do on the reclining seat. She pushed these away; she had no wish to see her mother thrashing in the arms of that man! No! No! She closed her eyes and saw her own bed.

She is twelve. Old serious face and dark anxious eyes below a dark straight fringe. She is staring at the old-fashioned brass bed covered with mosquito netting. Its brass posts gleam in the half light of the cavernous bedroom. She moves forward, touches its starched white sheet with all its creases smoothly ironed out. The whole bed smells of a fresh starchy fragrance.

"Oi! Girl! Wash your hands and feet. Don't dirty the bedsheets. This used to be Old Madam's bed. You are not to dirty it. This mansion is not like your farm," Ah Siew Chay wags a finger at her. "The bathroom is over there."

The amah goes out, closing the door behind her. She sticks out her tongue. Peeps into the toilet. White porcelain bowl which flushes down water. She pulls the chain. Water gushes out. She plunges both hands into the toilet bowl. Yea, she rejoices, can wash hands too. No more green bottle flies! No more smelly shit!

"Aiyah! I say farm girl is farm girl! Don't know anything nae! This is not for washing hands, aiyah chin-sai! For you to sit and do your big-do! We have no buckets here!" Ah Siew Chay shouts at her.

Ah Siew Chay had changed over the years. Certainly, the amah was downright snobbish when Suwen first came to this mansion, peering down her nose at her literally. In front of her mother who had become the new mistress of the Ong Mansion after the Old Madam's death, Ah Siew Chay and the other servants had addressed her as "our young miss". But behind her mother's back, they had called her, "Oi! You!" or "That farm girl". Whenever she was served a Chinese delicacy like bird's nest soup, Ah Siew Chay would mutter, "A cow chews on an orchid and knows not if it is grass or bloom. Aye, wasted, wasted."

Then, one day, she broke the brass poster bed. Everyone was shocked. In a fit of fury, she had jumped on the bed and broken its springs.

Bounce! Bounce! Up and down, she jumps on the bed. Do not dirty the sheets, did you say? Dirty! Dirty! Dirty! There! There! She hears herself screaming at the top of her voice. There is a loud crack. The bed springs snap and she collapses into a heap of tears, white sheets and mosquito netting. Her mother rushes into the room.

"Aiyah! Why are you so careless?"

"Why did they ask me to do this, do that? Like I am their bondmaid? No servants, ah? Why keep calling me?"

"Why you talk like that, Suwen? Have you no manners? They are your aunties."

"They don't treat me like their niece. They don't ask the others to empty their spittoons and ashtrays. Get this! Get that! They ask me! I have to study too, you know!"

She is sulking among the sheets and lengthening shadows in her room. Shades of whites and greys in the dusk of evening. The door opens. Her mother enters with the man, followed by the chauffeur and the gardener. She rises in her grey dress of childish sorrow and hurt pride. The men dismantle the brass bed, remove it and install in its place a brand new modern bed of brown varnished wood.

"Come and say 'thank you' to Uncle. He has bought you a new bed. Now don't pull a long black face. Those aunties won't be coming for mahjong for a long time, lor!"

She sees herself smiling and hugging the man in white shirt and grey trousers.

She grimaced as if struck by pain, willing the darkness to flood her mind. See nothing. Hear nothing. Dark empty chasm. The blackness of inner space. The blackness which one sees when one closes one's eyes, willing the mind to lay still, not think, just fall asleep. But her mind would not lie still. Out of its dark depths rose images and scenes from long ago. Grey scenes like those in silent films, the figures moving slowly and sluggishly.

She is watching a black and white Hong Kong movie of the sixties. Alone in the dark cinema. The film ends.

The crowd streams out and disperses. The cinema lights are switched off. She looks anxiously at her watch. At fifteen she is still a timid girl. The cars get fewer. The Indian watchman walks by. And still there is no sign of him. Twelve midnight. The road is deserted. She stands under the street lamp. A car whizzes past. She counts the soft ticking of her watch. Then his white Mercedes stops in front of her. She gets in.

The building housing the Solomon Maternity Home is a study in cream, white and beige. Shades of beige walls, cream-coloured beds, white sheets, white-clad nurses, doctors and ochre-coloured floor tiles. She walks into her mother's room. Her stepsister, newborn, swathed in white, pink face protruding, is lying in the cot. "Did Uncle come home last night?" her mother asks. "Yes," she lies. "What time?"

"I don't know. I was asleep."

"Aiyah, you are so useless! Ask you to do something so simple. Just see what time he gets back. And you fall asleep."

She opens her mouth but shuts it again. No use talking.

"I have my reasons, I ask you to keep your eyes open and look out for me. You are fifteen. Not a small girl now. If I draw you a man, I don't have to draw his intestines also, right?" Her mother's voice rises to a shriek. Almost.

"He is seeing another woman! I am here. I cannot go and stop him! So if he goes out, you follow! Follow him. He needs company all the time. If you are with him, then he cannot go after those vixens, you say right or not?"

The sea off Changi is a monochrome of blue. Blue-green waters under a blue-grey sky. Their canoe is a dark-blue crescent bobbing on the blue-green waves.

Her stepfather's friend, the woman in intense cobalt-blue, stands poised upon the canoe, straightens her arms and dives into the blue waves. Her sudden movement causes the canoe to wobble from side to side. The boat overturns. A dark-blue greyness washes over her. Salt stinging her eyes and throat. She flails her arms helplessly. A strong arm envelops her, pressing against her breasts. She is clinging to him, and he holds and presses her frightened body against his, pressing her against his chest as they tread water, two blue heads bobbing upon the blue sea. He swims with her back to shore. "Wait here. I will go and help Miss Yoke." He pats her head. "You okay!" She nods, grateful that he has saved her from a watery death in those dark-blue depths. She is shivering with fear, exhaustion and an inexplicable exhilaration. Like a streak of azure through the grey skies. He has held and grasped her virgin vulnerability, and she is wet. And cold.

Suwen woke up in a cold sweat and switched on her bedside lamp. 4 a.m. She got up, took a drink of water and tried to read, reluctant to get back into bed lest those dreams came back to haunt her sleep again.

Was she a sex-starved adolescent who had been badly brought up, as the gossips had implied? Or was she plain stupid and naïve? She could not face the answers; all she saw in her mind was a gangly sixteen-year-old, hunched and stooping to hide her budding breasts, desperately wanting to remain a child forever.

"You are sixteen already, mah! Not a small girl any more. And people have mouths. They will talk about you. Where are you going to put your face then?"

After the birth of Sulin, her mother's tune had changed from "Go keep Uncle company" to "Don't play with him so much. You are a big girl now." But she had wished all her young life for a family with mother, father and siblings. At that time, she did not see how others saw her as a big girl, too old to be Ong Tay Luck's daughter; he was, after all, only twenty-nine and a half. Thirteen and a half years older than her sixteen. But she was young and naïve. She had thought her mother had wanted her to be close to the stepfather. To be his daughter. And she had, in her naïvety, tried to re-enact what she had read in the novels on perfect family life. Every evening, she waited eagerly for him to come home. She prepared and served him his cup of tea. With both hands like a filial daughter. He patted her head and chatted to her about this and that, in English, so that her mother was soon left out of their conversations. She felt special and useful; here was something she could do: give him an intelligent audience, she had thought in her young mind, though not in such terms. He taught her how to swim after that dreadful accident in Changi and brought her to the Chinese Swimming Club every week. From swimming lessons, they moved on to badminton and the two of them played badminton every evening before dinner.

"Heh-heh-heh! Our Tay Luck goes home early these days," Gold Teeth laughed. He was a garrulous old man with an eye for women. "He is not going home to play with his baby daughter. It is to play with his big daughter. Heh-heh-heh!"

"Aiyah! You shut your mouth, and you don't talk, ah, no one will say you are dumb!" Gold Teeth's wife chided her husband whose loose talk, especially after a few drinks, was well-known in the Ong clan.

But the harm was already done; the blighted seed had already been sown. By the time the dreadful incident occurred, all the Ong relations were ready to blame her.

"You think Suwen is stupid? You really think she did nothing? But men, ah! You don't do anything, you don't give any signs. They will not come near you," an aunt said.

"The servants know everything. Ask them. They saw," another aunt claimed, "The girl throws a pillow at him, they say. He throws back. They play pillow fights. You tickle me here. I tickle you there. So? Sure to lead to trouble, you say right or not? One male, one female. Some more he is not her father."

"Aiyah, but our Tay Luck should have more sense, mah!" another relative tried to be more objective. "First of all, he is older. Secondly, he is her stepfather. And as the Cantonese say, one step across the bed and threshold, you are the parent. Right or not? And also the girl..."

"Oi! Listen, ah! Men are men. I say the girl should have been careful. And her mother too. Her mother has eyes, right or not? She can see for herself. Why did she let them play like that?"

"Oi! You women don't make me laugh!" Gold Teeth joined in. "She is a young chick still. He only touch-touch, right?"

That night, and many nights before, various scenes and snatches of conversation overheard or imagined came and went in her dreams in which thought and vision fused and melted; what she thought had happened returned and presented itself to her in ways she had not thought of or imagined before. Was it hindsight, she asked herself. In her memories of those dark days, she was forever returning to the past and not making any progress forward; two steps backwards for every step forward, on and on and on, treading a machine which kept rolling backwards just as she was desperately trying to move forward.

Throughout her long dreary years in the boarding school of the Convent of the Sacred Heart in Stonybrook, she was dogged by a deep sense of shame and wrongdoing. Sister Clare, the young Eurasian novitiate with clear loving eyes like those of a cocker spaniel's, drew her out and made her talk. They went for long walks through the woods and took weekly trips into the village.

Then, one day, without warning, Sister Clare was transferred out of the convent to London's East End to prepare for her mission to India, she was told. There were no goodbyes. It had all been so sudden. One moment she had a warm and loving friend who held her hand and gave her hugs, and the next, she was gone.

"Can I see her? Just once. Please, Reverend Mother."

"I'm afraid not, dear. Sister Clare is extremely busy preparing for her final vows."

"Can I phone? Just once, Reverend Mother."

"I think it will be good for you to join Mr and Mrs Hutchinson this summer. They're bringing a group of Sixth Formers to the Isle of Skye. It will be most interesting and educational for you. I've already put in your name."

She withdrew deeper into herself. She made no friends during her two years in the school although she had classmates and dorm-mates with whom she went shopping or cycling. She went for walks in the woods by herself and took up sketching and painting to fill the lonely days of the next two summers when most of the girls went home to their families.

After her matriculation exams, she went to Durham University to read English and the History of Art in the Western World. She shared a bed-sitter with a Cantonese girl from Hong Kong who spoke little English, and stoically settled down to a routine of lectures, library and long walks. What sustained her, especially during the cold dreary days of winter, was the memory of her illiterate grandfather who had brought her up on his vegetable farm; the light in the old man's eyes when she recited her first nursery rhyme, "Baa, Baa, Black Sheep", in incomprehensible Cantonese-accented English. "Por-por!" he had called out to her grandma, "Come and listen to our Suwen! Come! Come!" That night when they were sitting out on the verandah, enjoying the warm tropical breeze, her grandfather had turned to her. "Suwen," he said, his voice gruff and serious as he spoke, "don't be like your mother. Study hard. Don't be afraid. If you fall, never mind. Grab a handful of sand when you get up. Life is like that. You fall, you get up. Your horse dies, you learn to walk."

The following year, the Hong Kong girl met a young man, also from Hong

Kong, and after that, she was seldom at home. Suwen had the bed-sitter all to herself most nights during which she read or painted. She had started taking painting lessons at an art school nearby. Once or twice the art students, mostly Caucasians working in advertising agencies, had invited her for drinks at the local pub, but she could not enjoy her beer though in that sort of company; it would have been useful if she could. The men and women in black T-shirts and patched jeans were friendly enough and she was invited to a few parties but, somehow, she could not let her hair down to drink, dance and talk brightly and wittily like those young Caucasian women. She seemed to shrink like a morning glory flower in the evening, having little or no confidence in her own ability to attract others and hold her own in conversation.

There were only a handful of Asians at Durham while she was there. And having paid several thousand pounds in fees, the Asian students were intent upon their studies and seldom had time for anything else. The only outgoing ones were the Christians who were eager to pull her into their prayer groups and Bible study groups. She avoided them, however, like the plague.

Her ambivalence towards men had been a problem and remained so throughout her years in Durham. Sex was perceived as a threat and the road to damnation. In her nervous anxiety and naïvety, she took to classifying the men she met on campus as either the quiet-decent type or the irresponsible-fast-worker type; all the Asian guys naturally fell into the former and all the Caucasians were grouped in the latter category. But the Asian guys were far too studious, reticent and dull, having little to say beyond the subjects of their study. She was attracted to, but avoided, the tall, good-looking, handsome, sharp-witted, more articulate and worldly-wise Caucasians. Their beer drinking, sensuous dancing, clever banter and sheer abandonment for the pleasures of the moment frightened her. She shrank from their cigarette-flavoured embraces, their "Hello, love!" and "Hi, darling!" (although she listened eagerly to their conversations and, sometimes, knowledgeable discourses on European painting and sculpture). However, though well-read in this area herself, she did not have the courage to join in their talks.

She spent weekends going for long solitary walks, sketching the bare trees in winter and the leafy foliage in summer. Slowly and painfully, she learnt to see the world, not in shades of grey and ash, but in the hues and shades of spring, summer and autumn: azure, lemon, mauve, lilac, fawn, russet, hazel, the dappled, mottled and speckled hues of the English countryside. She saw her world in English colours and vowed to return to the East and see Asia anew in the Asian colours of vermilion, carmine, crimson, emerald, turquoise, ivory, saffron, citron and gold. She trained her eyes to look at horizontal and vertical patterns, lines, curves and shapes, gradually coming to the realisation that the eye did not simply receive light. It interpreted and reordered perceptions and descriptions of our world; pigments and brush strokes, the solidity of one's colours, the tessellations of lines and dots, and the variegated hues of light and shadow could express one's anguish or serenity. At first, she tried to see what the English painters saw and painted but her work was a miserable failure. Then she tried, and tried, again and again, each attempt nudging her closer to seeing what her own eyes saw and reordered in her Eastern mind. The image was new to her, and feebly rendered in paint, but her art teacher was full of encouraging praise. She promised Dave Buckley that she would not give up, whereupon the old man removed his beret and hugged her. "Paint what your Eastern heart sees," he murmured.

Then in the summer of her third year, she enrolled at King's College in Aberdeen for a short course on modern British literature, just so she had somewhere to go in summer, and while she was there, she met Mark Campbell. She had read Sunset Song and was able to converse knowledgeably with him about Lewis Grassic Gibbon, the Scottish writer ignored by the English and London. Mark must have been impressed for he took her on his motor bike to visit the church where Gibbon was buried. On another Saturday, he brought her and Sushila to an art gallery to view the Scottish masters. Then, over mugs of steaming strong tea in the cosy tearoom run by a retired teacher and his wife, they had discussed the cultural domination of the English in Wales and Scotland. Mark told them stories of Marie Antoinette and made them laugh. She, in turn, told them about Yang Kwei-fei and Tzu-hsi, the last Empress Dowager of China.

When Mark got into trouble with the British Council authorities over his weekend escapade with Sushila, she had stood by him. Later, he showed his appreciation by taking her for a walking tour of the Scottish Highlands that very summer after the course was over. It was her first ever holiday and one which she enjoyed thoroughly. They became good friends and had remained friends ever since, she insisted, to quieten the little voice whispering in her mind that it was otherwise. They had kept in touch with each other over the years, but he did not tell her, and she had not asked about his relationships with other women. She had no right to ask him; they were only friends, she reminded herself, and all the more so now that Jan was engaged to Zul, and she was thrown more and more into Mark's company in college.

She was restless. Whenever she reached home, she wanted to go out again, and wished she had somewhere to go to. Nica was not in town. She had gone off to Manila with Robert. And Jan was in a world of her own, leaving the college as soon as the bell rang. Suwen kept herself busy, staying back in college for as long as she could. But it was of little use. She could not concentrate on her marking. Reading her students' essays was becoming excruciatingly long and dull work. And, to make matters worse, she could not paint and she could not sketch. She had no inclination to do anything except to walk; walking aimlessly through the city, looking for things to buy, just so that she did not have to sit in her flat alone. Her habits and routine, no, her life had been disrupted and changed by Jan's pending marriage, she fretted. The marriage itself was not a surprise; she had always known that it would happen some day; and yet, when that some day arrived, she found that she was still not prepared for it. But could anyone blame her? For the past few years when Zul was away in the States, she and Jan had gone to the movies and theatre together, attended art exhibitions, had tea, lunch and dinner together. Now all these activities would cease; oh yes, they would, no matter what Jan had promised and protested. She might be a lonely woman but even lonely women could still be clear-eyed and clear-headed about such promises from a friend about to be married. Her life would not be the same, she realised, and wished without much hope that her feeling of having been a stopgap and a spare tyre would disappear. It had been niggling her all week, chipping away at her self-confidence. What she dreaded most, however often she tried to push the thought away, was returning to her former state of emptiness and the feeling that she had been abandoned like in her first year in England. It was the worst year of her life then. She remembered with some pain that winter morning when she had stood alone under the dark wintry branches of a solitary ash in the garden of the convent in Stonybrook, hoping for one last glimpse of Sister Clare. That winter, she was taught one of life's bitter lessons to never, never, never invest all of one's feelings in one person. Never put all your eggs in one basket. Learn to live alone and you won't get hurt. But every day, Jan's little smiles, her glowing face and eyes which seemed to shine with an inner light were confronting her with something else: involvement did not necessarily lead to pain. She envied her friend and resented that happiness had come to Jan so easily. It was so unfair! But this was hardly a feeling which one would readily admit to oneself, much less to others. One's best friend was getting married and one ought to rejoice and wish her happiness, not begrudge her. Besides, Jan was nearer forty than thirty. "And about time she settles down; she's a lucky woman," Mrs D'Souza had clucked. And the likes of Mrs D'Souza were all for marrying, naturally, for Mrs D'Souza had just celebrated her silver wedding anniversary with a mass in church and a grand bash in a hotel. "We have so many good-looking and intelligent women in Singapore. Like all of you in this staffroom. Why our young men don't want to get married sooner is something I cannot understand. I asked my son one day. But he just shrugged. Maybe you girls should be like us, you know, in the old days. Be a little helpless. Pretend lah! Then maybe the men will feel brave and come to your help. Give them an excuse to come to you. It always works. Trust me," Mrs D'Souza giggled coquettishly. But Mrs D'Souza, matron of matrimony, had no idea how vulgar and embarrassing her kind of talk could be, teaching them such low-down tricks to ensnare the men and perpetuating the myth of women as artful deceivers.

But say what one would, Mrs D'Souza belonged to the marrying kind, the kind which could never conceive of life alone, and she, Suwen, belonged to the other kind, the kind who was nearer to forty than thirty, the kind who might never conceive and who would have to face the prospect some day of growing old alone. But she preferred the phrase "growing old single". The word "single" was not as frightening as "alone" or "lonely". Thinking of oneself as a single, one could quite easily assume that one would have some friends. A few close women friends even if one had no men friends.

She thought about the men in the college with whom she could have been friends: Mr Quek, English Lit, fair of face and soft of voice, nyet! She was not drawn to men with soft features; besides, Mr Quek was only interested in getting his students through the examinations. He saw his job as printing and distributing tons of notes and instructing his students which phrases and words to underline. Mr Tong, the Maths teacher, was stocky and dull. Mr Tan, Econs, was forever talking about stocks and shares, and smelling faintly of cheap tobacco. He had switched from cigarettes to a pipe during one of the government's "No Smoking" campaigns. The younger men, those in their twenties, were not bad, but one could cry over the male teachers in her age group. She could not bring herself to talk with them for more than five minutes without thinking that they were blinkered and limited. The only topics which fired them into anything like intelligible speech were soccer, cars and car prices, parking problems, daft students, computers and computer games. She had given them up long ago. She might as well go and play "Trivia". With Mark and Dave Scott, the other expat teacher, she could at least talk about, and explore, if not discuss in depth, Chinese and European art, culture and politics.

She had gotten into the habit of taking her coffee breaks with them, partly to make sure that she was not seen with Mark all the time. Dave probably knew this, but he went along with it anyway. She knew that the other teachers were whispering and speculating about her and Mark. But this no longer bothered her. Not the way it used to. It was quite a change, she had to admit, compared to what she had felt several months back. She did not know when her feelings had changed nor how they had changed, and put it down to having grown a thicker skin and getting used to the knowing smiles and teasing remarks. As far as she could tell, Mark was not affected at all; more likely, he was living in blissful ignorance of what was going on in the staffroom.

This had seemed to be the case because one morning, either out of caprice or design, Mark had called for her at her garage apartment. At 6.45 a.m.

"Mark! You're crazy! What are you doing here?" she asked when she found him standing at her door.

"Didn't you say that you liked early morning walks?"

"Yes, but I didn't expect this!"

She was pleased, nevertheless, and they had gone for a stroll through the Botanic Gardens, breakfasted on roti prata at a hawker centre nearby and afterwards, Mark had taken her to college in his car. After college that day, they had driven back to his house in Holland Village. She had stayed for tea and was surprised to find that she was no longer nervous being alone with him in the house.

Mark came again two days later, and the next day and the next, and throughout the college's examination and marking period. She woke up each morning at 6.15, knowing what to expect, having something to look forward to and glad that there was someone with whom she could talk quietly and walk through the gardens slowly and companionably. She had been unaware of this aspect of herself which desired the comfort of familiarity and routine. How easy it was for human beings to do things out of habit, she mused, to meander down the same lanes day after day, safe in the knowledge that one would always have a companion. No doubt there was something to be said for habits and routine but she did not like this growing desire in her to cling to the comfort of familiarity.

"Let's go somewhere else this Saturday," she suggested to Mark.

"Sure. Where would you like to go?"

"The Chinese cemetery."

"What?"

She laughed. She liked the surprise in his voice and the way his dark brows frowned above his scholarly-looking glasses. "Your brows are dark for an angmoh," she had told him once. "It's my Italian genes. You forget, Su, that I'm Irish-Italian-Scot." How lightly he was wearing his cloak of multi-cultural heritage.

"Where's this wonderful graveyard of your Chinese forebears?"

"Off Sime Road. Very peaceful and quiet."

"Well, well, the inscrutability of Chinese women," he muttered under his breath.

"If you think I'm inscrutable," she laughed, "wait till we go to the cemetery. There you'll definitely encounter the inscrutability of the Chinese. All the gravestones are inscribed with Chinese characters."

When Saturday came round, he picked her up at 6.45 as usual and they drove to Sime Road. The sky was a cool light blue with wisps of white cloud, and the grass in the cemetery was glistening with the previous night's dew. They strolled side by side, down the sandy lane, past stacks of moss-covered granite slabs outside a row of attap huts.

"These are the stone carvers' workshops," she explained as Mark peered into their dim interiors. "The stone carvers chisel the Chinese characters onto these granite slabs and make them into headstones. The characters are painted red or gold."

It was still early and the carvers had not arrived yet. Other than the two of them and a few birds, there were no other living souls. A thick foliage of bush and trees had screened off the roar of the traffic along Adam Road; the cemetery was an oasis of peace and quiet filled with the muted presence of the dead. They strolled down the lane winding between the graves, shaded by the saga trees, vivid with red seeds.

"You really don't mind walking in a cemetery?" she asked.

"No," Mark drawled in his broad Scots, grey eyes twinkling wickedly. "One gets used to it. Singaporeans are a crazy bunch. All my Chinese friends drag me to the cemetery for their cultural reawakening."

"You're always teasing me."

She boxed his arm lightly and he returned the favour with a playful tug of her hair. She tried to give him another box but he dodged and ran off like a child. She gave chase till, breathless, she had to stop at the crest of the slope, catching her breath in the shade of the banyan tree. Mark had always had a playful streak which would break out when one least expected it. During their walking tour of the Highlands, they had had to share a room one night when all the B & Bs in Wick were fully booked. The North Sea wind and an icy cold drizzle had chilled her to the bone. The B & B had only one room with a double bed. They took it. "Great, we're having an affair," Mark had chaffed her. That night, he had curled up next to her. She must have stiffened her limbs for he said hastily, "Relax, I'm not going to harm you, child." The next morning, when she woke up, she had found herself lying in his arms. She'd leapt out of bed at once. "Gosh, I was stoned. Did I rape you?" Mark scratched his head, grey eyes gazing at her wickedly; she threw a pillow at him and, instantly, she'd remembered with a stab of pain and shame that it was what she had done with her mother's husband.

"This is all your doing, you know. D'you remember bringing me for that long walk in the Highlands?" she asked when he joined her under the tree.

"How can I forget?" he murmured, looking down at her, grey eyes clouding with wistful memories.

She felt the warmth spreading on her cheeks. "Anyway," she continued quickly, "I was so very impressed. All that wide open space. And those hills." She shook her head. "I'm so envious of you Scots. You people have so much land. Green hills and valleys for miles. And clear blue skies above. That was a beautiful summer. The image of that vast empty wilderness stayed in my mind for months. That was what I missed most when I came back. So I used to come here. Not quite the Scottish Highlands, I know," she said with a laugh. "But it's land devoid of traffic and people. The dead are silent and there's this wide open space."

What she did not tell Mark was that she had gone there with her memories of that beautiful summer, and amidst the silence of the graves, she had displayed before her mind's eye images of those green hills to soothe her heart which had missed him sorely. The graves and their dead had served as potent reminders of the fleeting nature of relationships which one had cultivated abroad. Nothing was permanent; all things were transient, these gravestones had reminded her even as she had clung to her memory of the Scottish hills. Greyish-green, bluish-green, yellowish-green, brownish-green; how does one describe the varied hues of the hills? Words were not enough. She tried the medium of paint and brushwork, but pigments and brush strokes could only recapture in mimetic representation what the eye saw, rarely what the heart felt nor what the nose smelt. She could still recall the faint stale smell of beer which had clung to all his sweaters that summer, the warmth of his grasp when he helped her climb the rocks and the sorrow in his voice when he recited for her his grandfather's poem lamenting the clearing of the Highlands by the English conquerors.

She pushed away these thoughts and the memory of how deeply she had missed Mark when she returned from Scotland. The first three months were the dark-grey months of hopeless waiting, sitting by the phone each night, hoping that he would call and knowing that he would not and pretending to herself that she was not waiting for his call anyway. She was exhausted by those mental games of deception. But such things Mark need never know, she argued with herself, for she had no intention of making herself vulnerable again. If that's what you want, why are you here? She heard the sardonic part of her self mocking her and saw through its eyes how she was seated close to Mark on a broken stone bench under the banyan tree. They were looking out at the spread of gravestones on the undulating slopes of grass, lallang and bush. She got up and walked over to one of the graves.

"D'you know I can't read these Chinese characters?" she said.

"You told me." Mark waited for her to go on.

"Mine's a lost generation," she began. "When I was seven, Malaysia became independent. It was known as the Federation of Malaya then. Singapore was not part of it. I was with my grandparents in Perak. We all had to study Malay in school. The national language. Then when I was twelve, I came to Singapore. They hadn't invented the second language or mother tongue then. Even when Singapore became part of Malaysia, we didn't have to study Malay if we didn't want to. Some of my classmates did Chinese. Mandarin, I mean. Others like me didn't do any other language. I just did English. Anyway I got marks like ten upon a hundred for Malay. So I was glad that I could drop it. But I didn't do Mandarin. I simply got A's for English. Now people like me are considered half-Chinese. Chinese who don't know their mother tongue."

"But is Mandarin your mother tongue?" Mark asked her. It was a question he would never dream of asking anywhere else, except in Singapore.

"No, Mandarin is not my mother tongue. My mother and grandparents spoke Cantonese. I grew up speaking Cantonese. But now they insist, at least that's what the press is saying, that Mandarin is our mother tongue."

"Aye, a misnomer."

"Yes, it's like saying that Hindi is the mother tongue of all Indians."

"But Mandarin is becoming the mother tongue of many Chinese children. There are statistics to back this up. I read it in the papers a few days ago."

"I don't know and I really don't care, Mark," Suwen was getting worked up, partly because she had some feelings about the language, but mainly because she would rather talk about this than let her feelings for Mark nudge her into an intimacy she might regret later. They had left the stone bench and were walking down a path of beaten brown earth winding between rows of ornately-carved gravestones. Mark pointed to their red and gold Chinese characters.

"Can you read some of them?"

"Shoo!" Suwen stamped her foot at the brown toad squatting in her path. The toad would not budge. "Shoo!" she stamped her foot again. The toad hopped up and landed back on the same spot again. "Stubborn thing! It must be a grandfather toad. Hard of hearing."

"Try a little Mandarin," Mark said. "It might hear you then."

"Zou-kai!" Suwen hissed. "Shoo! Kwai-zou!"

The toad jumped up and hopped out of her way.

"Well, it understood you! Your Mandarin must be pretty good," Mark laughed.

"No, we're like strangers. It doesn't understand me and I don't understand it," Suwen muttered, intensely aware of the gravestones mocking her ignorance of their ancestral words. "I can only read one or two of these characters. Like 'fook' for luck and prosperity. Quite a lot of names with 'fook'. They probably needed a lot of luck in those early days," she laughed to cover up her own sense of unease. "Too bad, I'm only literate in English. And even that, I'm not so good."

"Now I wouldn't say that if I were you," Mark gently reminded her in his teaching voice, forgetting for the moment that she was not his student. "You seem comfortable speaking English. It's not a foreign tongue to you the way French is to most English people."

"Right, it's not foreign. I think in English. I can't think in Mandarin or

Cantonese. But I don't feel English, you know what I mean?"

"Like Naipaul, Narayan and Maxine Hong Kingston."

"I don't know. I feel more English here than when I was in England. When I was over there, I felt most un-English. And yet, I wasn't feeling all Chinese, you know. Chinese like the people from China, Huang and Chin. D'you remember them?" But before Mark could reply, she had carried on as if the words were rushing through her head. "Huang and Chin came to my room in Aberdeen to celebrate my birthday. That night there were different kinds of Chinese in my room. Besides Huang and Chin from Communist China, there were Lui from Republican China, Taiwan, the two Cantonese girls from Hong Kong and Khoo from Malaysia. And there were three of us from Singapore. And we were all speaking English. But different accents. Then this Huang stood up. He raised his glass and made a speech. Something about all of us coming from one family. He was talking like a pompous little minister. I'm sure back in China, he must be a party cadre. He said that the rest of us were daughters of China, married into other families. Your family now is your husband's family, he said. But we will always welcome you when you return to China for a visit. Like a married daughter coming back to visit her parents."

"That's an interesting concept."

"Ya, we Nanyang Chinese in Southeast Asia are their married daughters. Married out already. Anyway I wasn't offended. The guy from Taiwan was peeved. I think that's because the Taiwanese still think of themselves as part of the Chinese mainland."

"Have you been to China?"

"No. I don't feel like going yet."

"Many American-Chinese are visiting China now. It's the thing to do, seeking one's roots."

"I know. But I think I should find out more about Southeast Asia first. This region is more home to me than China. You see, we immigrant Chinese are a funny bunch. Those of us who are English-educated know more about Henry VIII and his six wives than about Rama I of Thailand. For example, if it weren't for the Hollywood musical 'The King and I', we wouldn't have known anything about King Mongkut either. Right? And the Chinese-ed. They know all about the Chinese emperors and philosophers. But nothing about the kings and sultans of Southeast Asia. Sad, isn't it? And we're supposed to be third or fourth generation at least. That's why I admire Jan. She's committed to Zul and his Malay community. She's already sunk her roots here. Heart, body and soul."

"I didn't think you'd feel so strongly about these things," Mark murmured.

"Actually, me too," she smiled. "I'd no idea that I felt this way. Really. Until I spoke with you."

Mark raised his brow and gave her a quizzical look behind his steel-rimmed glasses.

"It's true," Suwen protested. "I don't know why. But every time I'm with you, I begin to think of these things. I feel very Chinese when I'm with you. But when I talk to Madam Tan Ai Mee in college, I feel that I'm not Chinese enough. I don't know much about Chinese customs and traditions. And I don't speak Mandarin. Speaking Cantonese doesn't count these days. At least not in Singapore. No dialects. Speak Mandarin. Then sometimes I think, so what? Why should I let the authorities define who I am?"

"Now, now, now," Mark was wagging a finger at her and shaking his head in mock despair. "That's what your government calls individualistic thought, it's not good."

"Yes, laugh, Mark. You can laugh because you're a foreigner. These things don't affect you. But it's not funny for people like me and Nica, you know. We've got to face this black-white thinking all the time. East is good; West is bad. East is disciplined; the West is permissive. More and more I'm beginning to feel that because I can read and think a thousand times better in English than I ever can in Mandarin, I am seen as being tainted. You know that? Tainted in the eyes of people like Madam Tan. But of course, I can't talk about this with Madam Tan. She'd just smile and say 'No, no' ever so politely. But inside her, she'd think of me as a gone-case. A yellow banana. You've never heard of this term?"

Mark shook his head, secretly admiring the strength he was seeing in Suwen for the first time. He couldn't remember when she had been this strong unless, of course, he counted the time when she'd hit his arm in Aberdeen.

"A yellow banana," Suwen was saying, "is an Asian, yellow on the outside but white inside. A WOG. That's how some of the Chinese-ed think of us. D'you know what Madam Tan told me one day? She'd been listening to Sue Tay talking to Jan. Then after that, she whispered to me in Mandarin: only in Singapore, you have two Chinese speaking to each other in English and not Chinese. Very shameful, she said. I'd wanted to remind her that thousands of Chinese-Americans spoke to one another in English, and it's no shame. Our language is our choice. And sometimes it's the result of a quirk of history. Like your colonial policies."

"You shouldn't let Madam Tan upset you. It's just her point of view."

"I know, Mark. I feel silly sometimes. But I was just trying to explain why I get riled sometimes. All this crap about our cultural heritage. I am as Chinese as my Cantonese-speaking grandparents have brought me up to be. And they were illiterate non-Mandarin speakers. And it wouldn't have occurred to anybody at that time in the fifties to label them as less Chinese or what! But nowadays, to be Chinese, you must know Mandarin and read these characters. How can? I can't read these. And my grandparents couldn't. And I bet you, ninety percent of those buried here couldn't read their own gravestones to go to heaven!"

Mark laughed. They had walked a full circle among the graves and were back under the banyan tree, at the top of the slope. He tried to pull her down to sit beside him on the stone bench again.

"No, thanks, Mark. I think better when I stand."

"Then I'll stand too."

"You know something? You can't even speak Gaelic, and you're a Scot."

"Now, wait a minute..." Mark shielded his face with a hand, "if you're attacking me now..."

"No! No! Don't tease, please. I was just about to say that millions of Scots can't understand Gaelic now. But nobody thinks you're less of a Scot."

"Wouldn't you say that Singapore is going through a phase which all immigrant societies experience? Searching for its roots?" Mark asked; he was more interested in talking about her country than about his own. "Most immigrants seek to return to the land of their forefathers. In spirit. This happens whenever they've done well."

"I know, Mark. But don't you think that the richer we get, the more we, Chinese-Singaporeans, talk as if all our ancestors had come from the educated class in old China? As if they had brought with them high Chinese art and culture? It's all bluff," Suwen dropped her voice instinctively as though she was afraid the dead might hear this and take offence. "It's true, Mark. Our immigration records tell a different story. Ninety-nine percent were illiterate coolies. The landless poor of old China. But we, their descendants, are clamouring for a return to the old values which these immigrants brought over. And what are these so-called old values? Not your Confucian high ideals, you know. But more of the survival values. Survival, hard work, thrift and the accumulation of wealth and property. Becoming rich and owning property were very, very important. And in those days, women like my grandmother fell into the category of property."

"Until recently, a wife was part of a man's chattels in Europe," Mark said.

"I know. You men are the same all over the world. In the early nineteen hundreds, thousands of Chinese women were sold by their parents and shipped over here. Twenty to thirty thousand each year. D'you really, really think all of them were virtuous wives and celibate amahs? Many of the women were sold into slavery and became prostitutes or bondmaids. Only a few hundred Chinese coolies became rich enough to go back to China for a wife. So what happened to the thousands of poor coolies then? They couldn't afford purity and virginity in a woman. I think," she whispered, "they married former bondmaids and prostitutes."

"It's no shame. I'm sure lots of families are like this," Mark smiled; he did not quite understand why Suwen was taking this so seriously. The issue of whether a woman was still a virgin on her wedding day had long ceased to be an issue in Western societies.

"I'm not saying it's a shame, Mark," Suwen said, her hands clasped under her chin as if she were battling for control of her feelings. She hoped that Mark could see that she was not running down the poor and the landless, hoping with some naïvety that, in some vague way, this exchange of perceptions might establish some sort of understanding between them. "Don't you see, Mark?" But she could see from his blue-grey eyes that he did not. She suppressed a sigh and went on. "You see, in Singapore, we tend to go on and on about our Chinese virtues and values. We talk as if our forebears and early pioneers were the carriers of high ideals and values, when in fact, they weren't. Most of our forebears came from the riffraff strata. The rough-and-tumble world of the poor and the lawless. But now that we, their descendants, have become rich, we talk all the time about the poets and scholars like Li Bai and the philosophers like Confucius. It makes me puke, d'you understand? I'm not looking down on the poor. My grandparents were poor. My mother was a lowly opera actress."

Mark patted her shoulders. "It's all right. Nothing to be ashamed of, Su."

"I know, Mark. I'm not ashamed of them. I'm just saying that we sometimes talk as if we didn't come from them. Of course, I don't expect," she added hastily, "every Chinese to go round saying that his grandpa was an illiterate coolie or that his grandma was a former prostitute or something. And, most likely, our grandparents didn't tell us the whole truth either. We Chinese are very good at covering up," she admitted with a laugh. "And if you think about it, why should our grandparents tell us everything anyway? Who wants to know such truths? It's better not to know. And this is exactly what we are doing. We don't want to know too much. Let's forget about those records of coolies and prostitutes, and pay more attention to poets and philosophers. But they are not our real forebears, are they?"

"You're against selective remembrance," Mark said cheerfully. How inviting the fair slope of her shoulders looked, he thought; he liked the way her dark tousled hair fell over her brow and which she would brush up with an unconscious sweep of her hand when she was agitated. "Every government rewrites the past to suit the needs of the present."

"Yes, I know. We remember some and forget some. What we don't want, we forget, cut it out."

"I doubt it's as clear-cut as that," he smiled.

"Of course it's clear-cut. In Japan, they cut out certain events from their history books. Someone told me, I think it's Nica who calls it cultural and historical lobotomy. They just cut out and leave out certain events as if they didn't happen."

She stopped to pick up a small stone and hurled it into the thick foliage beyond the graves. The leaves and branches parted as the stone fell into their midst, but they sprang back just as swiftly to their original positions, and the foliage looked the same as before, as though no stone had passed through it, and the stone was lost and hidden among the grass and bush. The toad on the grass had not even budged; it squatted under the banyan tree, quite unimpressed.

Mark's eyes followed the slope of her shoulders to her soft brown arms and the curve of her back. She was standing with her back towards him, gazing down at the undulating expanse of grassland, dotted with the graves of her Chinese ancestors. How thin and lonely her hunched shoulders looked, he thought; was she borne down by some sort of distress which as yet he had no name for? Very gently, he turned her to face him and took her into his arms, kissing her hair, then her shoulders. His mouth sought hers as their fingers laced and intertwined like the filaments of aerial roots from the banyan tree. "No, Mark," she broke away from him. "I'm...I'm sorry." She turned and started to walk down the slope. He followed. In silence. One after the other, in single file, they walked between the rows of silent dead. He felt the gaze of her ancestors and regretted his own lack of self-control.

Many years later, in a painting entitled "Elegy in a City Cemetery", Suwen's recollection of this moment was transformed into an elegant study of a graveyard done in blue monochrome.

In the painting's foreground were rows of Chinese graves, nestling peacefully among tufts of blue grass and blue bush, their grey-blue headstones arching gracefully across the frame. Beyond the graves rose the banyan tree against a light blue sky bathed in the light of an early morn when the sun had not yet arisen. Upon closer examination, the viewer could see that beneath this deceptively simple painting of a tree were the tangled filaments of aerial roots hanging down from its branches; roots, leaves, bush and grass intricately woven into a pattern of blue-green, blue-grey, blue-rust, cobalt, turquoise, cerulean and azure with patches of deep-blue sapphire reminiscent of the treacherous depths of the oceans. "The artist has skilfully suggested an underlying sense of anger and unease among the tombstones," an art reviewer wrote in *The Straits Times*.

PART 6

Sepia Prints out of a Biscuit Tin

It rained throughout the months of November and December. The northeast monsoon brought grey skies and wet days. The afternoons were long hours of dreary wetness with water dripping from the eaves of roofs, from the ledges of windows, from trees lining the roads and from clothes one had forgotten to take in, and there they had hung upon the clothesline all afternoon, those limp skirts and T-shirts, drip, drip, drip, in this season of damp and ennui. The winds and rains had brought with them the grey clouds and the damp. Especially to the old, the single and the lonely. The crowds flocked to the brightly lit shopping centres where, for a few hours of mindless spending, one could drown one's fears and loneliness in the steady stream of human traffic and sugar-sweet jingles of Christmas spending. Most of Suwen's friends had gone off for their annual vacation now that the college had closed for the school holidays, Mark had gone out of her life and had taken off for Bali and Surabaya. And Jan, she did not bother to find out where Jan was, probably somewhere in Lake Toba with Zul's family, she thought. She could not settle down to anything serious. Her mind flitted from her paints and canvases to her books and paraphernalia of painting and sculpting. Half-finished pieces of work and abandoned projects with half-formed concepts lay about her garage apartment. She had not the heart to begin packing even though her mother was determined to move out of the mansion before the year was out.

On one wall hung a large piece of canvas, almost covering the entire wall. It had been hanging there since November; bare like my life, she thought, and waiting for something to happen. But nothing had happened all day. The sky outside her window was grey and overcast, with a soft rain falling intermittently, the kind which never seemed to stop. During the past few nights, there had been squalls and sumatras, and the trees were slashed. She had awoken one morning to find large fallen branches outside her garage apartment. A huge leafy branch from the angsana tree had lain across her path like a road blockade. For days, her paints would not dry and her clothes smelt of damp. It was depressing and her spirits lay heavy upon her, and she had neither the inclination to meet nor the desire to speak with anyone she knew, except the servants. To them, she would chat amiably whenever she went into the mansion's large kitchen to collect her meals on a tray. She ate alone in her garage, cocooned and shielded from the outside world.

In the mornings, she went for long solitary walks, cutting across the mansion's extensive grounds and the Botanic Gardens nearby, usually avoiding the other early strollers. She tried not to think or remember, keeping her mind and eyes busy and focused upon the Gardens' rich flora. A strong breeze was blowing among the angsana and acacias; her mind recorded this fact. Their wet yellow blooms came cascading down in showers of gold and covered the footpath in front of her; her eyes recorded this fact too, like an inquisitive worm hungry for visual details. Large drops of rain fell from the trees onto her hair when the wind blew, but she did not mind getting wet. The rain cooled her tired head. She sidestepped the numerous puddles in her way, and seeing a snail, stooped to admire its slow but determined progress towards the black twigs and brown leaves lining the footpath, leaving a thin trail of mucus glistening in the grey half-light of dawn. She walked down the footpath alongside a large drain, a pavement of broken concrete slabs, hemmed in by acacia bushes. She stood on the path for a long while, hands thrust into her windcheater, watching the swirling rainwater gushing down the drain, carrying with it the brown leaves, turning and twisting in the current, and clinging desperately to the drain's mossy sides before being swept away by the water's flow. All life clings to its former state, she thought, the fear of change being universal.

Her phone rang. It was Nica asking why she hadn't been down to the studio for her sculpting sessions.

"Want to see a play or not? Done by the Stage Club," Nica invited her.

"No, thanks. I don't feel up to it."

"What?" Nica shouted. Suwen could hear the blast of a rock band in the background.

"I said I'm not feeling up to it!"

"Why? What's bugging you these days?"

"I don't know! Must be the usual end-of-the-year ennui. Feeling kind of empty."

"Oh, for crying out loud! You sure know how to pamper your own feelings! Are you missing Mark?"

"NO!" Suwen yelled into the mouthpiece.

"Hey, there's no need to shout. I can hear you. Mark called me before he left for Bali. He sounded real low. What've you done to him?"

"Nothing!"

"You didn't give him a reason to go off like this, did you?"

"I don't know."

"You're sure you don't know? You're always keeping things from me, I know you."

"Sure. I just want some time to myself. I need to think about my project."

"Okay, okay! I got you loud and clear. You want to think. Alone." Nica sounded peeved. "I know all about your project. It's to paint the past, right? Your family's past or whatever past lah! But surely there's no need to be so bloody uptight about it! You don't have to confess your dark secrets to me or to anyone, you know!"

"I know, Nica. I'm sorry if I sounded abrupt."

"I know. But remember this, girl. Whatever happened to you could happen to anyone else too. We're not all that unique, you know. However much all the Ah Bengs and Ah Huays would like to think so!"

"You've been drinking, Nica. I know it when you start talking like this."

"Hey, so what if I am tipsy? You know that I am still talking sense, drink or no drink!"

"Where's Robert?"

"How the f--- do I know? Am I his bloody keeper?"

"Have you broken up with him?"

"Hey, you people like to imagine things. You like to imagine, ha, that the past is dead and fossilised. Can't be changed. You're wrong! All of you! The past can be changed. Whoosh! Gone! See? I don't know Robert now. He doesn't exist. I have erased him from my memory, d'you hear?" Nica shouted drunkenly. "Our memory is a sieve, and we are the sculptors, shaping and reshaping the remains of our past."

"Nica, you're drunk. Shall I come over?"

"NO!"

The phone went dead. She tried calling Nica's apartment many times but no one picked up the phone. She tried again the next day and the next. She gave up after several days.

So, that's how we lose our friends, Suwen thought bitterly, through phone calls which go unanswered, through marriage, silence and, generally, through bumbling of one kind or another. And so the gulf grows and grows till one is alone. Utterly alone. Mark couldn't have loved her, she told herself. If he did, he would not have given up trying to call her on the phone. But why did he just phone? Why couldn't he simply have come over to her apartment, ring the doorbell and stand resolutely on the doorstep till she opened the door? They hadn't quarrelled. Nothing of that sort had happened. But he had allowed this gulf of silence to grow between them, a yawning gap which grew more unbridgeable as each day of silence passed by. Why didn't Mark say something to get them talking again? Men are so annoying. She had never seen this side of him before. He moped. He kept quiet. He avoided her. And before she knew it, the school vacation was upon them and he was off to Bali. She was annoyed with herself for being annoyed. She shouldn't let Mark's silence disturb her peace, yet, the niggling thought that she might have some deep feelings for Mark continued to plague her. She was irritated that she was this weak: it was an unforgivable vulnerability and she ought to be stronger. She would not be one of those women who bent over backwards to accommodate a man because she feared losing him. And she was not one of those who ran after white men or angmohs either. Neither was she going to placate famous temperamental artists. It was time for her to do her own thing, define her own space and develop her own art, she thought resolutely, and at this point, she had neither the means nor the inclination to determine how much of her resolution was simply a reaction to gossip in college about her and Mark, and how much of it was due to the artistic fire in her soul.

So be it, she thought. If Nica chose to avoid her, there was nothing she could do about it. And if Nica chose to think that she was working in secrecy on a project about the past, she might as well try to find out as much as she could of the past. But whose past? She mulled over this question during her solitary walks to stop herself from thinking too much about Mark. Not her own past; no, it should not be about her own past, she decided firmly. Art must not be simply autobiography. Then she thought of her grandparents on the farm back near Kuala Jelai. And a horrible thought came into her head: if her grandfather had been an impoverished vegetable farmer, then in all likelihood, if one were to go by the statistics, her grandmother was never a virgin and was, in all probability, a former bondmaid or, worse, a prostitute who had worked in the mining towns of Taiping and Ipoh! She took a deep breath as if to steady herself. While Suwen's line of thinking and logical deduction were bold, she was not bold enough to delve deeper into the matter. What if her fears were confirmed? What good would such a confirmation do? she asked herself and could not come up with a satisfactory answer. And that was when she decided to visit Ah Siew Chay again.

She went to the servants' quarters to look for Ah Siew Chay, the old amah of the Ongs. If anyone knew about the history of the Ongs, it would be Ah Siew Chay. She had been with the Ongs for more than fifty years, since the birth of Ong Tay Luck. If her mother's husband was a man with a heart, Suwen thought, he would not have agreed to chuck Ah Siew Chay out of the mansion and into an old folks' home. But since he had no heart, it had been decided that Ah Siew Chay would leave for the old folks' home before Christmas.

"Ah Siew Chay!" Suwen called out to the myopic amah peering near-sightedly into a biscuit tin.

The narrow bedroom was sparsely furnished with a bed, a chest of drawers, a table pushed against the wall and two cane chairs and some stools. Under the table were boxes and cartons of various sizes, stuffed with all manner of things wrapped in newspapers and plastic bags.

"Ah Siew Chay!" Suwen called again and came into the room without waiting for an invitation.

The old amah started and peered, scowling, through her thick glasses at the intruder.

"Nae! You! How many times nae I have to tell you not to creep up on me like this? My spirit nearly flew off. You did nae knock. You did nae learn manners on the farm, meh?"

Suwen shook her head and gave the old lady a sheepish smile. Ah Siew Chay was getting the times and scenes from the past mixed up with the present once again. It was quite impossible these days trying one's best to remind her that the ignorant farm girl had since grown up into a knowledgeable woman.

"Ah Siew Chay," Suwen said, pronouncing each Cantonese word clearly and loudly for the amah had grown deaf with age. "I haven't seen you for many days."

"I got work," came the gruff reply.

"Why are you working so hard still?" Suwen refused to be discouraged.

"Give more work to the young maids in the kitchen. If not, ah, how can they grow thin as a towgay stalk like you?"

The small cataract-covered eyes peered through the thick glasses, the glint of irritation creeping into them, and with it, clarity of mind. Only one person dared to tease her like this.

"Ah Suwen! What are you doing here?" she smiled at last.

"I come to see you, mah!"

"Aiyah! Your mouth, ah, is always full of sugar. You think now I old, ah, I forget things. But I can still remember my farm girl. Always asking me about this and that. What do you want, ah?"

"Nothing!" Suwen protested. "What are you doing with that tin of photographs?"

"I have to start packing, ah! All my things."

"Aiyah, Ah Siew Chay, why don't let the maids pack for you? Ask them to do the packing and cleaning, mah!"

"Aye, easy to say do nae clean, let the maids clean," Ah Siew Chay lapsed into the distinctive Cantonese of her Toong-koon village in Canton. "They say, nae, I nag them. They call me 'toong-koon-por' behind my back! They say my eyes are nae good. But like this morning, I go to the front door. I looked up. Ha! The red cloth is nae straight. Ah Hiong, I said, straighten nae red cloth. Very nicely, I say, good luck comes in straight as an arrow. But if the door is nae straight but crooked, good luck can nae come in, you say right or not? But that Ah Hiong! She said, your eyes are nae good! The cloth is straight, nae crooked! I am the one to hang the red cloth this morning so I know lor! Like that, she spoke to me. No big, no small! No old, no young! No respect! And I have worked here for so long since Master Tay Luck was born. Aye, if Madam Sia Liew were alive, nae ah! I will slap that Ah Hiong for her, ah! She can nae answer back like this! So rude, ah!"

"Sit down, Ah Siew Chay, please sit. Have a drink of tea," Suwen calmed her down. "Look, your Madam Sia Liew is smiling down at you," she pointed to the large black and white photograph of the mother of Ong Tay Luck.

"Aye, your mother's mother-in-law, ah, is blessed by the gods. She was a bondmaid. Then a concubine. And our Towkay Ong Ah Buck liked her. You can be a towkay's concubine, ah, and still not be liked by the towkay, ah! But she was liked. She looked after him when he was hurt by the rickshaw coolies," Ah Siew Chay said, returning to the Cantonese spoken by the people of Hong Kong which was plainer than her mellifluous Toong-koon village variety.

"You have not told me very much about my mother's mother-in-law. You were her personal amah, so you would know more about her than any relative in the Ong family, ah," Suwen said craftily, hoping that flattery would launch the old amah into storytelling.

"You are right, ah! I know more about our Madam Sia Liew than anyone else. Even more than what her only son knows, ah!"

Suwen's ploy had worked. The old amah poured out the entire collection of old photographs which she had kept in the biscuit tin. Black-and-whites and faded sepia browns. Suwen sorted them into little piles. Some of them looked familiar. Like those her mother had thrown out because there would be no place for them in the new house. Her mother had kept only the grand and the grandiose. And these she had framed and displayed in the mansion's so-called "ancestors' gallery". But what her mother had thrown out, Ah Siew Chay had salvaged and hoarded in biscuit tins and cartons. The superstitious amah could not bear to throw away the likenesses of those she had served for fear that bits of their spirits, captured in these photographs, might be dispersed and lost to their owners forever.

"Ah Suwen, you see this picture here?" Ah Siew Chay thrust a black-and-white photograph into her hand. "This one is Madam Sia Liew when she was young. And this baby is our Master Tay Luck. One month old. And that is me carrying him."

The photograph showed a much younger and fuller Ah Siew Chay with well-oiled hair, plaited into a pigtail. She was standing next to her mistress, seated on a high-back rosewood chair. The baby boy in Ah Siew Chay's arms was dressed in an embroidered jacket and embroidered cap of rich brocade. But below the navel, he wore nothing except for a triangular amulet for warding off evil spirits. Ah Siew Chay was holding the boy facing front so that anyone looking at the photo would have no doubts as to his gender. The baby's mother, Madam Sia Liew, was staring out of the photograph. She looked young and nervous. Her hands clutched the armrests of the rosewood chair. On each wrist was a thick gold bangle. And at her feet was a porcelain spittoon with a floral pattern, the symbol of wealth among the Southeast Asian Chinese at the turn of the century.

"Aye, Madam Sia Liew had a lot of fook, ah. You look at her face. You can see, mah. And her arms. Like a rich woman and towkah-leong."

Hindsight is a powerful eyeglass which distorts, Suwen thought with some amusement as she listened to Ah Siew Chay's description of her mistress. The camera had frozen for posterity the image of a young woman from a well-to-do family, giving one the impression that she could be the daughter of a rich towkay. "With a lot of fook," according to Ah Siew Chay. But the reality at the time when Madam Sia Liew was young and alive hardly matched what the photograph seemed to suggest. "Madam Sia Liew had a lot of fook. So she did not have to work, ah? Like Towkay Ong Ah Buck's first wife?"

"Aye, no, how can? Madam Sia Liew was a bondmaid and the first wife, Madam Geok Neo, was the daughter of a rich towkay. Aye, not the same. Madam Geok Neo never forgot that Madam Sia Liew was her slave girl before she became her husband's concubine. Every day, she scolded Madam Sia Liew and sometimes beat her. All these Madam Sia Liew told me. We were close. Like godsisters."

"Even after Madam Sia Liew was her husband's concubine, Madam Geok Neo can still beat her?"

"Aiyah, can! Madam Sia Liew was her former bondmaid, mah! But, if you ask me," Ah Siew Chay dropped her voice to a confidential whisper, "the reason is that Madam Sia Liew was very young. Same age as Madam GeokNeo's eldest daughter, mah! So, if at night Towkay Ong asked for Madam Sia Liew, the next morning, aiyoh! There will be trouble. Madam Geok Neo will scold and beat her. Very hard life she had, ah, my Madam! Had to sleep along the corridor, outside Towkay Ong's room."

Suwen examined the young girlish face in the photograph. It had the stiffness of one who was not at ease in front of a camera. And, perhaps, not at ease in her finery.

"Yes, aiyah! True, she was not at ease. You think a concubine like Madam Sia Liew wore nice clothes like this every day?" Ah Siew Chay exclaimed. The old amah was quite exasperated that Suwen did not seem to understand the hardships of poor bondmaids and concubines. "It was only after the birth of Master Tay Luck that she got to wear clothes like this. And that only because Towkay Ong liked her. She used to wait up for him every night."

"Why?" Suwen asked.

"It is the duty of a concubine to wait for the master. Madam Geok Neo would beat her if she slept and Towkay Ong was not home yet. Then one night, lucky she did not sleep. Towkay Ong came back with blood streaming down his face. It was the night when the rickshaw coolies, ah, many years back before the Japanese war, and they burnt the rickshaws made in Japan.

Aiyah, that year was very bad for rickshaw owners, ah! The crowds burnt many rickshaws. Towkay Ong Ah Buck lost many rickshaws, ah! But that year was a good one for Madam Sia Liew, nae. The gods in heaven opened their eyes and ah, blessed her. That year, Towkay Ong Ah Buck built her a room. She did nae have to sleep on the floor outside his bedroom any more. But then, Madam Geok Neo did nae like that and there were many fights and quarrels."

The Story Of The Bondmaid And The Towkay's Daughter

One night, Sia Liew was waiting for Towkay Ong as usual, lying on her bedding, outside his bedroom. Like a faithful dog, she still had no room of her own. And on that particular night, Mistress Geok Neo was sleeping in the children's room. Sia Liew was numb with shock at the sight of the bleeding head. She helped Towkay Ong Ah Buck, her master and spouse, into his bedroom. Then she returned with a basin of hot water. She sponged his head and wiped off the blood with hot towels. Then she made him comfortable on the bed and tiptoed out of the room. When she returned, Towkay Ong Ah Buck beckoned her. She sat on the edge of his bed and asked, in a soft whisper, "Are you feeling better? Shall I wake up my mistress?"

Towkay Ong shook his head and put a finger to his lips. He moved closer to her and lay his head on her lap. He closed his tired eyes. Sia Liew brushed aside a damp lock of hair and dabbed away a thin trickle of blood. Her master and husband uttered a soft moan and clung to her, shivering like a child.

"I saw them kill Lau Goo, my best friend," he said in a hoarse whisper. "Those sons of dogs beat him with sticks and steel bars. They burnt my rickshaws. Five thousand dollars," he groaned and burrowed his head into her bosom, swollen with milk for the baby due in a few months' time.

"Don't leave," Towkay Ong ordered his concubine as he closed his eyes and slowly sank into a fitful sleep. Tongues of fire leapt around him. There were blazing fires everywhere. He saw twenty Made-in-Japan rickshaws go up in flames. All the way down South Bridge Road and Tanjong Pagar Road, rickshaw coolies were attacking people and smashing up anything imported from Japan. His head was throbbing with acute pain. The blood rushed to his head; only the gods knew how many of those rickshaws were his! Those sons of pigs and dogs, ah! He heard once again the rapid pounding of hoofs, the murderous yells of the bandits as they galloped through his village back in China. He cried out in his sleep. His concubine hushed and soothed him, and he clung to her young and courageous body, burrowing his head between her breasts to shut out the petrifying screams ringing in his head. The bandits were raping his mother and sisters in the courtyard. His father's head was smashed. Those curs had bludgeoned his father before his horrified eyes. He hated China, oh, how he hated China! Spasm after spasm shuddered through his body. Sia Liew held him close and grimaced with pain as her master tightened his iron grip round her. Not a word passed between them; she simply held him close to her, closer than she had ever dared to do before. He had never, never needed her like this before, clinging to her like this, so intimately, and stirring in her heart feelings she had never known. She felt her heart would burst that night as she lightly stroked her master's shock of greying hair. How fast he had aged these past weeks of lockouts and riots. She wanted to be needed, to be needed by a man, her inarticulate soul wept as she hugged his sleeping figure and held him close to her bosom.

And that was how her mistress, Madam Geok Neo, found her when she burst into the bedroom at five o'clock the next morning.

"Sia Liew! What are you doing? Go and boil water!" Madam Geok Neo hissed.

Sia Liew silently pointed to the sleeping form lying on her lap.

"I said to go and boil water!" Madam Geok Neo hissed again and yanked her from the bed.

Towkay Ong's head hit the hard edge of the bed. "Poo-bor-ah!" he swore. "What are you two sows doing here? Can't you let me sleep? Out! Out! Out! You sluts! Out of my room!" he cursed and swore at them.

But his invectives and curses could be as much due to irritation and broken slumber as to an unconscious desire to create distance between him and his woman, brushing aside his weakness and the intimacy of the previous night. Who could tell what an unschooled and illiterate Chinaman felt? All we know from fiction is that no Chinese man in those days would dwell upon and mull over such trivia like man-woman or husband-wife relations. It was enough if each partner did his or her duties as prescribed by tradition and custom.

Towkay Ong Ah Buck left his family residence as soon as he was dressed, and stayed away for three days and three nights. Madam Geok Neo fretted and cursed her husband's young concubine. She took the rod and caned her too. Sia Liew cried and broke a cup. She was caned again and pinched till her upper arm was covered with blue-black marks. "Cry! See who dares to come near you! You slut! You who have no shame! Did I call you? Answer me! Did I ask you to go inside and spend the entire night there? You think I am blind? I don't know your tricks, you slut?"

To make matters worse between wife and concubine, Towkay Ong returned home on the fourth morning with two carpenters in tow. The carpenters went into the living room of the shophouse (this happened before the Ong Mansion was built) and put up partitions for a small cubicle.

"Oi! Tell me what for, this extra bedroom?" Madam Geok Neo demanded of her husband.

"For Sia Liew, mah!" he snapped back. "She's big with child. You cannot expect her to sleep outside your bedroom forever!"

"Right, you have drunk the slut's spittle! Do what you like! I hope the gods in heaven will open their eyes!"

When the cubicle was ready, Sia Liew shifted her meagre belongings into it. It was a tiny airless room with no window. The space between the matchwood thin partitions was just big enough for her dresser and an old four-poster, a discard from one of Madam Geok Neo's daughters. The bed sagged but Sia Liew did not mind; it was heaven compared to the hard wooden floor. The bed was pushed against the wall facing the doorway, and the space between the bed and the partition was just wide enough for a body to move about. The bulge inside her body was growing bigger. She could feel her skin stretching tautly over it.

When Sia Liew sat on the four-poster for the first time, the first thing which rushed into her head was, "Get off! The mistress will scold you! This is not yours." This was quickly succeeded by the second thought: "Ah, but now this is mine! This bed and this room, mine!" Her soul sang. She peeped through the curtains over the doorway to make sure that no one was about, then, very quietly and gently, she closed the bedroom door and returned to sit on the bed, savouring her unprecedented sense of privacy. "Mine, mine, all mine," she sang inside her head, bouncing slowly upon the bed. Bounce! Bounce! Bounce! It was an incongruous sight, this tiny woman with the bulging pregnant abdomen bouncing on the bed like a child testing a new toy, her face, a vision of innocent beatific joy.

On the wall opposite her bed, Sia Liew had hung an old mirror above her dresser, a piece of glass discoloured by water marks. She gazed at her dim image and peered into her own dark eyes. They gazed back at her, dark with tiny dancing lights as if they were harbouring, behind their pupils, little impish elves. Her eyes' secret liveliness thrilled her; they were such a contrast to her haggard face, particularly the downward turn of her mouth. There was an angry red welt on her throat where Madam Geok Neo's cane had hit her.

Every afternoon when Madam Geok Neo was taking her afternoon nap, Sia Liew would go into her tiny cubicle and stealthily lock the door. She found herself turning towards the mirror whenever she entered the cubicle to try and catch a glimpse of herself. But it was not vanity which drew her. It was the amazement of self-discovery at seeing herself. She had never owned a mirror and had never been allowed to groom herself in front of one because, according to her mistress, there was no need for a bondmaid to preen herself like a duck pretending to be a swan. But now, things were changing in the shophouse. She had a cubicle of her own and a mirror of her own, and no one had thought of taking it away. No one had scolded her for looking at herself. And so, closing the bedroom door stealthily, she stood in front of it for as long as she could, in fearful joy, lest someone should suddenly burst into the room and catch her looking at herself. It was because she was afraid that her mistress or the grown-up daughters of her mistress might catch her looking at herself that every peek into the glass at her own reflection held so much thrill. It was the thrill of a secret vice and secret self-assertion. The slave was beginning to see herself as a separate, distinct and unique entity, quite different from the way her oppressors had viewed her.

Gradually, as the bulge in front of her grew heavier, the image peering out from behind the glass began to smile. Then, one day, she noticed that the corners of her mouth had turned up. She could not remember when those corners had stopped their downward turn, when they had straightened out, at first, into a thin line of lips and then, several days or perhaps several weeks later, the thin straight line had curved upwards. Today, her image in the mirror was smiling. She was taken aback. She put her face closer to the mirror. Her image in the glass smiled back. She smiled too and it grinned. Almost mischievously. Positively wickedly. It seemed to be whispering to her: you are like them, char-boh-kan or bondmaid, you are like them. They have two eyes; you have two eyes. They have two ears and you have two ears. Your mistress has two eyes and you have two eyes. She has a mouth and you have a mouth. But, ah! Your eyes are shining and your mouth is smiling! Her spirits soared and her soul began to sing the song of youth and resilience. And through staring at herself for long stretches of time, she became intoxicated by the feeling that she was better looking than her ageing mistress. She might be her bondmaid and lowly concubine, but so what? Her master and husband liked her and favoured her, she sang inside her heart. And the more she looked at herself in the mirror and admired her own dark dancing eyes in a face that was younger than her mistress's, the louder her soul sang. There's a difference between her and me. Her and me! I am young and pregnant, and she is past bearing children.

It was not that Madam Geok Neo was barren but that Towkay Ong Ah Buck had stopped visiting his wife in her bedroom after she had borne him four daughters and three sons. Of the three sons born to her, only the birth of her eldest son, Ong Tay Ik, was celebrated with a grand feast. Tay Ik was the first male of the next generation, born after she had had a number of miscarriages. After his birth, her husband, in a gush of gratitude, had bought her a bondmaid as a present. This bondmaid was Sia Liew, a child of ten or so. At the age of sixteen, Sia Liew became her husband's concubine but she had been barren until a few months ago. Ha! Madam Geok Neo thought, the young vixen had not lived up to her name of Sia Liew, the pomegranate, symbol of fertility. But now that the young vixen was expecting, she was beginning to put on airs. Especially now that she had a cubicle all to herself! Madam Geok Neo fumed. That chit of a slave would not have caught Ong Ah Buck's eye if she, Geok Neo, had not raised her to her present status! Ingrate! She spat into the porcelain spittoon at her feet.

"Sia Liew!" she called.

"Coming, Madam!" Sia Liew waddled into the living room.

"Our Ah Loke has to go and look after her sister. Her sister is sick. From today, you take over her work. Go to the market in the morning and cook for the family. Do you understand?"

"Yes, Madam."

This was a full-time job and a heavy responsibility. Ah Loke was the family's old amah. Her job was to go to the market daily (in those days before-the refrigerator became a common part of the household) and cook for the family and the workers in the rickshaw repair shop downstairs. Sia Liew had been her kitchen help, but she had never ventured to the market (freedom of movement not being a basic right of bondmaids and concubines) nor handled money before. However, she had a quick mind and learnt fast. By the third morning, she was enjoying her new-found freedom despite the back-breaking task of carrying a heavy basket of meat, fish and vegetables from the market in Chinatown all the way back to Telok Ayer Street, with enough food to feed at least twenty workers and members of the Ong family. She was eight months pregnant, but she was used to hard work, and she liked having money to spend as she deemed fit even though she had to account for every cent she had spent to Madam Geok Neo.

"This fish costs one-fifty? Are you lying, Sia Liew?"

"No, Madam. He wanted one-eighty. But I bargained," Sia Liew protested.

"Come here! Undo your pants. Shake them out."

Sia Liew did as she was told; she untied the string which held up the pants of her cotton samfoo and shook the garment in front of her mistress.

"Now your shoes. Take them off."

Sia Liew took off her black cloth shoes and shook them. Bits of street gravel fell out. But no coins. Nothing else.

"Hmm! All right, you can go. But don't think I am blind, ah! I will check you suddenly. And if I find that you have stolen some marketing money and hidden it, ah! You just wait and see what I will do to you. Do you hear me?"

"I hear you, Madam."

She accepted the body search and all the indignities which went with it as part of the price she had to pay for the few hours of freedom she was enjoying daily at the Chinatown market. On most mornings, she would pretend that she was a towkay's wife and the mistress of her own household with money to spend in any way she liked. She strutted down the five-foot ways with her pert little nose up in the air and pushed her way through the crowds. The hawkers, the butchers and the vegetable sellers called out to her, "Towkay-neo! Towkay-neo! Come, come! Very cheap!" How they bowed and scraped before her, and she let them, fot she had the power to dispense or withhold the money in her purse. The power of money was highly intoxicating. She had discovered that the smell of cash and the feel of cash in one's pockets could go a long, long way in shoring up one's self-esteem and the respect of others. And so she strutted about the market with head held high and her abdomen sticking out like a huge pumpkin.

After two weeks with no news from Ah Loke, Madam Geok Neo sent for Sia Liew.

"Go to Carpenter Lane and look for her. It is not far from the market."

"What do I say to her, Madam?" Sia Liew asked.

"You have no head, ah! Why! Tell her to come back at once! I want her here!"

Her trip to Carpenter Lane marked the turning point in Sia Liew's life. It was an event which we would call "fate". It was fated, as if the gods in heaven suddenly opened their eyes, Ah Siew Chay said. After that, things happened so fast, it was as if the spirits were guiding her.

There was a gambling den at the back of the tenement house where Ah Loke had rented a cubicle. The shop in front, on the ground floor, was used for selling coal, firewood, stoves and kerosene lamps. Among the customers who came and went, some would slip behind the grimy red floral curtain to climb two flights of stairs and walk down a dark airless corridor to the cubicle at the end of it. Everyone in Chinatown, including the policemen on the beat, knew of its existence. There were gambling dens in every lane in Chinatown, wherever Chinamen congregated. Gambling was a Chinese passion.

The cubicle reeked of putrid urine, sweat, phlegm, liquor and cheap tobacco. A gas lamp hung above the heads of the sullen men and women standing in twos and threes, waiting for the betting to begin. In the centre of the cubicle was the gaming table with a large china bowl. A wiry man with long thin arms poking through the sleeves of his cotton shirt was clacking a pair of dice in his hands. The men and women crowded round the table. They had that sullen watchfulness and dark concentration in their eyes, the mark of the avid gambler. They spoke in hoarse whispers as they placed their bets. Sia Liew was squeezed among them, between Ah Loke and her younger sister, Ah Siew Chay. A man next to her coughed and spat into the spittoon. Crumpled bits of paper, cigarette butts and half-burnt matchsticks were strewn over the floor.

Ah Siew Chay pushed a piece of paper into her hand. She was ten years younger than Ah Loke and had worked as a high-class prostitute's maid in Keong Saik Street. Her dark eyes were alert like a sparrow's, darting about the room.

"Try your luck, Sia Liew. They say beginners always win," she whispered.

"I am scared," Sia Liew said.

"Never mind. Try," Ah Siew Chay pushed the piece of paper into her hand again. "Here, take this."

"What do I do?"

"Aiyah, see these pictures? Nah, use this pencil and make a cross like this. On any three pictures."

The piece of paper had pictures of a crab, a crayfish, a prawn and several Chinese characters. However, she could not read any of them. Hastily, at Ah Siew Chay's urging, she crossed out three characters and Ah Loke handed the paper to a sullen man in a blue coolie shirt.

"Ahem! Oi! Oi! We begin," the thin wiry man at the gaming table called out. A hush fell upon the crowd in the cubicle. The air was thick with smoke from the cheap red tobacco favoured by the coolies. As the bets were being made, the men and women surged forward, nudging against one another like so many piglets fighting for the sow's teats, Sia Liew saw the pair of wiry arms raised above the heads of the crowd, reaching up towards the gas lamp above the table. She heard the click-click-clack of the dice knocking against the sides of the china bowl. Ah Siew Chay, familiar with such gambling dens, pressed forward, craning her neck to see the gaming table. Then she clutched Sia Liew's arm.

"Aiyah! The gods, ah! You win! You win!" she shouted.

Ah Loke pushed her way into the crowd. She too shouted, "Aiyah! True ah! You win, Sia Liew!"

Sia Liew felt her head was floating away. She was light as a feather as if the other parts of her body had detached themselves and were floating away too.

"Help! She's fainting! Help!" she heard someone crying from a long way off, just before she sank into oblivion.

When the smoke in her eyes cleared, the man in the blue shirt handed her a wad of dollar notes. The gods, ah! Her heart leapt at the sight of so much money. Sixty dollars!

"All yours," Ah Loke was grinning. "You won it."

"I told you. Beginners always win. You got a triple win, ah!" Ah Siew Chay exclaimed. "All the three characters came in. You crossed out three and you got three. Wah! The God of Wealth, ah, is smiling on you today. Try again."

"Wait, Ah Siew. Don't rush her. She fainted," Ah Loke cautioned her sister.

"Aiyah, she was just excited. You must try again," she turned to Sia Liew, "Your luck is good today."

"But first, put aside your marketing money. If Madam Geok Neo finds out about this, she will kill you," Ah Loke, the more cautious of the two sisters, advised her.

Sia Liew, however, did not need much persuasion. She was willing to bet again. The prospect of winning and the possibility of being in the grip of this secret vice thrilled and excited her. It brought a flush of colour to her face and a sparkle in her eyes. Her hands felt damp and she was perspiring.

"Are you feeling all right?" Ah Loke asked her.

"Don't worry, I am all right. I want to play again."

At Ah Siew Chay's urging, she betted a few more times each time, betting with all the money she had won. And each time, Tua Pek Kong, the god of wealth and good fortune, smiled upon her, and she came away with a very thick wad of dollar notes on the first day of gambling.

Her heart was pounding furiously on the way home. "Lord Buddha, have mercy. Please protect me," she prayed fervently. The money clutched in her sweaty palm was enough to buy food for the family for a whole year.

"Don't forget! Don't tell Madam Geok Neo, ah! Hide it somewhere!" Ah Loke had shouted after her. Ah Loke had refused to return to the Telok Ayer shop. She had saved enough money to return to China to visit her aged mother. The amah was afraid that if she were to go back to the shophouse, Madam Geok Neo might prevent her from making the trip home.

"But what do I tell Madam Geok Neo?" Sia Liew wailed.

"Tell her I am very ill," Ah Loke instructed.

"Come back tomorrow and play again," Ah Siew Chay whispered. "You have good luck."

As Sia Liew hurried home, clattering on her wooden clogs, her head was feverish with fear and excitement. Like a child trying to hide some terrible deed which it had done and was anxious that its stern parent should never find out about it.

"So where is Ah Loke? Does she still want to work or not?" Madam Geok Neo demanded when Sia Liew reached home.

"Ah, ah, Madam. Ah Loke is very ill."

"Hmm, look at you. So big already. Due soon. Tell her I give her three more days. She must come back after three days. Else I look for another amah. Tomorrow, you go and ask the vegetable seller. See if she knows of an amah looking for work," Madam Geok Neo ordered. "Anyone. Find someone quickly."

The next morning, Sia Liew left the house as usual. But this time, she rushed through her shopping in the market and did not waste time haggling and bantering. Then she hurried to the den in Carpenter Lane where Ah Loke and Ah Siew Chay were waiting for her.

"Quick! I want to play again," Sia Liew said.

She won again and doubled yesterday's winnings. When she left the den, her eyes were shining with a new-found pride. When she rushed home, clattering down busy, noisy South Bridge Road, her feet felt light and the baby inside her did not weigh her down as before. She was going to be rich, she thought, and her head was filled with visions of gold bangles and jade pendants.

"Did you find someone else?" Madam Geok Neo demanded.

"Ah, no, Madam, not yet. But Ah Soh, at the vegetable stall, she said to let me know tomorrow."

The next day, and the next, and several days after that, Sia Liew rushed through her shopping in the market and hurried to the den in Carpenter Lane. Sometimes, she lost a bet; but most of the time, she won handsomely.

"Quick! Quick! I want to play!" she called out to Ah Siew Chay each time, as soon as she entered the den. Her dark eyes glittered with a hard light. Like a hunter's before the kill. The blood rushed to her face, her heart pounded rapidly, but her hand was steady when she crossed out her chosen characters on the betting script.

One day when she had won some money again, she exclaimed, "Aiyah! Ah Siew Chay, why don't you come and work for Madam Geok Neo? Then we can be together, mah!"

"Now that's an idea," Ah Loke said. "Why didn't I think of it before? I don't want you working in Keong Saik Street when I am in China," she told her younger sister.

And that was how Ah Siew Chay came to work for the Ong family.

Sia Liew made several more trips to the gambling den before her son, Ong Tay Luck, was born. The boy was dubbed "the son who brought silver and gold". When he was born, Sia Liew had won and saved more than one thousand five hundred Straits dollars. A very grand sum in those days.

"What are you going to do with the money?" Ah Siew Chay asked her.

"I shall buy a large piece of gold and keep it for my old age, lor!" Sia Liew answered brightly. She could not buy any gold ornaments and wear them without Madam Geok Neo asking questions about them. Madam Geok Neo respected neither the persons nor the properties of others and she was bound to make enquiries. Sia Liew could not risk this. Besides, her master and spouse, Towkay Ong Ah Buck, had already rewarded her with several gold rings and gold bracelets for giving birth to a son.

"Aiyah, Madam Sia Liew," Ah Siew Chay shook her head. "Please forgive me if I say you do not think fast."

"Think what?"

"Did nae you hear our Towkay Ong sighing these days? He, ah, wants to buy motor buses, right or not?"

"Aye, our Ah Siew Chay, I am not as stupid as you think! I know Towkay Ong wants to buy buses. But I have only one thousand five hundred dollars, ah! A lot of money to us. But what is that to our Towkay Ong?" Sia Liew asked.

"Listen to me," Ah Siew Chay whispered as she sat down beside her young mistress. "I have worked in Keong Saik Street houses for many years. I have seen, ah, how those koo-leongs work and wheedle money and favours out of the men who came to these houses. Be nice to him. Speak softly. Ask him about his business. Show him you also share, ah, his many worries. Rub him a bit. Rub here, rub there and talk to him, mah! Don't be like a piece of wood. Then when he is rested, tell him you want to do business too. Give him your one thousand five hundred. Tell him it is to help him to buy buses. Not enough. Very small sum. But tell him, it is from your heart. I swear he will not forget it."

"How come you know such things about Towkay Ong?"

"Aiyah, Madam Sia Liew! You don't know very much about men, ah! Towkay Ong used to visit the friend of my former mistress, mah!" Ah Siew Chay revealed. "I listened to them, I know. He is a kind man."

"He is good to me," Sia Liew murmured shyly. "Every Lunar New Year, he gives me some money secretly."

"That is why I say he is a good man. Give him your money to help him buy his buses. If he does not treat you even better after that, you can chop off my head, ah!"

When Ah Siew Chay was recalling this part of the story in her old age, she had insisted that Madam Sia Liew, the concubine, had prospered as a result of her advice on how to please men and win their favours, things which she had learnt through serving her former mistress, a well-known call-girl in the notorious Keong Saik Street in the Chinatown of long ago.

There were several faded sepia-coloured prints which showed groups of men, women and children posing in front of a motor bus from the prewar period. There was one photograph of Ong Ah Buck and his four "official" sons. These were the three sons from his marriage to Madam Geok Neo and the son of his concubine. The photograph showed Towkay Ong dressed in a Western suit with bow tie and black leather shoes, looking like an English-educated Baba gentleman entering the world of modern business and industry. He had grown stout and portly with hair thinning at the crown. Madam Geok Neo's three sons stood in a row behind their father. The eldest, Ong Tay Ik, wearing thick glasses, was the scholar in the family and the apple of his mother's eye; son number two, Ong Tay Yee, would soon be a trader, wheeling and dealing in the far-flung islands of Indonesia; and son number three, Ong Tay Sah, became the family's tinker and repairman. And, finally, there was son number six, Ong Tay Luck, the young son of Sia Liew who stood beside his father.

"Why so funny? This jump from three to six?" Suwen asked Ah Siew Chay.

"Aiyah, nobody told you this, ah? Our Madam Geok Neo, up to her dying day, refused to recognise the other sons of Towkay Ong. All by his mistresses outside, mah! There's a son number four and a son number five. But they do nae come to the mansion. I heard from one of the relatives. Aye, they are now businessmen. Doing even better, ah, than Master Tay Luck."

Had the sons not been named in the old peasant way in numerical order, Suwen mused, no one would have known, just by looking at the photographs, that Towkay Ong Ah Buck had more than four sons. But the dialect names of Tay Ik (Number One), Tay Yee (Number Two), Tay Sah (Number Three) and Tay Luck (Number Six) said far more than what was revealed in the picture.

What was also hidden was the strain of rivalry, jealousy and jockeying for influence among the women in Towkay Ong's life. He must have been like the lone cock in the farmyard amidst a harem of hens. Suwen shuddered at the thought as she studied his balding pate.

"It was I who taught Madam Sia Liew how to win the old towkay's heart, ah!" Ah Siew Chay repeated, her mind clear and lucid when recalling the distant past but vague in matters of the present. "You look at these two photographs. Look."

The first one showed Madam Geok Neo's jowly face marred by her harelip. But, nevertheless, she looked resplendent in her silk embroidered jacket and skirt of black silk, her bound feet shod in embroidered shoes.

Her hair was immaculately coiffured and decorated with jade and gold hairpins. She sat on a rosewood chair with hands resting on her lap, exhibiting the jade and diamond rings and her jade and gold bracelets. Standing beside her seated figure was Madam Sia Liew in a simple floral samfoo, looking like a plain countrywoman. The second photograph showed a dramatic change. Madam Geok Neo and Madam Sia Liew were both seated on rosewood chairs like sisters or equals. And what was even more conspicuous was the similarity in their dressing. Both wore the traditional silk samfoo jacket and ankle-length black skirt of Chinese gentlewomen living in China, just before World War II. Suwen noticed that they were even wearing the same number of pearl and diamond necklaces, jade bangles and diamond rings. But Madam Geok Neo's thickset figure looked as if it was suffering from gout and was too heavy to get up without help. Her eyes looked out of the photograph without lustre, staring blankly at a point beyond the camera. In contrast, Madam Sia Liew looked radiant. She had blossomed into a buxom matron.

"When this photograph was taken," Ah Siew Chay said, "our Madam Sia Liew had just given birth to her daughter, May Lan. And ah, as I told her time and time again, our Towkay Ong was kind. He never forgot that Madam Sia Liew, ah, gave him her savings. One thousand five hundred dollars. Not enough to buy a motor bus. But it came from her heart, you say right or not? So he was grateful and gave her many, many gold ornaments, ah!"

"Wah! She must be very happy then. One son, one daughter," Suwen exclaimed, wondering at the same time why she had never heard anyone mention the name May Lan.

"Aye, you can say our Madam Sia Liew was happy here in this picture. The bondmaid was blessed. Aye, if only May Lan did not run off!"

"Why did she run off? Is that why no one talks about her in the family?" Suwen was extremely curious.

"Aiyah, not for me to say! Very long story, ah! She went off with Tay Ik. Joined the koong-chang-tong like him!"

What? Two members of the Ong family had run off into the Malayan jungles to join the Communist Party of Malaya? Now that was something she had not known. Suwen pestered the old amah for her story and dug into the biscuit tin for pictures of those two.

One picture showed a fifteen-year-old girl in the white shirt with metal buttons and pips and white skirt of Yock Eng Girls' Chinese High School. She had straight hair and a dark straight fringe just above her pair of intelligent-looking eyes which gazed out fearlessly at the world. The only surviving photograph of Ong Tay Ik who was many years older than his half-sister, May Lan, was that of an earnest, bespectacled schoolboy in the uniform typical of the Chinese schools of the thirties and forties: white shirt with a row of metal buttons down the shirt front, a metal button on each flap of the shirt pockets and two metal pips on the shoulders in mock military style.

"How did he get involved with the Communists?" Suwen asked Ah Siew Chay.

"Aiyah, that cousin of his, lor! Ong Kim Hock, mah!"

"Uncle Kim Hock? He doesn't look like a Communist."

"Cheh! You, ah! You think people in the koong-chang-tong have special looks, ah?"

But Suwen had met the man several times. Ong Kim Hock, sixtyish and portly, was a businessman operating a chain of Chinese medical halls. He had never struck her as a political fanatic. He was always talking about business, prices of stocks and cars. Very boring, from Suwen's point of view, and she had never exchanged more than a few words with him.

Today, surely, people would find the likes of Ong Kim Hock and Ong Tay

Ik irrelevant and outdated, Suwen mused as she drove down Orchard Road, stopping now and again at the traffic crossings to let the shopping crowds surge across the road. December: the season of annual sales and bargains. Crowds of people rushed from one shopping centre to the next. New shopping centres were always being built and older ones, demolished and rebuilt. No building along Orchard Road would last for a hundred years. Unlike Harrods in London. She thought of the buildings she saw in London and some of its dingy cobbled lanes. The nineteenth century houses. The house of Charles Dickens. Trafalgar Square. The Tower of London. MacKenzie Lane with its cobbled stones in Aberdeen. Its fishermen's pubs along the wharf. Everything had smelt of history. British grandeur lay in the past, ours is in the present, she thought grandly as her eyes swept down Orchard Road. She had been away far too long and had grown up without knowing many things about the island's recent past, she had confessed to Uncle Ong Kim Hock last night. Very wily of her, but that was the only way she could think of to make the old man talk.

"Most people, ah, like this," he'd murmured politely when she called on him. "Sometimes they know, but they don't want to say. Sometimes, it is better not to say so much."

Ong Kim Hock spoke in halting English. He had been educated in the Chinese schools, he told Suwen, and had started to pick up English through the radio when he was in prison.

"How long were you in prison?" she'd asked.

"Five years, eight months and twenty-three days. Not very long."

"Oh, but that's a very long time, Uncle."

The old man shook his head and gave her a self-deprecating smile as if to say that the length of his incarceration should not be a matter of concern or importance.

"Some people in prison longer. A few still inside."

"What did you do inside?"

"I read. I studied English."

"They let you listen to the radio?"

"Ya, but only language lessons," he smiled and averted his eyes to look at her. "I studied Economics."

"The prison authorities gave you books?"

"No, no! My family. Members of my family brought me the books. Every three months. Later. After three, no, more than three years. Then they let us read the newspapers. With some news cut out. Newspapers with many holes. I read that," he laughed a little at the memory.

"Did you get to see or meet your…your…" she was searching for another word other than "prison mates".

"You mean my friends? Those inside with me?"

Suwen nodded. And it did strike her at the time that part of their conversation had been like talking about death without mentioning its name nor dwelling upon one's fear of it. At least that was how she had felt. In all probability, Uncle Ong Kim Hock had not felt anything. He was quite matter-of-fact about the whole thing.

"We were not allowed to meet other prisoners. Only guards and officers. I lived in a cell by myself. Quite dark. My eyes became bad. Very bad lighting," he shook his head. "Then I had an eye disease. They let a doctor see me."

That explained his peculiar squint. One of his eyeballs seemed stationary, showing very little movement. Each time he looked at her, he averted his head and at first, she was under the impression that he simply could not bear to look at others directly in the eye.

Ong Kim Hock was not a frequent visitor at the mansion. Few members of the Ong family wanted to be linked publicly with someone detained for his political activities. Besides, all the older members of the Ong family knew that Madam Geok Neo had cursed Ong Kim Hock with her last breath. The old madam had blamed her nephew for her eldest son's disappearance.

"During the war," Ah Siew Chay told Suwen, "we did nae know. Could be the Japanese soldiers, could be the Communists. Nobody knew. One day, he was gone. Madam Geok Neo asked many people. Gave people money to go find him. Aye, nothing. Nobody heard of Ong Tay Ik. Some people said he changed his name. Aye, now you see why I say, aiyah, our Madam Geok Neo, a towkay's daughter, had a hard life in the end? Fated."

The Medical Hall of a Thousand Fragrances along South Bridge Road had been demolished by the Urban Development Authorities a few years ago. But before its demise, it had been the lifeline to China for the Chinese illiterate like Ah Siew Chay. It had linked the amahs and coolies in Chinatown to their ancestral villages in mainland China. It was their bank, their post office and their clinic, all rolled in one. It was owned by Ong Kim Hock's father. When Ong Kim Hock was a young man in his twenties, he had helped his father run the shop. Ah Siew Chay had used it to send all her parcels, letters and money home. The Chinese medical hall was part of an extensive network of herbal establishments throughout the Nanyang, with connections stretching as far north as Beijing and as far inland as Wuhan and Szechuan. It was the veritable meeting place, not only for amahs and coolies in Singapore, but also for the clerks of Chinese trading houses, the merchants, the shopkeepers, the itinerant traders, members of clan associations and the Chinese press. Proprietors of other Chinese medical halls in towns and villages as far-flung as Surabaya, Jogja and Palembang in Indonesia, and Kota Bahru in Peninsular Malaya would come to the shop to buy their herbs, drink a cuppa with the proprietor and his son, Ong Kim Hock, and collect or pass on the news and gossip of the day. It was a well-known fact in the city that the medical shop was the place to go if one wanted to know about the state of affairs in Beijing, Shanghai or Canton, who was in or who was out of favour with Sun Yat-sen or Chiang Kai-shek or the goings-on of the notables in the Kuomintang or Communist Party. Often the news would reach the medical hall first before it had even reached the desk of the Commissioner of Chinese Affairs in the Straits Settlements.

Behind his beatific smile of the Laughing Buddha, Ong Kim Hock, with smooth round face creased in a smile at all comers into the shop, was an extremely alert young man. He kept his eyes and ears open and was extremely discreet. This latter quality had made him almost indispensable to the important men and leaders in the Chinese community. All sorts of letters and missives passed through his hands; the Chinese-educated as well as the illiterate did not trust the colonial postal services, staffed, at the time, mainly by English-speaking Babas and Indians. Various correspondence and despatches between the heads of the factions, clans and associations were handed to him to be discreetly stuffed into the packets of herbs to escape the detection of the British Special Branch. And the Chinese leaders could rest assured that their directives and the herbs would reach all the towns and villages in the Malay states and the Straits Settlements, wherever there were large communities of Chinese immigrants.

Ong Tay Ik must have been a young man in his twenties when he came under the influence of his older cousin, Ong Kim Hock. The two of them had studied in the same Chinese clan school and had gone on to Chinese High, the premier Chinese school on the island at that time where the Chinese-educated elite were bred and nurtured. They had memorised the same Confucian classics, recited the same patriotic verses in Mandarin and were taught by teachers from mainland China, dedicated to the overthrow of the Western powers and the Japanese devils. They grew up in the belief that they had a duty to save China or Chung-kuo, the Middle Kingdom, which was their beloved motherland and home of their ancestors, great poets and philosophers, decadent emperors and great reformers like Kang Yu-wei and Sun Yat-sen.

Judging from the only photograph of him which had survived the war, Ong Tay Ik was an earnest and idealistic young man, like so many of his generation.

"Our Towkay Ong did nae want to have his pictures in the house, ah!" Ah Siew Chay said. "Madam Geok Neo cried and cried. Very sad day it was for us when we dug a big hole and buried Tay Ik's photographs. Aye, like he was dead."

"Why did the family do that?"

"Oi! Japanese devils! Very cruel! Our Towkay Ong was afraid. He got to think of the rest of the family, mah! If the devils had found out, wah! They would have killed all of us!"

After high school, Ong Tay Ik had to put aside his plan to study in Shanghai. There was a war on in China and the likelihood of a Japanese advance southwards into Thailand and Peninsular Malaya was imminent. Ong Tay Ik got a job with the Chinese press, with some help from his cousin. From December 1941 onwards, he made frequent trips up north as far as

Perlis and Kelantan. The Japanese Imperial Army had already started the bombing of Kelantan. But the people in Singapore were kept in the dark about the extent of the destruction and the confusion reigning in the British forces. It was around this time that Ong Tay Ik was inducted into the Malayan People's Anti-Japanese Army and, through it, the Malayan Communist Party. He acted as Ong Kim Hock's courier, and through his frequent trips he was able to keep various pockets of party members informed.

One can imagine the mixture of helpless fury and frustration which Ong Tay Ik and others like him felt as they watched the Japanese Imperial Army steadily advancing down south after their successful bombing of Kota Bahru. And the Japanese had also managed to sink two prized British warships, the Prince of Wales and the Repulse.

"Just look at those angmoh blockheads! So strong their navy! And still they cannot fight the devils!" Ong Kim Hock raged.

Ong Tay Ik nodded, puffing hard on one of those cheap local cigarettes he had learnt to smoke since joining this "invisible" anti-Japanese force. His dark eyes had grown thoughtful. He did not want the Japs to win this war. But, like Kim Hock, he could not help but feel the gleeful malice of the slave in watching his master's downfall. And as the days sped by, the January communiques of 1942, brought down by their own couriers, were beginning to read like deficit columns for the British forces, all losses and very little gains. But the local English press was puffing up every hit made by a British bomber.

"Pooi!" Ong Kim Hock spat. "Lies! All lies!"

They were standing in the warm shade of a warehouse at the Tanjong Pagar wharf, away from the screaming crowds rushing up the ships.

"The angmohs are pretending to be calm. But look, they are sending their women and children away. As fast as they can. Look. Look at them. Scrambling up the planks like frightened rats!"

"Are they going to lose?" Ong Tay Ik turned to his cousin. The question itself had an incredulous ring. In his mind, the British were still impregnable. "Is defeat possible? I mean...we did not expect this."

"I know. But all things are possible under the heavens," came his cousin's sagacious reply, and with it, his smile of the Laughing Buddha.

Ong Tay Ik gazed at the pinched faces of the white-skinned women hustling their children up the gangplanks of the waiting ships. In the harried days which followed the debacle of the British retreat from Malaya, Tay Ik worked tirelessly, day and night, with Ong Kim Hock and other comrades who did not seem to need more than an hour's sleep. He was hungry for action and consumed by passion. Like many idealistic young Chinese men of his time, he was burning with the passion of youth for the ideals of liberty, fraternity and nationhood. These ideals were so deeply engraved in his heart that, like the Chinese hero, Yue Fei, who had the characters "Spirit of Loyalty and Service to the Nation" carved upon his back by his patriotic mother, Ong Tay Ik's heart grieved for the lost glory of his motherland. This was the China he had read about in the Chinese classics as well as in the writings of modern Chinese thinkers and reformers like Lu Hsun. In joining the Communist Party, he found himself in the thick of things. He collected gossip and information from all manner of sources, sifting the chaff from the grain, and each new day he saw more clearly the stupidity of the British administrators in Singapore. There was utter chaos and confusion in the weeks and months before the surrender of Singapore. Trenches were dug and trenches were filled in various parts of the city. Chinese and Indian coolies were ordered to dig in the sweltering heat while in the municipal offices, under the whirring electric fans, British officials argued and countermanded one another's orders. Ong Tay Ik spat out his disgust.

His thick gob of green phlegm hit the wall of the warehouse and slithered to the ground where it lay sizzling in the noonday heat.

Ong Tay Ik had a head-on clash with his father on the day *The Straits Times* published a report praising Towkay Ong Ah Buck for his generous donation to the British Defence Fund. His half-brother, Ong Tay Luck, had come home excitedly waving a copy of the Chinese newspaper which carried a photograph of Towkay Ong and a translation of the English report.

"Oi! Look! Look! Our Ah Pa is in today's papers!" the young and naïve Ong Tay Luck was stabbing his stubby finger at the picture which showed their father shaking hands with an Englishman. All the women of the household gathered round him. His sister, May Lan, tried to snatch the paper from him.

"Tay Luck, read it to us," Madam Geok Neo ordered.

"Support for War Fund," Tay Luck read in Mandarin. "A very good effort was made by Mr Ong Ah Buck. His transport company, the largest Chinese-owned company on the island, has been a consistent supporter of the government's war fund. Mr Ong has been contributing five dollars for each of the twenty buses owned by his company. This letter which came with his latest cheque expresses regret over his delay in sending his monthly contribution. The delay had been caused by the enemy's bombing and destruction of some of his property."

There was a long moment of silence after Ong Tay Luck had finished reading the report. His stepmother, Madam Geok Neo, his own mother, Madam Sia Liew, and all the servants like Ah Siew Chay had not understood a single word of his beautifully enunciated Mandarin.

"Say again in Hokkien, son," Madam Sia Liew coaxed.

"Aiyah, you read she-sher-she-sher! I did nae understand!" Ah Siew Chay laughed.

"Right! I tell you in Hokkien," Ong Tay Luck who was a natural mimic was only too happy to oblige the womenfolk. He could see that his mother was very proud of him.

"The newspaper says, ah, our father is a patriot," he spoke rapidly in the Hokkien dialect. "A good man, ah! Always gives the angmoh money. The angmoh fight the Jepun people, our father pays them. He gives the angmoh money to buy the war planes and guns, ah!" Then he mimicked his father thanking the British governor in the picture for being so gracious as to accept his small donation. "Our Ah Pa said, ah, aye, thank you so much! It is an honour, an honour, Your Highness, Our Gracious Prince of the island, please to accept my humble sum of money. Not big sum. Just small sum. Right, right," he nodded his head in exactly the same way as Towkay Ong. The women squealed; his mimicry had sent them into fits. Madam Geok Neo, usually stern-faced and dour, laughed till the tears rolled down her face. Madam Sia Liew laughed till she had to hold on to her daughter, May Lan, for support.

The women were in hysterics.

"Our Ah Pa is a fool!" Ong Tay Ik had burst into the room at this juncture. He was waving a copy of the same Chinese daily.

"What do you mean Ah Pa is a fool?" Ong Tay Yee, his second brother, asked. He too had bought a copy of the Chinese newspaper.

"Can't you all see?" Ong Tay Ik asked angrily. "The angmoh dogs are using Ah Pa! It is angmoh propaganda! For their own good! But Ah Pa doesn't know it! But they are using him to show that we Chinese here support them."

"So what is wrong with that? Our Ah Pa gives the angmoh money and they praise him. Fair exchange, mah!" Ong Tay Yee grinned. He was Madam Geok Neo's second son, the one with a sharp eye for business, and not one to delve into the ins and outs or pros and cons of something as complicated as politics. He was very different from the ascetic, scholarly Ong Tay Ik. His philosophy was simple: live and let live; do not peer into the muddy waters.

"Wah-pia! You blockhead! You really think that the angmoh devils care about us, Chinese?" Ong Tay Ik challenged his younger brother, lapsing into the cruder Hokkien dialect the family used at home. "Open your eyes wide, ah! Those angmoh dogs have drugged us, Chinese, with opium! Since the eighteenth century! Stolen our national treasures! Taken our land! Thieves and devils they are! English, German, French or Japanese! What is the difference? All thieves! F--- their mothers' asses all!"

"What? But the angmohs here protect us from the Japanese devils, right?" Ong Tay Luck asked.

"What do you know, boy? Last night, I saw three thousand street watchers take up their posts. All members of the Chinese Mobilisation Council! Any angmoh dogs among them?" Ong Tay Ik asked rhetorically. "Listen, brother! The other day the Governor's house was also bombed. And the next day, I heard him on the radio. He said, his own words, ah! I will stay. We will stay together. Fight together. His very words, ah, in the Chinese report I heard! European and Asiatic together. My wife and I are proud to share your danger and trials. Pooi! You are another fool and stooge! Our Ah Pa is foolish enough! He will land us into trouble one day, I tell you! I know!"

"You son of a bitch! What do you know?" Towkay Ong Ah Buck's face was dark with rage as he fixed his eyes upon his eldest son. He had heard everything from the next room and he could no longer contain himself. "You unfilial dog! I have tasted more salt than you have eaten rice. You are not afraid of being struck by lightning? How dare you talk about me, your father, like this? Your mother did not teach you? You did not learn respect in school? I have not gone to school, ah! But I still know what the saying 'respect your elders' means! Without me, the old fool here!" Towkay Ong struck his breast and glared at his son, "you think you would have the good fortune to go to school? And stuff your head with all these learned rubbish? You think I don't know what you people say about the angmoh dogs? All hot air and talk! So many years the scholars and officials talk! But common people like us starve in China! Bandits rob them! Rich men rape their women! Their fathers and mothers clubbed to death! In front of their eyes! And what do scholars like you do? You stinking fool of a mother's ass!" Towkay Ong banged his fist hard upon the table, a bowl crashed onto the floor. But no one dared to pick up the pieces. "I came here as a young boy. I was safe. I worked my butt off. I built up this family! This business! The angmoh prince honoured me! And you! My flesh and blood laugh at me? You go round this city today. Who will know you? You or me? You all have money and face today because you are my sons! Don't forget this!"

Ong Tay Ik was not cowed by his father's outburst. He knew that, sooner or later, things would come to a head between them. He was not a trader like his brother, Tay Yee. He was not interested in advancing the family's interest and increasing its wealth. His father and brothers had been corrupted by capitalism and, therefore, they did not mind being stooges of the imperialists, he concluded.

"Ah Pa, our people in China are dying. For every inch of earth they wrest from the Japanese devils, they shed an ounce of blood," he began.

"Don't you dare lecture me!" Towkay Ong yelled.

"Ah Pa, I am sorry but I was not lecturing, but..."

"What! This is not lecturing me? Then what is this? Begging me to forgive you? Poo-bor-ah!"

"Our Tay Ik, keep quiet. Please do not talk back to Ah Pa. Please, I beg you," Madam Geok Neo's anguished voice was heard at last. The rest of the family dared not speak.

"Ah Boo, I respect you. And I respect Ah Pa. But times have changed. He must respect my views too."

"F--- your mother! You son of a bloody sow! May the Thunder God strike you!" Towkay Ong swore like a rickshaw coolie, spitting out the same curses which his Hokkien ancestors had used to rave and rant against the misfortunes of life. "Accursed dog! May lightning strike you dead! For turning the heavens upside down, ah! Oi! Oi! You all listen ah! Now a father must respect his son, oi! Now sons are the heavens and parents are the earth! We must listen to our children now! Is this what all that learning has taught you?"

"Ah Pa, please listen..."

"No! You listen! You stinking pup! You think I don't know what you are doing? You go and join those people in the koong-chang-tong! You don't think about this family? And your duty to this family! If the angmoh authorities find out..."

"They will never find out!" Ong Tay Ik replied, perhaps haughtily.

Towkay Ong raised his hand and slapped his son's face. Ong Tay Ik steadied himself against the table. Then he turned and left the room without another word.

But the next morning, Madam Geok Neo rushed out of her bedroom, howling that her son was gone! Clutched in her hand was a hastily scribbled note about "not wanting to put his family in danger". It was signed by Ong Tay Ik and it had the chop of the Malayan People's Anti-Japanese Army. Beneath the chop was a quotation in Chinese which read: "To die for peace and justice of mankind, for national liberation and for a cause is the distinguishing character of the servicemen of the Malayan People's Anti-Japanese Army."

Towkay Ong, in a fit of rage, snatched the note out of his wife's hand and tore it to shreds. "If the Japanese devils find out about this, we will all be dead! The egghead! From today, I have one son less! Burn all his pictures," he ordered his weeping wife.

Ah Siew Chay's eyes were watery as she painfully related how, one by one, Madam Geok Neo lost her sons through the turbulent years of the

Japanese Occupation.

"Those devils took away Towkay Ong's new mansion. Just built. We were all going to move into the new house, ah! For the New Year. Then the war came. Every day the bombs fell. Very frightening. We went to stay on a farm in Yio Chu Kang. Then one day, Master Tay Yee did nae come back. We waited and waited. Towkay Ong looked for him everywhere. Did nae find him. Many months, we waited for some news. Then Cousin Kong found out that the Japanese devils had taken him."

Madam Geok Neo became quite ill during the Japanese Occupation years. She was on the brink of despair and suicide. One year after Master Tay Yee's disappearance, her third son, Master Tay Sah, was killed in a bombing raid. Madam Geok Neo went berserk; she howled and beat her breasts. She clung to one of the legs of the family altar and banged her head against it, rattling the shrines of the ancestral gods.

"Open your eyes, you gods! Open your ears! Aiyah! Why don't you all kill me with a bolt of lightning? Kill me! If I have done wrong, kill me! Don't kill my sons!" she screamed, and went on knocking her head against the altar till she bled. Drops of blood dripped on the floor. When Madam Sia Liew tried to comfort her, she lashed out at her husband's concubine. "You fox-spirit! You witch! Get away from me!" She snatched a bowl of fruit from the altar and hurled it at Madam Sia Liew. "You two-faced snake! Your black heart is happy now! Your son is now the heir!"

"Madam, please, Madam! My son is also your son," Madam Sia Liew tried to console her. "We have been through so many years. What is mine is also yours, mah!"

"Pooi! You sweet-mouthed witch!" she spat into Madam Sia Liew's face. "You have put a curse on my sons and me! You gods, ah! Oh, my father and mother in heaven, ah! Open your eyes and ears! I have three sons! Now I have only one! Protect our Tay Ik, ah! Wherever he is, keep him safe! He is the only one left. If anything should happen to Tay Ik," she sobbed, "that will be the end of this accursed family! The end, ah! The end of our family, ah!"

"Shut your filthy mouth!" Towkay Ong Ah Buck could not take it any longer. His hands were trembling with impotent rage at the war which had already robbed him of two sons. Both were fine young men. And the fate of the third, his eldest whom he had disowned, was unknown. "You are the accursed one, not me! Not this family! You Ongs are cursed! I took your father's surname when I agreed to marry you! But I am still a Lim. My parents sitting on this altar are Lims. We Lims are not cursed! I have many sons! Do you hear me? Tay Luck is here. And I have other sons outside! My flesh and blood! They are not dead! Not dead! Hear me?" He brought down his fist so hard upon the table that the cups and plates rattled.

"I know! You filthy old tortoise! Who doesn't know? Everyone knows about your bastards! Your bitches drop them off everywhere! You wear a green cuckoo cap upon your head! Do you know what people are saying behind your back? That you killed your sons! If not for you, ah! My sons will still be alive! Tay Ik will be here! Not lost out there! I hope, old tortoise, you can sleep at night! I pray to the ancestors, ah! That you can close your eyes at night and not see my dead sons' faces! You have brought this upon us! Upon me! I blame you! I curse you! May you never, never have a good night's sleep!" Madam Geok Neo flung away all notions of wifely respect and duty; she cursed her husband and his mistresses, the tears streaming down her grief-stricken face. "O gods in heaven! O our ancestors of the Ong family! Look at him, ah! He who bears our surname! He has disowned one son and sent two sons to their deaths, ah!" Madam Geok Neo beat her breasts. "Take pity on me, gods in heaven! I have married someone, ah! Someone who wants to play the big and important man, ah! He gave money to the angmoh devils! Who can tell, ah! Maybe the Japanese devils found this out, and now they have taken their revenge! They killed my sons because of their father!"

Towkay Ong Ah Buck rushed forward and gave his wife such a hard slap on the face that the blow sent her sprawling across the floor. For a full minute, no one moved. They were stunned into silence. This had never happened before. Towkay Ong had never raised his hand against the daughter of his benefactor.

Madam Geok Neo let out a howl of anguish. A horrible, almost inhuman cry of pain and anger. Master Tay Luck and his sister, May Lan, tried to help her up. But Madam Geok Neo's body had grown large and heavy over the years, and her small bound feet could hardly support her. She pushed away the children of her husband's concubine, and called all the more loudly upon the gods and ancestral spirits to witness the cruel blow she had received from the ingrate. Before the family's shocked eyes, she knelt in front of the altar and loosened her long grey locks. She flung away her gold hairpins and let her grey hair fall to her waist. She tore off the collar of her samfoo jacket and kowtowed three times to the gods. She knocked her head upon the hard concrete floor and keened sorrowfully for her sons and family. She called their names and wept for the babes she had suckled at birth. She tore open her samfoo jacket and showed the gods upon the altar the pair of withered breasts which her children had sucked dry. She wailed for the sons she had bounced upon her knee and for the young men who had supported her in her old age as she swayed upon her tiny bound feet.

"O gods in heaven have mercy on me! Who will look after me? Who will come when I call? Who knows how I feel?"

Madam Sia Liew knelt and keened with her mistress. But Towkay Ong turned and left the room, taking Master Ong Tay Luck with him. Ong May Lan, a girl of thirteen at the time, rushed out of the room and returned with two cups of tea on a tray. She knelt before the two weeping women.

"First Mother! Mother! You are both my mothers! The one who bore me in her womb and the one who taught me right from wrong! Both are my mothers," she cried. "I will always be a daughter to you both."

The two women clung to her.

Ong May Lan took over the task of running the household from her mother, and with the help of Ah Siew Chay, nursed Madam Geok Neo as well. Madam Sia Liew and Ong Tay Luck had to help Towkay Ong get the motor buses running again. But things were not the same as before. Bombed wreckage blocked the roads. Japanese soldiers were manning the numerous roadblocks and checking the movements of the population. Ration cards were issued to control the distribution and consumption of food. Ong May Lan and Ah Siew Chay joined the queues of women outside the licensed shops, clutching their ration cards to buy their meagre supplies of rice and sugar. In the markets, food prices soared; a bunch of green bananas cost a third of a teacher's pay, and meat was entirely out of the question.

"Only the Japanese soldiers and officers have food to eat," Ong May Lan said.

"Shhh! Keep quiet! You want to die, ah!" Ah Siew Chay scolded her.

The Japanese Military Police, the dreaded Kempeitai, had gone about its business swiftly and silently, striking down the dissenters like Ninja warriors in the night, so that, in a very short time, the entire population knew who was in charge. Ong May Lan and her brother, Ong Tay Luck, had joined several thousands who had lined the roads, watching in wary silence as the last of the British and Eurasian soldiers marched down the hot tarmac road on their way to wartime internment. Stern-faced Japanese soldiers had scanned the impassive faces of the crowds standing stiffly in the noonday heat. As the days dragged into weeks and then months, the Kempeitai tightened its hold upon the city's life. No one dared to breathe a word of protest lest someone else reported him to the Kempeitai. Neighbour turned against neighbour for a pound of pork. The Kempeitai were masters in the art of buying information. According to Ah Siew Chay, a black van would roll down a street slowly, and behind its curtained windows was an informer who might point an accusing finger at another man. And instantly that other man would be plucked out of the crowd and whisked away, never to be seen again.

So most people lived quiet desperate lives, waiting and praying for the end of the war. Towkay Ong, never a strong advocate of dissent anyway, did as he was ordered. When the Japanese authorities ordered him to reopen his motor repair workshops and to keep his buses and lorries running, he did so. When the Japanese Imperial Army ordered him to use his buses to carry its civilian employees from the city to the military camps, he did so too. He was like a man whose life's sap had seeped out of him. Almost overnight, his hair had turned very grey. Gaunt and bent, he went about his work, a stern silent figure who shunned talk. By the second year of the Occupation, many of his cronies had either died, gone missing or gone into hiding. He refused to talk about the sons he had lost and the son he had disowned. In his heart, he clung adamantly to his belief that it was Master Ong Tay Ik's Communist connections which had set the Kempeitai on the trail of his other sons. So Towkay Ong did his best to cultivate Japanese goodwill.

At times, he wondered if his friends and associates had betrayed him. Some of them had gone into hiding in Indonesia. He cursed himself for not following suit when he had the chance. He should have left with them instead of staying on this blasted island, "Syonan!" He spat out the loathed name. His friends had slipped away without a word. So much for their friendship then! The bitter worm of betrayal gnawed at his heart as the Occupation entered its third year. He lived aimlessly from day to day and left the running of his business to Madam Sia Liew and a few trusted workers.

The war years were Madam Sia Liew's good years. She was young and had the energy to see to the nitty-gritty of keeping the business going despite the deprivations of war. When she started, she could not read. But by the end of the first year, she had learnt how to read the accounts with the help of Mr Lau, the accountant. Master Ong Tay Luck also benefited from the Occupation. He grew up quickly during the war years and was a technical wizard without any formal training. He could make worn-out vehicles move again and fashion much-needed spare parts out of old bits of metal and discarded pipes and chains. He kept the buses and lorries running despite the dearth of rubber tyres and petrol. In the second year of the Occupation, a Japanese colonel of the Imperial Army was so impressed with Ong Tay Luck's improvisations that he gave Ong Prosperity Company the contract to service all the army's non-military vehicles. "Because of this, ah, our Ah Pa was not taken in by the Japs, ah! You think they didn't know he licked angmoh boots? And gave large sums of money to them?" Master Ong Tay Luck would ask his audience in later years when he recounted the story of the company's prosperity. Most of what he said could be discounted as speculation based on hindsight. But what was clear to all and sundry was that his connections with the Japanese military had brought the family rice and meat during the lean years of the Occupation. The family was given extra rations of rice and pork for services rendered to the Japanese Imperial Army. Behind many closed doors, it was whispered that the Ong family, like so many immigrant Chinese turncoats in Singapore and Malaysia, were "the wipers of Japanese bottoms", and that was why they could eat any amount of pork while their relatives were dying of malnutrition.

Naturally, nobody said such things openly, and nobody had ever refused the rice which Madam Sia Liew doled out to friends and relatives who came to beg. Towkay Ong Ah Buck did not ask any questions. He ate what was placed in front of him, without seeing, without tasting and without a care for what he ate. Madam Geok Neo was too sick to eat most of the time, and Madam Sia Liew was far too proud of her son to sense that anything could be wrong. The transport company was doing well and the family was eating well, so what could be wrong? The only person who did not touch the rice and the pork was Ong May Lan. The stubborn girl stuck to her diet of potato gruel and tapioca till her face and body grew mealy and bloated, and she was weakened with constant purging. "Fool!" her brother muttered under his breath. He saw no sense in his sister's punitive self-sacrifice. "Do you think the angmohs will thank you? You will be dead before you become a heroine!"

Ong Tay Luck had his father's practical entrepreneurial streak. Rice was rice and profit was profit; where these came from did not matter the least bit to him. One ate to keep oneself alive and one worked to make money, and that was that.

But to his sister, Ong May Lan, the act of eating "Japanese-contaminated rice" was tantamount to an act of betrayal. She would be betraying the lives of thousands of Chinese and non-Chinese who had fought and died to defend their motherland and this island. She had read the books her half-brother, Ong Tay Ik, had left behind. During the long dreary hours, cooped up in the farmhouse in Yio Chu Kang, she struggled to understand the works of Marx and Lenin and the essays of patriotic writers and reformers from Kang Yu-wei to Mao Tse-tung. She thought frequently about her eldest half-brother and the husband of her half-sister who was taken away in the middle of the night. Her eyes reddened and brimmed with tears. Brother Tay Ik was not dead, her young and tender heart cried; he could not be dead! She continued to read his books by candlelight and, gradually, her eyes turned myopic even as her mind and spirit were fired and hammered into steel by the power of the printed word. And she resolved in her young mind to join in the oppressed people's struggle to free the world from the stranglehold of the imperialists. After the war, in the late nineteen fifties, Ong May Lan left home and had not been back since. "She, ah, did nae say a word. But I think she went to join the koong-chang-tong in the jungle, ah," Ah Siew Chay said. And Ong Tay Luck had never discussed his sister's whereabouts with anyone; like any cautious Chinese, he kept whatever he knew in his heart. Not even his wife knew what he thought about his sister.

In the last year of the Occupation, Madam Geok Neo took a turn for the worse and a Chinese physician was called in. The grey old gentleman placed his fingers on her wasted wrist and listened to her pulse for several minutes. She had not been eating and sleeping well; her pulse was faint and she suffered terribly from prolonged coughing. Her cheeks were sunken and there were dark heavy bags beneath her eyes. The physician prescribed a tonic and strengthening soup of herbs. But it was wartime and herbs were scarce.

"Try, Sinseh. Please try and get the herbs," Madam Sia Liew pleaded.

"Aye, Madam, it is the war," Sinseh Lau sighed, gently blowing away the steam before sipping his hot tea. His eyes, which were watery and constantly shifting, had a perpetual indecisive light in them. "Herbs are hard to come by. Not impossible, but very expensive, Madam."

"But what about my First Mother's illness? Is there cause for serious concern, Sinseh?" Ong May Lan asked the physician, using the formal Hokkien dialect to impress upon him the degree of the family's concern for Madam Geok Neo's well-being.

"Aye, Miss Ong, concern. There will always be grounds for concern," Sinseh Lau shook his head gravely, talking in the gentle noncommittal manner which was typical of many in his profession. "We must ease that cough and cool down the fever. I have some herbs left. Not much but I can give them to Madam. Aye, but with no more supplies from China, ahem! They will be costly. Very costly."

"Don't worry, we will pay you for the herbs, Sinseh," Madam Sia Liew assured him.

"No, no, Madam! I am not worried about payment," Sinseh Lau assured her in return, bowing most courteously. "I only meant to let you know the situation. Ahem, as you know, this war is into its third year, and, er, we all need to feed our families. I have five little ones at home. My grandchildren, Madam. Hungry all the time," he laughed nervously and covered his mouth with his hand. Ong May Lan understood his plight at once. The harsh deprivations of the Occupation years had forced the respected physician to beg for his grandchildren. She went into the kitchen and returned with a bag of rice and a slab of salted pork for the poor man.

"Oh thank you, Miss, thank you, thank you!" Sinseh Lau clasped her hands in both his own.

"Sinseh, no need, no need," May Lan murmured, confused and embarrassed by the old doctor's effusion of gratitude. That bag of rice and pork from the loathed enemy for which she had held her brother in contempt would now be used to save some children from hunger.

Three days later, Ong May Lan changed her mind about her brother again and regretted having felt sorry for holding him in contempt. He deserved it.

"Poo-bor-ah! You moronic sow!" Ong Tay Luck yelled at his sister. "Just what did you do? Nothing left! I could have sold that sack of rice for a tidy sum on the black market! And you! Poo-bor-ah! You gave away my rice!"

He would have hit her had not their mother cried out then. The two of them rushed into Madam Geok Neo's room. A serious attack of coughing was making her retch in pain. She was gasping for breath. Madam Sia Liew and Ah Siew Chay were struggling to help her sit up in bed.

They sent for Sinseh Lau but there was little else that he could do for the patient. The high fever was wasting her body and she was declining rapidly. She had been fretting and pining for her sons. There had been no news and she feared that their bodies could be rotting somewhere in the jungles without a proper burial. Whenever she thought about this, large silent tears would roll down her wasted cheeks, and she simply could not understand why her acts of duty as wife and mother had not brought her the blessings of the gods. In all her years as the daughter of a rich towkay, there had been no spiritual anticipation of suffering; she was not prepared for the hard blows which life had dealt her, and she had none of that Buddhist detachment from material life to prepare her for this slow and agonizsng undermining of her hopes and expectations. All she saw, with the uncanny lucidity of the dying, was the unfairness and injustice inherent in life; only the scum and rats could prosper and thrive. She viewed Ong Tay Luck, her concubine's son, with loathing. "Rat!" she hissed. If he and his mother were expecting her to die soon so that they could divide up her wealth, she would keep them waiting for as long as she possibly could! Let the gods send her to hell! She was past caring. All she wanted was that, one day, her husband's concubine and son would suffer terrible deaths! Rage coupled with malicious thoughts and the grip of a high fever had brought an unnatural brightness into her eyes. It gave her the sudden strength to sit up when Towkay Ong Ah Buck came into the room.

"Ha! He's waiting for me to go too!" Madam Geok Neo cried out in her delirium. "To go and leave him everything! My father's wealth! Don't forget! I will take it, ah, with me!" She cursed and swore at the whole family.

It was unbearable. She went on in this state for several days. Dreadful symptoms of her coming dissolution emerged amidst rumours that the Western forces were winning the war at last, and that the hated Japanese invaders would be forced to surrender. This would have been unthinkable three years ago. The family waited with bated breath. Daily, Madam Geok Neo's coughing fits lasted longer and her shortness of breath grew more frequent as her delirium grew worse. Towkay Ong refused to enter the sick room. He seemed to have shrunk and dreaded being left alone at night; Ong Tay Luck had to sleep in the same room with his father.

Just before her death, Madam Geok Neo asked for Ong Kim Hock, her dark malevolent eyes following his every move when he came into the room. She saw not the nephew, linked to her by blood and family ties, but the loathed fiend who had lured her eldest son, Ong Tay Ik, to his death. If not for him, her dark accusing eyes seemed to say, her eldest son would be by her side now. "You, ah! You killed my son!" she gasped, her chest rose and fell with each tortured breath. "I, ah, I will not close my eyes. I, ah, I will take every cent with..." The dying woman could not finish. She fell back suddenly, her hands clutching at the empty air. Her married daughters were hastily summoned into the room. She was convulsed by an indescribable pain just before her breathing ceased.

The next day, when the rest of the family were busy preparing for Madam Geok Neo's funeral, Ong Tay Luck bounded into his father's room. "Ah Pa! Ah Pa! The Japanese devils have surrendered!"

But Towkay Ong Ah Buck did not live to see the end of the war. He had died in his sleep. The whole family was shakened and, hastily, they summoned the temple's priest. Towkay Ong Ah Buck was buried beside his wife, Madam Geok Neo, in a simple funeral in Peck San Teng Cemetery.

PART 7

Brown Eye of History

One day, in a sudden change of mood, Nica turned up at Suwen's garage apartment. And as far as Suwen could tell, Robert Lim had already been relegated to the past. Part of Nica's forgettable past.

"Hey, I don't cling to anyone. Memories are malleable; can be moulded to suit the present. Anyway, I'm here because it's just occurred to me that you might be moving out of this place soon. Right?"

"Yes, but not till next year. After Chinese New Year," Suwen laughed. Nevertheless, she was pleased to see her friend and art mentor again. "So, is that the only wind which blew you here?"

"Ah, you shrewd thing. Frankly, I'm curious. What have you been up to? I'm your art tutor, right? Don't you think you should tell me? I know the Arts Council is planning something big and you're interested, right?"

Unpredictable, blunt and to the point, that was Nica. Suwen settled into the window seat, spread out the photographs and captions she had written before telling her mentor the story of the Ongs.

"I'm exploring the idea of marrying two mediums – the word and the picture – to make art."

"Oh?" Nica had already settled into one of the beanbags scattered about the room. At the same time, she had not failed to note, in her own shrewd way, that Suwen was looking very photogenic on the window seat, a sketchpad propped on her knees. But she was not sketching or drawing. Just talking and looking out of the window at the angsana trees. Sunlight filtering through their foliage. And spread out at her feet, the faded photographs out of a biscuit tin. Fragments of an amah's memories. Of bygone days and of people whom she had never met. Mere shadows of the past. Like wayang kulit. But the figure on the window seat was solid, real and flesh-warm. With a history. Nica studied Suwen's face, the way she would a model for one of her sculptures. She made mental notes of the facial features, glancing up now and then from her beanbag on the floor. The face was attractive, though not pretty. The oval face and full lips hinted at softness and vulnerability. The dark eyes beneath the fringe of straight black hair were constantly shifting from clarity to perplexity as if their owner could not quite make up her mind on their perception of things. The figure resting against the window frame was a curved line at rest, curving inwards, with limbs curled close to the body, the sketchpad propped on the knees like a shield to ward off the outside world. Without looking up at Suwen again, Nica recreated in her mind's eye the softness of the olive-coloured face, the bridge of her nose, the dropped eyelids, the full lips of the closed mouth, the curved spine at rest and the angles of her knees and limbs, propping up the sketchpad to hide from view her small and vulnerable breasts. Suwen was afraid and inward-looking, Nica thought, but pretending that one was a pupa in a cocoon was no help; not if one wanted to be an artist. She waited till Suwen had finished telling her story and they had looked at the photos and read the captions. "What d'you think? Do they make sense?" Suwen asked.

"Sure. You've reduced the entire history of the Ongs into a litany of causes and effects."

That was how Nica had launched her attack on the pupa in the cocoon.

"Why do you say that?"

Suwen looked perplexed. She sounded agitated. She had not expected praise. But she had not expected such harshness either.

"Why not? Other than that bit in the gambling den with Lady Luck, the story is a listing of who did or did not do what! So Madam Sia Liew suffered like a slave. So the gods smiled on her and she prospered in the end. Madam Geok Neo beat and ill-treated her husband's concubine. So she was punished by the gods. Her sons died. Such poetic justice only exists in fairy tales. Anybody's life and history are surely more complex than cause and effect, no?"

"But cause and effect is the easiest framework to handle. Then I know which drawing or photo comes first."

"Right, Su, I know. You can arrange events more coherently within such a framework. But the question is – should artistic convenience override artistic truth?"

"But I wasn't even thinking of such things," Suwen wailed. "I was just simply tracing events in the family. Using whatever I found in Ah Siew Chay's biscuit tin. Not cause and effect, and all that!"

"But it sure came across like that." Nica was beginning to enjoy herself. "Didn't I try to show you once that sequence determines focus? The way you've told it, it does seem as if the towkay's daughter suffered because of her wickedness. And the bondmaid was rewarded with a business and mansion because she had suffered."

"But the gods didn't reward her as such! Towkay Ong did! For all we know, Ah Siew Chay might be right. Madam Sia Liew did well because she'd learnt from Ah Siew Chay how to please old men. All those funny things which prostitutes and mistresses had to do to earn their keep! And then, as you can see, it's not a happily ever after story, what!" Suwen protested. "I mean look at the man! Ong Tay Luck. He was a wretched son! He didn't make his mother happy. He's not making my mother happy. And he's selling off the mansion. The family business is going down the drain because of him!"

"Exactly! I agree, Su, I agree!" Nica laughed; she had succeeded in provoking Suwen who was now seated on the beanbag beside her. "You've just proven me right. There is a cause and effect theme in your storytelling. You yourself just said that your stepfather is the cause of his own bankruptcy. To put it another way – we can say that his profligacy is the cause of his bankruptcy. Oh dear, it even rhymes! What d'you say, eh?"

"I don't know what to say. What can I say anyway?" Suwen was peeved. "You insist on seeing things that way. That wasn't my intention when I arranged the whole stupid thing!"

"Geez! Easily provoked, aren't we?" Nica regarded her protegée with indulgence. "Don't you see? I was just trying to point out that artistic intention cannot determine spectator response. I can read anything into what you draw. That's why I said in one of my talks last year that the picture is superior to the word. If it's good, it strikes you instantly, and it's a medium which gives scope for interpretation and ambiguity. You should just paint or do a montage. Why write at all?"

"No, no, you don't understand, Nica. I, er, I've been thinking about this for some time..."

"Since when?"

"Since, well, er, since our painting trips in Tanjong Pagar."

"What? That long ago?"

"It's not that long ago. But since then, I've been thinking. I'm not sure, but it's just that I'm beginning to feel that the word is as important as the image. I know, you have always said that a good picture is worth a thousand words. But then the word creates the myth, and it's another way of crystallising the past."

"Ah so! That's it. Mark said something like this, didn't he?"

"What? You don't think I can think on my own?"

"C'mon, Su! That's not what I said. You know it. But I do remember Mark reading something about myth and history to us some time back. One of our Saturday nights."

"I can't recall."

"But I can."

Nica had a wicked gleam in her eyes. Her approach to human discomfort was sometimes akin to that of a child who, crouched by the drain, would pick up an ant and pull off one of its tiny legs, just to see how the helpless insect would react. One has to be objective to be an artist, she often told her art students. Objectivity is not the prerogative of the scientist. The artist, too, must study her subject objectively in order to paint it.

She picked up one of Suwen's sketchpads. Scribbled in Mark's scrawl were these words which she read aloud, without looking at Suwen:

> And yet, to be forever
> Trapped in the timeless present,
> With no past
> To set us free,
> With no myth or image
> To sustain us,
> How bare and bald
> Life would be...

"It's Mark's, right?" she asked the still silent form, curled into an even tighter knot on the beanbag beside her. "Mark's back from Bali, you know."

"So?" Suwen looked up.

"Nothing. Just thought you might like to know."

Nica wondered if there was really nothing between the two. Suwen was either being difficult or incredibly shy, or worse – emotionally retarded. Behaving like a shy naïve eighteen-year-old instead of thirty-something-plus! There were plenty of single women like her, thirty or forty-something, silly and prim in their virginal purity: Oh dear me! Really, you know! I don't know about such things. I've never gone all the way with a man. You all must educate me! She had heard one giggly forty-something say. The poor darling, a regular Sunday service churchgoer, probably never knew the difference between petting and f---ing, and was easily shocked at the things the youngsters did nowadays! Nica had no patience with such female dodos. She hoped Suwen was not one of those although she had never heard her talk in such a silly way.

"What're you going to do with this story and these photos in the biscuit tin?"

"Don't know. Maybe a collage or something. Or maybe paintings with stories to tell."

"Paintings with stories? You mean marry the word with the image?"

"Why not? I read somewhere that picture-making is as primeval as word-making. Which came first? Our creation myths or the pictures in the caves of early man? No one will ever know, right?"

"Gosh! What are you doing? Storytelling or painting? Which is which?" Nica asked.

"You know, I've been thinking too, that, that we tend to categorise all the time in Singapore, I mean we like to put things into categories. Must we classify each medium so starkly? I mean why can't I paint and tell the story of the early pioneers at the same time?"

"Sounds like you are doing a propaganda piece. Our Early Pioneers or The Pioneering Ongs."

"Why are you so against it?"

"I'm curious. The Ongs are not even of your blood. So why them?"

"But what's wrong with painting or writing about someone not related to me by blood?"

"Nothing wrong. It's just that if you can paint the Ongs, why not paint others as well? Why the family of a failed towkay? You talk about art being a subjective thing. But this is not subjectivity. Subjectivity implies choice. That you have chosen this among many options. But in this case, you did not exercise choice. You painted this family because it's the only one you happen to know. You happen to have some of their photos. That's all."

"I don't know any other family, Nica."

"So? You can't find out about others? C'mon! Ferret things out from other people. Other races. An artist shouldn't be so myopic and subjective. Art must offer a wider perspective of things in Singapore."

"I don't understand you. You're talking as if you are going to fight me."

"No, no! I don't want to fight with you. What I meant was this. Why paint just a Chinese family if you're talking about pioneers?

"Why not? I'm a Singapore Chinese. What's wrong with painting those I know well? I don't know the other communities so well."

"Well, my dear, and verily, verily, I say unto you," Nica held out her hands in a theatrical gesture and intoned like a priest delivering a sermon, "if you want to enter the kingdom of New Art in Singapore, you will have to paint and reach beyond your ethnic group. Paint those you do not know well, for in learning to paint them or to write about them, you will get to know them better. End of sermon."

"Honestly, I wasn't looking at art that way."

"Very few do. But don't you agree? The Singapore artist must see beyond his clan and his race. Society can be ethnically myopic. But the artist shouldn't. If society looks right, the artist should look left. And then right. And back and front too. To link the past with the future."

"I don't know, Nica. I don't think I understand you completely. My prof in England used to tell us, just paint what your eyes and your heart see."

"Nah! That's a romantic view of art." Nica dismissed it. She had moved away from that ideal, she told Suwen. She was seeking pure form and objectivity in art through intelligent perception; and she had already planned some lectures on Pure Form in Modern Art.

"But some of us are not abstract, not analytical. Please don't forget that," Suwen pleaded. "We need room to grow too. And, and there's nothing wrong, right? Painting coolies and towkays and people like Ong Tay Ik and Ong May Lan."

"I didn't say that it was wrong. It depends on the art form. But why them?"

"They dedicated their lives to the overthrow of the British. They fought for the Communist cause. We don't agree with that, I know. But they passionately believed in what they were doing. For all we know, they could still be in the jungle up north. I was very fascinated with Ong May Lan's story. Ah Siew Chay told me about her. D'you know that she returned to school after the war? Then she became a student leader in the late fifties. In Yock Eng Girls' Chinese High School. The one near Hollywood Cinema. During the Hock Lee Bus riots, she accused her own brother, Ong Tay Luck, and her mother of being corrupt capitalists. She went against her own mother and brother to fight on the side of the workers. It really shocked the family then. She and her fellow students barricaded themselves in school and fought with the police. She had a very colourful life. Later, she was detained by the Special Branch for a year. After her release, she slipped across the Causeway into the

Malayan jungle. No word from her since. She didn't even come back when her mother died. I want to paint her. She's got the kind of commitment we don't see in the English-ed. People like us."

"We're not that stupid. I would never do a thing like that. What for? They lay down their lives for a cause. Then what? People forget about them after a while. Even their own families. They're faggots which history has burnt and turned to dust."

"That's it, you see. People forget them. And, and you talk about looking left. This is looking left, right and front and back. The Ong May Lans and Ong Tay Iks are part of our history. They stand for something, don't they? Like the courage of conviction and self-sacrifice? And they were willing to suffer for their cause."

Suwen found herself arguing with Nica and trying to explain a period of history during which such single-minded dedication to a cause had been the hallmark of a certain type of Chinese education. Chinese students at that time were taught by teachers from China, teachers filled with hate and anger over what the Western powers and Japan had done to the China before Mao. And these teachers had filled their students with the resolve to fight for a motherland which these students had read about in their Chinese books. She had pondered over the value of her own English-stream education. Which was the better of the two? She had had several years in the convent schools and a few more years studying in Britain. But compared to the Ong May Lans in the Chinese stream, she had no political sense and no political will. Beyond a vague desire for a balance of power between the rulers and the ruled, she was contented as long as she was left alone to pursue her own interests. To be left alone, to be as private as she wanted to be. This was the closest to a political statement of sorts which she could come up with if pressed. Group life and the herd instinct scared her.

"I think we've been lucky. The Chinese-ed suffered great pain. Take Sulin, my half-sister. My mother sent her to a Chinese school. Because she didn't want another daughter like me – foreign, she said. Then Sulin went on to Nantah. But after her graduation, she couldn't get a job. She had to work for her father's transport business, and she hated it. But it was either that or be a

Chinese language teacher. And she didn't want to teach. She was very unhappy, and she and I couldn't talk. Not like you and me. She felt inferior to me. Which was ridiculous. She had a Master's in Chinese Lit. Now it's not so bad. She's married and gone to Perth. But before that she was very bitter over Nantah."

"That place was crawling with Communists and their sympathisers. It had to be closed,"

"I know, but it's a case of the mind seeing it but the heart feeling something else, isn't it? We can't get rid of bitterness with reason. Nantah was her alma mater. And even my mother used to boast that when she was a famous opera singer, she'd helped raise funds for the university. It was a big event at that time. You should've read some of the letters I read when I was working part-time at the Economic Research Centre. I remember this one distinctly because it was so poetic and tragic. Wait. Ya, it went something like this: 'It is evening. I walk along the Singapore River and watch the sun set. I think of my aged parents. They have sacrificed so much for me. But I cannot repay them for I have no job. Please, help me get a job, sir. I have thought of committing suicide many times. But I cannot die. My parents are old. They depend on me.' My colleague translated it from the Chinese. We showed it to our boss. He couldn't help. He was just conducting a survey for his PhD thesis and he didn't expect these people to write like this. So the job survey ignored such things."

"Oh dear! You amaze me," Nica said. "Why d'you think of all these things? What for?"

"I don't know."

"That's exactly what I'm afraid of. You don't know."

"What d'you mean?"

"You go and dig up these old ghosts, what for? They're dead!"

"But they were real people once. I would like to paint real people. People with a history, not, not some nameless model who sits for me for a fee. Art devoid of a sense of history is an abstraction, isn't it?" She paused, tentative and waiting, letting this sudden utterance slowly shape itself into a new perception in her mind. She had never consciously thought of art like this before; this was a new thought curling itself round her like a confident lazy cat.

"Having a sense of our country's history means having knowledge of its politics as well, d'you know that? And local artists should stay clear of such things," Nica said.

"Then, if it's going to be like this, we will never be passionately involved with this island. And serious art is about passionate involvement, isn't it?"

"No. Serious artists paint seriously," Nica smiled, her eyes lighting up mischievously again.

"There you go again. Teasing!"

"No, no, sorry lah! I couldn't help smiling. You looked absolutely serious," Nica laughed. Then, looking serious herself, she continued "My dear Su, involvement is a limited commodity. We artists are mortal too, you know. If we get involved in too many things, our art will suffer. Besides, why get involved in things which will land us into trouble?"

"Oh," Suwen was disappointed. "I was right then. We English-ed lack commitment."

"Now you don't have to be so insulting."

Nica was peeved. Suwen had studied abroad. She wasn't here when the government clamped down on university students in the sixties. That was why she was talking like this! She didn't have to go through that period when, except for a loud-mouthed minority on campus, the majority of students avoided political involvement like the plague. The government was young. It needed to prove itself, and some of its VIPs were suffering from paranoia. Every bit of criticism was seen as a cannon blast from the enemy, did you know that? She asked Suwen. Don't rock the boat, the students were warned by their politicians. Be careful. PAP spies everywhere, the students warned one another. So-and-so is on scholarship, probably a party cadre. So she, Nica, had stuck to her books and textbook definitions in History and Political Science classes. She was not a fool. She got high grades. And she stayed away from the loud-mouthed minority which tried to get students like her to take part in current affairs discussions and fight against student apathy!

We are not a political group, the loud-mouths explained. But who would believe them? They discussed Communism and Socialism. And in those days, such discussions outside of tutorials automatically defined one as a political. Stay clear of them, her father had ordered. And, for once, she had agreed with him.

"You haven't the foggiest idea of what the local campus scene was like then! You were blissfully away. You didn't have to breathe in the paranoia. It was in the air. The campus grapevine was full of stories. Some Malaysian students were deported. One lecturer was even forcefully carried across the Causeway when she refused to leave. Then Dr So-and-so's contract was not renewed because of some of his lectures. I didn't know any of these people. I just heard. Which was rumour? Which was fact?"

It had been impossible for students like her to tell rumour from fact. The wisest thing to do was to look out for oneself and to keep one's mouth shut. One knew for a fact though that the PM was intolerant of fools. But the fools themselves gave him plenty to be intolerant of! Suwen was not around to see those fools throwing paper planes in the lecture theatres to express their displeasure with the Admin. Infantile! Those guys in the Students' Union! The PM was right to cut them down to size. And Suwen had not seen what she had witnessed once when the PM cut down a highly respected lecturer and reduced the chap from man-size to mosquito-size at a public forum. It was a terrific piece of theatre, she told Suwen. The public interrogation and debate which followed was at once intimidating and humiliating. Bit by bit, the audience saw how, first, the man's ability to reason and think, then, the man's mawkish sentiments for the unborn, and his questionable loyalty and national identity were ripped from him. And the man was shown to be a quivering, snivelling worm beneath. One month later, the campus grapevine reported that the lecturer had resigned and left the country for good.

"How terrible," Suwen murmured. "This is the first time I've heard about this. Nobody told me. How can the PM do this to the man? And at a public forum some more!"

Nica, however, had no sympathy for the lecturer. The guy was a moron. Only a moron would challenge LKY without doing his homework thoroughly. Know thy enemy. That was her dictum. And knowing full well the kind of temperament the PM had, that lecturer should never have expected anything other than harsh words and hard-headed argument.

"But the stupid man thought he could get away with throwing a verbal Molotov cocktail! Of course, he got a hail of bullets from an M16! What did he expect?"

"You, ah! Really, Nica!" Suwen laughed. "I'd never have thought of describing it like this!"

"Okay, so I exaggerated a bit. But the PM's tough. And we needed a tough guy then," Nica insisted. "D'you remember the riots? How old were you then? I was in Pre-U."

Nica remembered the riots vividly. She was only seventeen when May 13 had exploded on the island's body politic like a pus-filled wound. She was in the back seat of the family car. Her mother was in front, next to her father who was driving them home. Curfew had been imposed and they had just an hour before the next curfew to get home. Her father had stopped at the traffic junction of Aljunied and Macpherson Roads. There were only a few cars and passers-by. All of a sudden, from out of the bushes, an Indian man ran out, bleeding from ugly gashes on his head and arms. He flung his bleeding body upon the car's bonnet. Her mother screamed just as shouts and curses filled the air. Passing cars honked raucously but none stopped. "Go! Chandran! Drive!" her mother screeched at her father, turning away from the ghastly face peering through the windscreen. The screen was splattered with blood. "Drive! Chandran!" Her father gripped the steering wheel. The car jerked forward so suddenly that the bleeding man vaulted across the bonnet. Their car sped down Aljunied Road. She turned back to look. But a gang of Chinese men, armed with iron bars and poles, had already blocked the unfortunate Indian from her view. Meanwhile, her mother was crying hysterically in the car. She remembered vaguely, Nica told Suwen matter-of-factly, that that was the day she had decided that she was neither Chinese nor Indian. She didn't care one way or the other who or what her parents were. Indian or Chinese, it did not matter when humanity itself was so hateful. The spectre of the bleeding man, his look of fear and hate gave her horrible nightmares. The man's screech for help in Tamil had so shaken her father that he became quite ill after that.

"Good grief, I didn't see a thing," Suwen murmured. She spoke like one who had been deprived. "All I heard were stories and rumours. I suppose we were isolated in the mansion. Many relatives stayed with us. Even the families of the maids and our Malay chauffeur. Ahmad even brought his father and mother, his wife, his two brothers and a sister. We felt protected. We had lots to eat. We children had a good time. I must've been fifteen or so, a few years after I left my grandparents' farm, I wasn't aware of anything terrible. My mother was happy; so many relatives, every day they played mahjong. But I remember seeing the PM cry on TV."

"Me too," Nica said. "We were stunned. But my father was the hero in our neighbourhood. We were one of two families with a TV set down our road. He brought out our TV set and put it in the garden so our neighbours could watch too. So every evening, our neighbours, all Chinese, came over to watch TV, curfew or no curfew. Our road was very quiet and peaceful. I don't remember seeing any cops on patrol. All I knew then was that we were a popular family. Everyone in Sennet Estate knew Dr and Mrs Sivalingam. I think we were popular too because we're a mixed family. I think, at the time of the racial riots, our neighbours saw us as a beacon of hope. Just a feeling. What d'you think?"

"I don't know," Suwen shrugged. "I was just thinking how difficult it is to portray what you've told me in art."

"You can't unless you can find a central image."

"I can try. For I really don't see myself painting spring blossoms, peonies and carps."

"Nor me. And no bare bosoms in batik sarongs either, right?"

The two of them had laughed, like kindred spirits with something in common then. Suwen felt it. Like the pull of a magnet for the needle. Was this charisma? She was not sure. But what she was sure of was that the two of them did not believe in painting stereotypes of bare-breasted Asian women to feed the tourist trade.

"That's it, you see," Suwen went on, "I'm neither here nor there. Neither traditional nor avant-garde. Sometimes, I wish I can just arrange a pile of bricks like Carl Andrea, and wait for some dumb museum to buy it."

"Fat hope!" Nica chuckled. Then turning serious again, her dark eyes glowing with intensity, she said to Suwen, "I want to sculpt the male form. In all its ugliness."

The next day, Nica visited her again.

Suwen made two mugs of coffee and handed one to Nica. Outside, it had started to rain again.

"My grandaunt from India will be here this Saturday," Nica said. "She used to live here before the war. One of the very few lady doctors at the time. She was a woman ahead of her time actually; had a mind of her own. During World War II, she fought against the British. She worked for Chandra Bose. You've heard about Chandra Bose? India's freedom fighter. I reckon you'd want to meet her."

"Oh yes! So I can see beyond my community, no?" Suwen smiled her appreciation; she did not doubt that Nica was pushing her to be a better artist.

"But I warn you," Nica was wagging a finger at her, "Mark will be there. He's back."

"So?"

"So? How do I know what's between the two of you?"

"Nothing's between us."

"That's what you say. But you can't fool me, Su," Nica went on in a sing-song voice, teasing her.

"Don't be an ass."

"Why don't you just kiss and make up?"

"Don't be funny!"

"I'm serious, Su. Life's short. Follow your feelings and intuition. That's the kind of path you like."

"And the path you like is teasing me."

Nica took a sip of her coffee and shook her head, "You're scared of your feelings. For a man. Aren't you?"

Suwen's grip on the handle of the coffee mug tightened. Was that a glint of malice lurking behind Nica's dark eyes? Eyes of mischief. Like those of an urchin teasing a hapless kitten. She'd seen such boys poking a half-blind kitten with sticks.

"You're acting silly, avoiding Mark like this," Nica was saying. "You do like him. But you don't want to admit it. Not even to yourself. D'you want to remain a virgin forever or what?"

"Oh, Nica! Must you always bring things down to that level?"

"What level? You talk as if sex is real low-down. We all have feelings and urges. Nothing to be ashamed of!"

Silence.

Nica lit a cigarette, drew it in and blew out smoke rings which wafted lazily through the cool evening air, specks of dust and memories rising. She finished the last of the croissants for tea, downed her coffee and stood up, flicking away some imaginary crumbs.

"Well, the rain's stopped. I must be off. See you on Saturday then."

Suwen cried a little after Nica had left. She did not know why she cried; she felt silly after that. It looked as if she was not only politically ignorant, but also sexually ignorant. Was she stunted as a woman in some ways? Did what happened in her teens make her shrivel up? Or worse still, she had blown things out of proportion; her fears and pain had been born out of a figment of her imagination. All through the week, she could not settle down to anything. Her brush and paints failed to calm her agitated spirit. So there had been an attempt to molest her or worse. But that was in the past. Why was she thinking and worrying about it, just because she was reluctant to meet Mark? What had Mark got to do with it? She waited anxiously for Saturday, dreading its inevitable arrival. Nica had asked far too many questions. The woman had no right! No right, she fumed.

"Go and see a shrink," Nica had said before she left. "Or better still confront your old man or your mother. Don't let them affect your sex life."

But why should she do that sort of thing? Confrontation and putting one's mother in the dock! That's American! It's what American celebrities do to their parents. Bette Davis and Joan Crawford. She was very sure that their daughters did not become the better for it. So why should she subject her mother, a famous Cantonese opera fah-dan to the same fate? Should one establish and publicise one's mother's wrongdoings in order to feel free to fornicate? Was that it? Was that what Nica had wanted her to do? Make it clear, once and for all, that it was actually the insecurity of the mother which had pushed the teenage daughter into the foggy realm of attraction between teenage girl and stepfather? She drew in her breath sharply, tossing and turning in her troubled sleep, and in the lonely silence of the lonelier nights in her garage apartment, with the rain drip-drip-dripping onto her roof, she slowly exhaled the faint possibility that a young and naïve farm girl, crouched in the shadows, watching an old man painting at the foot of the stairs which led to the Nam Sun Hotel, had been drawn to the young man who was in the hotel with her mother. For hours till the sun had set. An eternity of waiting when one was only a pubescent twelve-year-old, alone in a strange town. But that young man in the hotel with her mother had power; and power attracts us as doth the candle the moth. With the blurring of the years, she could not say for certain, with one hundred percent certainty, that her feelings had been daughterly and nothing more. But she was not one of those people who could talk things out in the way social workers and counsellors had urged their clients to do. She was a silent sufferer, not given to confiding things in family or friends, agonising over the past in private or conveniently forgetting about it altogether as if these things had not happened. However, there were things tucked away within one's nocturnal mind, squeezed and hidden in its tiny crevices, those small, very private secrets of girlhood which would make the grown-up woman blush should these furtive feelings and desires creep out surreptitiously into the daylight of one's reason. Like when one was fascinated by the dark curly hairs on a man's chest, the mix of his aftershave and body smells, the manly warmth and push of his body when he touched her during their wrestling and pillow fights. She could feel the burning of her cheeks in the dark of her nightmares and restless nocturnal yearnings. Instinctively, her hands reached up to cup them. "But why are you taking all the flak? Speak up! What are you afraid of?" Nica was her ruthless interrogator, even in her dreams. "Think!" Nica pointed a pistol at her head. Strong arms sheathed in green military fatigues tore off her clothes. "No! No! No!" she cried out in her sleep. She was her mother's daughter. Still Asian enough to believe that children should respect, not strip off, their parents' illusions. Illusions made the past bearable, she was pleading with her tormentors. What was the point of telling one's parents that they were bad parents? So, you beat me; you torture me; you allow others to molest me! May guilt and disquiet accompany you to your grave! Would saying all these words help? She questioned her interrogator. Should she kill her mother with these words? Oh, you ageing opera star! You were on the decline so you clung to him. Years younger than you. Then you used me to anchor his affections for you! What's the point? Her mother was slowly being killed already now that the Ong Mansion had been sold. Only the West relishes sordid confessions and confrontations. People in the East don't! No, they don't! The uniformed women, moving with the blind efficiency of machines, twisted her arms backwards. She fell to her knees and cried out in pain. She pleaded with her tormentors. She could not kill her mother. Her mother needed her, more than anyone else in the world. When her mother was huge and pregnant, when every part of her had swelled and ballooned out like mounds of unsightly flesh, her mother had clung to the man's car. A grey BMW. The man was on his way out to visit his mistress. The man had revved up his engine. But her mother clung on. The car moved forward. Her mother was dragged along the road. She saw her mother drop to the ground in pain. The car drove off. She rushed to her mother's side. "I'm all right, Suwen, I'm all right," her mother said. "I still have you. I have a daughter still." Her mother had clung to her. That same night, she had heard her mother praying to the family gods to bless her with a son.

When Sulin, her half-sister, was born, Suwen had stayed the night in the maternity ward, silently sharing her mother's keen and bitter disappointment.

When Suwen saw Mark in Nica's living room, she knew it was not going to be an easy evening. Among the guests were several artists she had met before, as well as the usual Saturday evening crowd. As she nodded and smiled her way across the room, she had the illusion of meeting several pairs of veiled eyes, discreetly shaded to mask any obvious curiosity about the sari-clad figure in the armchair.

Nica introduced her to her grandaunt, Dr Susantha Menon, and she shook hands briefly with the frail old lady. Mark came over and said hello; then Nica called him away to help with the drinks. She sat on the sofa with Jan and Zul.

"Zul is going to interview Dr Menon tomorrow," Jan whispered.

"I'm sure you're happy to be back in Singapore after so many years," Naidu, a regular in the Saturday group, said.

"Oh yes, I'm happy to be back, of course. To see my family and friends. But I can't recognise many of the old places."

"How d'you feel about Singapore now?" Jan asked.

"Oh, my feelings about Singapore are mixed," Dr Menon told them in her strong Indian-accented English.

Sounding almost like a character out of a Narayan novel, Mark thought as he tried to catch Suwen's eye. He wondered if he should have called her earlier and offered her a lift, and toyed with the idea of asking her out after the night. Nica would approve; she had been very attentive all week. He could not resist her invitation to come and meet her grandaunt. A woman who had actually helped to train a regiment of Indian women to fight the British in World War II. Meeting the old lady this evening had upset all his impressions of dusky demure ladies in saris during the time of the British Raj. He simply could not imagine now how this soft-voiced, silvery-haired lady with such fine smiling wrinkles and those thick bifocals could ever have been an army captain. Mark was held by her dark-grey eyes which were bright and alert as a sparrow's and openly curious about the people in the room with her.

"Singapore has certainly changed. Almost beyond recognition," Dr Menon was telling the group. "When I was living here, before the war, we didn't mix this much. Oh no, the different races lived quite separate lives. Apart, with very little contact."

The thick bifocals turned towards Mark; he smiled at them and glanced round the room of Asian faces: Suwen, Nica, Jan, Zul, Naidu, Bob Tan, Dave Wong, Michelle D'Souza, a blur of faces.

"The first thing that struck me about Singapore now is the number of young people like you. All different. Sharing a common history," Dr Menon went on.

"Except Mark, Auntie," Nica quipped: "He's British. From the other side."

Mark shrugged and shook his head amidst the laughter. One had regrets about one's country's past, but it was not of one's making. Should one apologise for one's country? For its greed and stupidity? Before he came out here, the British Council chap who met him briefly had advised him to watch out for some of the locals who were, well, one might say, sensitive. Politics, race, language and religion, particularly politics, were things one would do well to keep out of. One should never be seen to be meddling in their local affairs, the bald-headed guy had advised him. No point in antagonising the authorities. They had no qualms about throwing out journalists who misbehaved, blacklisting the media and labelling others as "undesirable". Very draconian measures indeed, the bald man had rubbed his nose as though he were delivering a half-apology. But there wasn't anything which anyone could do really; the island is an independent nation, he went on to explain, and one had to respect one's neighbour. Certainly, it was quite different from what it used to be when Singapore was part of the myth of British invulnerability and empire. Colonial society on the island had been highly stratified then, he had read in Noel Barber's book. Even though it had been described somewhat ironically as "an arsenal of democracy" in which:

> The British were the highest in Singapore's caste system. The lowest were the 12,000 Eurasians, products of liaisons between Europeans and Asiatics such as English and Chinese, Dutch and Malays, known contemptuously by the same word used for a small whisky – a stengah or "half". Whatever his qualifications, an Eurasian could never hope to earn more than half the salary of a European. The only exceptions were the Babas, for more than a century the favourite "children" of Britain.

If that was indeed a fact of the colonial past created by those bloody English snobs, thank God for the present, the Scottish side of Mark exclaimed, and Nica whispered into his ear, while helping him with the drinks, that the

Eurasian community had produced some of the best legal and medical minds on the island.

"Singapore must seem strange to you now," Mark said politely to the old lady as he handed her a glass of juice.

Dr Susantha Menon looked out of the window of her grandniece's apartment, the towering blocks of offices and flats glowing in the distance.

"Singapore is a very new and very young nation," she paused, looked at the faces before her, and added, "and very brave too. Every major community is represented in your government." She turned to Jan and Zul. "You're a very lucky people. I don't see that happening in India and Sri Lanka in my lifetime." An almost inaudible sigh escaped her lips before she turned to Zul again, who was writing a feature on her for his paper. "During my younger days, it would have been unthinkable for a Malay to marry a Chinese, or a Chinese to marry a Malay. He would be ostracised by his community. So I was very pleasantly surprised this morning when Nica took me to the Cricket Club for lunch. I was amazed by the changes in your society. Nica introduced me to two lovely Chinese women. Mrs Fernando, wife of a Eurasian judge, and Mrs Sandosham, wife of an Indian lawyer. Then Nica said to me, look over there, Auntie, Mrs Mah and Mrs Tay. I looked, and she said, no, no, Auntie. Not the Chinese women. Over there, the other side, the two Caucasians talking to the Indian lady by the window. And she introduced the Indian lady as Mrs Natalie Tan, and the Caucasians as Mrs Mah and Mrs Tay. Imagine this old lady's surprise and amazement!"

Delight and laughter ran round the room. "Yeah, Auntie, we Chindians and Eurasians will change the world!" Nica quipped.

"Chindians?" Mark was puzzled, and so was Dr Menon.

"Oh ya, I forgot. That's the term we give ourselves, Chinese-Indian or Indian-Chinese. People like me," Nica grinned. Her grandaunt smiled indulgently at the young people.

"Dr Menon, why don't you tell us about your wartime activities?" Zul asked.

"Please call me Aunt Susantha if you like, I stopped practising many years ago."

"Nica said you had a clinic in Serangoon Road."

"Yes, I had my practice in Little India and my best friend, Dr Letchmi, had her practice in Geylang. Letchmi knew Dr Chandra Bose, the Indian nationalist leader. She was the one who got me interested. She was young and idealistic. And so were many of us. We all wanted to do something for India. Free our country from British rule. We had meetings and talks in each other's clinics. All girls. We'd read about Gandhi, Nehru and Bose. For many, many months after the war broke out in Europe, the Indians here were worried about a possible Japanese invasion. Many families sent their women and children back to India. Indian men who'd worked for the British talked about quitting the service. I remember I was sort of vacillating. Letchmi and I. We'd been educated in schools run by the English missionaries. Very decent people. I grew up with the ideals of noblesse oblige, fair play and loyalty. My father too had been reluctant to abandon ship so hastily. But I changed my mind the night I accompanied my father to the Governor's ball held in the Raffles Hotel."

Dr Menon pursed her thin lips and Zul saw the fleeting look of displeasure, or was it disdain, in her eyes.

"My father, Dr K Menon, was head of the surgery unit in St Andrew's Hospital. I can still remember that night at the Raffles. The last ball before the Japanese came. Raffles Hotel was a blaze of lights. The British still believed that all would be well. There were lights among the palms and bougainvillea bushes, and two rows of Malay and Indian constables in splendid khaki uniforms. They were lined up along the driveway, standing rigidly, to wait for the Governor and his party to arrive. There were many guests inside the hotel. As usual, they stood together with their own kind. Can you imagine Singapore colonial society standing under the glittering chandeliers of Raffles Hotel?" Dr Susantha Menon laughed at the memory. "There we were, Asians and Caucasians, as divided as Sir Stamford Raffles had wanted us to be. Didn't the great man allot Little India to the Indians, Chinatown to the Chinese, Geylang Serai to the Malays and the choicest acres of Tanglin and Queen Astrid Park to the English?"

As her grandaunt talked on, Nica could almost see with the clairvoyant clarity of the artist, the Raffles ballroom in 1940.

Her great granduncle, Dr K Menon, had bowed to the English lady on the other side of the room. The blond-haired woman had acknowledged it with an imperceptible nod. A slight inclination of the head and she had moved away.

"Whew! I need air, David. There're just too many of them in the same room."

"Sarah, please!" her husband hissed. "This is the Governor's ball. Do mind what you say."

"But I can't help it, darling, if my nostrils do act up a bit. They are of a delicate nature."

"Well, old chap! Where've you been? Haven't seen much of you at the club lately," Mr Elliot, the Under-Secretary for Commercial Affairs greeted David Richardson and his wife. David was from Bower and Scott Trading with offices in Hong Kong and Shanghai, Buck Buckeridge of the Singapore Fire Services joined them.

"Hello, Buck. What's this I hear about an auxiliary fire service?"

"That's the AFS, sir. Mostly volunteers."

On the other side of the ballroom, Colin Mason, the assistant editor of *The Malayan Tribune*, was passing his tin of Players round a group of Asians. Ha'aji Yaacob, the representative of the Malay and Arab traders, politely declined the Englishman's offer of cigarettes. Colin nodded amiably and moved on. He was a rare breed. In the ten years since he had been there, he had made it his business to know everyone and mingle with them. Damn the blokes at the club. He knew that, even though those blokes were sticky about the club rules and had insisted that he should resign from the Tanglin Club when he married Abigail, they were secretly envious of him. Abigail, born of a Portuguese father and a Siamese mother, was not only a beauty, but a good wife and mother as well. Those dowdy matrons and their sods could have Tanglin for all he cared!

In the meantime, Mr Thiagarah was shaking hands with Ha'aji Yaacob. But once the social obligations and exchange of pleasantries were over, each walked back to his own group. Mr Thiagarah joined Mr Krishnan, president of the Indian Association of Traders and Merchants, and Mr Govindasamy, the proprietor of a major textile trading company in Serangoon Road.

"Are you sending your families back on the next boat?" he asked the two men in Tamil.

"These are restless times, Mr Thiagarah. My wife and children will be safer in my father-in-law's village," Mr Krishnan said. "I've booked their passage."

"I hear the whites are also sending their women and children home to England. In fact, many have already gone," Mr Thiagarah pulled at his tie. The crowded ballroom was warm despite the whirring electric fans above them. People spilt into the garden and courtyard.

Just behind them, the distinguished-looking Mr Sequiera, a descendant of one of the famous Portuguese conquerors of Malacca, was heard saying, "Don't worry. Churchill will keep his word. England will protect us. She has guaranteed our safety." Then lowering his voice dramatically, he winked at Colin Mason. "I took the liberty of glancing at this morning's dispatch."

In those anxious times, such an indiscreet admission was forgiven and welcomed, for the colony was hungry for news. And as the assistant to the Postmaster General, the Eurasian was an important source of news and rumours about the decisions taken in Whitehall.

The young and attractive Dr Susantha Menon stood close by the side of her father, feeling a little out of place in the glitter and pomp of British officialdom. Everyone seemed to look uncomfortable and tried their best to hide it. Over at one corner, near the entrance, were the Chinese men, many of them in ill-fitting suits and bow ties.

"That's the group from the traders. They can't speak English. The Chinese lawyers over there are the ones who speak English fluently," Dr K Menon told his daughter.

The young Dr Susantha Menon noticed that, except for a few gadflies like Colin Mason and Mr Sequiera, few guests left their ethnic groups for long.

"My dear chappie," a small dark-haired man slapped the arm of the Lieutenant-Colonel from the RAF. "The Nazis will go through the whole of

Europe like a hot knife through butter, is that not so?"

"Mr Rafaella, the borders of Italy are closed. Our chaps are monitoring the situation," the English officer replied stiffly.

"But what about this yellow peril in the East?" Mrs Richardson asked the two men in a shrill voice fraught with anxiety.

Her husband should strangle her for shaming him like this, Susantha Menon thought savagely. She had noticed that the group of Chinese barristers was listening with obvious discomfort over Mrs Richardson's phrase "yellow peril". The whole room had heard her.

"What's your assessment, old chap?" the irrepressible Italian trader asked.

"Yes, Lieutenant-Colonel, how safe are we?" Sarah Richardson demanded.

"Well, Mrs Richardson, I dare say this island is very well fortified. We have nothing to fear. I wouldn't go so far as to say like the rest of them over at the club who claim we are impregnable. But if, in the remote likelihood of those Japs coming and banging at us head-on, they are going to end up with some pretty sore heads."

The group round the Lieutenant-Colonel, which had swelled by now, laughed heartily at his picture of Japanese defeat.

"You're damn right, sir. We're near impregnable. What with those two battle cruisers on the way and all," Mr Richardson joined his wife. "That's what I keep telling Sarah here. We have nothing to fear. Two of the best battle cruisers will be sent out here to protect us, I hear."

The Lieutenant-Colonel nodded, and the company was visibly cheered by his confirmation of this piece of good news.

Outside, the band had struck up. A whisper ran round the room that Sir Shenton and his wife had arrived. Groups separated and rearranged themselves. The Caucasian women patted their hair and the men straightened themselves. The Asians crowded to one side of the ballroom until a red carpeted aisle separated them from those with pale skins. Susantha Menon watched with great amusement as the hotel's Hainanese waiters scurried round the room, whisking away the half-empty glasses left at the corners of the banqueting table. Only the English, other Caucasians and a sprinkling of Asian dignitaries had been invited to the banquet. The rest of the Asian crowd would have to content themselves with the singular honour of shaking the Governor's hand, after which they must politely take their leave.

Dr Susantha Menon was standing just outside the anteroom reserved for members of the press corps. Colin Mason and several English reporters were at the bar. The Asian reporters who did not drink generally and who were not offered any had moved away from the bar. They stood, bunched together, waiting, but not talking, for there was no common tongue among them. Susantha Menon knew that the British colonial administration was not what it appeared to be; it was manipulative. It had encouraged the growth of the vernacular press, by which term they meant the Malay, Tamil and Chinese newspapers, because they gave the colonial government a hint of what "the ground" felt.

She noticed that Mr Naidu from the Tamil press was skirting apologetically round the English reporters at the bar. Colin Mason finally noticed him.

"Naidu chap, what is it?"

"Ahem," Mr Naidu coughed and apologised for the intrusion. "Bad throat, sir. But I overheard, eh, one of you, gentlemen, one of you had mentioned Dr Chandra Bose."

"Well, what about it?" one of the Englishmen asked him irritably.

"I say, I say! The Bose fella? Captain from the Indian Army. Up to no bloody good, he and his kind!" one of the red-faced guzzlers told the group.

A second fattish face, pallid and simmering like a milk pudding over a slow flame, nodded his agreement. Several meat-red faces hovered round Mr Naidu.

"That lackey isha ridiculoush asha that shalf-naked fella whash-hish-name!"

"Gandhi," Colin Mason supplied the name.

Mr Naidu left the press room without another word.

"And so did I," Dr Susantha Menon told the group gathered round her. The old lady's eyes flared up momentarily before her fine wrinkles spread and fanned out in a smile. "Dr Bose was a very charismatic leader and a fiery speaker. So when Dr Letchmi told me that he'd asked her to lead the Rani of Jhansi regiment, I joined too. We were one thousand strong."

"D'you think, er, you did the right thing, Auntie? I mean," Suwen, feeling Mark's eyes on her, struggled for the words, not wishing to give offence. "I mean I remember reading in a history book, a reference to Chandra Bose. It, er, it wasn't at all flattering."

Dr Susantha Menon smiled and turned to look at Mark pointedly. "To be sure, girl, how could it be otherwise? History of the war had been written by the English."

Mark nodded his agreement, without taking his eyes off Suwen. She had refused to meet his eye throughout the talk.

"But to answer the question on everyone's mind," Dr Susantha continued, "yes, I did the right thing. Collaborating with the Japanese was a political convenience. My aim was to help free my country, India."

"My professor in Columbia was a great fan of Mark Twain," Zul said, "and he used to quote this: 'the very ink with which all history is written is merely fluid prejudice.'"

"I don't get it," Suwen looked at him.

She had left Nica's apartment with Jan and Zul, leaving the party earlier than the other guests; Zul because of the article he had to write for his paper the next day, Jan because of Zul, and Suwen left because she didn't want to leave the party with Mark. Not tonight, she thought, she wasn't ready; what it was that she feared if she were alone with Mark, she could not say. But she did not want any surprises, she told herself. If she was being unfair to Mark, she was sorry; she'd seen the way he'd tried to catch her eye and knew, with a heart which skipped several beats, that he did have some feelings for her.

"During Dr Menon's time, protecting the British Empire equalled fighting for freedom, fighting against the Japanese," Zul tried to explain. "In World War II, I think, if you fought against the British, you would be seen as a traitor."

"Even though you were fighting to free your country from being a British colony?" Jan asked.

"Yes, even that."

"But Dr Menon looked so serene, so at peace, when she answered your question, Zul. I think she really and truly believes that she and her friends did the right thing," Suwen said. "But I must admit it did shock me a little, you know. Especially when she was describing how her regiment had sabotaged the British Army supply lines. Shocking!"

"It shocks us now," Jan added, "but at that time, they were fighting for the independence of India, and Japan was an ally. Their ally."

"I know, but why ally with Japan? Lots of Indians here fought the Japanese. There was a regiment with Sikhs and Rajputs, I think. And, her actions shocked me because I know about the terrible things Japanese soldiers did," Suwen pointed out, recalling the stories of the dreaded Kempeitai. The Ong family had lost two sons and a son-in-law because of them.

"Actually, if we look at it from the point of view of the nationalist movements, Gandhi, Nehru and Chandra Bose had one thing in common. They all wanted Indian independence. The only difference is that Chandra Bose used Japan and Nehru used Britain," Zul said.

"Ya, I suppose so. If Japan had won the war..."

"Chandra Bose would've become the first PM of India instead of Nehru. Right, Zul?" Jan asked.

Suwen saw the look of understanding which had passed between Jan and Zul. She saw her friend's glowing face and envied her happiness. Jan was happy despite the thousand and one changes and adjustments she had to make. Was Jan being too accommodating so early in the relationship? Suwen wondered. Jan was even going for religious classes at the Muslim Converts' Association and she wondered if Jan's approach to religion was not one of utility rather than of faith. But, she quickly corrected herself, who was she to judge? Faith is a matter solely between oneself and the Almighty.

"Most of the accounts of the war here, in Southeast Asia, were written by Westerners. Australian POWs," Zul was saying as they got into his car and drove off in the direction of the Botanic Gardens. "And because the Western powers were the winners of World War II," he continued in the voice of a Political Science student at a debate, "and because they ended the Japanese Occupation of Southeast Asia, we regard them with more kindness. This is not wrong. But we forget sometimes that the British and the powerful American media had shaped the way we looked at the war and the role of the Westerners.

The way they conducted the war here."

Zul revealed that his aged father had entrusted him with his private papers, written in Malay, a veritable record of his father's work and observations.

"My father had always wanted to write a book about his wartime experiences. But he never got started. He told me in hospital last week that Allah in His Infinite Wisdom guided him to do other things. Like bringing up his children properly."

"Why don't you translate some of these papers into English and get them published?" Suwen asked.

"Ya, why not do it, Zul? Bapak is too ill to do it now. Why don't you write a story on him or something? Like the one you're doing on Dr Menon," Jan added.

However, Zul found out that it was much easier to write about others than to write about one's parent. So, it wasn't until one year after the death of his father that Zul wrote a story for the papers entitled "Notes for a History Book which Never got Written".

NOTES FOR A HISTORY BOOK WHICH NEVER GOT WRITTEN

My father had always wanted to write a book on the Japanese Occupation from the point of view of a Singaporean Malay, but he never got down to it. He told me that Allah in His Infinite Wisdom had guided him to other tasks. However, he was disturbed by the stream of popular books and films by Westerners in which the British and Americans, naturally, took centre stage. "What about us?" my father asked. "In these American and British books, you get the impression that we, Asians, except for the Japs, were just bodies. Masses of bodies killed and maimed. Caught in the crossfire of war because we happened to be there. An island on which the British wanted to stake their reputation. Singapore, the impregnable fortress of the British in the Far East!" My father's indignation and disillusionment increased with his years. As a young man, he had been inclined to view the British more kindly than me. He saw them as the protector of the special rights of the Malays. As he grew older, however, and as he read more widely, he began to see more clearly

British machinations and manipulations of the Malay sultans and their people. He wrote several articles for the Malay press, one of which I have reproduced below:

> Not only were we, Malays, taken in, but English-educated Indians and Chinese alike had tended to view the British colonial rulers more kindly than their Dutch or French counterparts. Most people of my generation think that the British colonial government was not a bad one; at least, it was fair and just. They gave us a good civil service and a sound education system, unlike the French and Dutch colonial governments. But, lately, my eyes have opened wider and, like a frog hopping out of the well, I have begun to see more things as I begin to read the official documents of the war years.
>
> What my old eyes see is that throughout the history of their presence in Southeast Asia, the Portuguese, Dutch, British and, later, the Americans, were colonial and imperial powers first (self-serving and looking after their own people first) and humanitarian governments second. This is inevitable for it is the nature of imperialism.
>
> I do not wish to be discourteous to the British. If the reader would read the following extracts, he will conclude like me that the British cared more for their own honour than for anything else in Asia.
>
> 10 Feb 1942 – Cable from Churchill to General Sir Archibald Wavell, Supreme Commander of All Allied Forces in the Southwest Pacific: "There must at this stage be no thought of saving troops or sparing the population. The battle must be fought to the bitter end at all costs...The honour of the British Empire and of the British Army is at stake."
>
> Wavell's Special Order of the Day: "Our whole fighting reputation is at stake and the honour of the British Empire...There must be no thought of sparing the troops or civilian population, and no mercy shown to weakness in any shape or form."

I humbly beg the reader to see that British honour and the British Empire came first, British lives came second and our safety and well-being came a poor third.

In January 1942 I saw, with my own eyes, hordes of British men, women and children leaving these shores. It is also true, of course, that many chose to remain on this island and other parts of Malaya. But by 1942, literally thousands of British civilians had left us. Then I found out, years later, that when London was bombed by the Germans, the English people had air raid shelters and English children were sent away into the countryside accompanied by their teachers.

We Asians in Singapore and Malaya had no such shelters. When the Japanese bombed Penang and Singapore, there were no air raid shelters. We had nothing to help us cope with the thousands dead and wounded. The bombing killed thousands of us, and disease took another hundreds of thousands. General Sir Lewis Heath, the man responsible for the defence of Malaya, north of Johore, ordered a complete evacuation of all Europeans; women and children first, secretly in the dead of the night, hoping that the Asian people would not know about it. But we knew. My friends and I in the newspapers knew about this. And as Allah is my witness, there was nothing we could do about it. We knew we would have to fend for ourselves.

I remember a radio broadcast by Sir Shenton Thomas, the Governor of Singapore then: "Let not the Asiatic population of this island imagine that one day they will find themselves abandoned."

We did not have to imagine it. We saw it with our own eyes!

My honoured readers may have studied history, but I think not many people know that just before the fall of Singapore, with the Japanese less than thirty miles away, the colonial authorities in Singapore were still haggling with officials in London over how much to pay our labourers employed in building defence works! Do you think that if we had had our own Prime Minister at the time, say, Lee Kuan Yew, he would have allowed this to happen?

Today, thirty years after the fall of Singapore, we Singaporeans should not take our independence for granted. May Allah in His Mercy and Kindness continue to guide us!

Hussein b Abdul Rahman
February 1972

My father used the war and its stories to teach his family the lessons of life. But of all the stories he told us, two have left their indelible marks on me. At the time, when my father was alive, I did not pay much attention to his stories, partly because he tended to ramble, and partly because I was impatient, being young, healthy and full of vitality. I had wanted to get on, into the future, rather than dwell on the past. The final lesson which my father taught me is that regret, when it comes, is always too late. So all I can do now is to share his stories with others.

Ah Hock

My father and his cousin, Fuad, rescued Ah Hock during an air raid. My father and Cousin Fuad were cycling home, going down Geylang Road in the direction of Geylang Serai. It was a hot and dusty afternoon. February had brought a dry and dusty heat to the city. For days, the sun had shone with no sign of rain. The grass by the roadside had turned brown and withered in its blazing heat. Geylang Road was clogged with vehicles and the traffic was chaotic. At the junction of Geylang Road and Aljunied Road, my father and Fuad had waded into a sea of people moving into the city or moving out of the city. Some were moving their families to the suburbs and others from the suburbs were moving into town. Rumours were rife. All the roads and lanes were jammed with wounded and dishevelled Indian and British troops. A fire engine came down the road, clanging helplessly, but none of the cars and lorries made way for it. It was each man for himself. Some people shouted that Indian troops were fighting the Japs along Upper Paya Lebar Road, and that the Malay Regiment had lost the battle in Pasir Panjang. There was chaos everywhere. People did not know which way to run. Sikh soldiers were clattering down the roads in light armoured tanks. My father heard gunfire.

Their way back to the kampong in Geylang Serai was blocked by debris, sandbags and hundreds of abandoned vehicles. Crowds of people on the roads were blocking traffic. The sudden wail of an air raid siren sent people screaming and running in all directions. Fuad and my father abandoned their bicycles and dashed for shelter. But my father fell. It was as if the sun had dropped out of the sky and he sank into darkness. When he regained consciousness, he found that he was lying underneath a Chinese man.

That man was Ah Hock. He had been hit by shrapnel and was bleeding profusely. My father and Fuad helped him up and took him home.

"Telima kasih, telima kasih," Ah Hock cried when he woke up after a long sleep.

"Boleh cakap Melayu?" my father asked.

"Sikit boleh, sikit, sikit!"

My father spoke to Ah Hock quietly in pasar Malay, I think, and as I imagine the scene now, I believe that it must have dawned on my father then that the essence of our communication lies not so much in words as in the feelings behind the words. "Hati yang baik." My father's kindly look and tone were received with gratitude; Ah Hock grasped his hand and murmured, "Telima kasih" over and over again, mispronouncing his Malay words and getting the intonation all wrong. However, that did not bother my father. Neither did it bother Ah Hock that my father's Hokkien had sounded terrible. Their feelings of sympathy as fellow sufferers gave their words a force which accurate pronunciation could never have.

After the war, Ah Hock returned to the kampong with two chickens and a big basket of fruit to thank my father for giving him food and shelter during the war. Thereafter, Uncle Ah Hock visited us every year, even in that year when we had the racial riots. Uncle Ah Hock spoke to my father in a rojak of broken Malay, pasar Malay and Hokkien all his life. He was not a highly educated man, and I suspect he was only semi-literate even in Chinese, However, he was a courageous and sincere man who did not let the strong hostility of his own community during the May 13 riots affect his relations with my father and Fuad. I remember that my father was very happy when Uncle Ah Hock came that year after the riots. He kept saying over and over again, "*Kalau benih yang baik, jatoh ke laut menjadi pulau.*" (If good seed in the ocean fall, an island will spring withal.) For no matter where the seed is sown, good blood will come into its own. And in my father's eyes, Uncle Ah Hock was a good seed.

My father also tried to teach us patience, tolerance and respect for others. "These things helped Tok to look after his kampong people during the war," he told us.

Tok, my grandfather, was the penghulu or headman of the village in Geylang Serai in 1941. At that time, my father, who was the only English-educated young man in the kampong, felt that he should help Tok. The villagers looked to their penghulu for advice and help to settle every conceivable problem. Life was hard and meagre that year. The British and Europeans were leaving Singapore by the thousands. Jobs were scarce; many had lost their jobs as gardeners and drivers. The mood that year was one of resignation. My father was also worried about whether the Japs would respect Tok.

"Think of Tok," my father said. "Look at the way he used to dress. Cheap cotton singlet and green checked sarong. And on his head a white cotton skull cap. For us, that is the sign of one who has been on the Haj, but to the Japs, it was nothing. In their eyes, Tok was just a poor Malay man."

But my grandfather was respected by his villagers. He was also respected by his children. He was a stern and strict father. For example, he rarely used the term "anda", a term of affection and endearment with his sons. Tok believed that for such words to have value, they should never be cheapened by inappropriate or frequent use.

I reproduce below my father's story of the meeting of kampong elders and young men, held barely a week before the Japanese Occupation:

> That night, the air in our kampong was heavy with the pungent smoke of the men's cheroots and anxieties. What could they do should the war reach this part of the island? Tok Imam, the religious leader, asked. He wanted to know how they could protect the women and children. And then there was the problem of food.

"In every war, there's famine and bloodshed," Tok said, sipping coffee out of a tin mug.

"That's true," Pak Senik murmured. He was the oldest in the village, and people listened to him because he spoke wisely. "*Gajah sarna gajah berjuang, pelanduk mati di tengah-tengah.*" (When elephants in conflict lean, the mousedeer gets killed in between.)

As the old men spoke that night, young men like me listened. The oil lamp hanging from the beam in the sitting room flickered in the warm night breeze. Our dark faces were tensed and taut. Many of those present were still talking about how their Sahib and Mem had left hastily. The orang puteh had left in fear, some of us said. The orang Jepun were dangerous. And the villagers were waiting for their penghulu and imam to tell them what to do.

"Ahem! Who can tell what this new overlord will do?" a villager said.

"Better that we don't do anything, then we won't offend."

"Do or don't do! The orang Jepun will do what all overlords do. Overlord us!" Aziz, the village wit, laughed.

The young men joined in. But theirs was the laughter of anxious men. The village elders smiled, their worried faces brightening for a while. They nodded to one another as if to say, the young bloods will have their jokes even at times like this; let them be.

"But from what I know, the orang Jepun are not against us. We won't be the ones to suffer. The Chinese will get it for China is at war with Japan. But not us. It's not our war. But while there's fighting, we can grow our own food," I said.

"Like tapioca and sweet potatoes?" Pak Jusoh asked.

"Ya, ya, good! Use the kampong land. Just do lah what our forefathers have done. Grow some yam, potatoes, chillies and some vegetables. Plenty to eat," Ahmad, the father of eleven children, was enthusiastic. Had not his own vegetable plot thrived? he asked his audience. And had not his home-grown fruit and vegetables helped feed his family? Praise be to Allah! He has blessed us.

"All this talk about growing food is very well," Pak Kasa raised his voice, "but what if we're bombed? This kampong will be burnt to the ground. All wood and attap."

"What are we to do?" Pak Kassim asked.

"We might still be bombed."

"Take our chances. Allah be with us."

"Then why move?"

The villagers argued late into the night. The men around Pak Kasa were in favour of moving nearer to the sea. But others like Wan Ahmad were adamant about staying put to grow their own crops. And young men like me were growing tired of pointing out to the elders that either way they would be caught in the crossfire of guns. It was war, what did they expect?

"When the elephants fight, the grass will be trampled on. Orang puteh or orang Jepun, they will trample us. We must take a common stand."

The elders agreed. Pak Kassim, seated cross-legged on the grass mat, made a fine speech about cooperation and gotong royong. Not to be outdone, Pak Kasa followed this with a speech on the need to protect young lives, holding forth with an eloquence never heard before in the kampong. One by one, the elders spoke, and the young men listened to them with patience and respect for this was part of our adat, our custom governing our social relations and behaviour. After the last speaker had spoken, the villagers turned to their penghulu.

Tok sipped his coffee and nodded to Tok Imam. He was a seasoned penghulu who knew that he had to have the support of the religious leader before anything could be done. Tok Imam, old and patient, a father figure to all the villagers, understood his headman's little nod. He had worked with Tok for many years and there had never been an argument between them which could not be settled over a cup of coffee.

"Allah, blessed be His Name, will protect us wherever we are,"

Tok Imam said quietly.

"Right, and so," our grandfather took up from where Tok Imam had left off, "I think we should stay put here and try to grow our own food."

In the beginning, I did not understand my father's story about my grandfather and the villagers. I had found it long-winded.

"What's the point of the story?" I asked him.

"The point, Zul," my father said, "is to show you and your brothers that people in my generation and in your Tok's generation never forgot their adat. Even at times of crisis. Everyone who had something to say was listened to. With patience and tolerance. Today, forty years after the war, we have become used to instant trees, instant noodles and instant coffee. Telephones which connect us to our friends at the press of a button. As a result, we have become impatient. We want things done quickly. We don't want to wait for others to speak their minds. We have become impatient with our old folks. But bear with us and listen. However humble and poor, however long-winded and stubborn. I know that some old people can be very stubborn. But if you listen to them, you might learn something useful and wise. Your decisions will be accepted. And there will be harmony. This is what Tok taught me: he who listens as he governs will grow in knowledge and wisdom."

My father was a patriot. He loved this island. He might not have accomplished great deeds like some other men, but for me, his son, he had left some very lucid thoughts and observations. When I think of him now, I realise that my father had lived through great political and social changes.

When he was a young boy, he was sent to the madrasah where he learnt to read the Koran and write the Jawi script. His seven-year-old head was turned towards Mecca. Then he was sent to Raffles Institution where he learnt to read and write English and sang "God Save the King". His mind was turned towards London then. When he was a young working adult, his world changed again. During the years of the Japanese Occupation, my father and those in his generation had to sing "Syonan", turn towards Tokyo and bow to the Nippon Emperor of the Land of the Rising Sun. "Those were terrible years," my father wrote in his diary. "The Japs tried to turn us 180 degrees round, from London to Tokyo. Singing songs in praise of Nippon was one of the most painful and degrading things we, Singaporeans, had to do. Just so we could survive. However, I thank Allah the Most Merciful that I am able to leave this world singing Tok Zubir Said's 'Mari Kita Ra'ayat Singapura'. Sung by all who have made this island their home and its history, their history."

A great man once said, "A country without a sense of its own history is not redeemed from its past. For history is a pattern of life's timeless moments, and our historical sense, the insight into these patterns."

So, while the light wanes over the Padang and the rain trees cast their long shadows on the grass, history on this island is here and now, and I intend to be a worthy part of it. Insya-Allah! Farewell, Bapak.

Zulaiman
Straits Herald

Later, Zul felt that his article had bordered on sentimentality. He was a little embarrassed by this exposure of his feelings, largely unforeseen by him. Jan tried to reassure and comfort him. But his father's death preyed on his mind. Was it guilt? Or regret?

Certainly, he regretted not taking the time off from his work to talk with his aged father more often. He regretted not knowing his father as well as he could have. The hollow he felt in the pit of his stomach was a great empty void which nothing could fill. He was angry with himself and was often short and sharp with Jan when she tried to be solicitous. Certainly, his dying father had thought about him; had thought about Jan and his coming marriage to Jan. For a long time, Zul did not show, not even to his brothers and sisters, the letter his father had written to him just before his death. Laboriously written on hospital notepaper:

My son, I am an old man inclined to worry. Sometimes, unnecessarily. Tonight, I share with you the fear and worry in your mother's heart and mine. Mak does not say what is in her heart sometimes, so I shall say it for her. Mak loves her children. She worries about all her children and grandchildren. I shall come straight to the heart of the matter. Mak and I know that what you feel for Janice is not *bagai embun di hujang rumput* (a transient love that will pass like dew on the tip of a blade of grass). You will marry her and you will have children. Mak and I worry that your children, that is to say our grandchildren, will be neither here nor there.

Air yang tenang jangan sanka tiada buaya (don't think there are no crocodiles because the water is calm). Let me tell you what I saw during the Japanese Occupation. I cannot forget the wartime troubles of the Eurasians. They were the products of mixed marriages. I was a reporter during the Japanese Occupation, and I covered the speeches the Japanese authorities made about the Eurasians who were ordered to assemble at the Padang. I heard too the speeches made by the Eurasian spokesmen on behalf of their community. It was like watching dragons turning into worms. These people had to grovel and appease their Japanese overlords in order to survive. For what else could they do? They were caught between the tiger and the crocodile in the river. The orang puteh had deserted them. General Sir Lewis Heath did not make plans to evacuate the Eurasians. Many of them had been abandoned by their English spouses, and the Japanese conquerors despised them. What could these people do? As I listened to the speeches that day at the Padang, my heart went out to these people, born of East and West. They were stranded on no-man's land by the war, and burdened with a history not of their own making; abandoned by one community and held in contempt by another.

My son, I dread the day when the Malays and the Chinese clash, like on May 13, which I pray with all my soul, Insya-Allah, will never happen again. But, if the dreaded unforeseen should happen, what will become of your children, my grandchildren? Will my grandchildren be torn and be distrusted by both sides? You are a newspaper reporter and no stranger to the kind of ethnic troubles found in different parts of the world. Have you and Janice thought about the kinds of problems your children might have to face, when you discuss housing, finance, career and the one thousand and one things which two persons about to marry like to talk about?

Please forgive an old man his pessimism. Do not think, my son, that I am going back on my word or withdrawing my blessing. I am not about to do that. Janice Wong is a fine woman. She has visited me regularly in hospital. Tonight, I am simply expressing an old man's thoughts and an old woman's worries. You have not told us very much about the parents of Janice Wong. Mak and I think that they are not happy about their daughter's plan to marry you. You are Muslim; they are Christians. And this can be one big area of trouble. Therefore, Mak and I were very, very happy, blessed be Allah the All-Merciful, when you told us that Janice would be taking lessons at the Muslim Converts' Association. Allah be praised. Tell Janice that I welcome her into the community of believers. May she grow in understanding of the faith of the Great Prophet. She has great courage and great love for you, my son; love and cherish her. The heart of the old is faint, but that of the young is brave. I admire the courage of youth.

May Allah the Most Merciful and Compassionate guide you and Janice always.

Bapak

Jan had always thought (in the way her Sunday School had taught her) that love in its purest form could overcome all differences and all difficulties. The lives of great men and women of mercy and compassion, the saints and missionaries, had shown how the power of love could transform human lives. Rather naïvely, she believed that faith in the One Supreme Omniscient, Omnipresent and Omnipotent Being could help human beings overcome differences and division. This was why she could not understand how she and Zul could have quarrelled over something as silly as what her father had said. The old man was prejudiced, and Zul had known this all along, so why did he get upset over it now?

"Maybe if you visit him and try to make up, you know, seek forgiveness?" he had begun innocently enough.

And she had replied, "But why should I beg for forgiveness? He threw me out of the house, remember?"

"I do remember, Jan. But it's part of our faith to beg for forgiveness and he's still your father. It'll be good if he comes to our wedding."

"He won't, I tell you."

"But you haven't tried. How d'you know he won't come?"

"I just know. No need to try. He's a stubborn old man."

"How can you be so sure he won't?"

"Sure I'm sure! He's my father. I know his nature."

"Maybe if we give him time…"

"No use! You don't understand! You're pushing me into another confrontation with him!"

"Look, I'm just trying to help."

"What help? Push me into yet another quarrel with my father?"

"That is not a fair statement to make, Jan," Zul almost gritted his teeth trying not to raise his voice. "I thought you might like to have your whole family at our wedding. Very few people from your side."

"Oh, so now it's my side and your side. I see! My mother and brother are coming. So's Aunt Ethel and Uncle John. If that's not enough, I'll invite the whole staff of my college! Big enough?"

"Why are you so reluctant about the old man? You said you were close to him."

"Well, things have changed, I am not now."

"Surely if you ask him…"

"No, Zul, no! For the hundredth time, the answer is NO!"

Zul waited until Jan was calm again.

"Please sit down. There's no need to stomp around like this. Are you hiding something from me?" he asked in the light of what he himself had done. He had not told Jan about his father's note to him.

"No."

"I hope we can be very frank…" he began.

"Look, Zul, if I go back and talk to him, he'd just say: I've got no daughter. If other people choose to reject their ancestors, that's their bloody business. If other people choose to leave their church and change their religion, that's also their bloody business. He talks like this, my father."

"Then he must have said more than this."

He looked at his wife-to-be, but Jan refused to look him in the eye.

"More than what?" she asked dully, looking out of the window of their newly-bought Housing Board flat.

"More than just converting to Islam. Isn't that so?"

"Why are you interrogating me like this? Like I'm a criminal or what?"

"Jan, I'm not blind. I know how people like your father feel about us. You don't have to tell me. I'm in the newspaper business. I know how some people feel. They don't say it, but it's there!"

"Look, I've said it before and I'll say it again! I'm against all my father's prejudices. So what're you getting so worked up for?"

"I'm not worked up! I want you to know once and for all! I know what your family and relatives think! Their thoughts stink! And you needn't hide things from me!"

"Don't you dare accuse me of lying! You know how I hate it! I have had to make a lot of adjustments. Can't you for once adjust to me and my needs?"

"I've tried my best."

"Oh sure! You are the one who has to leave the family, right? You are the one who has to change his religion, right?"

"Hey, hey, I'm not forcing you. If you still have doubts and you don't believe..."

"Shut up! What d'you take me for? If I still don't believe, d'you think I'd carry on? You think I'm a spineless jellyfish?"

Jan stormed out of the room and slammed the door. She had to learn to control her tongue, she reminded herself too late.

Zul threw himself into the armchair, gloomily listening to the muffled sobbing in the next room. Like rain outside one's window. Let her cry, he thought savagely; tears do not solve anything. He was shattered. They had never quarrelled like this before. And over something they had agreed never to quarrel about. Two people in love, he fumed. Educated and rational! How could he! He blamed himself. How could he let the prejudices and cock-eyed beliefs of others mar his feelings for Jan? They had come this far. This far! He was mad with himself for losing his perspective. He loved her. Their love is the rock upon which they will build their life together, Jan had told him and he had believed her.

But we deceive ourselves if we imagine that beneath our feelings of passion and affection is a strong and sound structure called love, a vast storehouse chock-full of affection, insights and sensitivities towards those we love. And he was painfully reminded of his father's proverb, "*Air yang tenang jangan sanka tiada buaya*" (don't think there are no crocodiles because the water is calm). There are problems in the most loving of relationships. The thing to do, he reminded himself, is to remember the relationship and not the problems, "*Terbakar kampung kelihatan asap, terbakar hati, siapa tahu?*" (Smoke is seen when a village burns, but hearts aflame, who will discern?) he added a proverb of his own. Inside his own heart, his feelings had been weaving and interweaving like smoke and flames in the heart of the argument. From one moment to the next, he hardly knew what was going on inside him and Jan. What foul words had fallen out of their mouths! What dark looks! They had said things, not because they had meant them.

All they had cared about was winning the argument. The nobler feelings of mutual respect and regard were all blown away in seconds. And what he had imagined to be their sound and sturdy structure was but a flimsy grass hut! Rumah attap!

The room darkened as the sun set, and in the brief tropical twilight just before the street lamps were switched on, the living room of the flat, their future marital home, was filled with the grey shadows of the past and his father's words of caution. The sobbing in the next room had long ceased, and his heart ached to be at peace with the woman he loved. Sighing, he rose from the armchair and went into the bedroom. One should cherish and respect, fight and forgive, and, God willing, this would be the pattern of their married life, like Mak's and Bapak's. And yet, different, he hoped.

PART 8

Paint...Scarlet
Painted...Red
Painter...Cheap
Painting...Porn

After Suwen had left the party that night with Jan and Zul, with hardly more than a "hello" and "goodbye" to him, Mark threw himself into the business of helping Nica to bring her grandaunt sightseeing. They brought Aunt Susantha to the Jurong Bird Park, "to look at the highest man-made waterfall in Southeast Asia," Nica announced with a wry smile and a faint twinkle in her eyes. "Everything that we boast of is man-made, Auntie. Cleanliness, law and order, and our tall gleaming towers of commerce."

They drove up to KL to visit Nica's parents. Mark was introduced to Dr Sivalingam and his wife. A delightful couple. He had found Dr Sivalingam highly entertaining and could not understand why Nica had to "flee her home", as she put it.

"I needed to grow up. Out of my father's shadow. He's a well-known neurosurgeon and he expects all his children to be doctors. I want to be an artist. A sculptor."

"And he doesn't approve."

"Right. He's very possessive and protective. Indian girls are over-protected if you ask me! Besides, I've already vowed to be neither Indian nor Chinese. I want to be my own person. You don't know how free I felt when he left Singapore to practise in KL."

Mark understood her and admired her strength.

After Aunt Susantha had left for India, Mark and Nica drove back to Singapore. A long leisurely drive. They stopped outside a kampong, on the way to Muar. Brown-skinned village urchins ran up to them with bunches of red rambutans.

"Very cheap! Very cheap! Three dollars only!"

Nica bought several bunches of the hairy fruit. That made the kampong boys very happy and they brought out some mangosteens and handed them out.

"Take! Eat! For you free lah! No charge," a tall lanky fellow, obviously the leader of the group, grinned.

Nica was delighted. Her eyes lit up. She laughed and thanked the boys and joked with them in pasar Malay. She broke open one of the mangosteens and, at her urging, Mark crouched gamely beside her by the ditch, and they ate fruit after fruit, sharing the juicy pieces of white flesh which Nica dug out of their maroon-coloured shells.

"Want to try durians? Very good ones!" the tall lanky boy asked.

"Ah, now I know why you gave us free mangosteens!" Nica wagged a finger at him. "You want us to buy your durians!"

"No, no! Don't say like that lah!" the youth pretended to be hurt. He beat his chest and muttered, "Sakit hati lah!"

His companions laughed and, joining in the game, they said, "But we like you! You look nice! He, your boyfriend ah?" They pointed to Mark.

Mark made a face. Then Nica joined the kampong boys in urging him to try some durian.

"Go on. Be a sport. Try a bit."

She held out the ripe yellow custard nestling in her hand. Mark took a bite of the soft, creamy fruit and inhaled the pungent fragrance for which he had no adequate vocabulary.

"How is it?" Nica asked.

"Mmm, it's out of this world. But it tastes good."

He made the thumbs-up sign and the kampong boys whooped with delight and offered them more durians.

"They're trying to make a fast buck," Nica murmured.

But she was in an indulgent mood that day and, since they were in no hurry, she asked the boys to open more durians. She and Mark sat on wooden crates and spent the afternoon eating durians, rambutans and mangosteens, laughing and joking with the village urchins. How pleasant the day was, Mark thought; the splash of dazzling afternoon sun, the cool jungle green, brown attap huts and, above them, the clear blue sky with just a wisp of cloud. During the drive back to Singapore, under a starlit sky, the two of them hardly spoke. There was no need for words.

Christmas was only two weeks away. Mark could feel the season's frantic pulse the moment he stepped into the Orchard Road area with Nica. This was the heart of Christmas buying and selling, with every department store proclaiming the Good News of sales and bargains.

"It's ridiculous," Nica was saying. "Why should an Almighty God submit himself to the trauma of birth and death? This idea of God coming into this world as a totally helpless babe is alien to the major religions in the East. I still can't understand it despite my convent education. Maybe deep down, I'm a Hindu. Like my grandma."

"Sorry, I didn't catch what you were saying," Mark stopped under the department store's ten-foot-high Christmas tree. The noise of the shoppers was deafening, and the saccharine-sweet carols from the loudspeakers were making civilised talk almost impossible. He was beginning to wonder if they would ever be able to find a suitable wedding present for Jan and Zul in this crowd.

"I was trying to tell you that most religions speak of gods as the Creator and Destroyer. Omniscient. So how does this fit into the Western image of God as a baby?" She pointed to the plastic doll in the crib.

Mark found himself looking at it with distaste. The manger was tacky with tinsel, gold stars and cardboard cut-outs of angels, shepherds and kings sheltering under the fir tree imported from West Germany. The store was promoting its German products this festive season, but the traditional German carol "O Tannebaum" sounded hollow in his ears.

His year in Singapore seemed to him to have been one long procession of colours and festivals: the red and gold of Chinese New Year, the white and green of Hari Raya Puasa, the Islamic New Year, the exuberant mix of gaudy hues of the Hindu festival of Thaipusam and the Chinese festival of the Hungry Ghosts. His Christmases and New Years in Scotland had paled beside these. It was mind-boggling for someone who had spent his entire boyhood in the quiet little town of Berwick-upon-Wye, near the Scottish border. On Christmas mornings in Berwick, the snow-covered streets were hushed, the air crackling with the cold. At a quarter to ten, the church bells began to ring. Every boy in Berwick could distinguish the peal of the bells. The heavy authoritative clang of the Episcopal bells was followed by the resonant chimes of the Wesleyan, the Congregational and the Baptist chapels. But the ringing of the great bell of the Parish Kirk, which rang out invitingly and yet commandingly over the town every Sunday and Christmas morning, was the summons which brought families of believers out of doors to church, chapel or cathedral. Berwick-upon-Wye had always been a small conservative border town. It had none of this metropolitan glitter, he told Nica. Little had changed over the years from the time when he was a boy. Except perhaps a few more strings of lights and neon signs down High Street during Christmas and in front of the pubs and beer gardens in McKenzie's Row.

But Nica was not listening. She was talking about the Creator as a baby again.

"A baby is like an idea," she slipped into her public-speaking voice. "Both can't dictate what's to happen to them. Before and after birth. The unborn and the newborn are the most vulnerable. Whoosh! And they are DNC-ed away. Some babies have been thrown down rubbish chutes or flushed down the toilets. Killed. Just like that! We're a ruthless people. We do the same to unpopular ideas, you know. If the powers-that-be think that an idea is dangerous, it's killed at conception. And if that same idea were to rise again like a Jesus Christ, ha! The higher-ups will call in the PR firms. And they dress up the dangerous idea as a Santa Claus! They neutralise it and make it absolutely harmless."

"Oh, I see," he murmured, more out of politeness than understanding. For him, Christmas was childhood and security. He was uncomfortable talking about the Baby Jesus in this irreverent way.

"No, Mark, you don't see," Nica insisted. "You don't want to see what the Western governments and vested interests have done to Christ and Christmas. In the long history of Christianity they have reduced him to this," she pointed an accusing finger at the plastic doll in the plastic crib. "The idea of an Almighty God deliberately making himself vulnerable, giving up his omnipotence for impotence, is a very subversive one, you know. It subverts all that Power and Authority stand for nowadays. Can't you see?"

"I'm afraid I am a bit thick today," he smiled and glanced at his watch. They ought to be looking for the wedding present.

"Look," Nica persisted, "if God the Almighty can humble himself and give up his power to serve his creatures, what d'you think God is asking the powerful in this world to do? Eh?"

"Cripes! Nica!" he threw up his arms in exasperation. "I need a cold beer before I think another thought!"

"Wham! Got ya!" Nica hooted with glee. "Sorry, Mark. I plead guilty to using you like a guinea pig."

She looked contrite but Mark knew by now that Nica loved drama and games.

"You see, Suwen is pursuing art as history or history as art, I don't know which is which now. So I'm exploring the artist as thinker or art as concept. Some call it conceptual art. How's that?"

"Well, I've been had," he groaned and laughed good-naturedly. He didn't really mind; Nica was a clever woman and a very accomplished artist. She was also one of the few Singaporeans he had met so far who could pursue an idea and explore it thoroughly in a conversation.

"Would you like to pose for me?" she was asking him. "Come, let's get you a cold beer before you turn into a frog, and then I'll proposition you." Nica steered him out of the department store.

They went back to Nica's apartment. "You can take off your shirt and jeans and hang them on the hook over there."

Nica fixed him a long hard stare. Mark took off his clothes as instructed. Her stare had bewildered him. It had nothing in common with the stares he used to get at the beach along East Coast. The girls at the beach usually averted their eyes when he returned their stares. But here was Nica looking hard at him, every part of him, fixing each part of his body, face, limbs, crotch, with the same long questioning stare which one would train upon a specimen. He felt belittled at that moment and regretted his decision to come and pose for her. And yet, he knew he would only sound silly and cowardly if he were to change his mind now. There was nothing for it but to go through with it. For Nica had already stepped forward, turned him around, and, on seeing his embarrassment, had proceeded to undress herself too.

Slowly, with great care and deliberation, she removed first her blouse, then her jeans, and lastly her bra. The garments dropped at her feet. Stepping out of her shoes, she led him by the hand and sat him down on the sofa.

"Now we are both nude and equal. And as you can see, I am no better than you. Sit in any position you feel comfortable in. I'll just pull back the curtains and let in more light."

Nica stepped back and looked at him, and he was glad that the apartment was on the twenty-first floor. No one could look in through the window.

"This is it, don't you see?" Nica was lecturing again. "Man's dignity is only clothes deep. Strip away the shirt, the tie and the business jacket. Take away the trousers and underwear. Strip every Prime Minister and President down to their puris naturalibus, and every one of their Excellencies is a flabby paunch, soft as my grandma's bum," she laughed.

A harsh brittle laugh, Mark thought.

"Are you sure you're strong enough to stand naked and pose before me?"

Her dark eyes challenged him. He was standing with his arms hanging loosely by his side. Man the naked ape. Nica motioned him to turn to the right, and then to the left, checking his profile. Satisfied, Nica turned away to rummage among her things for a sketchpad.

Mark shook his head as if to clear the cobwebs inside it. He needed to see things more clearly. He lacked clarity and knowledge, the kind which came only after years of residence in one place. He was too new to Singapore. That's the problem with being an expat on this island. One could be taken in by the bright cloudless skies, days of sun and heat, and the blinding brightness at noon. On such days, one sees the stark outlines of the tall buildings and the islands offshore, as far away as Johore and Indonesia. Then, all of a sudden, the skies darken and the islands and buildings are hidden. One looks out of the window of one's highrise apartment. One sees the well laid out city below. The miles of tarred highways, street lamps, flowering trees, office blocks and the constant stream of cars attesting to the high level of prosperity. And the telephone operator speaks to one in plain English. One feels at home. But walk down any one of the main thoroughfares, past the plate glass and metallic fronts of the offices, turn down a sidelane, and one is suddenly flanked by decrepit shophouses and Chinese temples flying the black and yellow colours of the medium cults. An old woman digs among the rubbish bins, salvaging cardboard cartons and other discards. At night, the girl in the leather skirt and boots, whom one dances with in the disco, confesses that she goes to a bomoh for amulets to ward off evil spells.

And right now in front of him was this well-educated Indian-Chinese girl, half-naked before his nudity. What was he to make of this? He had assumed that the island's populace was a modern people governed by ancient Asian values, that is if one believed the local papers. His perceptions of Asia and Asians were fast crumbling. Just before he came out here, he was sent an ad: "Asian women are pretty, petite and pleasant. Write to the Asia-America Friendship Bureau or call us toll-free for an introduction." He had since found out that these Asian women were mainly poverty-stricken Filipinas seeking a better life in the West.

In Berwick-upon-Wye, there was only one Chinese family and no Indians. The Indians he had seen on TV were West Indians rioting in Brighton and London. Very different from the ones he had seen here, praying in the Hindu temples, quiet dusky ladies clad in saris as bright as a parrot's feathers. And now seated on the sofa, nude, he was posing for this dusky artist, whose talk was as sophisticated as those London girls he had met in the West End.

Nica reminded him of Sushila Sanjay, the woman who was half Indian. Sushila too had a strong sense of who she was and what she wanted. No man could make her do what she did not want to do. And he was drawn to Nica in precisely the same way that he had been drawn to Sushila. Their strength attracted him. Their lean dancer's bodies were athletic triumphs of fitness arching over his pale frame. His fingers probed their deep and slippery insides, reliving the blind tactile pleasures of his adolescence. Having been raised by strict puritanical parents who had sent him to boarding school at an early age, he had suffered throughout his boyhood in silence the tormenting of boys bigger than him. He was an only child, and he was painfully shy of his small build, average height and his ignorance and lack of interest in kicking a ball or wielding a bat. He had preferred to spend his afternoons walking through the woods, looking for squirrels and birds. The boys nicknamed him St Francis. Later, he convinced his parents that he was destined for holy orders, and spent two years in the seminary before he could pluck up enough courage to leave. By the time he moved out, ready to live in the secular world, he was convinced that he was destined for a dull single life, burdened by an insecurity about his own masculinity. He was a singularly shy young man. It took a chance encounter with Monica Davis, and another two years of struggle and agonising before he dared to believe that he could be attractive to women. Today, after many years and many other willing, smooth-skinned women, he still could not say that he was proud of his own body the way athletic males usually were. But he was determined and willing to shed his inhibitions; so Nica had no trouble persuading him to pose for her.

"Don't worry, you've got magnificent thighs," she was clucking appreciatively like a connoisseur.

"Really?" He was beginning to throb.

"Do you like it when I do this?"

Her voice was low and husky, one he'd never heard before.

"Yes, yes." His own voice sounded hoarse.

"And this way?"

"Yes, yes. Oh, God, yes."

"You love Suwen, don't you?"

"Yes, and I shouldn't be doing this. But no, carry on, yes, yes…" he was groaning. The pleasure was unbearable.

"What a magnificent charger. Now if you can just hold still, I'll do a lightning sketch of you like this. Phallus erectus."

Then. And only then did it dawn on him that this had been her purpose. The sketch.

Years later when she was a well-known artist in her sixties and a grey-haired woman with dark teasing eyes, Nica wrote in a letter to Jan:

I saw no harm in doing it. Really. It was Art as Vengeance. One. The whites had exploited us, Asians; so I, in turn, exploited a white man. Two. The male has exploited the female body since time immemorial. So what is so shocking if a female artist exploits the male body?

But at the time this happened, Suwen simply could not see Nica's action in this light.

to be without feelings
is to be safe;
to be aware,
to feel deeply
is to court danger
to oneself...

Suwen scrawled in her sketchpad and flung it away. She was disgusted with their frivolity. With Mark for having toyed with her feelings. Night after night, she had tortured herself with images of the two of them together. In her dreams, she saw Mark dancing with his bitch-goddess. Nica was in black lace, swaying to the rhythm of an inner music which she, Suwen, could not hear. Moonlight streamed into the room of mirrors. Mirrors covered the ceiling and the walls. The floor was a huge mirror, bouncing off images of their naked writhing bodies, white and black, pink and chocolate brown. Image after image of their naked togetherness mocked her. She cried for them to stop dancing but no one heard her screams. No one heeded her cries. On the walls, a hundred, no, a zillion million images of Mark's naked body taunted her. He was bending and arching over Nica, pushing and bearing down upon her in an ecstacy of desire. She turned away, but whichever way she turned, the lovers were there. To her right and to her left. Behind her and above her. But in front of her was the wall of plate glass, and behind that wall was Nica in the flesh, twirling in circles within circles of concentric browns and ochres, her dark fingers seeking his white flesh, gripping the pistil of his manhood, harder and harder, he grew taut with pain and pleasure, pounding and twisting till he cried out soundlessly in an explosion of legs and limbs, red and black. A brilliant mess of scarlet pain and vermilion ooze.

Her brush was hurling itself ferociously across the canvas like a reckless driver hurtling down the racing track, bent upon suicide, the world exploded into blood. A thousand million drops of carmine and scarlet. She saw her hand holding her brush. Her brush wriggling and writhing in serpentine coils of orange and black, and pink, hot angry pinks, spiralling up stairways of hate and plummeting into the whirlpool of deep violent greens. The lovers' moans pursued her, pounding against her ears, rising and falling in a crescendo of exaltation and confusion. Mark, oh, Mark! I hate you! I despise you! I loathe her!

She woke up in a sweat, and wondered numbly at the pieces of her jealous self splattered upon the canvas hanging on her wall. Did she cry in her sleep? Did she shout? She did not know. Why did Mark do it? The question screamed inside her head. The veins at her temples throbbed in the heat. Every part of her was aching for him. Why did he do it? Why did he cheapen himself, his body and her love? Why? Why? Why? She asked over and over again, painting in a frenzy of strokes. Her body racked with her broken sobs.

She would never forget the evening she called at Nica's apartment.

"Look," Nica had enthused, "aren't these great?"

What Suwen saw was a series of charcoal and pencil sketches of a Caucasian male body in all its magnificent and grotesque glory. The eyes of her body saw for the first time the naked sinews, the lines and angles of the man she secretly loved; the arch of his spine, the veins and sinews of his thighs caught in the moment of desire, his muscles flexed taut in one sketch, and relaxed in the next. In another sketch was the hairy texture of his chest, the loose skin of his torso and crotch. The eyes of her mind burnt at the sight of his taut phallus, curving upwards above the wrinkled texture of the scrotum, partly covered by the light-coloured hair curling around it. She forced herself to look at sketch after sketch, excruciatingly beautiful and perfectly executed. The magnificent purity of line and curve assailed her artist's eyes. In her mind, she was like a schoolgirl, feasting her gaze for the first time upon Michelangelo's David, aged by time. She felt the burning of her cheeks, the quickness of her pulse and the sudden inhalation of her breath. The eyes of her soul were full of agonising admiration for the artist. For her charcoal study of a mature male.

"Look at this one. See this sketch? I'm very proud of this one. Well, I shan't tell you how I got him to arch like this. Shall I leave it to your imagination?" Nica teased.

And she remembered thinking that Nica's eyes were mocking her ignorance and pain.

"I'm going to leave it like this. Hanging in space. What d'you think? You know my stand, right?"

But Nica did not wait for an answer, she rushed on, so pleased was she with the sketches.

"A work of art should have spaces, don't you think? Unfilled and uncluttered like a painting of the Zen artists. With room for the viewer's imagination, A half-empty canvas is better than one filled with the artist's ego strokes. I say let the spectator have room to recreate for himself the painting before him and see what..."

"Why are you doing this to me?"

She found her voice at last and cut Nica off in mid-speech.

"What?" Nica turned to face her.

"What have I done to you?"

"What are you talking about?"

"I'm talking about these sketches! These! These! Why did you use Mark? Why him? You've got so many others to choose from! Why him? And not Robert or John or Dan?"

"How do I know? I asked him. He agreed and posed. Robert has left. And, besides, you know that I've never done male nudes before."

"I am well aware of that."

Her reply was cold. But their argument did not stop there. If it had, she wouldn't have been so troubled. Nica was sharp as a knife, slicing through everything she said. She hated her but she also admired her. Nica was straightforward, open and candid about her motives and desires. She, Suwen, was crooked and more self-deceiving by comparison, never quite clear about what she wanted or hated until her dormant serpentine self reared its ugly head to strike at the object nearest to it. She hated conflict and argument. All her life, she had run away from quarrels and confrontations. Especially with her mother. In school and at work, she had always maintained what she primly called "the balance and harmony of the yin and the yang", calm when others were angry, ruffled when others were calm. So when Nica had taunted her with not having the guts and courage to follow her instincts, urges and passions, she had remained silent.

"Why don't you do something, eh? Fight back. Argue with me, for God's sake! Challenge me. Don't you even want to fight for the man you love? If you love him, that is!"

Yes, she loved him! But no! She couldn't say that. She wasn't sure of his feelings and her own feelings. What she was sure about was this: she did not want to fight for him. She would never stoop to fight with another woman over a man. It's degrading. If a woman has to fight with another woman over a man, then her relationship with the man is worthless! There is something innately wrong in two women reducing a man to the level of a prize to be fought for! Aren't we regressing? Fighting and quarrelling over a male was the sort of thing one's mother and grandmother did in the bad old days when the male was supreme. In the Ong household, Madam Geok Neo had bitched against Madam Sia Liew, wife and concubine fighting shamelessly for the favours of Ong Ah Buck! But then, he was their sole breadwinner! The male today is not the sole breadwinner. He preens himself before us, but should we scramble and climb over one another for him? What for? For his seed? In her unexpressed anger, she vowed that she would rather that pride be the cause of her downfall and spinsterhood her future. She maintained her stony silence, and let Nica rave on.

"You're being foolish, Su, I tell you. Mark is no young David. As you can see from the sketches. And you're not a blushing schoolgirl any more. He's had experiences. He's forty. I don't know about you lah! You seem to have none. But surely you realise that virginity is not that hot in the West. Not even in the backwaters of Scotland. For them, a woman who's had experiences is not necessarily bad and immoral. She's just someone with a past. Don't you have a past?"

She must have appeared startled, for Nica said immediately, "Oops! Sorry, I didn't mean to startle you like this. I forget. I am the woman with a past. You are the woman with purity."

Nica's laugh grated, her lips curling in a sneer. She'd found her stony silence offensive perhaps.

"Ha! I know you! You judge me as a woman with a past. You don't say it. But it's in your eyes. But tell me, what good is virginity at thirty-nine? What is it worth?"

Nothing! Nothing! Nothing! She screamed the answer in her head. Nothing! SDU doesn't even organise functions for people her age! Youth is king, youth is queen in Singapore, don't you know?

"Gosh, you teacher types," Nica was taunting. "Frigid in the body, frigid in the head! Here's a guy crazy about you. And you about him. If not, d'you think you'll be so hopping mad just because I sketched him without his clothes on? But cripes! What d'you do? Nothing! Absolutely nothing! The guy's been mooning about you for a year out here. All you did when you were with him was to moan and groan. Not over sex. Geez! But of all things! Over art, language, history, all the cerebral blah-blah-blah! So what d'you expect the guy to do? Rape you? Christ! You're a stupid woman!"

Familiarity breeds security, not contempt, Suwen thought as she gazed with relief at the scene in the Keppel Road Railway Station. Nothing much had changed since the fifties. There were the usual disorderly queues in front of the ticket booths. The ticket and customs officers still wore the same khaki-coloured uniforms.

Above the crowd was the familiar wall mural of tin miners, dulang washers, rubber tappers and padi planters; a myriad of minute mosaic tiles had gone into the making of the mural, a tribute to the work of the humble folks. She drew comfort from that work although it had little artistic merit. But the mural served its purpose, reminding people like her that Peninsular Malaysia was still the home of simple rural folks, the home of farmers and rubber tappers, the homeland of her maternal grandparents, and part of her own roots. Neither Communist China nor the literary China found in Chinese literature was her spiritual home, she concluded. Standing amidst the noisy crowd waiting for the afternoon train to Kuala Jelai, she had the curious sensation that she was going home at last.

The noise around her was a continuous din of babies' cries and the chatter of the excited adults in a babble of tongues. The fat Chinese man next to her yawned. He shoved a stubby forefinger into his mouth and dug out a bit of food. He flicked it off his finger and the bit of food landed at Suwen's feet. She edged away from him. Her eyes scanned the faces of the uncouth crowd, noting details of nose, eyes, cheek bones, hair, anything. Anything to fill the idle mind. Keep it busy. Keep it thinking about other things. Fill its greedy crevices. Trivia: railway timetables, number of public toilets, number of bawling babies, old women in blue samfoo, people who dig their noses in public, who blink incessantly, who talk incessantly, etcetera, etcetera! Keep looking and counting. Keep busy. Keep moving.

There was a hiss of steam and the squeak of metal upon rails. The slow afternoon train had arrived; it was the only one which stopped at all the small towns. The crowd surged towards the customs counters. The Indian man in the khaki uniform made a chalk mark on her backpack and waved her on. She squeezed past two families blocking her way. She clambered on board the train. The first carriage was full. A large family group had put their bags and packages on all the seats. "Taken, taken!" they said. Typical Singaporean kiasu behaviour. Chope and reserve everything for one's own kind, she thought wryly.

She went into the next carriage. And the next. And the next. Packed with the bodies of excited children and anxious adults. But this was the price one had to pay for travelling third class, she sighed. It was the class she used to belong to whenever she travelled with her grandparents in the fifties. "Never go first or second class," her grandma used to say. "If the Communists want to bomb the train, they always bomb first and second class. That's where all the gwailo are." Her grandmother's advice was typical of the sort of folk wisdom born out of the twelve years of Emergency and guerilla warfare in the Malayan jungles after the Japanese conquerors had left. The Commies always bombed coaches with white men in them.

When she reached the sixth carriage, she finally found two empty seats. She took the one by the window, unstrapped her backpack and shoved it under the seat. Only when the train was moving out of the station, past the lines of track and the fuel tanks, did she feel the stab of regret. She had chosen silence and had refused to take any of Mark's phone calls. The persistent ring of the phone had tormented all her waking and sleeping hours. The anguish: to answer or not to answer. The constant pacing up and down. The arguments and counter-arguments raging day and night inside her head. Ha! Goodbye to all that!

But she knew she was deceiving herself. Do not think. Do not recall. She was bringing herself perilously close to tears. Fill the mind with facts. Facts are comforting.

Fact number one: life is unfair.

Fact number two: regret is useless.

Fact number three: a good horse will never return to old pastures.

Fact number four: to rest the mind, think of something else.

Like one cannot choose one's parents. Where the hell was the man whose sperm gave her life? This was the question in her mind. But aloud, she had merely asked, "Who is my father?" And her mother had cried. And dinner became like the Last Supper. It was actually the last meal they would ever eat in the old mansion because, the next day, the movers would take away the furniture and boxes of stuff. Her mother's face was grim. Sulin and her husband, back from Perth, tried to cheer her up but they failed. The man, Ong Tay Luck, had very conveniently taken himself and his belongings to the house of his Number Four mistress. He did not want to see the movers and packers doing their work. Having to sell the mansion had been a heavy blow.

But he had only himself to blame, said her mother. He was blind to the deviousness of Number Two's son, she sniffed. I told him so! But he didn't want to listen! Well, that was her mother's version of the family's decline, but she doubted whether things would have been any different even if the man had listened to her mother.

Ah Siew Chay was absent from the Last Supper. Which was a mercy. The aged amah had wanted to stay till the very last but her mother had whispered that she wanted Madam Troublesome out of the way. Would she please...? And she had to agree. At the St Theresa's Home for the Aged, Ah Siew Chay's eyes had turned misty. The old amah held on to her hand as the two of them sat on the white metal bed, a typical institution bed. "Aiyah, like in the hospital," Ah Siew Chay fretted.

"Come and see me, Suwen? You can or cannae?" She could, she lied. But not so soon. She veered closer to the truth for it would have been cruel to make her old amah wait in vain. She had to go away for a while, she told the old woman who clung to her all the more. Mother will come and see you soon, she assured Ah Siew Chay. "Aye, she will nae come." Ah Siew Chay dabbed away her tears with the corner of her samfoo jacket. "She does nae like me. I was Madam Sia Liew's maid. Not hers. She always think me a snake, ah. I do nae mind, what to do?" Liar, she'd thought but what was the point of challenging an old amah's mendacity? What was real to old folks were the memories lodged in their heads. Their versions of history and their own past. These they would bring to their graves. "I did nae forget. I can remember still," Ah Siew Chay said. "I can remember when I was a girl in my village, ah. I was married. Once. I did nae tell you. A long time ago. Very long. I was only fifteen, ah. But I did nae like him. He was a butcher. Old as my father. He had a foul mouth and a heavy hand. People said he beat his first wife to death, ah! I got scared. I cried. But my father did nae listen. Sold me to the butcher. So I ran away. I hid inside a well. My aunt helped me. She brought me to the harbour and that was how I got here. Aye, I did nae marry. Look, I am still not touched, ah. No man, aye, has ever seen these." Ah Siew Chay had pulled up her samfoo jacket then, revealing two very small, light brown and delicate-looking nipples. Small as a young girl's and just as flat. The body of the seventy-seven-year-old amah, long hidden under layers of cotton samfoo, was fair with tiny wrinkles, a sharp contrast to the deep ugly ones on her face. Ah Siew Chay had seemed proud of her virginal nipples. But, poor, poor soul, Suwen thought, they were all she was left with besides the memories. And even the latter would fade with the decay of brain cells over time.

Suwen gazed out of the train with unseeing eyes. So, of what use are chastity and virginity if at the end of one's life, all one retains is a sense of waste? Disuse? Unuse? The questions plagued her hard-won sense of equanimity. Of what use are breasts which no man will see and fondle? No babe will suckle? Two untouched, undefiled, shrivelled breasts. Are these the symbols of purity? They can't be now.

Not now. Things have changed. And yet...she sighed. Here she was in twentieth-century Singapore, a woman and an artist whom the Singapore man-in-the-street had decried as geh angmoh (a pseudo-Westerner) in their letters to the press after that disastrous exhibition. Just look at herself! She was still worried about not getting married. Worried about missing the boat or being left on the shelf! A trap! It was a mental trap! It was exactly the kind of thinking which had trapped many like her into a prison of fear and anxiety. It was the kind of male-dominated perception which saw women as goods left upon the shelf if they remained unmarried. Or as flowers waiting to be deflowered by the bee which could flit from bloom to bloom while the flower just waited. Gosh! She had to be careful. What was she to do? What could she do? She disliked this way of looking at things as much as Mark did. But a woman in her late thirties had to be more cautious about giving away her heart to a man. The pain, if he treated her heart lightly or if he flung it away, would be unbearable. Utterly devastating. More so, far more so, than if she were in her twenties, young and resilient and still highly desirable in the marriage market. There she went again! Falling into that kind of thinking again! No, no, no! But she would rather die than suffer another betrayal. Public rejection of her art – that was something she could handle. Fame lasted only but a week anyway. And so did public disapproval for that matter! It didn't matter; they could approve or disapprove as long as she could carry on painting. But private rejection of her intimate self and affection – she didn't even want to think about it any further.

She sank into her seat, exhausted by the mental picture of chaos in her mind. Given the frailty and vulnerability of her heart, it would matter, and matter to a degree unimaginable to a man. Especially if that man were a Westerner, a white man used to dealing with white women who take their virginity and chastity far more lightly than Asian women. Most white women, if not all, in matters of sexual equality merely wanted to be like the men, treating their own sex organs like so many hands and feet, a physical limb to thrust into a body or be thrust into by another body. God, God, God! She was getting more and more prejudiced the more upset she got! She must stop. Simply stop thinking.

The train rolled across the Causeway and stopped at the Johore Bahru station. People got off and people got on; then the train rolled out of the station, leaving behind the ugly town. It rolled past the ugly telephone poles, the junkyards of abandoned vehicles, straggly bush, dirt huts and dirt tracks. She was leaving its ugliness behind her. Far behind her. The vulgar crowds at the art exhibition flashed before her eyes. She had not expected to win nor attract so much public attention. Outshining Nica's charcoal sketches which had won the judges' commendation and even the approval of some critics. Her oil painting, however, was the topic of controversy. She felt misunderstood by members of the public. And betrayed. Nica had exhibited the man she loved and yet no one had said anything against her other than that the sketches had "true artistic merit", in the words of one critic. And yet ... the thought that Nica's model was the man she loved, oh, the very thought of it, of seeing his private parts displayed in an art gallery of the National Museum, to be gawked at by the public! No, no, no! She could not and did not go to the gallery for the prize-giving ceremony.

The telephone poles continued to flash past her unseeing eyes. The buildings of the town were giving way to the plantations of oil palms, rubber and coconut. Long straight rows of palms and trees stretched as far as the eye could see. The sun was shining in her eyes, a white ball of heat hanging in the clear azure blue. Her eyes were dimming, threatening tears again. She shut them against the light. But the darkness in front of her eyes brought no peace.

Could it be that she was dismayed and distraught by the public's hostility to her painting? Anguished at her own act of betrayal. She had painted those writhing figures in a blaze of vengeance and hate. She had avenged her jealous spirit in a frenzied fit of copulating brushes and exhibited its result. Have you no shame? she asked herself a hundred times in pain. How deceitful and self-deceiving she had been. She was no better than Nica. Her tears were flowing freely now. She knew she was once again running away from shame. She, not Nica, was the exploitative artist feeding off the flesh of others. The vulture of human failings and decay. If only Mark would come after her and save her from herself and her pain. But it was a wish as fleeting as a breath of wind, and she would never admit to it again. Not even to herself.

The picture of a withered spinster purveying her impoverished past with regret flashed before her eyes. It is a myth, she told herself firmly. And yet the sudden thought that this might be her bleak future made her turn to look round the train carriage. Hoping to find what? Mark? She caught herself wondering as the polite noncommittal faces of her fellow passengers returned her look of bewilderment. She should get off the train at the next stop and go back, she thought, reckless, wild and desperate like a caged animal. If only one did not have to act and choose. Every action and non-action brought its own train of consequences. Should she or shouldn't she? The train chugged on relentlessly. Mercilessly.

She was changing her mind with each turning of its wheels. She would forgive him; no, she would not forgive him. Her mind swung like a pendulum as she clung fiercely to her pride. It had been hurt; damaged beyond repair. She would rather choose pain and loneliness than a cheap reconciliation with Mark simply because she feared being alone and single. A part of her agitated spirit yearned for the fluidity of loneliness and rootlessness; to go where she chose, to paint what she saw and felt, and to suffer the choices she had made. Ultimately, she was Suwen. Alone.

Epilogue

He went up the broad carpeted stairs leading to the Art Gallery of the National Museum. The lone girl manning the reception counter smiled at him. Behind her were the congratulatory baskets of flowers. He noticed that some of the yellow chrysanthemums had turned brown at the edges. He signed the Guests' Book in his elegant handwriting: Mark Campbell, friend of artist.

"Do as you wish but I won't be there," she had said, her voice laced with frost. "I've got a train to catch."

He wandered into the next room and the next. Then he saw it, hanging at the far end of the main gallery. It dominated and filled the entire wall. The splashes of reds, greens and pinks, hot angry pinks, mocked his eyes and challenged him to a scrutiny of their shapes and lines. He stood in the middle of the gallery, deserted because it was mid-morning on Monday, and peered at those leering shapes and shadows through his steel-rimmed glasses. He saw their pattern after a while, the mass of phallic curves, pale, arching upwards between the dark, full, rounded breasts, hanging like ripe fruits of brown, cinnamon, russet and auburn, shading into deep chocolate before the greedy white mouths reaching up to suck them. He was amazed at the boldness of her brush strokes, their vibrant colours seemed to throb with such life and energy. Such abandon! There was a wildness in the movements of the semi-abstract human shapes. A female Picasso without the sharp angles and triangles. Her sensuous curves and arches were bathed in dark shimmering colours. Was there a suppressed sexual energy? Who could he ask to verify his feelings and perceptions? Nica had taken herself off to London. He could follow her if he wished. He thought about their heated argument a week ago and her persistent refusal to fit into his life. "I need to be in control," she'd said. And in the meantime, Suwen had already left for some god-forsaken town near the Malayan jungles in search of her roots. He could follow her too if he wished, and found himself dithering between the cool greens of Berwick-upon-Wye in summer and the dark dank jungle-green of the Malaysian Peninsula.

And so life simmers on in the golden heat of desires and half-desires, between impulse and indecision, he mused as he nodded to the girl at Reception and walked down the stairs into the brilliant sunshine.